follow the money...

I shuddered. Ginny's accident *had* been an attempt at murder, and she was still in danger, danger of dying before she had the chance to get better and live. She was in danger of dying the way Madeleine had, a victim of an apparent accident, a senseless waste of human life.

People murdered for three reasons. Revenge was out. Love was out. Only money remained.

The train pulled into the City Hall–Brooklyn Bridge station and I got off as if I were sleepwalking. I emerged into a blast of arctic air and snowflakes large as cotton balls. The cold jolted me awake and I headed toward Centre Street. I was, for the moment, technically homeless.

But I was alive.

Praise for HOMICIDAL INTENT:

"HOMICIDAL INTENT candidly and vividly illustrates the legal and emotional tightrope that must be walked daily by the forensic psychiatrist."

—Karen Irving, author of *Pluto Rising*

homicidal intent

vivian chern

A DELL BOOK

Published by
Dell Publishing
a division of
Random House, Inc.
1540 Broadway
New York, New York 10036

Author photo by Michael Shnaidman

Cover photo by Adam Smith/FPG

ISBN: 0-440-23720-3

Printed in the United States of America

Published simultaneously in Canada

September 2001

10 9 8 7 6 5 4 3 2 1

OPM

for michael

homicidal intent

prologue

The boy had curly blond hair. His blue eyes were huge, and they watched me from the witness stand as if I were the only person in the crowded courtroom. His mother had chosen a navy blue blazer for him, to go with the white shirt and striped tie. I peeked at her, sitting with her husband and their lawyer. She must have felt my eyes on her, because she turned and gave me a wan smile. The husband's hair was neatly cut, and he was wearing an unaccustomed suit and tie. The parents wanted to be presentable for their son's unexpected appearance on the witness stand, in this most publicized and controversial trial of the year.

I was sitting behind the prosecutor, in the first row of observers. With difficulty, I unglued my eyes from the boy's. I knew what he was going to say. I looked instead at the flags behind the judge, the United States flag and the New York State flag, the judge sitting between them like an apology. I glanced down at my clasped hands, then back at the judge, his fringe of gray hair and bushy eyebrows almost making him into a caricature. Here comes the judge. Here comes the witness. Here comes the verdict.

"You may begin," Judge Hershkovitz said to the pretty attorney in her red suit.

"Jason," she said gently, approaching the witness stand, "would you tell us in your own words what happened on the afternoon of December twenty-third?"

I thought I could hear the heartbeat of the reporter sitting next to me. In the back of the room, somebody coughed. A pencil scratched somewhere down my row, probably a courtroom artist sketching. I felt as though I aged a few years as I waited to hear the boy's words.

"I shot that gun," he said quietly. "I shot it at Amanda. Her friends . . . they laughed at me. I shot them too. I wasn't sorry then," he said. "But I'm real sorry now."

A buzz started in the back of the room, fading away before it reached me. Nobody in the front row would dare to talk.

"Order," the judge said, banging his gavel.

"I killed Jessica and Hannah," Jason said. "I killed Miss Lopez. I had to." He had tears in his eyes. "I took that gun, and I put it in my pocket, and I took it to school that day, you know?" He was looking at me again, and I felt my eyes fill too. "I didn't know it was wrong. I didn't know, Mom, Dad." Jason looked at his parents. The mother dabbed at her eyes with a crumpled tissue.

"Could you tell the court what kind of feelings you had been having in the weeks before the shootings?"

"Feelings?" The boy gave what almost sounded like a laugh. "I had no feelings. I hated everybody. Even my mom and dad," he added, in an even lower voice. "I'm lucky I didn't shoot them."

The buzz started again for just a second; by the time the judge dropped the gavel it had already stopped.

"Jason," the lawyer said, "do you think you can read this article aloud, like we discussed?"

"The one that describes what I . . . how I . . . you know?"

"Objection," the other attorney said.

"Overruled," Judge Hershkovitz said. "You may proceed."

Jason surreptitiously stuck a finger inside his shirt collar, as if he could loosen the tie and the choke hold of the trial at the same time. He was too young to be in a courtroom. He should have been in school diagramming sentences, or outside playing soccer, or practicing the clarinet or playing Nintendo, or whatever kids were playing these days. He should never have gotten hold of a little nickel-plated revolver and he should never have used it to shoot four people. But here we were in court, and it was all because of him.

" 'New York City, December twenty-third,' " Jason recited. "Should I have read that part?" He looked worried.

I saw his mother's head nod yes as the lawyer said, "That's fine."

Jason resumed reading. " 'Three die in shooting; one critically injured.' " Jason breathed audibly. So far the words were just old news. I knew that certain parts had been highlighted for Jason to read for the greatest impact. The judge glanced at his watch. The reporter sitting next to me whispered, "I can't believe they're letting him do this." I just nodded and looked back at Jason.

" 'The atmosphere of festivity turned to one of horror at Manhattan's most prestigious public elementary school today, as a twelve-year-old boy opened fire on schoolmates and teachers at the annual holiday party.' " Jason stumbled over some of the bigger words, then regained his composure and continued. " 'Eyewitnesses saw the boy pull a small gun out of his pocket and take dead aim at another twelve-year-old, classmate Amanda Frost. By the time police and security officers arrived at the scene, three people were dead.' " Jason's voice quavered. A tear glistened on his left cheek. All around me, people were silently wiping away tears, even though we all had known for a long time how this story ended.

" 'Although hysteria was rampant in the crowd of more than a hundred pupils and teachers, the shooter was observed to walk calmly to the buffet table for more popcorn after emptying the gun.' " Now Jason's voice broke completely. "I did that?" he said, openly crying. "That was me?"

"Do you think you can continue?" Judge Hershkovitz asked in a grandfatherly voice.

Jason shuddered, nodded, and continued in his shaking voice. " 'The boy was cold and unmoved as police took him into custody. He showed no remorse. Already the Manhattan district attorney's office has indicated that they wish to try the twelve-year-old suspect as an adult. Experts are excitedly debating the child's fate.' "

"Thank you, Jason," the judge said.

"Nothing further, Your Honor," the lawyer with the red suit said.

"Your witness," Judge Hershkovitz said.

The other lawyer looked at Jason, and then looked at the jurors in their box. The attorney knew what to do.

"No questions, Your Honor," he said.

I listened to the whispers and the murmurs that I knew would come.

"You may step down," the bailiff said, and opened the little door for Jason, who ran into his mother's arms. I squirmed on the wooden bench as I watched the lawyers shuffle papers and the judge sip from his water glass. My testimony would be next. I closed my eyes and breathed deeply, trying to calm the herd of elephants that always thundered through my stomach right before I had to testify in court. Once I reached the witness stand I would be all right. I heard the judge say, "The court will take a ten-minute recess," and I heard myself let my breath out in a rush. I wanted to get up there and get it over with, at least get the beginning over with.

Ten minutes to kill. I kept my eyes shut. Without warning, I was taken back to that day four months ago, when I had first become involved with this case.

It had been snowing, that day. I kept my eyes closed against the sunny April skies and the few still-leafless branches that brushed the high courtroom windows. For a second, it was as if the past four months had never happened. My eyes flew open, and I sat up straighter on the hard wooden bench. It was almost time.

chapter one

I was defrosting in the bathtub on the coldest and snowiest night of the year. The tub was a little crowded. I perched my feet on Greg's chest, wiggled my toes, and admired the pedicure I had gotten that morning. Greg didn't even crack a smile.

"What?" I said.

"Nothing."

"I thought you liked this time of year. The lights, the decorations. I feel like a little kid."

"You don't want to be a kid these days." Greg splashed some water on his face, rinsing off the bubbles. "I got a new case today."

"That boy?" I asked, knowing immediately the one he meant. The city hadn't announced its final choice of prosecutor yet, but I had suspected that the case might become Greg's. Despite his dark coloring, in the district attorney's office he was the proverbial fair-haired boy.

"Yeah. Can you imagine? Barely twelve and already a murderer. And he's being tried as an adult—by me. It's going to be tough." He picked up a handful of bubbles and slathered them on his face, as if donning a mask to hide his defeated expression.

I watched the steam rise toward the ceiling. Maybe love wasn't enough to counterbalance the sordid events and disturbed people that were our daily bread. Every day, something new happened that I found impossible to forget. Sometimes I wondered when my brain would run out of room for my collection of horrors.

"What's he like?"

"The Devinski boy? Seems like a regular kid. Kind of angry."

"Did you meet the parents?"

"Not yet. I don't think they want to talk to me. They are only communicating through their lawyer."

Greg paused, and I waited for what I knew would be his next words.

"I can't wait to go up against her." His usual enthusiasm crept back into his voice, exactly as I had expected. Natalie Diamond was well-known as an ambitious, utterly ruthless criminal defense lawyer. She was very much in demand by New York's criminals, at least those who could afford her astronomical fees. The fact that the Devinskis had retained her to represent their son had been on the news within hours of the school shootings. But what worried me wasn't her legal prowess or that she was going to make Greg's life miserable in court.

"Any chance that he'll plead guilty and spare you the trial? After all, everyone knows that Jason Devinski shot those girls. A hundred witnesses saw him."

"I think they're going to go for your favorite defense."

"An insanity defense? He's only twelve. By definition, I would say he doesn't have the same capacity as an adult to distinguish right from wrong. But the chance of him being mentally ill . . . I don't think so."

I worked with some pretty shady characters in my private forensic psychiatry practice. The criminally insane were always challenging and never boring. But I rarely worked with children and had never been involved with either the prosecution or the defense of child murderers.

"Are the parents divorced?" I asked.

"I don't think so," Greg said, with a strangely satisfied look on his face.

"It's a horrible case. And bizarre. So many kids killing other kids, or their parents, or even strangers, lately. And all of them have been out in the boondocks. Here in the city, I guess I thought we were at least immune to murderous children."

"A lot of cases in Arkansas and Michigan." Greg ticked off the locations on his fingers as he spoke. His nails were bitten even lower than usual. "One in Ohio, one in Oregon. I'm probably missing some. Don't forget Colorado, the worst one. And now this one, in Manhattan."

"Somehow, I never thought that we'd have a kid shooting into a crowd in New York. School shootings always seemed like a problem that wouldn't reach us here."

"It's a national trend now. I wonder why."

The water had started to get cold, and the romantic aspect of our shared bath had chilled off long ago, when we started talking about Greg's case. I was a bit disappointed that our bathroom had just become our home office. Now I was not only thinking about Jason Devinski, the murdering little boy, but simultaneously of Natalie Diamond, the famous photogenic lawyer. I wanted to remind Greg that I had an exciting and glamorous career too. Or at least to remind myself.

"I got a job offer today," I said as I got out of the tub and reached for my bathrobe. Greg was right behind me, eager to relight whatever flames had been doused by the bathtub conversation.

"Doing what?" he asked, standing close behind me and kissing my neck.

"I got a call from this pharmaceutical company. They asked me if I was interested in being a consultant for them." See, I'm cool and important too, I was saying. "They even said they're going to send some opera tickets over for us. As a sort of bonus."

Greg wasn't listening. He kept kissing. "Tell me later. You know what they say about all work and no play." I didn't point out that one of the perks of private practice was the ability to control my own schedule, and that I had taken the opportunity to give myself a week off, starting about two hours ago.

"You're going to be seeing a lot of Natalie Diamond," I said, stepping away.

"Are you upset about *that*?"

I couldn't say anything. Guilty as charged.

"Tamsen, let's get this straight right now. Natalie and I are on opposing sides of this case. I barely know her."

"I know," I said. "I'm just je-n'secure." It was a word we had invented, meaning "pretentious and insecure."

"Okay, so now where were we?"

"They wanted a consultant for their new medication," I said.

"That's not what I meant."

I had almost forgotten what I wanted to tell him when I heard the intercom buzz from the kitchen. I was tempted to ignore it, but women have difficulty ignoring stimuli like crying babies and ringing doorbells. It's an evolutionary protection for advancement of the species.

"Yes?" I shouted into the intercom, while Greg reached for his sweatpants.

"There's a gentleman here to see you," the doorman said. "A Mr. . . . " He conferred with somebody. "Mr. . . . " The doorman made a sound that sounded like a growl with a cough in the middle of it. "Can I send him up?"

"I don't know him. I don't know who he is." I was still a bit disoriented. The blood that had rushed away from my brain was having trouble finding its way back.

I heard voices in the background again, then a new voice, deep and resonant despite the distortion of the intercom system, said, "Dr. Bayn? I'm an associate of Ginny Liu's. May I come up?" Ginny Liu was the pharmaceutical company representative who had stopped by my office earlier that morning, bearing gifts of pens, drug samples, and encouragement for me to provide the requested few hours a week of psychiatric consultation for her department. The voice must belong to the messenger who'd brought over the promised opera tickets.

"Come on up," I said reluctantly, and ran into the bedroom to put on some clothes.

When the bell rang a few minutes later I had put on some fuzzy leggings and an oversized sweatshirt, cozy hanging-out-at-home-why-are-you-interrupting-me clothing. People in this city don't just casually drop in on each other, especially not on Christmas Eve, and especially when you've never even met them. Why couldn't whoever it was have just left the envelope with the doorman?

I opened the door to a tall, well-preserved middle-aged man. He wore a snow-dusted black cashmere overcoat and held an expensive-looking pair of leather gloves, the kind with the stitches hidden on the inside. He didn't look like a messenger.

"Dr. Bayn, thank you so much for seeing me." He held out his hand, which was as smooth and manicured as his tanned face. His smile revealed perfect white teeth but didn't seem to reach his blue eyes. The man looked as perfect, and as nondescript, as a crash-test dummy. "Parker Grandines. Ms. Liu found you for us."

"Grandines?" I repeated. I shook his hand, sure that surprise was written all over my face. I've never been good at poker, and not just because I keep forgetting the rules. "You mean you own the company?" In response, he handed me a card: *Parker Grandines, Chief Executive Officer, Grandines Pharmaceuticals.*

"Grandines is a privately held company," he replied. "It's been in my family for, oh, two hundred years, in one form or another."

"Umm. What a . . . surprise. That you're here, I mean. To see me." Surprise was putting it mildly. It's a wonder I didn't tip over and fall unconscious, from the shock of having the CEO of Grandines Pharmaceuticals appear on my welcome mat.

I was looking at a rich man, Old Money, the kind of person I read about but only occasionally met.

I took his fancy coat and offered him a seat on our sofa.

"I know how unusual this must seem to you," Mr. Grandines said.

I nodded. Greg stood in the hallway leading to the bedrooms, watching us. I didn't think that Mr. Grandines had noticed him.

It went against everything I had been taught since birth to not offer Grandines a drink or coffee, but I hadn't invited him and the suspense, as they say, was killing me. Greg disappeared from my view for a moment. When he returned, he had put on a shirt. He came right over to introduce himself.

"Ah, yes, the prosecutor," Grandines said, nodding. "Quite a case you've got there." It seemed like everyone in the world but me had watched the news and already knew that Greg was prosecuting Jason Devinski.

"May I offer you a drink?" Greg asked in his best unaccented English.

Grandines asked for a scotch, which went with the perfectly tailored dark suit and, of course, those gloves. I was amazed when I saw Greg pour two glasses from a bottle that I knew had been a gift from a victim's father, a hundred-dollar bottle of scotch that had been a thank-you for a life sentence without parole. Greg brought me a glass of red wine. What a lovely intimate holiday gathering.

"When Ginny mentioned that you were a forensic psychiatrist"—Grandines paused briefly for a sip of scotch—"I didn't understand why she thought you'd be appropriate for us."

"Ah, you were wondering about how dead bodies and tracking down psychotic killers fit into your marketing plan," I said.

Greg laughed. Grandines's unspoken question was one I answered practically every day. "Forensic psychiatry is the application of psychiatry to legal matters. The word 'forensic' comes from Latin; it means 'in the forum.' 'Pathology' is when you cut up dead bodies." I paused, then added mischievously, "Of course, most pathologists don't actually cut up dead bodies. They interpret slides from the tissues of people who are still alive. And who hope to stay that way."

Now I'd confused him thoroughly. I almost laughed. Sometimes I felt like I was on a mission to teach people the meaning of the word "forensic." Once they heard it, they rarely heard the word "psychiatry" following it. Everyone automatically thought of scary stories featuring serial killers, and old television shows featuring wise medical examiners.

"Now I know," Grandines said. "And we felt that your experience testifying in court and explaining psychiatric concepts in words that the average citizen could understand would be perfect for us. We just lost our previous psychiatrist, after almost fifteen years. Our team leader, actually. We need someone to work with our Curixenol team. Ms. Liu thought you'd be perfect. It's a part-time job, ten to twenty hours a week. We wanted someone fairly young, you know, and, ahem, attractive." He looked at Greg, who just smiled back pleasantly.

"What's the emergency?" I was flattered that they wanted me, but I was suspicious. *What's the catch?* was the question I was really asking.

"Well, you know that Curixenol is going to be launched right after the first of the year," Grandines answered. "There will be press conferences, newspaper stories, lots of attention focused on our revolutionary new product. We thought it best that our spokesperson be a physician, a psychiatrist. We don't require anyone with pharmaceutical-industry experience."

He mentioned an hourly rate that almost made me fall off the sofa. I glanced at Greg, who shrugged his shoulders as if to say, "Do whatever you want."

"We particularly like your forensic background," Grandines told me. "Not that we anticipate any legal problems with this drug. But we like having somebody who knows how to talk to lawyers." He said it with such a straight face that I couldn't even meet Greg's eyes for fear of bursting out laughing. Greg and I had passed the talking stage long ago.

"Could I think it over for a couple of days?" I didn't need to think about it. I was always looking for extra work that paid well, that was flexible and clean and didn't involve filling out endless forms. My plan was to be a successful famous forensic psychiatrist by the time I was forty, the kind of expert witness who'd get called to evaluate people who try to kill the president, or who lead cults or hijack airplanes. Any media exposure would help me reach my goal.

"That would be fine," Parker Grandines said. "Fine. Again, I truly apologize for barging in like this, but it was impossible to find a messenger on Christmas Eve, and I was in the area. It was a pleasure to have the chance to meet you for myself."

He stood up to leave, and as he put on his coat he pulled an envelope out of a pocket. "Oh, yes, I almost forgot. I wanted to give you these tickets that Ms. Liu promised you. To the Met, next week. After the dinner. You will be attending, won't you?"

"We'll be there," Greg said, probably noticing that I was too astonished to speak. "Thank you."

We showed Grandines out, then went into our tiny kitchen. I poured myself another glass of wine and sat at the kitchen table to watch Greg cook.

"I can't believe he came *here*. Why would he? These important CEO types never get involved with lowly psychiatrists like me."

"Wouldn't you have met this guy at the dinner, anyway?" Peppercorns crunched beneath the blade of Greg's knife.

"No. Those dinners are marketing things. The main guys would never come to an event like that. They have salespeople who run them, like Ginny Liu."

The dinner Grandines had referred to was coming up the following week, in a well-reviewed restaurant. All the pharmaceutical companies liked to arrange dinners, outings, and activities where a bunch of doctors would be a captive audience. They would use the time that we spent devouring our entrées and desserts to pitch—and push—their products. Occasionally the drug companies would throw in a bonus, like a concert or a show. But as physicians, we understand the attempted seduction to be exactly what it is: advertising. The company bigwigs never attend those programs, and Grandines hosted dinners for their one other psychiatric drug regularly.

The drug company dinner probably wouldn't be as good as the dinner I was about to eat. I sat silently sipping my wine as Greg trimmed the steaks of fat and speculated about what would make the president of a company make a house call on Christmas Eve.

"It must be part of their marketing campaign," he decided. "Or maybe there's some regulation that they have to have a physician on their team, or something like that." Now he was coating the steaks with the peppercorns he'd crushed earlier. He poured oil into the pan and, after a few moments, added the steaks, which sizzled so loudly I couldn't hear his next words.

"It was too weird," I said finally, looking apprehensively at the gigantic butcher knife he had picked up again. I was always sure we would end up in the emergency room instead of at the table. He interpreted my look correctly, and set the knife down carefully on the counter.

"That he came here, I mean," I continued. "And those opera tickets. How did he know that I liked opera?"

Greg removed a carton of heavy cream from the refrigerator. "So are you going to do it? Sounds like they really want you."

"Why not? I think it will be a good medication. Or not bad, anyway. And it's great money! I have to thank Ginny for recommending me."

"What's this medication for?" Greg asked.

"It's supposed to be an antidepressant that treats alcoholism. It's an SSRI. Selective serotonin-reuptake inhibitor. You know. Like Prozac. They're focusing on the alcoholic crowd. Since lots of alcoholics are depressed . . . I guess it will work on some of them."

"Are you hungry?" Greg asked, changing the subject abruptly, as he often did, a technique he'd undoubtedly learned in court.

"Starving."

"Okay, watch." Greg held a lit match to the pan. Blue flames leapt out for a few seconds, like an aura, then died down. The first time he had tried flambéing, he'd set fire to the filter in the exhaust hood above the stove.

He transferred the steaks to plates that had been warming in the oven, then added the heavy cream to the drippings in the pan. I watched as he stirred and shook. Finally he took the plates out of the oven and poured the sauce over the steaks.

"It's ready," he announced proudly. I poured him a glass of wine and prepared to feast.

"Why don't you just quit and open that restaurant you keep talking about?" I asked rhetorically. "Then you wouldn't have to worry about prosecuting children." But I knew he never would quit. Cooking was just a hobby for him. A useful hobby, but he didn't love it the way he loved the law.

The dinner was too delicious to be part of a normal person's repertoire. After we ate, we cleared up the kitchen and moved into the living room with the rest of the wine. The usually incredible view of lower Manhattan was shrouded in a thick white veil.

"So, um, you want to do me a favor?" Greg said, his head in my lap.

"What kind of favor?" I was stroking his thick dark hair, the way I knew he liked. I thought I knew the kind of favor he had in mind.

"Not that you need the business, now that you're going to be a rich drug company psychiatrist. But you think you could evaluate this kid's parents for me?"

"What?" I thought that the topic of the murdering twelve-year-old had been put to bed for the night. Now I understood why he had looked so pleased earlier, when I had asked him if Jason Devinski's parents were divorced. He already knew he'd hooked my interest. "But you always say I shouldn't consult on your cases. That we shouldn't work together anymore."

"This one is different. I need someone reliable. I just

want you to find out if there's any family history of violence, anything like that. I could get you court-appointed."

"I think I'm a little too, um, close to you. You should get some other psychiatrist."

"I don't trust any other psychiatrists. I trust you."

"I'll think about it," I said.

"Okay, think about it. Later," he said. "Now, think about this . . ."

Well, that part's private.

chapter two

When we woke up Christmas morning we were amazed to see that over a foot of snow had already fallen. Outside the window, snow still fell, but without the energy and sassiness of the night before. Now it was coming down straight, like rain. Like it meant business. The city below seemed deserted. The record snowfall guaranteed that we'd have to spend a cozy day in the house. At ten o'clock sharp, the phone rang.

"Good morning, honey, did I wake you?" My mother has some strange idea that as long as she waits until ten A.M. to make a call, she's excused in case she happens to wake someone up.

"We're up," I said. "Now."

"Do you have a lot of snow there?" My father had picked up the extension.

"We have the same amount of snow as you." They live on the Upper East Side, in the same building as the office they let me share. All of Manhattan is only thirteen miles long. It doesn't contain different temperate zones.

"So, what are you doing today?" my mother asked.

"Nothing special. We're snowed in." Obviously I was exaggerating. It was still possible to get out and walk around.

"I'm just worried about the party," my mother fretted. "What if people don't come because of the snow?"

"They'll come."

The point of the call was to remind me for the hundredth time to bring my extra-large coffee maker tonight. They'd probably remind me twenty more times before the day was out. I promised to remember and hung up.

I was brushing my teeth, barely aware of the television droning in the background, when I heard Greg say, "I don't believe it."

"Don't believe what?" I mumbled around a mouthful of toothpaste.

"Remember that other child murderer? In Lexington, Kentucky? Last summer—that twelve-year-old? He killed his whole family, and then wouldn't talk to anyone for months. Today he finally agreed to talk to a psychiatrist. Everyone is excited—he wouldn't even talk to the defense attorney until now. They've been finding him incompetent to stand trial for months."

Competency to stand trial is a legal decision made by a judge, after hearing testimony from psychiatrists. This child in Kentucky had refused evaluation. Now possibly he would go to trial.

The world had become a complicated and hostile place. Innocent children had no reason to kill. They could barely understand the permanence of death. Yet all these prepubescent boys suddenly had access to weapons and no remorse. Jason Devinski was just the most recent in a wave of violence washing over this country in the most unexpected way, at the hands of children.

"Did you ever think of killing anyone when you were a boy?" I asked Greg, after he'd watched the rest of the story from the comfort of our bed. Details, at this time, were scarce. When I heard the word "psychiatrist" I tried not to perk up my ears.

"Of course. I played with guns and swords. Games. Pretend. Not real."

"This Devinski kid, Jason, does he have a history of anything? Learning disabilities, or abuse, or anything? Is he adopted?"

"Not as far as I know. His father is a college professor. I don't remember what the mother does."

"It would be interesting to talk to them," I admitted.

"So you'll do it? You'll evaluate the Devinskis?"

"As long as you inform the judge that we're living

together"—oh, how I hated the sound of that—"and he doesn't think it will be prejudicial, I'll do it. Oh, God, what am I getting into?"

"It'll be fine," Greg said. "Fine. Come here."

"I'm going to make coffee."

"Make coffee in five minutes." He held the covers up so I could get in beside him.

"It's only going to take five minutes?" I couldn't help laughing.

He gave me a big grin. "Don't you want to find out?"

He got my mind off the news.

We eventually moved into the kitchen, our second-favorite hangout, and I ground coffee beans while Greg inventoried the refrigerator. We had acquired one of those old-fashioned aluminum percolators that makes espresso on top of the stove, and after many false starts, I finally had the proportions and timing right. But even the strong coffee didn't distract me.

"I keep thinking about that poor family. Sometimes I hated my parents, but I never considered murdering them!"

"I never hated my parents." Greg would never say anything bad about his parents, since they were both dead. Survivor's guilt. "Kids get angry, I know. They can be really cruel to each other. But to kill your friend? To murder your own mother and father and brothers?"

"You knew I'd see those Devinski parents," I accused.

"Of course I knew. I wouldn't have asked you otherwise. You can't resist a puzzle."

I got up from the table and started preparing breakfast. Eggs, toast, and fat-, cholesterol-, and pork-free bacon. After all, it was a holiday. Later, like all good Jews, we were supposed to go to the movies and go out for Chinese food. But a glance out the window told me that we were probably in until the evening.

I had just joined Greg at the table when the phone rang again. Startled, I jumped up to answer it. I wasn't expecting any calls of holiday cheer. The caller ID said "Unavailable."

"Oh—hi. May I speak to Gregory, please?" The woman's voice held a note of confusion.

I handed the phone to Greg.

"Hi, how are you?" Greg's voice was bright, and he was smiling.

"Yes, sure, oh, okay, no problem." Pause, pause. "Yes, Umm. Hmm." Pause. "No, it's fine, I said. It's even better. I'll get it to her sooner." Pause, pause, pause, as I drummed my fingers on the table, watching our breakfast get cold. "Yes, okay, you too." Long pause. "Sure. See you then." Longer pause. "Okay, Natalie, bye."

"Natalie Diamond?" I asked as Greg hung up the phone. "What did she want? Why is she calling you here?"

"She wanted to know if it was okay to bring by the parents' psychiatric records today. She got them last night."

I was so shocked that Natalie was coming over to our house that for a moment the phrase "parents' psychiatric records" didn't even register. "She's coming here? Today? In this weather?"

"She said that her daughter is with her ex-husband and she has nothing to do. So she's working. Wants to go out and get some air."

I'll give her some air, I thought, but Greg said, "What?" so I guess I was savagely muttering.

"Nothing." Greg and Natalie seemed to have a pretty close working relationship for two opposing attorneys. Then I remembered: "The Devinskis have psychiatric records?"

"Apparently. You'll have them in"—he glanced at his wrist, devoid of a watch, then looked at the microwave, which showed the time—"about an hour."

Most of my forensic experience evaluating parents had been as they were divorcing. Those cases were battled in civil courts, away from public attention, unless the participants were especially famous or the circumstances of the case particularly awful. But after seeing firsthand the hatred of people who once loved each other, it wasn't a giant leap to children unhappy enough, or unstable enough, to kill. Unhappiness so ugly it turned criminal.

I didn't dress up for Natalie's visit. When the doorman buzzed from downstairs to tell us Miss Diamond was coming up, I was sitting at the computer in the second bedroom, now our study, looking busy. Actually, I was looking for honeymoon cruises, but Natalie didn't need to know that. I let Greg answer the door, while I pretended to be immersed in the specifics of regular ships versus sailing and the Caribbean versus anywhere else.

"Tamsen," Greg was calling, what seemed like an hour after the doorbell had rung, and after I had been hearing low voices and laughter for a long, long time. "Come here."

I went out into the living room and was surprised to see that although Natalie looked good, her features were quite ordinary. "Hi," I said, politely offering to shake hands.

The hand that shook mine was small and icy cold. "This is convenient," Natalie said. "A live-in psychiatric expert." Was that a hint of snootiness that I heard in her voice?

"Would you like some coffee?" I asked, expecting her to refuse.

"Sure. I'd love some." She had already taken off her full-length shearling coat, and now she bent over to pull off her boots. I couldn't decide if she was being polite by not tracking in snow, or rude by making herself at home. She was wearing jeans and a bulky sweater; unfortunately, she was one of those women who could look sexy in a potato sack. I could tell she was wearing makeup, although I bet Greg thought she was *au naturel*. Silently, I went off to make coffee. In the regular coffee maker. No special gourmet espresso for her.

"I don't mind at all," Natalie was saying. I watched her from our open kitchen area. Her face was plainer than I remembered from television, very small and fine-boned and symmetrical, the kind of face that looks better in photographs and on screen than in real life. "Use whatever expert you like. I have no preference. I don't think that the parents' histories are relevant. This isn't an abuse-excuse case. Something else is going on here."

I listened hard as I stood on tiptoe to retrieve a glass platter on which to arrange some cookies that one of my patients had baked for me. Natalie couldn't have reached that high. Try as I might, I only heard snippets of their conversation.

I brought out the coffee and cookies on a pretty tray and sat down on the sofa next to, but not right next to, Greg. Natalie was sitting on the other arm of the L, in what was usually my place.

"I'm really interested in what you're going to think about these parents, Tamsen," Natalie said, suddenly contradicting her earlier statement. "I have Dr. Bluecorn examining the boy, of course, and I'll probably have him evaluate the parents as well, just for another opinion. Victor spoke highly of you."

The world of forensic psychiatry was relatively small, and so I knew Dr. Bluecorn well, although not quite well enough to call him Victor. I doubted Bluecorn had ever spoken highly of anyone other than himself, but at least he wasn't interfering. Was Natalie being condescending? I couldn't tell. Since I was now a court-appointed independent expert, both sides would try to use my findings to their advantage. It was in her best interest to be nice to me.

"Is there a court-appointed expert assigned to evaluate Jason?" I asked. Natalie had made it clear that she'd hired Dr. Bluecorn privately, which was fine with me. A criminal defendant had the right to hire his own experts. But if Dr. Bluecorn was working for the defense, then who would be working for the court? Bluecorn had trained all of the available experts. It was a strange situation, which didn't bode so fantastically for the case.

"Not yet," Natalie replied noncommittally. "I'm sure Greg will let you know when someone is appointed." Something in her tone disturbed me.

"I hope you don't have a problem with, you know, the fact that Greg and I are engaged," I said. "I told Greg that he should look for another psychiatrist, but he likes working with me."

"Oh, no, it's fine. You have a good reputation. I know you'll say what you think, not just what the prosecution wants you to say."

"The prosecution has no preconceived ideas about this case," Greg said, "other than the fact that ninety-seven witnesses saw the Devinski boy kill those girls."

"Yeah, well, there is that," Natalie said, with, could it be, a dejected sigh? I couldn't believe that the three of us were sitting around my living room in a snowstorm on Christmas Day having this discussion. "Still. There must be an explanation. Did you hear about the boy in Kentucky?"

We talked about all the recent child murderers who had been in the news far too frequently lately. Finally, Natalie got up to leave.

"Nice meeting you, Tamsen. And listen, these psych evals are very informal. You're court-appointed. We probably won't even need to put you on the stand. After all, I doubt the parents had anything to do with this boy's craziness." She shook her head as she bent over to put on her boots. "That kid got crazy all by himself."

chapter three

My visit with Natalie had gone better than I had expected, all things considered. At least she had brought me some potentially interesting reading material. Greg settled down on the sofa with a beer and some pistachio nuts that I didn't even know we had. Even on Christmas Day, he found a game to watch. I propped myself up on the arm of the L and picked up the first folder.

The chart I was reading concerned somebody named Karen Marulli. All of the entries had been signed by a Dr. Bergman. The record predated Karen's marriage to Devinski, Peter, subject of the other chart. A quick browse showed me that Karen's records stretched back all the way to her college days and continued almost to the present.

"This seventeen-year-old single white female presents to the student health center with complaints of insomnia, irritability, and dissatisfaction in relationship with boyfriend." The photocopy I was reading was of a record that was thirty years old, but shrink-speak hadn't changed much. I glanced at the end of the note. *"DX: Brief Reactive Depression and Situational Depression."* We no longer used those diagnoses, as per the *Diagnostic and Statistical Manual of Mental Disorders,* currently in its fourth revision, but Dr. Bergman had probably done a fair job of describing young Karen Marulli's problems.

I flipped through the notes. In her freshman year of college Karen had gone to approximately ten therapy sessions with Dr. Bergman, then stopped. I forced myself to decipher the photocopied doctor scrawl. Nothing special. Karen sounded like a typical adolescent adjusting to college. She worried about exams and boys. In the last few progress notes, reference was made to "Bill." The final session's notes said, *"Spending more time with Bill, no longer feels need for psychotherapy in light of new boyfriend."*

The next set of notes was dated two years later, and included a thirty-day psychiatric hospitalization. *"Broke up with boyfriend,"* was her chief complaint. I read further and saw that Karen and Bill had broken up, and she was devastated and thought about killing herself. *"+ suicidal ideation, without plan or intent,"* the chart reported. So Karen was one of those sensitive people who feels like killing herself in response to stress. I wasn't sure if she had really suffered from a major depression or if she had been "acting out" in response to the breakup. It's hard to interpret old records, with their old-fashioned diagnoses and limited explanations. I saw that she was in treatment for at least seven years after that, but the only reference was a note in what I assumed was Karen's handwriting: *"Psychoanalysis with Dr. Bruce Bartholomew (deceased), age 20 to 27."* I could ask Karen about those years in treatment, but Dr. Bruce had surely taken the juicy details of her life to the grave with him. Then came a gap of several years. The next stack of photocopies was in yet another handwriting. Dr. Helen Tamassi had treated Karen with psychotherapy and medication. Karen was started on antidepressants shortly after giving birth to her son Jason. Since then she had tried every antidepressant that came on the market. About four years ago the frequency of visits and the length of notes both dropped precipitously, and the handwriting changed too. Seemed that Karen's managed-care health insurance company had referred her to a Dr. Shilpa Singh, who saw her twice a year and refilled her prescriptions. I wondered if Dr. Singh was at this moment racked with guilt about not seeing her patient (I assumed Dr. Singh was a woman) often enough or thoroughly enough to know if something was wrong at home, something that maybe could have been prevented.

In the whole folder, I didn't see one direct reference to Jason or Peter, and although a couple of entries read,

"Increased work stress," nothing mentioned what kind of work Karen did. We've become very symptom-oriented in psychiatry lately, but I'm not very comfortable with the "new psychiatry." I believe that we are products of our environments, not just our genes or our brain chemistry, as important as those factors have been proven to be. In my opinion, every therapy is a family therapy, even if the rest of the family is dead and gone. Today, medication is supposed to solve everything. I wondered how Karen was feeling now about the panacea of medication. I had seen countless patients who insisted, no matter what the evidence was to the contrary, that the right medication could fix all their problems. On the other hand, Karen had been in psychoanalysis for seven years, so she probably knew the limitations of both. Maybe. The pharmaceutical industry could be extremely convincing when it came to selling their products. And soon I would jump on the latest bandwagon. . . . Still, we needed medications in psychiatry. They just weren't the entire answer to the world's problems.

I felt a hand on my shoulder. Greg was standing beside me.

"Anything interesting?" he asked.

"Yeah. Did you know that Jason Devinski's mother has been in psychiatric treatment of one kind or another since she was seventeen?"

"Really?" Greg sat down next to me. I scrunched into the back of the sofa to give him more room. He started nibbling my earlobe.

"Don't you ever think of anything else?" I said. "Look. This is very interesting."

"Told you it was a good case for you," he said, between nibbles. What could I do? Officially I wasn't working.

Life was finally good. Greg was soon snoring on the couch, the remote clutched in his hand. I turned off the television and opened Peter Devinski's chart.

Peter's chart contained records from the age of twenty-five to right after his marriage to Karen, when he was thirty-seven. One flip through the pages told me everything I needed to know. Peter was a recovering alcoholic. He had been in and out of rehab programs for about twelve years. Then suddenly, I saw the notation *"Refer to group treatment,"* and the chart ended. No notes from the group therapist, if there had been one. No further information. No nothing. Peter's case was closed.

That was strange. I read the early notes and saw detoxes, rehabs, references to "Bipolar—Depressed" and "Depression and Anxiety." Peter had been tried on various antidepressants, Valium, other tranquilizers. He had been detoxified from alcohol repeatedly. But the documented history of his alcoholism seemed to stop right after his marriage to Karen, thirteen years ago. What a success story. Lots of men only start drinking when they get married. Look at my father. It took him years to discover alcohol. I glanced at the empty beer bottle lying next to Greg on the sofa, and said out loud, "Nah."

So both Devinskis knew the ins and outs of psychiatric treatment. I wondered how their histories had impacted on their son. I wondered if Jason had been a wanted, planned child, if they had ever tried to have another, if they had a good relationship.

I took the beer bottle to the kitchen and pitched it into the recycling basket. You could drink every day and not be an alcoholic, just like you could work every day and not be a workaholic.

I had worked enough for a holiday. Outside, the snow had stopped, and a few feeble rays of sun poked between the clouds. I went into the bedroom to prepare an outfit for my parents' party, a task I dreaded and always left for the last minute. I pulled out the black dress, the high heels, and all the accessories that I hoped would make me glamorous, and arranged everything on top of my dresser. My side of the bed beckoned. I lay down for just a little nap.

chapter four

I woke up in the dark, totally disoriented. I had been
dreaming that I was swimming upstream in a river. So subtle, and hard to interpret. I groped my way into the bathroom and heard Greg's voice: "Good, you're up, we have to
get ready."

We got ready. I always hated the part right before we
left, when I was sure that I looked hideous and that everyone there would hate me and reject me. I had tried to train
myself not to bite, not to let myself fall into the preparty
anxiety trap, but it never worked completely.

The dress was black velvet, very tight, short, and held
up by thin sequined spaghetti straps. I have no idea what I
was thinking when I bought it. Now I slipped into the dress
convinced that I had dissociative identity disorder, formerly
known as multiple personality disorder, and that I had pur-
chased the dress as another personality. The shoes were
black satin with a couple of sequins to give them that elegant flair. I put gel in my hair and arranged it so that it fell
dramatically over one eye. I worked like an artist trying to
finish a canvas commissioned for a hated despot, drawing
and patting and stroking and rubbing creams and powders
onto my face with the intensity of someone who knows his
work has to be perfect, but hates it just the same. I told
you. I'm je-n'secure.

Greg made an appreciative noise as I turned to
face him.

"Am I okay?" I asked.

"You'll do," he said, winking. He had this wink that was
like a posthypnotic suggestion. Wink, and I would fall at his
feet and do his bidding.

I remembered the coffee maker. We decided to try for a cab. The one we found drove us uptown quickly through the freshly plowed streets. I was amazed that the snow-plows had been out, since it was the biggest holiday of the year. The doorman on duty in my parents' lobby was a young guy from some on-again-off-again European country. He spoke no English and didn't recognize me, so I had to show him my name on the guest list that my father had spent a month preparing, alphabetizing, and cross-referencing.

Sofia the cleaning lady had happily agreed to come to the party to help, and she'd brought her friend Eva. The two women had presumably spent Christmas in the bosom of their Polish compatriots but, like the snowplow drivers, wouldn't turn up their cute button noses at the chance to make an extra buck. Christmas night is a great time to have a party: an escape from all that forced family togetherness for some, a cure for meaningless aloneness for the rest. We paused in the hallway to hang our coats on the rack sent up by the super for the occasion. Judging by the number of coats, not too many guests had canceled because of the weather. I shoved the hanger between a black mink and a black shearling. I kind of doubted the wisdom of leaving a mink coat in a hallway, even on the Upper East Side, and even with the Bosnian defense forces guarding the door downstairs.

Finally, I could procrastinate no longer. I pushed open the door clutching the coffee-maker box in my arms, sort of shielding my cleavage from that first, revealing exposure, and instantly collided with Natalie Diamond.

"Did I hurt you?" I inquired politely, once I had recovered from the shock of seeing her in my parents' home. She was rubbing a bare shoulder where it was quickly turning the same red as her very small, clingy . . . well, you couldn't really call it a *dress*. I checked the corner of the box I was carrying. A little dented. *Oooh, good, I hurt her,* I couldn't help thinking. "What are you doing here?"

"What are *you* doing here?" she said, looking up at

Greg, who hadn't said a word. Probably overcome by the sight of her mostly naked body right here in front of us in living color.

"I live here," I said. "I mean, my parents live here. This is their party. See? I brought them my coffee maker."

"Oh. Well. I'm here with a . . . date."

"Oh. Okay, well, see you." I ducked into the kitchen before she could add anything else. It was clearly Greg to whom she wanted to talk anyway. I handed over the stupid urn and grabbed a little hot dog wrapped in dough from one of the Polish ladies as she rushed out to serve the guests.

Not an auspicious beginning. But I had to admit that my parents knew how to throw a party. There was always plenty of good food, lots to drink, and usually quite a few interesting people mixed in with the usual family friends and business colleagues. I set out for the living room to find out who was here, and especially, who had brought Natalie.

I snared a little square of pumpernickel, thinly smeared with butter and covered with a slice of smoked salmon. A handsome blond man with slightly Slavic features and wearing a tuxedo asked me nicely: "You would like a drink, miss?" A Polish bartender, courtesy of Sofia, no doubt. I almost asked for a glass of wine, but I realized that it was already a vodka kind of an evening.

"A vodka tonic, please," I told him. Didn't the Poles invent vodka? No, actually I think I read that it was the Native Americans who invented it, but they never got the credit for it.

As I waited for my drink I scanned the huge living room and spotted my mother in a scarlet blaze of sequins, in a corner holding court over a group of dark-suited men, none of whom I recognized. Probably some guys from the managed-care network for which she had recently signed on as a consultant. My father was leaning against the baby grand piano that nobody ever played, talking with another group of people, mostly old friends of my parents whom I've known since childhood. This decision was a no-brainer. My father's group won. I hate managed care.

I kissed the air next to all their cheeks, answered their questions as patiently as I could, as I looked around at the guests, trying to guess which one had brought Natalie. Finally I asked my dad.

"Gordon Ranier," he said, as if it should have been obvious.

"Who is he?"

"My agent," my father said.

"You have an agent? For what?" It wouldn't be entirely out of character for him to decide that he wanted to play professional basketball.

"My book," he said. Loudly.

"What book?" I asked, as if on cue. We had an audience already.

"I'm working on a new book. About violence against women," my father announced. "A self-help book. You know, to help women leave the men who grieve them and find kind men to love them."

I could hear the quotation marks as he spoke. His first self-help book had been published about fifteen years before. It was still in print. For quite a while it had been joined every couple of years by a sequel, but four years had passed since the last. I'd always thought that if the advice he offered helped, his readers wouldn't need to buy the sequels. Even though I believed his theories were a crock of you-know-what, they *had* paid for my college and medical school. They had also sent my father on frequent national publicity tours, after any of which, I knew, my mother would have been entirely justified to leave *him*. Still, you had to give the guy credit for getting published in English when it wasn't even his first language.

"Well, congratulations," I told him as his friends began pelting him with questions.

"Let me introduce you," my dad said, suddenly benevolent. "Gordon. Come here for a minute." A forty-something guy with distinguished gray streaks in his dark hair looked up from a crystal platter of Belgian endives with cream cheese and red caviar. Natalie's "date" was tall, handsome, and, well, looked like he was *somebody*. As he approached us I felt a little flutter in my chest, right around where the black velvet met my skin.

"Gordon, I'd like you to meet my daughter, Tamsen. She's a psychiatrist too. She has quite a busy forensic practice."

"Very nice to meet you." Was that a trace of English accent in those honeyed tones? My father's literary agent had lost the endive along the way, and now transferred his drink to his left hand so he could shake with his right. The palm that grabbed mine was cold and a bit damp, but not unpleasantly. His grip was strong. His blue eyes looked down into my brown ones, then unashamedly took in the cleavage, dress, and everything else. Wow. This guy was on the prowl, and not even trying to hide it. I hastily pulled my hand away.

"Forensic psychiatry, what an interesting profession." Gordon moved closer to me, speaking in a low, confidential voice. If I were an editor, I would buy any book he sent my way. He was so transparent, yet that little flutter kicked in again. Move over, leading man *du jour*. If Gordon had told me he had a whole row of Academy Awards on his mantel, I wouldn't have been surprised.

"Oh, I see you've met," a woman's voice said from somewhere near my elbow.

I felt an arm around my waist and looked up to see Greg leaning against me. "Gregory Jolson." He held out his hand toward Gordon. The introductions were made all around.

"I'm thinking of representing Natalie for a book that she wants to write on the Devinski case," Gordon told us. "I was thrilled when she called yesterday to tell me her idea. A book about the inner workings of the defense of a violent child. Good thing we had an excuse to meet right away, isn't it?"

I stared at Gordon. So Natalie had called him yesterday. Was she trying to find ways to get inside information about Greg's planned prosecution of her young client? Or was she just trying to find ways to get close to Greg?

"My interest is popular nonfiction," Gordon continued. "I have big plans for your father, Tamsen. What about you? Ever been interested in writing a book about your work?"

If anybody ever published a book about my work, I'd be sued for sure, I refrained from saying. The subject matter was too sensitive, even if people did give up their right to confidentiality when they agreed to an evaluation with a forensic psychiatrist.

"Natalie was telling me a little bit about the case," Gordon went on, obviously not as interested in my work as he'd been in my body. I've never been able to figure out, even though I'm supposed to be an expert at understanding human emotions and behavior, how I could wish for men to be attracted to me, and at the same time be totally freaked out and suspicious when they paid more attention to my boobs than my brain.

"I'm evaluating the Devinski parents," I said, probably in an attempt to remind him that there was more to me than perfume and a short dress.

"What's wrong with them?" Gordon's smooth voice sharpened slightly.

"I don't know yet," I said.

"They have a long psychiatric history, both of them," Natalie said.

I didn't like the way this conversation was going. "I need to see them first." I kept my voice noncommittal. "I'll have a report ready in a couple of weeks." I needed to change the subject. "What exactly does a literary agent do, anyway?"

"I represent authors who want to get published," Gordon replied. "I studied English once, but it . . . didn't work out. I wasn't cut out to be a writer myself."

Here came the "let's confess to the psychiatrist" part of the evening.

"Why not?" I asked, ever the good doctor.

"Hmmm," Gordon mumbled. Then, "Notice what I'm drinking?" He held out his glass, full of ice and lemon, with a bit of something red on the bottom.

"Blood?" I said, then wished I'd kept my mouth shut. But I couldn't help it, the guy was as predatory as a vampire.

Fortunately, he just laughed. "Tomato juice," he said, drawing out the *a*. The British accent was back. I was fascinated, and repelled, simultaneously. Greg's arm tightened around my waist. His other hand held a glass of what looked like whiskey.

"At the time I had a little . . . chemical dependency problem. I don't have very clear memories of those days. I was in a graduate school for a while. But fortunately, that's all in the past, now.

"I got treatment, and my wife got pregnant. My son Oliver is just around the same age as Natalie's young client. What a tragedy, that the Devinski boy should have grown to be so warped. My Oliver is a tremendous boy."

"And where is your wife this evening?" I inquired as politely as if I were asking about the health of the Queen.

"Oh, we divorced. She and Oliver are back in London."

I glanced at Natalie, who was standing close to Gordon with a shrimpy yet possessive stance. She was gazing at Greg as if he were the prize behind Door Number One. How did she manage to make two men feel so handsome and important at the same time?

"So you want to write a book on the Devinski trial?" Greg drained his glass. "You seem pretty optimistic. Maybe there won't even *be* a trial. And anyway, how do you know this case will have the magnitude you want it to have? Couldn't you at least wait until it starts?"

"It's a hot publishing category. I have the name. People would buy it." Natalie was vehement in her defense, just as I imagined she'd be in court.

"And would you actually do the writing, also?" I asked sweetly.

"We haven't worked out the details," Gordon said, missing the point. "But I'm certain that this will be a huge case. Tremendous." One of his favorite words, obviously. "I did a little writing when I was in graduate school. I can help her."

Suddenly I had to get away from Natalie and Gordon. I excused myself and went to get another drink. Greg followed me loyally.

"Let's get something to eat," he said, with his usual assumption that the food was actually the reason we came. He was blessed with an excellent metabolism and a genuine love of exercise, so he could afford to be a foodie. I was more the genetically-engineered-for-any-possible-famine type, although I fought it bravely. Still, I had to eat dinner, didn't I? This crowd contained enough interesting people to keep me away from Natalie for the rest of the evening. I could eat and schmooze. So that's what we did.

Greg and I finally got home sometime after midnight. We were just tipsy enough to enjoy the taxi ride home together. By the time we pulled each other into bed I had forgotten all about Natalie, Gordon, and the Devinskis. It was only as I drifted into sleep that I wondered, illogically, what Gordon's missing ex-wife and the tremendous Oliver were doing right now.

chapter five

Three days later I'd had about as much leisure time as I could stand. Tuesday morning I said to Greg, "I'm going to the office. I'm going to schedule the Devinskis' evaluations." I knew we were theoretically on vacation, but I wasn't a good vacationer. I hadn't had enough practice. Maybe I needed a hobby.

Greg admitted that he was planning on "just stopping by the office for a minute," himself. So we set out, a little later than usual, for our respective offices.

I could have called the Devinskis from home, but it was a beautiful day, very cold, with snow still on the ground but a sky as blue as a child's drawing, strewn with fluffy clouds. I caught an uptown train and emerged strangely energized on Seventy-seventh Street.

I called the Devinskis from the office. Karen answered right away. I explained who I was and what I wanted.

"Oh, Tamsen," she said. "You don't mind if I call you Tamsen, do you?" They all did that. "It's been so awful. My managed-care company referred me to a social worker for psychotherapy, but I really don't feel up to it. Plus, this woman I work with just went out on emergency medical leave and I have to cover for her. They all know what I'm going through, but I really need to keep my job so we can afford that lawyer. Oh, God," she said, and sighed, then gave a little croak, as if she had run out of gas.

I waited to make sure she was finished, then asked her when would be a convenient time to come in.

"Not today. I'm going crazy with this presentation. How about tomorrow? Do you want us together or separately? 'Cause Peter could come today, if you need him. Peter," I heard her calling. "Pete, come here for a minute."

"That's okay, Mrs. Devinski." I always did that, I called them Mr. or Mrs., and they always called me by my first name. "Your husband can come at the same time as you, if you want."

"Please, call me Karen," she said.

We made an appointment for ten-thirty the next morning. Then I puttered around the office, watering the plants, sorting the mail, and reading the magazines that we subscribed to, supposedly for the waiting room. I was surprised when the phone rang. It was my line. I picked it up before the answering service could get it. May as well save the twenty-five cents it would end up costing for them to answer and then page me.

"Dr. Bayn," I said, half expecting a patient needing a refill on a prescription, even though I was pretty good at preempting those requests.

"Yes, hello." The voice was youngish, female, confident. "Is this the answering service?"

"This is the doctor," I said.

"Oh. Hi." She sounded relieved. "Hi. My name is Gwendolyn Conklin, I'm a child psychiatrist in Lexington. Lexington, Kentucky. Call me Gwen." She pronounced it "Gwin." Her voice had a twang that I guessed was all bluegrass. "Okay, this is why I'm calling," Gwendolyn said. "I have a practice here in Lexington. Mostly kids. I do a lot of work for the courts. So the other day, I'm sitting around with my family, opening presents, having a nice holiday." Here her voice took on a sarcastic note. "If you're into sitting around with a bunch of relatives, each of whom knows best about how you should live your life." I knew instantly what she meant. "I'm pregnant," Gwen said. "You have to forgive me. I know I'm being a bitch. I have, like, *no* impulse control left. I just say whatever comes into my mind. But at least *I* haven't shot anybody—yet.

"Anyway," she continued as I sat down at my desk, getting ready for what I thought might end up being a good story. "I get this call from the Lexington DA's office that they have this kid they need me to see. His name is Sammy Towland. Maybe you heard about him out there?"

"The boy who shot his whole family last summer? The one who asked to speak to a psychiatrist on Christmas morning?"

"Yeah, that one. I didn't even know about it, the fact that he and the grandmother had agreed to talk to a psychiatrist, I mean. I knew about the shootings, of course. But my parents and my husband are, like, in this conspiracy not to upset me. It's my first baby. I'm thirty-nine. They think I'm much too old and fragile to be doing this."

"The DA wanted you to evaluate Sammy Towland as soon as possible," I guessed.

"Yeah. So of course, I said yes, and man, you should have seen the scene at my parents' house! All hell broke loose. Like I should be in suspended animation somewhere, waiting to give birth, my brain on ice."

"Did you see the boy? Sammy?" The way she told it, her family problems were almost as interesting as that murderous little boy.

"I saw him, all right. He is one cold little kid. No remorse, none whatsoever. It's like whatever was in him that made him human, it's gone. Sammy's like a little robot kid from some movie about after the bomb."

Gwendolyn Conklin sounded like one of those Appalachian storytellers I had heard about, spinning out her tale into one hell of a long-distance call.

"So let me tell you how I got to you, Tamsen. Or do you prefer Tammy?"

"I hate Tammy," I said.

Gwen laughed. "Good thing you don't live in Kentucky, then. Anyway, I called the prosecutor's office in Manhattan to find out who was evaluating that Devinski boy, your child murderer. They told me it was Dr. Bluecorn. Is he the same one who wrote that textbook, the big red one?"

"The forensic psychiatry book? Yeah, the same one. He didn't write it, he just got a lot of people he knows to write it for him."

"Bluecorn's out of town until after the New Year. But the woman I spoke to knew you were going to do the parents, so they gave me your number, said maybe you could help me."

"How can *I* help you?"

"Something is damn strange with that Sammy Towland. The grandma, she's one of those sweet old ladies with blue hair, even though I guess she's no more than fifty-five or so—she told me that Sammy was always just the sweetest little thing, no problem at all, really good with his schoolwork, played all nice with his little brothers. Grandma swears that only recently, when he started to reach 'pubery'—that's what she called it—he started stayin' in his room alone all the time, actin' all weird, losin' touch with his friends."

"What did she say about the parents?"

"Oh, you know, how they-all were such good parents, never raised a hand against their kids, hardworkin', God-fearin' kind of folks."

"Think they were?"

"Well, I really couldn't tell you, since they're dead. That's what you're gonna tell me about the Devinski parents."

"What do you mean?"

"Since I can't meet with the Towlands, I thought I could learn a little about the Devinskis. Just for my information. You know."

"It's a different kid," I said, baffled.

"Well, I know. Let me tell you what I did, just as part of my research. You'll keep this between us, right?"

"Of course." I could envision Gwen as an old lady, rocking on a porch in front of a one-room shack, long white hair in a braid, with a bunch of scraggly barefoot kids clustered around her: *Now, chilluns, y'all listen to old Grannie Gwen; she's gonna tell y'all a tale gonna chill your marrow right outa the bone. . . .*

"I went down to the hospital to see if the parents had any old charts in medical records. And guess what?"

"They did?"

"That daddy was a big-time drinker. He was in for detox maybe five times."

"You think Sammy's father drank, that he used to beat the kid or something?"

"Maybe. I mean, we do have other hospitals. He could have gone to some program somewhere else. Or he could have given up, just stayed a drunk. If he was drunk and abusing the kid all the time, who knows what might have happened?"

"Where did he get the gun?"

"Sammy, you mean? Honey, this is Kentucky. We got guns."

I considered for a second, then said, "As long as we're keeping this confidential, I may as well tell you. The Devinski father was an alcoholic too. But he supposedly stopped drinking about the time that his son was born. Before, even."

"Yeah, so it's supposed to be some intellectual challenge to say that these kids who grew up in alcoholic families have problems. Like we didn't know that."

"I've seen lots of kids from alcoholic families. Most of them don't become vicious killers when they hit puberty." Truth be told, I was a kid from a partially alcoholic family. The daughter of what's called a functional alcoholic.

"Well, you have another explanation?"

"I don't have any explanation," I admitted to Gwen. "But I'll tell you what, I'll give you a call after I see Jason's parents, and let you know what I think."

"Great."

I took her numbers and wished her luck with the case and the baby.

"Thank you," she said. "I'm gonna need all kinds of luck with this kid. Usually they don't care what the psychiatrist thinks. They just want you to see the kids so it will be, like, on the record. But in this case, suddenly everyone wants an explanation. An' it better be good!"

chapter six

After I hung up with my new friend Gwen, I chose a few magazines to take with me and put on my coat. I had almost made it out of the office when the phone rang again.

"Hello, this is Daphne Williams calling on behalf of Mr. Parker Grandines." The caller's voice was satiny, her articulation superb. Even with secretaries, Mr. Grandines obviously had impeccable taste.

"Yes?" I replied profoundly.

"Mr. Grandines would like to arrange an appointment to meet with Dr. Bayn, and for her to meet some of our staff. Would she be available around two o'clock?"

"This is Dr. Bayn," I said. Will there ever come a day when I can answer my own phone and people won't automatically assume I'm the receptionist? Then Daphne's request hit me. "Today?"

"Today," Daphne replied, unruffled.

I looked at my watch. I would have to go home to change, but I could make it.

"Okay." I wrote down the address, which was downtown, not far from my apartment. Only after I'd hung up the phone and was on my way home did I think that perhaps I should have played a little harder to get.

The man sitting to my right on the subway was reading a beautiful newspaper printed in various colors of ink. Photographs of Jason Devinski and his four victims were prominently displayed on the front page, but unfortunately, the paper was written in the intriguing characters of some Asian language that I couldn't read. The man on my left held up a paper printed in mundane black ink on a faded grayish background, but at least the words were in English.

This newspaper featured photographs of both Jason Devinski and Kentucky's Sammy Towland. "The Murdering Boys," the headlines dubbed them. The similarities between the two shootings, and their appearance in the media around the same time, had of course encouraged the press to link the crimes, even though there was no conceivable association between them—beyond the obvious. Kids all over the country were shooting each other, but so far the search for a variable to connect them all together had been fruitless.

My seatmate's newspaper used the occasion of the Kentucky shooter's request to talk to a psychiatrist to rehash Jason's crime, which had been truly horrible. He had come to his school holiday party, all dressed up in corduroy pants, a new white shirt, and leather shoes. He had been a good student, but lately he had been a little "isolative," one of those bogus psychosocial mumbo-jumbo words that only means "isolated." He entered the school gym with the rest of his sixth-grade class, got himself some popcorn and a soda, and talked briefly to his classmate Amanda Frost, taller than him and "strangely seductive" in her shiny red party dress (this last bit from the male gym teacher).

When Amanda walked away from him to join a group of friends, Jason had pulled a little gun out of his pants. *"I thought it was a toy," said a classmate, whose parents refused to let her be identified.* Then Jason walked right up to Amanda, pointed the gun at her head, and fired. She was still alive, one-eyed, on life support, and she was expected to survive. After Jason shot Amanda, he kept shooting into the terrified crowd until the little gun was empty. Amanda's two friends, Jessica and Hannah, had already been buried in the frozen ground. A teacher, Carla Lopez, thirty years old and recently married, had also been laid to rest. A color photograph showed Jessica's grave, covered with flowers, stuffed animals, and candles. And snow. I closed my eyes, hard, and breathed deeply through my nose until the urge to scream passed, and then I didn't read over the guy's elbow anymore.

I got off the subway shivering long before I reached the street. I was used to seeing psychiatric patients who were also criminal defendants, who had committed violent crimes. I was even used to seeing drug-abusing criminals with no official psychiatric disorders, who thought they could beat the system by faking insanity. But somehow the murders that occurred during drug busts or barroom brawls, or even the crimes of passion committed by fully grown men who should have known better, failed to evoke the same response in me that these little murdering kids did. Was it exposure to too many violent cartoons and movies, like some people claimed? Could the violence be blamed on working mothers, another popular theory? I pushed my way through the crowded streets that seemed suddenly to be filled with prepubescent boys. Would one of these children be next to pick up a gun?

I always had a tendency to overidentify with everyone. I identified with the victims. I identified with the perpetrators. I even identified with the witnesses, although that's a little harder. You don't usually get the feeling that the latter are really grieving or horrified. Usually my impression is that the witnesses are in a state of there-but-for-the-grace-of-God grandiosity that makes them say really stupid things on national television. I wished that Jason Devinski and Sammy Towland had never done what they did. I kind of wished I hadn't been drafted into their sagas. I was a relatively young woman, finally planning my wedding and starting—I still thought of my life as not having quite yet started—my real life. I didn't want to be drawn into anybody's disaster right now. And with the good fortune of this Grandines consulting job, I could justify turning away a forensic consultation now and then.

But then again, it was a big case. Everyone in the city—in the tristate area—would be following it. The only other time I had gotten involved in a big case, my practice had doubled within days of the verdict. It had been great for me, for my career, for my ego. I was so ambivalent. I hated tragedy, but I loved attention. And I had this niggling little egotistical muse that whispered to me, "You can figure this out, make it all better." Whatever "this" was.

By the time I unlocked the door to our apartment I was mentally kicking myself for not making a holiday reservation for some tropical paradise. Greg had scheduled a few days off also, but I guessed that by now he had firmly reinstated himself at work. His prestigious position as the second in command of the Career Criminals Unit of the Manhattan district attorney's office was one of those plum jobs that put him in the spotlight of every major homicide investigation in the borough.

"Hey." Greg was home, sitting on the sofa with a huge file open on the coffee table in front of him. "Wanna collaborate?" He gave me that hypnotic wink.

I laughed and threw my coat over a chair in what we euphemistically called our dining room. I sat next to him, putting my icy hands on the back of his neck and kissing him the way that, until I met him, I thought was reserved for times when the lights were out and I'd had too much to drink. "I love you," I said without even meaning to.

"I love you too," he said. "Take your clothes off."

I gave an inadvertent and unladylike snort. "I was just going to make us some lunch. I have a meeting at Grandines at two."

He closed the folder and stretched. "Lunch sounds good," he said, with that wicked grin, green eyes laughing. "One of the many advantages of working from home. You control all the interruptions. Anyway, you're going to have to change to go to Grandines, so you may as well . . ."

I laughed again and went into the kitchen to make tuna sandwiches. In between bites I told Greg about the phone call from the psychiatrist in Kentucky.

"So," I concluded, "since the parents of her kid are dead—"

"Since he murdered them," Greg interrupted.

"Since he killed them," I agreed, "this psychiatrist, she wants to talk to me about the parents of our kid." I was using possessive pronouns because that's how psychiatrists tend to talk: "My old lady," "My kid," "Your manic-depressive." It's a subtle form of jargon. "She hopes she can learn something about her kid's family situation by comparing it to a similar family's . . . a family that produced a child murderer."

"You think there are any similarities?" Greg asked me. "Lexington, Kentucky? Could you even find it on a map?"

"Of course I could," I bragged.

"If it were one of those geophysical maps with no state lines on it, could you find it?"

"That's beside the point. Listen. That father had a long history of alcohol abuse. This guy, Devinski, he's a recovering alcoholic."

"I thought that alcohol caused brain damage in the people who drink it, not in their offspring."

"Except for fetal alcohol syndrome. It's caused by the effect of alcohol in utero."

Greg looked at me quizzically.

"If a pregnant woman drinks a lot of alcohol, her baby can end up with brain damage, and certain deformities. It's a syndrome, a collection of physical findings that occur together. Like, a lot of times, fetal alcohol syndrome babies don't have this. . . . It's called the philtrum." I reached out and touched the little indentation above Greg's upper lip. "But that's the least of their problems. They are usually retarded or have behavior or learning problems."

"Retarded? I hope you're not going to say that in court."

"It's a medical term. Nothing offensive about it. Mental retardation has its own code numbers for insurance purposes, and that's exactly what it's called. Mild, moderate, severe, profound. Each one gets its own number."

Greg scowled. "Jason Devinski is not retarded. And anyway, it wasn't Jason's mother who was alcoholic, you said it was his father."

"Yeah . . . a recovering alcoholic, which supposedly means he's sober. Anyway"—I decided to lighten the mood—"didn't you ever hear that saying 'Insanity is hereditary, you get it from your kids'?"

That got me a smile, at least. "So, Mr. Assistant District Attorney, my question for you is, can I talk to this Gwendolyn about what I find out about the Devinskis?"

"You will anyway," Greg said. "You think I don't know how you psychiatrists gossip about all your cases?"

"Oh, like you lawyers are any better." People always talk about their work. It's a fact of professional life. You go out to lunch with someone, maybe an old friend that you happen to bump into when you go to court to testify, and next thing you know, you're swapping horror stories and tall tales, anecdotes with miniplots, about borderline patients, emergency room incidents, and legal nightmares. But implicit in all this storytelling is the simple fact that the information never can, and never will, be used by the listener for anything other than entertainment.

What Gwendolyn wanted was a little different, however. What would the repercussions be if she used my evaluation of the Devinski parents as a "Source of Information" for her evaluation of little Sammy Towland?

"You can get the Devinskis' permission, Tamsen. Otherwise, any discussion you have with this other psychiatrist has to remain unofficial. Maybe instead of talking to you, she could find some articles on the families of children who murder. Actually, maybe *you* could find some articles too. It could help us."

My potential role in this disaster was getting bigger by the minute. "Maybe." I shrugged noncommittally. Research was not my forte. I stood up. "I'm going to get ready."

Grandines Pharmaceuticals was waiting for me, and I was cutting it kind of close. I put on a black suit with a pale silk blouse and black heels, appropriate corporate-type clothes for meeting with pharmaceutical-company executives. The secretary with the smooth voice had asked me to bring a copy of my CV, so I printed one out as I reapplied my makeup. I wore elegant little pearl earrings, even though my natural preference was for long dangly exotic ones. I hoped I could look as sophisticated as the secretary sounded.

I took a cab. I must have lucked into a random lull in traffic because I got to the Grandines building with almost twenty minutes to spare. Following the instructions I had scrawled on the back of an envelope (recycling, I liked to tell myself, not disorganization), I signed in at the security desk, then took the elevator to the twelfth and top floor.

I stepped from the elevator into an enormous reception area, designed to make me pause and notice it, which I dutifully did. A curved, polished wood desk displayed a name tag that read "Ms. Clothilde Simmons." The wall behind her was wainscoted in dark and shiny wood, topped with a burgundy and gold wallpaper. Crown molding completed the effect. Clothilde looked like a model; that is, she looked like a skinny seventeen-year-old blonde dressed up and made up to look thirty-five. I felt as if I had stepped on to a sound stage.

"I'll tell Ms. Williams you're here." She spoke with some kind of accent or affectation to her speech that I couldn't quite place. She pressed a button and mumbled something into an intercom. "Please have a seat, Ms. Bayn. Ms. Williams will be out shortly." *That's Doctor Bayn to you, kiddo.*

The reception area in front of the elevators opened on to a glass-walled waiting lounge furnished with several overstuffed sofas and little side tables. The magazines were new and organized in wooden racks. A tall table in front of the windows held a massive arrangement of fresh flowers, just in case the panoramic view wasn't enough for the casual waiting visitor.

I wondered what kind of offices filled up twelve floors. While I admired the scenery, the sparkling water of New York Harbor, still ice-less, the sun reflecting off the glass of the downtown skyscrapers, I thought about what pharmaceutical companies actually did. I had taken psychopharmacology in college, and pharmacology in medical school, and in my residency, psychopharmacology courses were part of the curriculum throughout all four years. I prescribed medications almost every day of my working life, and I certainly liked to reap the perks of being on the drug companies' marketing lists. But I had never really considered how drugs were developed or how they were brought to market.

The door opened and a woman stepped into the waiting area. Seeing me, she walked over briskly with a welcoming smile on her red-painted lips.

"Dr. Bayn?" I recognized the smooth voice from the phone. She held out her hand, which immediately added ten years to my original guess about her age, which had been thirty. Women can get face-lifts but their hands rarely lie. "Welcome. I'm Daphne Williams, Mr. Grandines's executive assistant. If you would follow me, we're all set up in the conference room."

I shook her hand obediently and followed her down a carpeted hallway. Despite the carpet I swore I could hear her heels clicking: she had that kind of walk. The red skirt with the black blazer and crisp white blouse made her look smart and fashionable enough to be Grandines's CEO. "I hope Clothilde didn't frighten you," she said. "Some of our visitors have been complaining. She's just a temp. She wants to be an actress. Thinks she's fooling everyone with that fake French accent. Parker wants me to get rid of her, but in the holiday season, it's difficult to find temps."

Daphne seemed nice enough. Maybe this Grandines experience would turn out to be a positive one. I had been— slightly and momentarily—intimidated by the no-expense-spared air of the building, the waiting area, and of course Parker Grandines himself. But apparently Daphne, like me, was unimpressed by pretension and wasn't afraid to admit it. I took a preparatory breath as she opened a door.

The buzz of conversation stopped abruptly when we entered. I looked around the room to avoid looking at the people it contained. From this angle the Statue of Liberty could clearly be seen in the distance. Before I could process anything else, Parker Grandines stood in front of me, his big hand outstretched.

"Dr. Bayn, thank you so much for joining us on such short notice. Please have a seat."

I sat in a wood frame chair with gray upholstery and wheels. The wheels glided soundlessly on the gray carpeting. The conference table was a huge wooden oval, and spaced around it sat four men.

Daphne said, "What do you take in your coffee?"

Relieved that the first question was such an easy one, I answered, "Milk, no sugar," and glanced at the foursome. Next to Parker Grandines was a man who could have been his brother, and in fact—

"This is my brother, Colin." Grandines began the introductions. "Colin is chief financial officer. That is my cousin Jonathan Grandines on his right, my brother-in-law Jackson Dwyer, and of course you know my right-hand man, Daphne Williams."

"Right-hand woman," Daphne corrected, her voice only slightly less smooth, as she handed me a ceramic mug of coffee and sat down beside me. She placed a little notebook in front of her on the table.

I took a sip of coffee so that I wouldn't be expected to say anything. I felt like a duck sitting on an ice floe with a bunch of penguins. I knew that I could swim, but I still felt out of place.

"Jonathan is nominally our head of marketing." Parker Grandines didn't merely speak, he orated. "Although he has several division heads working under him. And Jackson, of course, is a physician. He is the global head of medical operations for Grandines."

"Really?" I said politely. "What kind of physician?"

"I'm an internist," Dwyer said. He was a tall, gaunt man with a shock of white hair, bushy white eyebrows that turned up at the ends, and eyes so pale they looked clear, like water in a glass. His voice, though, was warm. "I haven't practiced in many, many years. When I married Alice, her father offered me a job here."

Parker Grandines must have seen the question on my face because he explained, "Alice was my older sister. She died two years ago. A stroke."

"I'm sorry," I said.

"Yes, well, back to business," Jonathan Grandines said, his first contribution to the conversation.

"We're extremely excited about the launch of our new drug," Colin Grandines said. "How familiar are you with its mechanism of action, and its clinical indications?"

"I was hoping to learn more about it at the dinner tonight." I smiled as wide as I could. Their drug was just another serotonin agonist, so I was sure I understood more about how it worked than they did. After all, I was a psychiatrist, and they were a bunch of businesspeople, except for Dwyer, who by his own admission hadn't actually practiced medicine in many years and had to be well into his seventies anyhow.

"Yes, well, good." Jonathan nodded. "Do you have any questions? We'd like to be able to count on you to come to some publicity meetings in the next few weeks."

"What would I have to do?"

"Oh, you know, talk to reporters about how you are giving your support to this amazing drug that will save lives."

"Because Curixenol will save lives," Dwyer interjected. "You realize that, don't you?"

"I . . . um, yes, of course." I drank the rest of my coffee, so I wouldn't have to elaborate. Something in Dwyer's voice had changed. I almost challenged him to explain to me how the drug worked and what the clinical indications were, but something in those watery eyes stopped me.

"Did you speak with Ginny Liu about Curixenol?" Parker Grandines asked me.

"Well, yes, we spoke about it. I asked for samples, but Ginny said they—you—weren't sampling yet, not until the official launch." Not that I'd expect Grandines to hand out samples before the drug was officially available in pharmacies. Ginny had given me samples of Grandines's other popular drug, Xixperdine, as a consolation prize.

"Did she say anything else?" Parker inquired.

"Not really," I said, wondering why he cared. Was he checking up on Ginny, on how she was doing her job? Was she up for promotion?

"It would be important for us to know, with this diversion business, now, if she took you into her confidence." Parker watched me closely.

"Diversion business?" I wanted to break his gaze, but felt I'd be giving in to something.

"Oh, we had a little problem with diversion of a shipment. A return. Nothing you need to be concerned with." Parker smiled and shook his head slightly.

"A shipment of Curixenol?" I asked, perplexed.

"Oh, no." Parker laughed. "We don't need to go into this right now." He gave the others a look that could break glass. "So, getting back to Miss Liu. We'd like to know what you discussed with her the last time you saw her, was it Friday? We need to know how much training we'll need to subject you to before you can start doing public relations for us."

"She just told me about this job, and a little bit about Curixenol. She left me some materials to read."

"What materials?" Jonathan's voice was like a knife. Parker glared at him disapprovingly. These people were not friendly. I didn't get it. Was it because I was a woman? A Jew? A doctor? Was it anger at their other psychiatrist for dumping them, that they were taking out on me? Or did their obvious anger have something to do with Ginny Liu?

"Marketing materials," I answered. I heard the slight snippiness in my voice as I asked, "Marketing, that's your department, right?" Jonathan nodded, chastised or something. I wasn't feeling quite so intimidated anymore.

"How did you develop Curixenol, anyway?" I asked.

"What do you know about how a drug is brought to market?" Dwyer asked me.

"Not much, really."

"First, a compound is developed by our scientists. I won't go into how that is done. It involves all kinds of studies about receptors and protein binding and other biochemical techniques that I'm really not familiar with."

"Yes?" He was the global head, yet he wasn't familiar with the process? Was that normal?

"Then the compound is tested in animals, mainly for

safety but if possible also for efficacy. Once we know it's safe, we start testing it in humans. And eventually, it becomes a drug. The FDA—Food and Drug Administration—gives its approval—"

"And voilà, we have a new drug," Parker interrupted his brother-in-law. "I'm sure you can discuss this with Dr. Bayn another time, Dwyer. She has to get going if she's going to make it to our dinner tonight."

"Will you be there?" I asked in surprise. I'd never heard of a pharmaceutical big shot attending something as pedestrian as a sales dinner.

"Oh, no," Parker Grandines said, a shade too regretfully. "I'm sorry we didn't find you sooner, you could have said a few words tonight. Our previous psychiatrist was slated to contribute something, but, sadly . . ." He let the words hang over the polished table.

Daphne stood, and all the men quickly stood too. I scrambled to my feet, feeling as if I were in temple following the instructions for silent prayer.

"Thank you so much for coming," Parker Grandines said.

I glanced at my watch. It was only 2:05. The meeting had started early and had lasted less than fifteen minutes. I shook hands all around and followed Daphne as she led me back to the elevators. Even the inside of the elevator was shiny polished wood. As the doors slid shut in front of me I let out a sigh of relief and leaned against the elevator wall.

What did this company want from me? Why had I been invited here today? I could buy the assumption that for some reason the company really needed a psychiatrist on the Curixenol team. But why would the four most senior members of the company need to meet with me? What secrets were buried in the marketing materials Ginny had left for me? What, exactly, was a diversion? What was I missing?

chapter seven

I went home, hoping to tell Greg about my meeting, but he was out. He must have run back to his office. By the time he came back, I was getting ready for the Grandines dinner and I had convinced myself that the meeting with the Grandines bigwigs had been only so that the other guys could meet me and give their stamp of approval. Probably the position they'd offered me was as a figurehead, nothing more. They hadn't even told me what they wanted me to say to the press or when they wanted me to start.

Greg forgot to ask me about the meeting. He seemed distracted but I didn't comment. Sometimes we just needed to give each other a little space. By the time he got out of the shower an hour later, I was ready to go out. I twirled around, showing off my new dress. I wore sheer black stockings and the sequined black shoes, and I knew I was outrageously overdressed for an early dinner with a bunch of psychiatrists. But it was worth it, to have Greg look at me the way he did. And after all, we were going to the opera, and there would surely be other dressed-up people there, because this was a holiday week and everyone was overdoing everything.

Greg looked handsome as always in a dark suit and a tie with little hippopotami all over it. You couldn't really tell, it just looked like a tie with a conservative small repeating design. He caught us a cab as soon as we walked out of the building. We sat close together, not talking, during the ride uptown, but I sensed that the earlier hint of tension between us had subsided.

The restaurant was called Nicoletta's and it was on the West Side about two blocks from Lincoln Center. We walked in and gave our coats to an attendant. I looked around at the crowd, not seeing anyone that I recognized. A small table near the entry had been set up with name tags, the way seating cards were laid out at weddings. I found ours. Greg's actually said "Gregory Jolson, Esq." So that was why Ginny Liu had asked me my "significant other's" name. They couldn't very well have a name tag that said "Guest," could they?

I looked around for Ginny. She had arranged the whole thing. I hadn't forgotten that she had recommended me to Grandines, and I wanted to thank her. I didn't see her diminutive frame anywhere, which seemed odd. Ginny was a small person, but she had a very large personality. And in general, the pharmaceutical representatives would always greet all the doctors individually.

Greg and I made our way through the crowd of middle-aged men and their frosty-haired wives. I nodded to a couple of people I recognized. As we approached the bar, I smashed right into a woman who turned around just as I tried sliding by. Whatever curses she had been planning to hurl at me died on her lips.

"Tamsen!" Dr. Lourdes Esposito gave me a hug and a kiss. "Wow. You look great! It's so good to see you. And who's this?" Lourdes had been chief resident in the emergency room when I was a young, raw attending.

I introduced Greg, and returned the compliment. Lourdes was literally glowing. She had lost weight, and her thick, glossy black hair was in a French braid that reached halfway down her back.

"Where's Nassim?" I asked her.

"He had an emergency," Lourdes replied. "You know he's in private practice now?" We caught up a little bit, and then she said, "And we have another surprise." She stepped back enough so I could see her stomach, like a basketball under her stretchy black dress.

"Congratulations!" I exclaimed, and Greg joined in. He didn't even know her, but soon he was joking with her and asking if he could feel the baby kick.

"Tamsen and I are going to be parents soon too," he said.

Lourdes's black eyes grew round.

"We are not," I said.

"We are," Greg said. "We are."

I thought it was a good time to change the subject. "Where's Ginny?" I asked.

"Oh, didn't you hear?" Lourdes paled, remembering. "Ginny had a terrible car accident."

"She did? How awful! Is she okay?"

"Actually . . ." Lourdes paused. She knew how sensitive I was. "She's in a coma. She had extensive internal injuries, and she broke both femurs. She might not make it."

"Oh, my God," I said. "How did it happen?"

"I don't know. I heard she had to stay late for a meeting on Christmas Eve, and so she was rushing home in that snowstorm. She crashed going into the Holland Tunnel. Her car got squashed between a bus and a van. She never knew what hit her."

"It happened *Friday*?" I felt as if someone had punched me in the stomach. Nobody at Grandines that afternoon had mentioned Ginny's accident. Were they such callous, money-oriented businessmen that they didn't even think to tell me that the person who had recommended me for their job had nearly been killed? So far this year was going out with a lot of bangs, most of them horrendous.

Lourdes had just started to reply when a woman's voice spoke over a loudspeaker. "Ladies and gentlemen, welcome to Grandines Pharmaceuticals' holiday party. Please take your drinks and find seats in the dining room. We'd like to get the presentation under way."

I sat with Lourdes at a table for six, while Greg went to get us our drinks. Looking around, I calculated that there must be about sixty guests. The restaurant was one big room, with stucco walls, red and white checkered tablecloths, and rustic-looking wooden tables and chairs that looked like they would have been at home in someone's summer house in Tuscany. Candles stuck on top of old

Chianti bottles flickered on the tables. Every table held a couple of red carnations in a vase. The effect was of an intimate gathering in some other country, a country where the families were huge. I kept thinking about Ginny.

"Was anyone else hurt?" I whispered to Lourdes.

She shook her head no, put a finger over her lips and pointed to the front of the room. A podium and screen for slides had been set up against one wall. Greg came back to the table and handed me a glass of wine.

"Good evening and thank you all for joining us tonight." The woman at the lectern was probably in her mid-forties, with frizzy blond hair pinned on top of her head. She wore a dark green suit with a darker green velvet collar. She looked somehow *wrong* for a drug rep. Usually they were younger, their hair always smooth and shiny, their complexions flawless, their makeup perfect. This woman looked pale and haphazard. I wondered if she was a scientist, not a marketing person.

"As you know, Grandines expects Curixenol to be a wonder drug for the twenty-first century. . . ." I zoned out. I tend not to listen to the presentations. I could read the package insert later. As far as I could tell, there was nothing particularly revolutionary about Curixenol. Grandines had just figured out how to carve out a new niche for their product. This class of drug worked for depression, for social phobia, for anxiety disorders, and for obsessive-compulsive disorder. Grandines Pharmaceuticals had—rather cleverly, I thought—added alcohol dependence to the list. The company had been premarketing Curixenol for months, and even the *Today* show had done a feature on it. It would have been nice if the program had offered me information that I didn't yet have, but I didn't learn anything new.

A waiter approached our table as the woman droned on, and handed around some menus. I studied mine by candlelight. Greg whispered to me, "What are you going to have?" I felt someone brush against the back of my chair and looked up to see Lourdes's husband slip into the chair beside her.

I sipped my red wine and dipped a piece of bread into

a little dish of olive oil. The oil had some herbs in it, and a lot of black pepper. This presentation was much more boring than I had expected. If Ginny had been doing it, she would have had us all laughing with her Viagra jokes.

"This company is cursed," Lourdes whispered to me.

"What are you talking about?"

"Don't you know who that is up there?"

"I have no idea." I realized belatedly that it was odd that the speaker hadn't introduced herself. I knew that Grandines had invested a fortune in this drug launch. I had expected a perfectly choreographed and executed presentation. What we were watching was worse than my lectures to the medical students used to be when I found out at 9:55 that I had to cover for somebody at 10:00.

"That's the mother of the boy who shot the girls and the teacher at his school last week."

"That's Karen Devinski?" I was too shocked to remember to keep my voice down. People turned to glare at me. Now I felt really bad. No wonder the woman hadn't introduced herself at the beginning of the presentation. And no wonder the presentation sucked. Karen Devinski had told me on the phone that she was extremely busy. She had mentioned someone on emergency medical leave. Now I was stunned to realize that Karen Devinski had been referring to Ginny Liu, the Grandines representative I'd first met during my training, and had bumped into so many times over so many years.

Up at the podium, Karen, mercifully, was winding down. "So, let me recap, you start with thirty milligrams PO"—by mouth, or, for Latin fans, *per os*—"daily, in the morning. The side effects to look out for are basically dry mouth, or slight nausea. Those side effects should resolve within two weeks. Then you can go up to the recommended daily dose of sixty milligrams. And just stay there.

"Ladies and gentlemen, I want to thank you again for being here tonight, and I hope that you will all find clinical applications for this new medication that will, ultimately, save lives." The applause was about as deafening as one hand clapping in the forest. Karen Devinski quickly stepped down from the spotlight and took a seat in the back of the room, where she busied herself packing up her slides. No question-and-answer period, unusual, but understandable given the circumstances. I was sure she didn't want to be here and didn't want anyone to know who she was. I excused myself from my tablemates and approached her.

"Karen?" I said hesitantly.

She looked up. Her eyes were bloodshot. Her green suit had a flaky white spot on the velvet of one cuff. What kind of company would force an employee to take on this kind of last-minute responsibility at such a horrific time in her life?

"I'm Tamsen Bayn. We spoke on the phone today."

"Hi!" Karen smiled, and for a moment I could see how she must have looked before her son had become a killer. "Oh, I'm so pleased to meet you. I apologize for the awful presentation. I had nobody else available, I had to do it myself."

Karen was either turning on the charm so I would like her, or she was doing something that was strangely common among people I evaluated for the court. She was responding to me as a psychiatrist, as somebody in whom she could confide her darkest secrets, and totally ignoring the fact that the information I gathered might one day be used against her in a court of law. I always informed evaluees that the interview was not confidential and that it was not a therapy session, but they rarely cared. When Freud first described transference, he knew what he was talking about.

It wasn't like me to be cold and distant. I sat down next to her. "I heard about Ginny." There was no prohibition against expressing my sympathy. "I'm so sorry. Have you seen her?"

"I stopped by the hospital yesterday on the way to the lawyer's office."

I nodded, to indicate that I knew who she was talking about, but not giving anything away. "I didn't know you were a drug rep."

"I'm not," she replied, with a tight smile. "I was, years ago. I've been with Grandines for over fifteen years. I'm their director of marketing for CNS." CNS stands for "central nervous system," and includes all psychiatric and neurological pharmaceuticals. "Although I know I don't look like it, tonight."

"You had to cover for Ginny?"

"Ginny is the district manager for Curixenol for this whole region. All my reps are either out doing other programs tonight or on vacation. You know, a lot of them are young, they have little kids, family responsibilities . . . I tried, but I couldn't pull someone off vacation at the last minute." She shook her head. "I guess I could have, under the circumstances, but I didn't even try. Old habits die hard."

"Have you heard anything at your company about a new psychiatrist for the Curixenol team?" I asked her.

"No," she said. "Nothing. I didn't think they'd really need anyone, and after what happened. . . ."

"What happened," I echoed, more sharply than I had intended.

"Oh, the previous psychiatrist just, well, disappeared. He was there one day, gone the next. A great guy, really. I heard he went to the Bahamas. I should have gone with him." Unspoken but understood were the words: *And I should have taken my son, before it was too late.*

"They offered me the position," I told her. "Ginny recommended me, they said."

"That's great," Karen said. "So we'll be working together, after this, well, you know."

I wasn't so sure that it was great. "It may be a conflict of interest. I'll have to check. I had no idea you worked for this company."

"I'm sure it's not. But we'll check. Grandines's legal department will check for you."

It was nice to know they had a legal department to consult. Come to think of it, I had my own legal department, waiting for me at the table.

"Aren't you going to eat?" I said to Karen. "Come and

join us." Well, why not? We still had two empty seats at our table. She hadn't pulled the trigger on those poor girls and their teacher. She had to eat. I wasn't going to interrogate her, and she looked so lost sitting in the back of the room when she should have been the center of attention. I stood up and she reluctantly followed me. The waiter was hovering nearby, so we both ordered.

The conversation stayed carefully away from Jason Devinski.

"What's diversion?" I asked Karen, after we'd discussed the bizarre snowstorm to death.

She looked at me blankly.

"In the pharmaceutical industry," I clarified.

"Oh. Diversion is when a shipment of drugs doesn't end up where it's supposed to be."

"Have you heard anything about a diversion problem at Grandines?"

Greg had been talking to Nassim about the football playoffs. His head jerked around and he said, "What?"

"Diversion—" I began, but Greg interrupted me.

"Conflict of interest," he hissed in my ear.

I shut up instantly. I had just landed two really cool jobs, I didn't want to lose both of them simultaneously.

"How's Ginny doing?" Lourdes asked Karen. I was grateful for the seamless change in topic.

"I'm going to go see her again tomorrow morning," Karen said. "Her poor husband has been keeping vigil at her bedside day and night. They've been together for twenty-two years." She told us how Ginny had met her husband on the first day of college. "They have two children. Their daughter is twelve, and they had a baby boy last year. They tried so hard for that baby. Ten years they tried. Excuse me." Karen swiped a tear that had silently made its way down her cheek and pushed back her chair. "Thank you all for coming. I've got to get going, now. I'm sorry that I have to leave you all alone. Nice meeting you." She stopped by the back of the room and collected her slides and projector. I saw her confer briefly with the maître d' before she vanished out the door.

chapter eight

Wednesday morning Greg woke up at his usual time of five forty-five and went off to the gym. Wind and rain rattled the windows. Vacation was over. Our sparkling evening at the Metropolitan Opera was just a memory now. I forced myself awake and reluctantly sat down on the side of the bed to put on my sneakers. I had no more excuses, and I still had one new slinky dress that I wanted to wear on New Year's Eve.

By eight o'clock I had exercised, showered, dressed, and made coffee. Greg called to tell me that he would be taking witness statements all day. In a normal case, the sworn testimony, equivalent to depositions in civil trials, probably would have come later, but in the case of Jason Devinski, the witnesses were on a school-year calendar, and the entire case was complicated by the fact that there were so many witnesses, and that most of them were minors. I had an appointment with the Devinski parents later, but I couldn't stop thinking of Ginny Liu. I had known the Grandines representative since I was a resident, in the casually friendly way you know people you see once every month or two, for not more than an hour at a time. I knew that Grandines Pharmaceuticals made mostly generic versions of popular drugs, but they had one patented antipsychotic medication, unspellably named Xixperdine, that was definitely a big money-maker for them. Until recently, Ginny Liu's entire arsenal of psychotropic medication consisted of Xixperdine. I'd wheedled some samples out of her last time—and I'd asked her for Curixenol too, but she'd informed me they weren't sampling yet. Samples were great—you could give them to patients to try a new medication, before asking them to make a commitment to trips to the pharmacy and, for those without a prescription plan, considerable expense. With this new Curixenol, a selective serotonin reuptake inhibitor with—maybe—the incredibly useful side effect of stopping alcoholics from drinking, the company would move out of the category of small pharmaceutical company. I personally had doubts as to whether or not a drug in this class could have the effect Grandines was claiming, but if Curixenol worked at all, I'd predict that the giants, the pharmaceutical conglomerates, would start placing their bids any day now. The current owners of the company would be rich beyond their wildest dreams. Poor Ginny, she had worked so hard for them, and to have something like this car accident happen to her was unthinkable. I decided to go visit her before going to my office.

Lourdes had told me that Ginny was in Bellevue, where she had been taken by ambulance after the crash. I'd worked there for two years after finishing my forensic psychiatry fellowship, but I didn't feel like stopping by the psychiatric emergency room or any of my old stomping grounds. As I made my way upstairs to the neurosurgical intensive care unit I passed some familiar faces and exchanged the usual holiday pleasantries.

Only two visitors were allowed in at a time, and only for fifteen minutes out of the hour, but I was a doctor, and still officially on staff as voluntary faculty. Ignoring the sick and recovering in the other curtained cubicles, I left my coat and umbrella at the nurses' station and clipped my ID card to my scarf. Ginny was lying on a raised hospital bed. Various bags were hanging from poles. I recognized what was basically a sugar-and-salt-water solution, and a collapsed plastic bag with yucky-looking beige goop smeared on the inside that I knew had contained TPN, total parenteral nutrition. Two men stood at Ginny's bedside. One was an Asian man wearing jeans and a sweatshirt. The other was a tall, distinguished Caucasian, in a familiar black cashmere coat and holding a pair of expensive-looking leather gloves in one hand. The other hand tapped on the bed rail. Parker Grandines was visiting his injured employee. I murmured a general "Hello," and turned to the younger man.

"Mr. Liu?"

The Asian man raised his eyebrows. "Ray," he said.

I introduced myself to Ginny's husband and told him that I just wanted to see Ginny for a minute, that I had always liked her and that I'd known her, although not well, for about seven years.

"She opened her eyes before," he said in a tired voice.

I looked across at Ginny. Once she had been a tiny firebrand, straight black hair cut in a short wedge, dark eyes blazing. I remembered the ring that she wore on her right hand, made of that extra-yellow Chinese gold and a piece of jade carved into a little dragon. Now her hands lay limply at her sides, her arms were dark with bruises from where intravenous lines had been inserted, and had infiltrated their contents under her skin. She already had a central line, right under her collarbone, into a large vein. Although no machines beeped at her bedside, I knew that Ginny was being monitored by telemetry and that the nurses could observe her vital signs without ever leaving their station. Ginny's head was bandaged and I knew that underneath the gauze her glossy hair had all been shaved off. But she was breathing on her own, and that was a good sign.

Ginny's husband stroked her pale cheek with one finger, and I thought I saw her eyelids flutter for a second. "She's beautiful even without hair," he said softly. Grandines took in a deep loud breath.

I looked at him again, and he held out his hand, the one that had been tapping on the bed rail, and said, "Dr. Bayn. Always a pleasure."

I shook the proffered hand. "It's nice of you to come see her," I said, privately wondering if he had actually known who Ginny Liu was, prior to her Christmas Eve disaster. "Did you just find out about the accident?"

"Yes, just yesterday afternoon," Grandines replied. "Late yesterday afternoon."

"I just wanted to see her," I said to Ginny's husband. "I don't want to intrude."

"It's time to go, anyway," a nurse said, walking over. "You can come back in half an hour. We're going to get her washed up now."

The nurses were probably happy, in their own way, to have this pretty young woman to care for, instead of the gunshot wounds, the cheating, drug-abusing husbands who'd had their brains bashed in with frying pans in the middle of the night, the detritus of the community, people who had nowhere else to turn. It occurred to me that Ginny gave the nurses hope. For once the nurses could hope for the recovery of a patient who really deserved to recover. Bellevue was a city hospital, famous for its psychiatric wards and for being a refuge for the unwanted and disenfranchised. As Ginny's condition stabilized, she would probably be transferred to New York University Hospital, just up the street, but a world away in terms of clientele and atmosphere.

I went out into the corridor with Ray Liu and Mr. Grandines, preparing to leave, but Ray said to me, "Did you go to the Curixenol dinner last night?"

"I did, actually."

"Ginny had been working so hard on that presentation," Ray said. "I think that's what caused this. She had been working too hard." He looked at Parker Grandines without expression, but it was clear whom Ray blamed for his wife's condition.

"I feel terrible about this," Grandines said. "I know I drive my people hard." A poor choice of words, under the circumstances. He winced. "We had a last-minute sales meeting. She must have been in a rush to get home."

Something bothered me about Parker Grandines. He kept turning up in the weirdest places, first my home, now Ginny's bedside. I got the feeling that he had come here this morning especially to make this speech to Ginny's husband. I had the irrational thought that Mr. Grandines was *spying* on Ginny, which of course was absurd.

"Has Karen been here yet?" I asked Ray.

"No," Ray said. "Is she supposed to come here today?"

"She mentioned she was going to stop by this morning. At the program last night. She did very well," I told Mr. Grandines, just in case he had heard how truly awful the presentation had been. Karen Devinski had enough problems. She didn't need to lose her job on top of everything else.

Just then Karen turned the corner into the visitors' lounge area.

"Oh, Ray, how are you doing?" she murmured, hugging Ray Liu as if he were a relative or a real friend. She stepped back and seemed to see me and Mr. Grandines for the first time. "Parker. How nice of you to stop by." Her voice wasn't exactly what you'd call warm.

"How are you holding up?" Grandines asked.

Karen shook her head and didn't reply. Her curly blond hair was still pinned in a frizzy mess on top of her head. She was wearing a long black coat over black leggings, black cowboy boots, and a thick black turtleneck. Even Karen's umbrella was black. I've heard a million jokes about how New Yorkers always wear black, but to me, Karen looked as though she were in mourning.

"Tamsen. I know Ginny would be so happy to know you came by to see her. Now I remember her telling me about you, about a year ago. I didn't make the connection until after we met."

I couldn't think of a response.

"Yeah, she told me when you joined your parents' practice, how she was rooting for you, because almost everyone she knew in private practice was middle-aged and out of date. She really liked you. *Likes* you," she corrected uneasily. "That must have been why she recommended you to Parker, when we needed a psychiatrist so quickly."

"I think she's getting better," Ray interjected.

"Yes, one can only hope so," Grandines said. Why did that man repulse me so?

"I'll be right back." Ray slipped away so quickly I didn't even see in which direction he had gone. Nobody made a move to follow him. After a moment, Karen spoke.

"Parker, maybe you know what Ginny wanted to tell me after the meeting? She rushed off so fast after she met with you that I couldn't catch up with her."

"I'm sure I have no idea," he replied.

"It was so strange," Karen went on, "to go into the office on Monday and get an e-mail from her, knowing that she was already . . . here."

"What kind of an e-mail?" I asked.

Karen glanced at me, then said carefully, "Nothing special. 'Merry Christmas, see you next week.'" She shrugged.

"Karen," I said politely, "I need to get to the office. And didn't you say you had an appointment too?" Why I was being so evasive, I had no idea. By tomorrow the fact that I had evaluated her would probably be in the newspapers.

"I haven't seen Ginny," Karen said.

"The nurse said we have to wait half an hour," I told her.

"In that case, I'll come back this evening," Karen said.

"I'm looking forward to working with you," Grandines told me. "In the meanwhile, I do hope you can help Karen's son."

So much for subterfuge. He knew I was evaluating the Devinskis.

Karen and I moved toward the elevators. "Do you mind if we ride uptown together?" she asked.

"Of course not."

"I would never, ever have hung out with one of my other psychiatrists."

"I'm not your psychiatrist. Think of me more as a detective, trying to figure out if anything in your life could have influenced what your son did. I'm court-appointed. I don't take sides. I'm just trying to gather information." I didn't know a gentler way to put it. My job had nothing to do with helping Karen cope, although if I thought she needed psychiatric treatment, I would certainly recommend that she get it—from someone else.

Outside, it was still raining, and the sidewalks were slick with melting snow. The wind beat at my red umbrella. "Let's take a cab," I said, reluctant to make the long walk to the subway.

"I was just going to say that." Karen stepped into the street. A yellow taxi miraculously appeared and we got in and listened to the prerecorded voice of some famous person I'd never heard of tell us to fasten our seat belts. The inside of the cab smelled like a wet dog. I gave the driver the address and turned to Karen.

"I'm not officially starting the interview or anything. But you have to tell me one thing."

She looked at me, not understanding. Her eyes were very blue, the red capillaries less pronounced than the night before.

"Why did you lie to Mr. Grandines?"

chapter nine

"I didn't lie," Karen said.

"I just got the feeling that you weren't telling him something about the message Ginny sent you."

"Oh, no. It was nothing secret. But it wasn't any of Parker's business."

I waited. It was none of my business either, but I bet she would tell me. People always tell me things, and not only because it's my job to hear them. And telling me about Ginny would keep Karen's mind off her son and his problems, a little good deed on my part that would no doubt not go unpunished.

"What did it say?" I asked.

"It just said, Everyone is buzzing about Jason. We really need to talk. And of course, Merry Christmas, I hope you liked your present, like I said."

The taxi splashed through what seemed like an entire river. I waited until we were back on terra firma before I continued.

"So what do you think Ginny meant by that? You really needed to talk about what? Do you think that your job is in jeopardy because of what Jason did?"

"How could it not be?" Karen's tone was bleak. "Listen, I can't say that we have financial difficulties, Peter and I. We have money put aside. But I need to keep working to pay Jason's lawyer. She's very expensive. As it is, the money for Jason's college will have to go to his legal defense. They can't fire me for what Jason did. Even if he's found guilty . . ." She paused. "I've been with the company a long time. If Grandines Pharmaceuticals gets sold, I'll get a bonus, a big bonus. Then I'll quit, or get laid off, and look for another job."

I thought about Karen's explanation. When I'd met her last night, she had seemed to genuinely care about her son. Obviously, I didn't have any children, and I sometimes thought that if I ever did anything notoriously horrible my parents would just abandon me. Still, the normal response would surely be to do whatever it took to save your child. I tried not to think about the one-eyed girl or her two dead classmates, or the dead teacher, or any of their living survivors.

The taxi crept through the jammed streets, full of snow, slush, vehicles, and pedestrians. With the exception of doctors, who have to travel from hospital to clinic to moonlighting job, New Yorkers seldom drive. We take buses or subways, or taxis. I somehow don't consider a taxi a real car. When I'm in one I never wear a seat belt or pay attention to the traffic. I always think that the taxi driver is experienced enough to keep me safe, which intellectually I know is ridiculous. Most of the city's taxi drivers come from other countries, where they'd had any of a thousand different occupations—but almost never taxi driver.

"Isn't it strange that Ginny had a car accident when she was so used to driving?"

"I was thinking about that," Karen said. "As a drug rep you spend almost all your time on the road. At one time, Ginny's territory was all of New Jersey. *All.* Can you imagine how much driving she did back then? And she never got so much as a speeding ticket."

I guess nobody ever wakes up in the morning and says, "Today is the day I'm going to change the habits of a lifetime and get into one of the worst car accidents in the history of the Holland Tunnel." Still, it sounded like Ginny had always been a safe and responsible driver, just as she had always seemed to me, in our brief interactions over the years, to be a responsible and reasonable person.

We rode the rest of the way in silence. The cab finally stopped on East Seventy-seventh Street, in front of a residential building with a white canopy and uniformed doorman. My office, or, more correctly, my parents' office that they were kind enough to share with me, was on the ground floor. My parents had bought the office years before, when we still lived in a two-bedroom, one-bathroom apartment in Washington Heights. While I was away at college, they'd bought an apartment on the fifth floor of the same building. It was a thousand times nicer than the apartment I grew up in, but I had never really lived there except for a few months this past fall after I sold my apartment and before I officially moved in with Greg.

A large man was sitting on the bench in the lobby right outside my office door. He had wet dark hair, shot through with gray, and a beard that looked like it had missed its most recent trim, and possibly the one before that. A pool of water had gathered at his feet where it still dripped off a giant black wood-handled umbrella and a pair of rubber-and-leather boots. For some reason, nobody ever sat on that bench unless they were here to see me or my parents. It was as if a large sign were posted above it, "Emotionally Disturbed People with Major Problems Only," even though the bench had been placed there by the building management and its twin sat sedately right across the foyer. Karen introduced the wet man as her husband, Peter.

"May I throw this piece of junk out in your garbage?" Peter asked the doorman. His umbrella was broken. That explained the wet hair.

I knew the office would be empty; my parents didn't use it much anymore. I showed the Devinskis in. After checking the expiration date on the milk in the little fridge, I made a pot of coffee. Soon the three of us were sitting in the consultation room. It's a great office, cozy and soothing, like a furnished cocoon. I wish I could say I had been the one to decorate it, but it was all my mother's doing. The Devinskis sat together on the couch, holding hands. They didn't look like the type of people who could raise a killer.

"Did you want one of us to wait in the waiting room?" Karen looked at her husband as if he were a lifeboat and the sofa were the *Titanic*. Her coffee cup sat on the end table, untouched.

"Maybe later," I said. I didn't need to stress them. As long as they weren't hiding secrets from each other, it didn't matter if each heard what the other one had to say.

"I wish it was something we did," Peter Devinski said. "You know? We left Jason with nannies, and of course we were older already when we had him."

"I was thirty-five," Karen added. "I'm forty-seven now. Maybe I had some genetic mutation that the amniocentesis didn't pick up."

"I used to drink." Peter's expression was pained. "You know all that. You saw the records. Maybe the alcohol somehow damaged my sperm." He looked uncertain, as if maybe he shouldn't have spoken what passed for a dirty word in some circles. "You're a doctor, right? An M.D. Not a psychologist." Obviously, my being a medical doctor made the tentative foray into sexual jargon okay for him.

"I'm an M.D.," I said. "I'm board certified in general psychiatry and in forensic psychiatry. Look, let me tell you a little about why we're here. The judge in Jason's case has ordered both of you to submit to a psychiatric evaluation, to see if maybe one of you has a psychiatric condition that might have impacted on Jason's actions."

They looked at each other. Peter held both of Karen's hands in just one of his big ones. I could almost smell their anxiety.

"Anything you tell me is not private. An interview with a forensic psychiatrist is not like a regular session with a therapist. The interview is *not* confidential and I will be writing a report to submit to the court."

Both Devinskis nodded. They had known all this when they agreed to our meeting. Although the judge officially ordered the evaluation, it was really a result of the desire of both attorneys, the judge, and the parents themselves to find some answers. Or at least to define some questions. I had never really heard of someone other than the defendant himself being court-ordered for an evaluation, but this case had so much in it that did not make sense.

"Now, about what you just said, about alcohol damaging sperm." I sipped my coffee as I tried to remember. Caffeine, too, has been linked to birth defects, although the validity of the research is debatable. "Sperm takes about two weeks to be produced, and to become ready to fertilize an egg. So whatever's in the ejaculate underwent its first cell division about two weeks before. A *history* of alcoholism wouldn't affect the genes that you pass on to your offspring. And anyway, I don't think that there's any evidence that alcoholism in the father produces any birth defects." I took a deep breath and looked at Peter, who'd seemed so distraught a moment ago. "But are you saying that you *knew* that there was something wrong with your son?"

"No," Karen answered quickly. "There was nothing wrong with Jason. In the past few months, he seemed more withdrawn than he used to be, that's all. He used to be a very outgoing boy."

"Tell me about him. I need to know whatever you can tell me about Jason, and yourselves, and his relationship with you. A child's relationship with the parents is so important."

"In my mind it's all like a bad dream, a terrible mistake." Karen's eyes glistened with unshed tears. "My Jason couldn't have done this. I don't even know how he got his hands on that little gun."

"It wasn't your gun?"

"We wouldn't have a gun," Karen said. "For what? We live in the city. We don't have a business. We're not allowed to have guns."

It's almost impossible to get a gun permit in New York City, but I knew many people who had managed to, and many more people who simply didn't bother with that step. Just because they claimed it wasn't their gun didn't mean anything.

"Why don't you tell me about how you met? The two of

you." Maybe I'd try conducting this interview on a happier note.

Now Karen was openly crying. "We met on a blind date. Is that important? Don't you want to talk about Jason?"

"Yes. But I also want to talk about you. The defense attorney would like to be able to say that somehow you were responsible for what Jason did—"

"Hey, wait a minute." Peter's voice rose. "I'm paying that woman to help my son, I'm not paying her to make *us* look bad. We didn't abuse him. I never even slapped him. I *loved* him. *We* loved him. We *love* him. I mean, if there's something *inadvertent* that we did, well, that's one thing. But we don't want a Menendez trial here."

"No." I shook my head. "I don't think that's what she means to do. She's just looking for a way out. The prosecutor is very unhappy with this case also. The judge, too, probably. Nothing like this has ever happened here before, and there's no clear history of behavior problems in your son, at least no history of anything that the press has latched on to." I waited to see if they would contradict me, but they were both nodding in agreement. My psychiatrist's intuition told me that neither of them had known that Jason had any problems or leanings toward violence. So many parents refused to accept any responsibility for their children's actions. These parents seemed to be simply bewildered and upset, not hiding anything. But intuition has been known to be wrong.

"Was Jason a planned child?" I asked. I turned to a third sheet of paper. I almost wasn't conscious of writing things down as I interviewed, but of course I had to document everything. After years of residency training, fellowship, and working, the one thing psychiatrists indisputably know how to do is take notes.

"Planned? Well, yes, of course, I guess you could call him planned," Karen answered. "We wanted him. But I wasn't like those women who could say, Oh, I think I'll have my baby the second week of February so it can be an

Aquarius. You know? Or let's squeeze him in towards the end of December so we can get our tax deduction. Things were going well for us, we stopped using birth control, and eventually we got pregnant. I got pregnant, I mean."

"How long did you try?" I asked, curious more because I was thirty-three and wondering how long it would take me to get pregnant than because I really thought it mattered.

"Not long, actually," Peter laughed, looking proud. "First shot out of the gate."

"*Peter!*" Karen reddened, but she looked a bit more relaxed.

We went through the history of Karen's pregnancy, had she taken drugs or medications, was everything normal; her delivery (NSVD, for normal spontaneous vaginal delivery); until we got to the part about her postpartum depression.

"But, you know," she told me, "I don't think I really had it. We lived in another state then. The psychiatrists there were very generous with the medications, not too interested in psychotherapy. You know, a different perspective than around here, at least for those days." She gave a grim laugh. "Today it's just pills, pills, pills, no matter where you go. Good for my bonus, if not for my brain." She paused. "So, I think after I had Jason, I was just stressed, having problems coping. I suddenly had this tiny creature who depended on me for everything. It was hard."

She went on to tell me that her psychiatrist had told her to stop breast-feeding so she could take the antidepressants, which she dutifully did, but "Not right away," she added, with a worried look on her face. "Could that have done something?"

I wrote down the name of the medication with a promise to look it up for her, but I didn't think that a couple of weeks of a couple of tricyclic-laced feedings a day would have made a difference. In any case, the influence of the medication on the baby would be for the child psychiatrist to determine, not me.

We went through the rest of Karen's history, and then I turned to Peter. He cheerfully reminded me that he used to drink, but he had solved his problem with the help of a great "shrink." He didn't think he had any other psychiatric problems, and according to his records, he didn't. All that meant for me, though, was that Peter had somehow mastered the problems which had contributed to his alcoholism—not that the problems didn't exist.

"Yeah," Karen said. "Funny. I think Peter's psychiatrist was the real reason we decided to have Jason."

"What?" I was confused.

"I don't mean that like it sounds," she said. "He was a terrific guy. He used to tell us this motto, 'Make up for lost time,' after Peter got sober. So we decided to have a baby. Poor guy."

"Poor guy?"

"Yeah, he had a stroke or something, when he was still fairly young."

"Was it while he was treating you?" I asked. "How horrible, to have your psychiatrist—die. Did he die?"

"Not right away," Peter answered. "But no, I'd stopped the treatment by then."

"You stayed in touch with him?" It isn't unusual for people to want to keep their old therapists informed of events in their lives, but it is highly unusual for the psychiatrist to reciprocate.

"I just heard through the grapevine." Karen shook her head. "A real tragedy."

"Horrible." I paused, then turned to Peter. "When you heard about your former psychiatrist's death, did you pick up a drink?"

"No," Peter said. "I guess I really was better. It hasn't been a problem for me to stay sober."

I wondered, but didn't comment. The ninety minutes I'd planned to spend with the Devinskis were up. "Thanks for coming," I said. "Oh, Karen. Do you mind if I ask you about something totally unrelated?"

"Depends what it is," she said, frowning.

"That psychiatrist who worked at Grandines. The one I'm replacing. Did you know him, by any chance?"

"Oh, sure. Antony Hastings-Muir. Nice guy. Really sexy English accent."

"What happened to him?" I asked.

"Nothing, as far as I know. He just left. His fiancée died suddenly a couple of weeks ago. A freak accident." Karen's eyes clouded over for a second. "Tony left the company right afterwards. He got a nice severance package, though, so I don't know if it was workmen's comp, or disability or something. This was going to be his first marriage. He was, oh, forty-five? Oldish, for a first marriage. But cute." She glanced at her husband.

"So he was with the company for a long time?" I was treading dangerously close to conflict-of-interest territory, but I thought I could get away with just a couple more questions.

"Yeah, Tony came here from England and did a research fellowship or something, then he got this Grandines job and stayed."

I glanced over my notes as I sorted the pages to file away. "Oh, one more question," I said. "Karen, did you go with Peter to his therapy sessions, when he quit drinking?"

"To Dr. Abitor?" Karen asked, and I wrote down the name after I asked her how to spell it. "Yes, I went sometimes."

"It was a group-therapy thing." Peter looked uncomfortable. "For alcoholics. I went. We went. I got better. Until now, I thought we had done pretty well for ourselves."

"You did." Talking with these two dynamic, articulate, attractive people, I had almost forgotten what their son had done, the reason we were here now.

Karen clearly remembered, however, because her expression altered. "Obviously we screwed up somewhere. What do you think we did?"

"I don't know," I answered honestly.

"And, oh, my God, look what time it is." Karen was looking at her watch, standing up and gathering her things together in a frenzy. "We have to go. We have to see Jason at one. Natalie is going to meet us there. Pete, come on."

"When can you come back?" I asked them, my pen poised over my appointment book.

"Tomorrow," Peter told me. "We'll be here tomorrow. Same time?"

"Sure, the same time," I said, watching them run out the door. I wrote their names thoughtfully on tomorrow's empty page. Their departure had been so hasty. Were they really in such a rush? Or was it something I'd said?

chapter ten

After the Devinskis made their departure, I sat at my desk staring out the window for a while. The air was gray with rain and fog. I winced as I heard a squeal of brakes, but happily, no sound of metal crunching into metal followed. I was getting hungry and I felt discouraged. Although the Devinskis had shared some intimate details of their lives, I was no closer to understanding what, if anything, had happened to Jason. In fact, we had barely mentioned him, because every time his name was spoken, Karen began to cry. Was she crying for herself, for her son's lost innocence, or for the lives he'd destroyed?

I was also itching to talk to this Antony Hastings-Muir, the psychiatrist who had worked for Grandines for so many years and left so precipitously. He'd known the Devinskis, or at least Karen. I couldn't really ask him about her without written permission, but I could talk to him about Grandines. Even if Hastings-Muir had moved, maybe his New York phone number was listed. I couldn't imagine that he could sell his apartment, if he owned one, in just two weeks, even though I had miraculously sold my apartment in one week. (But still. You have paperwork and a closing. It takes a long time to actually be free of your real estate.) I picked up the Manhattan White Pages and looked up Hastings-Muir. To my surprise, an Antony was listed. It had to be the right guy; even in New York there couldn't be two people with such an odd name. I called the number and got a recording: "Hey, this is Tony. Please leave a message." I hung up before I could hear him say, "After the beep." I had no idea what I wanted to say.

The voice definitely had a British accent, not as strong as the ones you hear on TV but unmistakably not American. I composed my thoughts and called back. This time I left my name and various phone numbers on the tape, asking him to please return my call ASAP.

I locked up the office and took the elevator upstairs to my parents' apartment, hoping they weren't home. I rang the bell and then inserted my key into the lock. They usually had food.

Just as I was pushing the door in, somebody opened it. My father was standing there, wearing a suit and looking like he was about to go to some important function, maybe a coronation.

"Where are you going?" I asked.

"I just came from the dentisht," he said. That's my father in a nutshell. Nothing like wearing a thousand-dollar suit to lie in a chair with sharp metal instruments all over your chest, and to get sprayed with water, and if you were really lucky, a little blood. "Come in, Gordon ish here."

Gordon Ranier, my favorite breed of predator? It was my day for Englishmen.

"How nice to see you again." Gordon held out his hand, so I shook it. As he had at the party, he gripped hard and strong and long. For some reason I was reminded of the boys in seventh grade who used to grab your hand and then tickle your palm with their middle fingers. I guess back then we all thought there was something sexual about it. Whatever sexual was.

"How's the book coming?" I asked him.

"Oh, excellent, excellent. We're almost ready to send it out." Gordon told me a little about my father's twelve-step program for liberating women from mentally and physically abusive relationships. I wondered if my father was going to let my mother read the book. I'd rarely met a man more egotistical, manipulative, and self-centered than my father. My mother was a sort of a door prize he'd acquired along the way. I was often curious why he'd never replaced her with a younger, blonder model.

"So, have you met with the Devinskis yet?" Gordon wanted to know.

"A little," I said cautiously.

"Any ideas yet?"

"Not really. How's Natalie's book coming along?"

"She's been far too busy to work on it. Interviewing witnesses, that sort of thing. And Dr. Bluecorn is still in Florida. When he returns, and evaluates the boy, then we'll have something."

How Natalie could think about writing a book about something that hadn't happened yet was beyond me. Unless she was going to market it as fiction, of course.

"How wush the dinner?" my father asked. My psychiatrist parents had been invited to the Grandines Curixenol extravaganza but, fortunately for me, hadn't been able to attend.

"Weird. You remember Ginny Liu, the Grandines rep?" When you work in a medical office for years and years, you get to know all the reps; they stop by every month or two, with the latest news about their products. A reminder service, so we continue to prescribe whatever it is they're selling. I don't mind. I told my father what had happened to Ginny, and how Karen Devinski had to cover for her and give the Curixenol presentation.

"I wonder if that's the case they were talking about on the news this morning," my father slurred.

"What case?"

"I heard," my father said, then dramatically rubbed his puffy jaw. "Something about the tragic accident in the Holland Tunnel on Christmas Eve was now definitely thought to be the result of sabotage and brake tampering."

"Really?" I breathed. I couldn't believe it. Somebody that I actually knew, a victim of an attempted murder. "So if somebody did something to Ginny's brakes—what did they say was done to the brakes, anyway?"

"They didn't shay."

"But whoever tried to kill Ginny could still be after her."

"They said that the victim's spouse was taken in for questioning."

"Ginny's *husband*? Oh, that's ridiculous. The man worships the ground she walks on."

"Listen, I'm just repeating what I heard."

"Is Ginny under police protection? How could somebody tamper with her brakes? How would they know that she'd get in such a bad accident, that she wouldn't just swerve into somebody in the parking lot at some suburban supermarket?"

My father cocked his head to one side in the thinking pose he'd cultivated for use on the daytime talk shows. "I don't know."

"Ginny is a district manager. Maybe she has a disgruntled employee after her."

Gordon pounced on that. "Really? Do you work much with disgruntled employees?"

I could see the wheels spinning in his devious mind. *Twelve Steps to Preventing Shootings in the Workplace,* a national best-seller.

"You know, when I worked in the emergency room, the only category of psychiatric patient that we always, *always* admitted was postal employees."

Gordon laughed, as I expected him to. I have a whole repertoire of cocktail-party chatter and amusing anecdotes for when I want to impress people with my professional experiences.

"So, lovely people, I was just going to invite your father here to come out with me for a bite of lunch. Tamsen, would you care to join us?"

"I can't have lunch, Gordon. I'm still numb. I can't eat for two hours." My father looked offended that Gordon hadn't remembered.

I wondered where my mother was. She would have to suffer all my father's wrath when the anesthesia wore off and the pain kicked in.

Gordon made a token murmur of regret, then turned to me. "So, Tamsen, shall we?"

And that, ladies and gentlemen of the jury, was how I came to be having lunch with the suave and debonair Gordon Ranier on a rainy December afternoon.

chapter eleven

Gordon and I left my father clutching his jaw and pouring himself a scotch. Outside the rain was still falling, and it had gotten colder. I don't know how Gordon ended up sharing my umbrella, but when I slipped on a patch of ice as we crossed Park Avenue, he grabbed my elbow to steady me, and then didn't release it.

I was so uncomfortable walking so close to him that I didn't even hear what he was saying as we made our way through the soggy streets. I knew exactly what he wanted from me, had known it from the minute I caught him staring at the décolletage of my black velvet dress the other night. Not that I didn't find Gordon attractive, but I wasn't interested. I was almost married, and I had waited for so long to find the right person. Gordon had no *right* to do what he was doing.

He led me to a restaurant on the corner of Seventy-seventh Street and Third Avenue. A curved, polished mahogany bar took up the front half, and even though it was lunchtime, the crowd was three or four deep. We were shown to a booth in the dining room. When I took my coat off, I felt Gordon's eyes burning into me like lasers. Everywhere they looked got warm.

I sat on the padded bench and briefly thought that I should have been shown, instead, to a padded cell. I was crazy for having lunch with this guy.

A pretty blond waitperson came over to us. "Would you care for a drink?" she chirped.

I perversely gave Gordon credit for not ogling her. He ordered a "tomaaaato" juice, and I asked for seltzer. I studied the menu while I wondered why we were here. Could it be only for the obvious reasons? My stomach growled, as if to convince me.

The waitress returned with our drinks and a basket heaped with bread. She took our orders and slipped away.

"So how were the Devinskis, then?" Gordon asked conversationally as he reached for a roll and his butter knife. "The father drank, you said?" I'd said no such thing to Gordon, but clearly he'd picked it up from Natalie. "Tough thing to deal with. I barely remember those years when I was drinking. I was different then. It was a difficult time for me, and I seem to have blocked out much of it."

Oh, goody. Yet another man who used lunch with a psychiatrist as an excuse to vent. I watched him devour his roll, and I took one myself. Gordon touched my left hand as it hovered above the bread basket.

"Beautiful ring. I didn't realize you were married."

"It's an engagement ring." I knew that many women wore my type of ring, a circle of diamonds, as their wedding rings. "I'm engaged," I added, stupidly.

"He's a lucky man."

"Thank you."

We both paused. I desperately needed to change the subject.

"I have a new position," I said. "A new job, I mean. As a consultant for a pharmaceutical company."

"Oh, very nice. What company?"

"Grandines Pharmaceuticals. Have you heard of them?"

Gordon's hand stopped in midair. "Grandines? Why, yes, of course I've heard of them." He set his glass down gently. "Weren't they on the news recently?" He reached for another roll. "Superb bread, isn't it?"

"Deadly." I tore a little piece off my roll. "On the news? Why?"

"I'm not sure. I think they had some sort of industrial accident? I heard something about a British bloke, which is why I paid attention. And something about some accounting problems or something."

Gordon's English accent was more foreign than usual today. Gordon had obviously come to this country as an adult; Greg had emigrated from Russia when he was ten, and his accent was usually almost undetectable. But it became more pronounced when he was stressed or uncomfortable. Something to ponder.

"I think I heard something about that."

"Apparently this Brit owned a home in Bermuda, and he moved there. I've been in this country for almost twenty years, so I know quite a few people in the expatriate community. But it was nobody I knew. It was funny, though—the newscaster used the Bermuda angle as a lead-in to the weather."

"The weather there must be beautiful. Do you know, um, why he left the company? The British guy, I mean. Did they say he was a psychiatrist?"

"A psychiatrist? Someone you know, then? A colleague?"

"Not exactly."

"The news report I saw said that this woman, this man's fiancée, also worked in the company." Gordon sipped his tomaaaato juice. "In a different department from the man. They showed her photograph on the telly. Blond, very pretty in an intelligent sort of way." He smeared more bread with butter. I had an irrational memory of a childhood book—could it have been my Girl Scout handbook?—instructing us that bread should always be torn, never cut.

"What happened to her?"

"Some sort of explosion in the lab. She was a scientist of some kind. A microbiologist? Maybe a geneticist? I don't really remember. Apparently, she was working late one evening and there was some kind of industrial accident. She was struck in the head by a piece of flying glass. One of those freak accidents. They tried valiantly to save her, but she died a few days later, without regaining consciousness. Quite sad."

"Grandines sure wins the prize for freak accidents."

The talk turned to Ginny, then back to the mysterious

Antony as our lunches arrived. I'd ordered a salade niçoise, with grilled shrimp and calamari in addition to the customary tuna. Gordon had a plate of something cheesy and drippy, oozing calories.

"Mmm, smells good," I said.

"Now, all we need is a nice Chardonnay." His blue eyes were bright as he sipped the last of his juice. "You know, if I hadn't gotten sober I probably would still be married."

We were back in *True Confessions* mode. I wasn't surprised. Dysfunction did serve a purpose.

"I worry a bit about Oliver," he added.

Oh, yes, his son, the *tremendous* one.

"Do you?"

"I worry about him growing up there without me, and with a stepfather. I'd love to bring him here, but I don't think I would be a very good father."

"Too many different mother substitutes for him here?"

"What? Oh, well." He laughed. "Is it so obvious?"

I hoped it was a rhetorical question. We finished our lunch, and I got up to put on my coat. I was going to catch the subway on the corner of Lexington, and we walked over together. The icy rain had turned to snow, and my leather-soled boots were no match for the sheets of ice we had to cross. Gordon offered me his arm, and I chose proximity over an impromptu skating lesson. Still, I was glad when we reached the freshly salted station stairs.

I let him kiss me on the cheek, old-friends style, and thanked him for the lunch that he had insisted on paying for. In a couple of minutes I was steam-drying on the downtown number 6 train. Carefully keeping my eyes away from other people's newspapers, I thought over my morning with the Devinskis and my lunch with Gordon. He had been entertaining in his own way, but the man made me nervous for reasons I hadn't completely sorted out. He'd seemed to know an awful lot of details about a story that had been only a lead-in to the weather.

I stopped thinking about Gordon as the train screeched into the Fifty-ninth Street station. I changed to a train that would leave me marginally closer to home. I emerged downtown ready for the long walk, but after a block of walking west into the wind, little bits of ice flying into my eyes, I hailed a taxi. I was spending that Grandines money already.

I was relieved to get back to my cozy apartment. The morning's rain and slush had not only turned to ice but was now already covered with at least an inch of new snow. You couldn't tell that underneath the pretty whiteness, treachery lurked.

I changed out of my black wool pants and the black sweater that had been the focus of so much of Gordon's attention, and put on some sweats, best for serious thinking. I called Greg at the office, but he was unavailable. Still meeting with all the schoolchildren, probably. Or deep in negotiations with Natalie. Oops. Shut up, brain.

As I made a pot of decaf I couldn't help thinking of all the coffee I had been making for people in the last few days. I had offered Ginny Liu a cup of coffee as I squeezed her in between two patients last Friday. Plying everyone with refreshments isn't so unusual for a psychiatrist. I'd read somewhere that Sigmund Freud himself used to offer his patients chicken soup.

Last Friday, Ginny had only been in my office for a few minutes, to tell me that she had recommended me to her company as a consultant. I'd been very busy that day with my regular, nonforensic patients, seeing all the anxious grandmothers who were about to have their children over for Christmas and the anxious daughters who were dreading spending the holiday with their parents. I wanted to make sure that everyone would remain stable during what was going to be a stressful time for them.

Ginny had urged me to pursue the consultant job, and had pressed some promotional materials on me. She'd seemed a little upset, but I thought it was because of the weather and the last-minute crush of work and preparations. I wasn't sure if she celebrated Christmas officially, but everyone always had some kind of commitments that day. What had she left for me to read? Just some glossy brochures and package inserts about the new drug, and a little squishy foam brain that said "Curixenol." And now they were saying that her accident had been intentional. Did she know something about Grandines that she shouldn't? Was she involved with some kind of diversion of drugs? She certainly hadn't mentioned anything about diversion. Ginny was a drug rep, a marketing person. How much was Curixenol worth on the open market? Not much, probably. And the generic medications which Grandines cranked out in their factories were definitely worth even less.

I decided to try again to reach Dr. Antony Hastings-Muir. Now at least I had a lead. I knew he owned a home in Bermuda. How would I get his number? I went into the study and logged on to America Online. I clicked my way onto the Internet and conjured up my favorite search engine. I typed in "Bermuda," and next thing I knew, the Bermuda telephone directory was on the screen in front of me. I love technology!

Bingo: Hastings-Muir, Antony. I copied down his number and address and logged off before I was tempted to waste time.

I entered the numbers and heard, "All circuits are busy now. Would you please try your call again later." I hung up in disappointment and relief, recalling how as a little girl I used to watch my parents phone various friends and relatives who had scattered all over the world, for holidays and birthdays and anniversaries and deaths. The calls were always serious, invested with a responsibility that necessitated much shouting into the phone. I hit redial.

On the second ring a male voice said, "Hullo."

"Hello, is Dr. Hastings-Muir available, please?"

"Who's this?"

"My name is Tamsen Bayn, I'm a psychiatrist in New York."

"Yes?"

"Are you Dr. Hastings-Muir?"

"That depends. What are you calling in reference to?" His voice was rough, not in texture but in tone, and definitely English. He sounded as though I were disturbing him, like I was calling to get him to switch long-distance carriers or something.

"I've just agreed to work for Grandines Pharmaceuticals. I was hoping to ask you a few questions—"

"Tamsen Bane, you said your name was? Never heard of you. Bane, B-A-N-E?"

"B-A-Y-N," I replied automatically. I'm used to spelling my last name for everyone.

"Bayn," the voice repeated. "It sounds Welsh. Are you Welsh?"

"I'm Jewish."

"Do you know what it means?"

"Bayn? It means 'heathen' or 'pagan.' My father pulled it out of a baby name book when he turned twenty-one. It used to be—oh, never mind. It used to be something really ethnic and impossible to spell." Little had my father known that nobody would have known how to spell his new surname either.

I heard him laugh on the other end of the line.

"You *are* Dr. Hastings-Muir, aren't you?"

"Yes, I am."

"So, like I said, the reason I'm calling is that I'm going to be working with Grandines on marketing Curixenol, and I had a few questions—"

"I'm sorry, Dr. Bayn. I can't help you. I no longer have any relationship with that company. Although I must tell you, the employee cafeteria is excellent."

"The cafeteria? What? No, I wanted to just ask you about diversions of—"

He interrupted me again. "It was a pleasure speaking with you. Good day, Doctor."

"Wait! One second—" But I was talking into a dead phone.

chapter twelve

By eleven P.M. I still hadn't heard from Greg. When I'd paged him at six o'clock, I was rewarded with a loud beep-beep-beep from the top of the dresser. I made dinner and ate it by myself around nine. Greg often worked late, but he always called, ever since the first day I met him. I could only think of one explanation. The explanation had long black hair and wore a size four, and I was getting more and more annoyed by the minute.

Eventually I must have fallen asleep, because at some point Greg came in and I felt him in bed beside me. He reached for me but I rolled away, turning my pillow over to its cool side and ignoring him. But by the time I heard his deep, even snores, I was wide awake again.

I went into the kitchen and made myself a cup of de-caf tea, which I took into the computer room. I couldn't sleep, and I wasn't going to read a book with a perfectly beautiful and independently wealthy heroine who, in addition to solving all of the world's problems and averting certain disaster, also gets her man by page 352, when my man had come in after midnight without so much as an apology. When the computer finally warmed up I typed in "Grandines Pharmaceuticals." I don't know why I hadn't thought of it before.

I found zero category, one official Web site, and one hundred and thirteen Web page matches for Grandines. A jackpot. I started clicking and scrolling to see what I could find on this corporation that had so unexpectedly blasted into my life.

Much of what I learned I already knew, and many of the references were things I didn't understand. I wasn't a sophisticated enough Internet user to search the list I had generated for "diversion" so I just looked for it with my tired eyes. In hit forty-three, I found it.

> Grandines Pharmaceuticals, a New York City–based company with offices and factories in New Jersey, Michigan, and Arkansas, filed a disclosure statement with the Food and Drug Administration today revealing that they have been experiencing losses as a result of diversion of shipments of returned, expired drugs. For the third time in as many weeks, an expired shipment of pseudoephedrine, slated for destruction at the company's Arkansas facility, failed to reach its destination. Pseudoephedrine is a nonprescription medication for cold and flu symptoms, which in this case was being sold as a generic product by a Midwestern drugstore chain. Vasily Stolnik, director of security for Grandines Pharmaceuticals, said that the company was doing everything in its power to track down the diverted returns. Stolnik added, "Thankfully, the losses were not of a controlled substance. Grandines is an established company, and we see no reason to allow this problem to undermine our confidence."
>
> Here in Washington, however, speculation abounds. It is no secret that pseudoephedrine is one of the key ingredients in methamphetamine, one of the most dangerous and easily synthesized illicit drugs in use in this country today.
>
> The Federal Bureau of Investigation (FBI) is currently awaiting the issuance of a federal warrant that will allow their involvement in an investigation that is currently being handled by the Drug Enforcement Agency (DEA). For Grandines, however, it appears to be business as usual. The company even plans to launch a new drug in the next few weeks.
>
> Although the company is privately held, a mild dip in pharmaceutical stocks followed the announcement. Industry analysts predict more turmoil until other,

larger, and public pharmaceutical companies clear
their year-end inventories.

Wow. Those were some diversions, all right. I scrolled
back to the top of the story. December 12, the *Washington
Post*. I rarely read newspapers anymore, except over people's
shoulders, so I didn't know if the local papers had picked
up the story. Who was this Vasily Stolnik? I hadn't heard
any mention of him when I was rubbing elbows with the
Grandines aristocracy.

After I had saved my Grandines list for later perusal, I
closed everything down and slid back into bed. I wasn't
tense anymore. Now I had something juicy to think about.

chapter thirteen

Greg hit the snooze alarm when it shrilled at five-thirty, rolled over, and swung a leg over mine. Still mostly asleep, I didn't immediately remember that he had breezed into bed after midnight without a word of explanation. His warm body enveloped mine. The windows rattled and the wind outside sounded like a pack of hungry midair wolves. Bed seemed a good place to be. But when the alarm went off again seven minutes later, I flinched and remembered.

"Where were you last night?" I asked.

"Hmm?" Greg was rubbing my thigh with his.

"Last night. Why were you so late? I was worried."

"Ugh," he mumbled, not fully awake. "Working. I tried calling you."

"No you didn't," I said, and slid away from him. Now he was lying to me. I couldn't take it. I wouldn't even think about it yet. I stood up and shivered, feeling in the darkness for my fuzzy slippers on the floor.

I knew I could use a visit to the gym to work off some of that excess hostility, but it was so miserable outside that I abandoned virtue in favor of a hot shower. As I stood under my private waterfall rinsing special overpriced color-enhancing shampoo out of my hair, I felt the shower curtain open. Greg stepped in.

"What's wrong, Tamsen? I did try to call you. There was something wrong with the phone. It would ring once, then click and go dead."

"I paged you. So there couldn't have been anything wrong with the phone. But your beeper was here."

"Don't be mad," he said. "I love you."

Every time I got mad, he told me he loved me. It was the most effective weapon in his arsenal.

I finished my shower and got out to dry off.

"No gym?" I asked Greg when he got out after me.

"Nah. I'm too tired. This case is driving me nuts."

"Tell me about it," I said, opening the door of my tiny closet to decide what black clothes I should wear today. I applied body lotion, rubbed it in, and started getting dressed. "You think you have problems. It's not enough that I'm evaluating the parents of a kid who killed three people," I said. "The mother of the child works for the same company that just hired me to basically do PR for them. Not only does she work for them, she's in charge of exactly the drug that I'm supposed to promote. Now I find out that this company is somehow involved with the FBI and the DEA because they managed to lose three truckloads of methamphetamine precursors. I think I'm having a little conflict-of-interest situation here, don't you? Oh, yeah, and don't forget who I'm sleeping with."

Greg was laughing out loud by the time I was finished. "You had a rough day," he agreed. "Let me tell you why I was so late."

I sat down on the side of the bed, prepared for the worst. Intellectually, rationally, as they say, I knew that the midst of trial preparation would probably not be the most opportune or the most likely time for two opposing attorneys to hit the hay together. But I was totally unprepared for what Greg said next.

"You're going to love this. Guess where Jason Devinski got the gun?"

"Where?"

"Wait, let me go back for a minute. The reason I was so late was because we were arguing motions, believe it or not, in front of a judge who thinks that this is the biggest, most interesting case he's ever had, and actually stayed late to hear them."

"But where did he get the gun?"

"I'm getting there. Connor—you remember Connor?"

"Of course. Your deputy DA. He's working with you on this case?"

"Yeah. Connor really didn't want us to let this in, because it kind of helps Jason's case, but, my feeling is, Jason's twelve: I'm going to let everything in. But we had to put in the motion, because the judge expected us to, and—"

"Let what in?" I didn't want to hear all the legal maneuvering. I hate that part of the law, the part about motions and technicalities. As much as I understand that the law cannot be the defender and upholder of absolute justice all the time, I am angered when it isn't, when it can't be. Which is often.

"The gun, silly. Where he got the gun."

"Don't call me silly." I was still prickly.

"It's a term of affection."

"The parents told me it wasn't their gun."

"Yes, I know, they told me that too. Natalie had them tell me. But they almost fell over when their son admitted *where* he got it."

"Tell me."

"At the company picnic," Greg said, his face serious. He looked tired, dark circles under his long-lashed green eyes, a growing number of silver hairs at his temples. His nails were bitten down so far I wondered how he was able to keep biting them. Greg believed in the power of the law. He believed in justice. But I could tell that he was having problems with trying a child killer as if Jason were an adult. This part of our jobs is the part that most people don't understand. There really are at least two sides to every story.

"What company picnic?"

"At his mother's company picnic. You know. Families are invited."

"Grandines?"

Greg nodded.

"So? I mean, from where? Who did he get it from?" Ooh, it frustrates me when I'm reduced to grammatical ineptitude.

"The company picnic was at the CEO's house this year. In August. His estate, actually. Somewhere out on Long Island."

"Grandines's house? Parker Grandines's house?"

"Jason said that Grandines was talking to him, and invited him into the library. He had all sorts of cool stuff in there."

"*Cool* stuff?"

"Jason's word," Greg said. "It was the biggest show of enthusiasm he's given us yet. He—Grandines—showed Jason some antique swords, and different guns in his collection."

"And?"

"Well, this is just what Jason said. Obviously, we'll never know what really happened."

"So?"

"The gun had no serial number. It was . . . Well, the best way to describe it is that it's a little semiautomatic pistol made to look like an old-fashioned nickel-plated revolver. A custom piece."

"And?"

"We subpoenaed Grandines. His people are negotiating."

"His people?"

"His lawyers."

"But, getting back to Jason," I said. Without noticing what I was doing, I'd begun pacing back and forth in the crowded bedroom. "He said he stole this custom-made gun from Grandines? Why in the world wasn't it locked up?"

"Jason said that Grandines unlocked the gun cabinet with a little key that he kept in the top drawer of his desk. Grandines locked up the cabinet, replaced the key, and then he and the boy returned to the party. Then Jason went back a few minutes later, found the key, unlocked the cabinet, and stole the gun. Then he put the key back in its place."

"And Grandines never reported the gun missing?"

"Nope. Which kind of makes sense, in a warped way,

since the gun had no serial number and couldn't be registered. It wasn't a real antique either. It was a sort of no-man's-land gun."

"Wow," I said. "So Parker Grandines knows—or at least suspects—that it was his gun that Jason used in the murders."

"I know this doesn't make any sense. But Jason says he thought that Grandines knew he was going to take the gun."

"Why would he think that?"

"Well, maybe little Jason really is paranoid. But I don't think so. He strikes me as very, very bright."

I didn't mention how paranoia and intelligence seem to travel together genetically. "But . . . did Jason plan to take the gun that day? Did he know there were guns on display in that house? And how did he know he wouldn't get caught?"

"That's another weird thing." Greg was knotting his tie, which today was covered with tiny little parrots. He liked to wear animals on his ties. He said it was because his workplace was a zoo. "Jason claims he got the idea from Grandines. Grandines told him that a crime committed with this particular little gun could never be traced."

"Yeah, maybe not," I said. "Especially with a hundred witnesses watching."

"Never mind that part." Greg put on his suit jacket, pulled something out of his pocket, stared at it for a moment, then crumpled it up and threw it in the general direction of the garbage can. "When Grandines went to replace the key to the gun cabinet, Jason swears Grandines looked at him and winked."

"Winked? At Jason?"

"Yeah. And that's how Jason says he knew he was supposed to take the gun. Five minutes later, he went back into the library and lifted it."

Now that part could certainly be interpreted to make Jason seem psychotic. The only problem was, why hadn't Parker Grandines said anything when he noticed his gun was missing? I didn't like the scenario one bit, and I said so.

"I don't like it either," Greg agreed. "But it moves Parker Grandines into our venue. We might be able to try him for conspiracy to commit murder." Before I could assimilate the enormity of those words, Greg continued. "And you know what the scary thing is? I really believed that kid, about how Parker Grandines wanted him to steal the gun. I could swear he was telling the truth."

chapter fourteen

After Greg left for work, I sat at our tiny kitchen table drinking my coffee and eating scrambled eggs. Greg had explained that he and the opposing counsel (i.e., Natalie) would discuss whether or not I should continue with the Devinskis' evaluations, given the potential for conflict of interest, but that he thought that the answer would be yes. They would clear it with the gung-ho judge today and get notarized copies of the written permission of everybody involved, including the Devinskis and Parker Grandines. In the meantime, I should continue with my evaluation, and "Stay away from that Parker Grandines. I don't trust him." Well, duh. I thought I should probably not accept the Grandines position, or resign from it, whichever was applicable, but Greg suggested that I wait at least another day to see how everything turned out.

It wasn't yet seven o'clock. From my vantage point on the tenth floor I heard a snowplow having a difficult time trying to scrape through the piles of ice underneath the snow. I dreaded leaving my apartment. I was just thinking about how I should have stayed in bed awhile longer, when a loud buzz startled me. The doorman, from downstairs.

"Yes?" I yelled into the intercom.

"You have a visitor," a voice responded.

I gave my second silent *Well, duh* of the morning, and said, "Who is it?"

"A gentleman. He says you should come down," was the answer.

Nobody ever visited us here spontaneously, and now here I was with two visitors in less than a week. Suddenly I was Miss—make that Dr.—Popularity.

"I'll be right down," I said, and traded my fuzzy slippers for a pair of shoes.

Two minutes later I exited the elevator into the lobby to see a tall man in a black overcoat and hat, holding a pair of leather gloves. My heart sank. Grandines, I thought, come to harass me again, and now with "Rule out conspiracy to commit murder" on his résumé. But when the man turned around, I didn't recognize him.

"Dr. Bayn?" the stranger said. He took off his hat, revealing thinning, graying red hair. His cheeks were red from the cold. "Dr. Tamsen Bayn? I'm sorry to barge in on you like this. I tried calling you, but I couldn't get through yesterday evening."

"Have we met?" I asked.

"No, not exactly. Jim Mahoney, FBI." He fished a slim wallet out of an inside pocket and handed it to me. I examined the FBI shield. It looked authentic, but who could tell?

"How can I help you?" I handed the leather folder back to him. I had always wanted to work for the FBI. Was there a handy serial killer who needed profiling?

"I'm just the messenger," Mahoney said. "All cases in which the FBI collaborates with the DEA get run by me first. I came to see if we could enlist your help. Do you mind if we go upstairs to your apartment?"

I must have looked nervous, because Mahoney said, "I understand completely, Doctor." He smiled. "Still, I'd prefer not to speak with you in such a public place." He glanced around the lobby. Two small sofas were wedged into a corner at right angles.

Mahoney took a seat on one of the sofas. I sat down cautiously on the other. "Don't worry. It's going to be fun."

"What's going to be fun?" I really didn't like the sound of that. Maybe he was a perverted old weirdo after all.

"Working for the FBI."

"What do you want me to do?" I wondered briefly if I had fallen asleep again after having breakfast. Or while having breakfast. Or maybe I even dreamed breakfast.

"We need some information," Mahoney replied.

I gaped at him with what I supposed was an expression of true idiocy, until suddenly it dawned on me.

"Grandines?" I asked, hoping I was wrong.

"Grandines." He nodded. "We heard you were hired by Grandines Pharmaceuticals."

"I heard about the pseudoephedrine," I said. "But I wouldn't have anything to do with that. I'm just supposed to be, like, a figurehead, a spokesperson, for this new drug of theirs. Nothing to do with diversions."

"You know the term," Mahoney said.

"They mentioned diversions. I wondered, so I looked them up, Grandines Pharmaceuticals, I mean. On the Internet."

"In this quarter alone, five shipments of Grandines-manufactured pseudoephedrine have gone missing. Returns. The company claims the drugs were all part of the same batch, so they all expired around the same time. Therefore—"

"They all needed to come back around the same time. But it's funny, I wouldn't expect there to be so many returns of pseudoephedrine."

"What do you mean?" Mahoney took a little notebook out of his pocket, and started making notes with a gold fountain pen.

"Nice pen," I said. The doorman stared at us openly.

"A gift from the bureau. Also functions as a radio transmitter and poison-dart thrower."

I almost believed him for a second there, too. "Okay, Mr. Bond. So, what exactly would you like me to do?"

Mahoney smiled briefly, then said, "Go back for a moment, Tamsen. You don't mind if I call you Tamsen, do you? You were saying about the returns, that you wouldn't expect large quantities?" A family of four came out of the elevator. The two little boys were arguing so loudly that I had to repeat my next words.

"Right. Because pseudoephedrine is a cold medication, and everyone catches colds. You'd expect that they'd sell out their orders, and have to reorder."

"Excuse me?" Mahoney said, over the din in the lobby.

I gave up. "Let's go upstairs," I said. I led the way to the elevator. As soon as the door closed behind us, I continued. "Pseudoephedrine is not like some of the more obscure psychiatric medications, or antibiotics, that have a really short shelf life. Plus, now, everyone knows that this drug is used to make crystal meth. Or whatever they're calling it these days. Crank, I think. Drug dealers—or suppliers, I guess you'd call them—synthesize the drug using something called the Nazi method. But I don't think it really has anything to do with Nazis. Still, methamphetamine is still not that popular here. In the city, I mean. Here it's still crack and heroin."

"Crack and heroin," Mahoney repeated thoughtfully. He wrote something in his little notebook as the elevator door opened. I led the way to my apartment.

"Coffee?" I asked after we entered, silently resenting my mother for raising me to be so goddamn polite.

"No, thank you."

I took Mahoney's coat and hat. He sat down at the dining room table without waiting for me to ask, choosing a location that was more businesslike than the sofa a few feet away.

I sat down too. "This pseudoephedrine, they watch it, in the stores. If somebody comes in and buys a few packages at once, they're supposed to be reported, I think."

"You're right." Mahoney nodded. "We—or more accurately, the DEA—have been monitoring people who buy pseudoephedrine in large quantities. But we don't have the manpower to watch every drugstore in America, and reporting buyers is voluntary."

The whole notion of synthesizing illegal drugs from over-the-counter medications amazes me. It's right up there with making bombs out of stuff that you could buy at any garden-supply center.

"So, we would like a contact inside Grandines," Mahoney continued.

"Industrial espionage? I can't help you," I said without hesitation.

Mahoney looked at me questioningly.

"I don't think I'm going to be able to keep the position. Or actually, accept the position. The Grandines position," I clarified. Quickly, I explained my conflict of interest.

He nodded and wrote down a few more things in his notebook.

"It would make sense for you to give up the job," he said. "It can't be good for it to get out that you're evaluating someone for the court while you're being paid by her employer, even if it is for some other reason."

I felt myself flush. Of course I couldn't do both.

"Have you accepted any payment from Grandines yet?"

I shook my head.

"How much are they paying you?"

I told him. His eyes widened in disbelief. "That's the going rate for a psychiatrist these days?"

"It's about six times the hourly rate of most moonlighting jobs," I said. "Why do you think I accepted it so quickly?"

Jim Mahoney's blue eyes twinkled. "So, does the bureau have to outbid Grandines to get you to work for us?"

"How do you usually pay your informers?" I asked, and in the back of my brain I heard someone say, *We don't like snitches.* I think it was Parker Grandines. Or maybe Humphrey Bogart.

"It depends," Mahoney said. "Actually, we don't usually pay anything. People like to cooperate with the FBI."

"Yeah, then you send them off to the witness protection program where they can only get a job flipping burgers for the rest of their lives."

"Don't worry, you're not a candidate for witness relocation." The humor seeped out of Mahoney's face. "I would like you to continue to do whatever Grandines is paying you to do. Don't worry about any conflict of interest. You have the United States Government behind you now."

My heart began to pound.

"A special agent named Kathleen O'Neill is in charge

of this investigation. Everything goes through her. I'd like you, if possible, to meet with her for a debriefing."

"Debriefing?" My mouth went dry. "What exactly are you investigating?"

"We're investigating the diversions. And an attempted murder."

"Attempted murder? Ginny Liu? I thought the police were investigating."

"The NYPD was, except the accident actually occurred in the New Jersey side of the tunnel. Truthfully, initially we were inclined to leave it with the NYPD and the Port Authority, but once we made the connection between the victim and the company we were investigating, we had no choice but to take over the case."

"So what happened? Who tried to kill Ginny? How?"

"I can't tell you that, Tamsen." Mahoney looked at me disapprovingly, like a teacher disappointed with his star student. "This investigation is strictly need-to-know."

"Need-to-know," I repeated, trying to win back the teacher's favor.

"Kathleen will give you a call later, to set up an appointment."

"Okay," I said. "I'll be at the office. With the Devinskis."

"Great. It's not confidential, your evaluation of them, right?"

"Not really. But if you're thinking that I can pick Karen Devinski's brains about this methamphetamine connection and then tell you what she said . . . I can't do that. Unless the information is relevant to my psychiatric evaluation of her. Unless she tells me she's been using methamphetamines or something."

"Ask her," Mahoney said. "Ask her if she uses drugs. And if she does, then you can ask her if she ever used at work or if she has a supplier there."

"I'll ask her. But I guarantee she hasn't and she doesn't. And I don't believe she knows anything about this diversion business. She's got much bigger problems to worry about."

Mahoney got up to leave, put on his coat and his grandfatherly hat. "She certainly does have bigger problems. Will you be going to Grandines again soon? Have they requested it?"

"Not yet."

"Ginny Liu's office." The pleasant, warm expression had vanished from Mahoney's face, blue skies turned to granite in his eyes. "Could you get in there and look around?"

"You're the second person who seems to think that Ginny has something to do with this diversion thing. How could it be? She's in a totally different department. She doesn't even handle those kinds of over-the-counter medications. *Nobody* handles them. I mean, I guess somebody handles them, but they don't have a huge marketing department with field representatives going around to doctors' offices to convince them to prescribe their generic versions of popular medicines. It's a sales thing, between the sales department and the pharmacies. I don't get it." Ginny Liu was a CNS rep. Why would she have any connection with a decongestant?

"Well, you know that her husband was questioned about her accident."

"I heard about it. I'm skeptical. He loves her." I looked away so Mr. Mahoney wouldn't think I was some simperingly sentimental female, even though I was. "Is that under need-to-know also?"

"Again, it's a matter of crossing the *t*'s and dotting the *i*'s."

My expression must have been one of "What the hell are you talking about," because he gave a weak laugh.

"Grandines is a family business."

"So?"

"So they never had a rule against husbands and wives working at the same company. Ray Liu's worked for them since he finished graduate school. In fact, he brought his wife into the company."

"So Ray Liu works for Grandines also. So what?"

"Tamsen, Ray Liu is the senior DEA compliance associate for Grandines Pharmaceuticals. Nationwide. He's in charge of every pill, every capsule, every molecule of controlled substance, that moves anywhere in this country that has any connection, however remote, with Grandines."

Slowly, I sat down on the nearest dining room chair. I put my hand on the table, to steady myself, and stared at the pile of mail in front of me, not really seeing it. Breathe in, I told myself. Now breathe out. Okay, in again.

Finally, I looked up. Mahoney had slipped off his coat again, and stood with it folded neatly over one arm. His hat was in his other hand. It was warm in here. Suffocating. I looked at the place where my damp fingers had left prints on the shiny cherry wood of the table. For a second I visualized myself cleaning, scrubbing, erasing any memory of this man and this conversation from my home.

"So Ray could have tried to kill Ginny," I conceded. "To shut her up. He could try again." And Ray had remained constantly by his wife's side since she'd been brought to Bellevue.

"Exactly. Now do you see why it's so important to have somebody on the inside? This Ray Liu has supposedly been cooperating with the DEA for months, and now his wife is in a coma. I don't really believe in coincidence."

"But . . . maybe it was somebody else . . ." What I wanted to say, but couldn't seem to articulate, was that maybe Ginny's accident had been arranged by somebody else, as a warning.

Mahoney read my mind.

"I don't think so, Tamsen." He shook his head sadly. "Ginny called our New York office just half an hour before she left work that day. She was ready to make a deal."

chapter fifteen

Before Jim Mahoney left, he assured me that Ginny Liu was under round-the-clock protection by specially trained FBI agents. I locked the door behind him. Here I was, all neurotic because Greg worked late without calling home, and meanwhile this *married* woman, mother of two, married to the same man for *eighteen* years, with him for *twenty-two* years, was almost *dead* after some inconceivably complex betrayals between husband and wife.

Do you ever really get to know a person?

I went over to the window and looked down. Cars were submerged under endless waves of snow. People trudged through drifts as tall as they were. I thought about just skipping the Devinskis for today and staying home. I had books, music, food, and a comfortable sofa. But even as I looked around the room, at the maple bookcase practically sagging under the weight of words read and unread, at the charcoal-gray L-shaped couch, the framed photographs and paintings on the museum-white walls, and the mohair afghan that my grandmother had crocheted for me years before, I knew that I would meet with the Devinskis today. Not only was it my job to finish my evaluation, but now I was extremely motivated to try to uncover more of the secrets of Grandines Pharmaceuticals. Karen Devinski had been Ginny's boss. Correction—Karen still was Ginny's boss. Karen had admitted that Ginny had tried to reach her on Friday and couldn't. Maybe Karen knew something that she thought was irrelevant, possibly because it had nothing to do with her primary concern, Jason.

For sure, Karen knew that methamphetamine can

cause violent behavior. I shivered as I stepped into the cold outdoors.

By the time I got to my office, snow was pouring down as if somebody had decided to make a movie about the tundra, first take in five minutes. I practiced a few words of Spanish with the chief doorman, Alfredo, before unlocking the door.

Inside I found my mother watering the plants.

"Hi, honey," she said. "I didn't know you were coming in today. Do you have any patients?"

Even though she was a psychiatrist, I could never seem to teach her that forensic evaluations were not "patients," but it didn't matter. I told her about the Devinskis. I had no "patients" scheduled until after the New Year.

"I hope they show up. It's awful out. Daddy and I were supposed to go away tonight, now I don't know if we'll be able to."

I remembered that they were going to Florida to visit some old friends. Every year the New Year's party changed locale, but my parents were incredibly diligent about maintaining their old relationships, most of which crossed the ocean back to their childhoods in Romania. I, on the other hand, seemed to change friends yearly. My girlfriends kept getting married, having babies, and moving to the suburbs, and I was like the obligatory spinster aunt that everyone forgot. Most of my medical school friends worked part-time, and most of my college friends didn't work at all. The only friend I could imagine wanting to spend so many New Year's Eves with was Gregory. And ironically, this New Year's Eve would be our first one together. But it was time, I told myself, as I did a hundred times a day. It was time to love the one I was with. And I did love him. What scared me wasn't the permanence. I was terrified that after I let myself love him, he would disappear. Because what if love really wasn't what it seemed to be?

"Can I ask you something?" I asked my mother.

"Sure," she said, turning toward the windowsill. My

mother had started out in her education planning to become a surgeon. Even though she had been forced to abandon that particular dream, she found dozens of ways to use her hands to make amazing things happen. From her I had inherited my ability to draw and paint, together with the practicality that made me abandon art for a career in medicine. Today, she was making cuttings from a plant with green and white leaves, sticking them into an old seltzer bottle with its top cut off. In this way, she had populated both her apartment and the office with lush, green foliage year-round. I often felt it was only me that she had never quite managed to nurture properly, even though I could never really identify what she had done wrong.

"Do you think it's possible to live with somebody for a long time and still not really know them?"

Her thin shoulders stiffened, and she turned around slowly. "Is it Greg?"

"No. It's just a general question."

"Well, then. Well, yes, of course. You know what they say, the wife is always the last to know." She paused. "It is Greg, isn't it?"

"No," I said, stung.

"That little lawyer girl was very cute," my mother said. She's astute enough to always say the one thing guaranteed to make me crazy.

"I'm talking about somebody else," I said. "This person seemed to have a really good relationship. Nothing to do with Greg, or me. You've met her, she comes to the office sometimes. Ginny Liu."

"The Xixperdine drug rep?" My mother wasn't up-to-date with Curixenol yet; but she wrote a lot of prescriptions for Xixperdine.

I nodded.

"Tamsen, honey, you can never guess what goes on behind people's closed doors. You of all people should know that."

"Why me of all people?"

"Just . . . the career path you've chosen, dealing with all of these criminally insane weirdos, waiting so long to get married . . ."

She'd have to bring that up. "I'm not waiting so long to get married," I pointed out. "I've only known Greg since August."

"You know what I mean. You could have met a nice boy a long time ago." She turned and started snipping more strands off her plant.

"I *did* meet a nice boy a long time ago. He died, remember?" I didn't add, "Lucky for me." I wish that Daniel had lived, but it had taken me years to admit to myself that a marriage between us would never have worked.

"You could have met another one."

"Why don't you like Greg?"

"I do like Greg. I just don't like the fact that you're living with him."

"Could we please not have this conversation again right now? I'm going to marry him, I'm not planning to live in sin forever." I took one of those deep, cleansing breaths I've been reading about. "I have somebody coming in for an evaluation in a little while. So, were you planning to, um, leave?"

"We're leaving tonight," my mother said. "Weather permitting."

"Have a good time," I said flatly, and waited to see if she'd leave the office or if I'd have to ask her again.

She set the cuttings on the windowsill and returned the scissors to the desk drawer. I watched as she went through the pile of mail from the last few days, then picked up a decorating magazine to take with her.

"Happy New Year, honey," she said, everything forgotten.

"Happy New Year," I echoed.

I watched the door close behind her, realizing how clearly she had answered my question. Of course you could live with somebody for a long time and not know him—or her. I had lived with my mother, or near her, my whole life, and even though I kind of thought I knew what drove her to say and do so many contradictory and frequently hurtful things, I never *really* knew why. My mother was one of the mysteries of life, to be tolerated and dealt with on her own terms, never on mine.

But now I was a big grown-up. I could handle her. And we can't always choose who we love.

I went into the tiny kitchenette to make coffee. Under the sink I found a paper-wrapped fake log, which I dusted off and brought into the office. They're foolproof; you simply light the paper with a match and in seconds you have a warm and picturesque fire. You just have to remember to open the flue, which I did, only seconds belatedly.

Most people who came here wouldn't get such special treatment, mainly because I didn't trust them not to throw themselves, me, or something else into the flames. My patients weren't dangerous, exactly, and neither were the people who were sent to me for evaluation, but psychiatry is by its very nature an unstable and unpredictable arena. I wouldn't leave scissors lying around on the desk either.

I had a secret agenda of course. I wanted the Devinskis to feel so good with me that they wouldn't notice that I was asking them questions about things that were none of my business, at least from the perspective of evaluating them for their prepubescent son's upcoming murder trial.

I fluffed up the pillows on the sofa and prepared three mugs for coffee. One of my mother's patients had brought a box of chocolate truffles, so I put some in a dish and set it on the coffee table. I was all ready when the buzzer rang at exactly ten A.M.

I opened the door with a big smile, and said, "Hi," even as I realized that I was welcoming the wrong person.

"FedEx," the man said, looking down at his clipboard. "For a Tamsen Bayn?" I could hear that the question was, "Am I pronouncing this correctly?" not, "Is she here?"

I took the clipboard and signed on the electronic dotted line. The delivery person handed me a large purple, red, and white mailer.

"Thanks."

"You stay warm, now," he said mechanically. "Bad day out there."

"Yes, it is. Bye. Drive safely." As I closed the door, the phone rang. I knew it was my line because my parents' was turned off, going directly to the answering service. I ran back into the consultation room to pick it up.

"Tamsen?"

I recognized Karen Devinski's voice immediately. "Running late?" I asked hopefully.

"Running so late that we can't make it. I'm really sorry. Can we come tomorrow? We have a crisis here with Jason."

"Crisis?"

"He's okay," Karen said. "But, I don't know, *I'm* not okay." She gave a shaky laugh.

"What happened?"

"I'll tell you tomorrow. Is tomorrow okay?"

"Sure, fine," I said, even though it wasn't sure or fine at all. Tomorrow was New Year's Eve, and I'd made appointments for some self-indulgent procedures to get ready for my evening out. I didn't want to become persona non grata in the manicurist underground.

"Could we make it really early?" I asked. "Eight A.M.?"

"Of course," Karen said. "No problem. Listen, we'll pay you for the appointment today, I know that's the usual routine."

"No, that's all right. The state is paying me. Just be sure to call me tonight if you don't think you'll be able to make it tomorrow."

We exchanged good-byes and hung up. I had just put a two-hour imitation log in the fireplace, so I supposed I was stuck here until the fire burned itself out. I'm too paranoid to leave a lit fire with nobody watching it. I examined my surroundings. The bookshelves held medical books, but mixed in were a few novels that had been left lying around. The velvet-covered sofa was inviting. The plants on the windowsill provided plenty of oxygen for me, and for the fire, to breathe or burn. I could think of worse ways to spend a couple of winter hours.

I got my book out of my bag and headed toward the sofa with my milky coffee. I had just gotten comfortable when I remembered I'd forgotten something.

The FedEx envelope was on the desk, where I had dropped it when the phone rang. I got up to retrieve it.

The return address said "HollowHill, St. George's, Bermuda."

I found the scissors my mother had put away and opened the heavy envelope with shaking hands. I knew only one person in Bermuda, not that I really knew him. Here was my answer about Grandines, about everything. I was right, something weird was happening there. He didn't trust the phones. He had written to me, instead.

I finally cut enough of the packet open to slide my hand in and feel for a letter. A normal-sized business envelope was inside the big one. I pulled it out, opened it eagerly, hoping for a long missive of explanation.

No letter. I stood perplexed, looking at the little folder of papers in my hand.

Antony Hastings-Muir had sent me a plane ticket.

chapter sixteen

The ticket I was holding was a full-fare, open ticket from New York's LaGuardia Airport to St. George's, Bermuda. For a moment I considered ignoring the obvious invitation and just hanging on to the ticket to use at my leisure, like when this whole mess had become a dim memory. But I'm the conscientious type. And although I wasn't certain, I supposed it was beautiful in Bermuda this time of year. It had to be better than New York under twenty inches of dirty snow.

Still, I couldn't just go tearing off to Bermuda on some sort of wild-goose chase. The man had refused to speak to me on the telephone. What would compel him to send an expensive ticket to a woman he had never met? Was he simply melodramatic? Or was the information he had so serious, so shattering, that it could only be conveyed in person?

Before I could do anything else, like call the airline to make a reservation, the phone rang again.

Greg's voice was agitated, unusual for him. He could remain calm during a bombing. "Did you hear about Jason?" I heard a babble of voices in the background.

"I heard that something happened," I replied cautiously.

"Jason met with the juvenile detention center psychiatrist today. He told her he wanted to kill himself. The psychiatrist is insisting Jason go to a hospital for evaluation and treatment."

"Well, he should go," I said, watching the blue flames dance over my pseudolog. "He didn't actually make a suicide attempt, did he?"

"No. But, Tamsen, this doctor here, her name is . . ." There was a pause while I heard him ask someone, "What was the name of that child psychiatrist?" I didn't hear the answer, but out of the chaos on the other end of the phone line I heard him say, "Statton. Elizabeth Statton. Do you know her?"

"Never heard of her. What did she say?"

"She said that maybe Jason was having a seizure when he did the shootings. Wrote it in his chart, in fact."

"Oh, that's ridiculous. Bizarre purposeful action of *shooting*? Where did she come up with that crazy idea?"

"All I'm saying is that we have just one more complication now to worry about."

"Okay, well, send him to a hospital, and I'll work on the family history of seizures and mental illness and drug abuse tomorrow."

"Drug abuse? Which one of them is a drug abuser?"

"Oh, never mind, it's just one of those things we look at and ask about." The royal medical "we," and with it came the sudden, and shocking, realization that I wasn't going to tell Greg about Jim Mahoney's visit. I was keeping a secret from my husband-to-be. "More complications," I said softly. I should have known that nothing good could come from working on the same case. I wanted to tell Greg what was happening in my life and as a result of my work with Grandines Pharmaceuticals, but I was afraid it would jeopardize my involvement with the Devinskis, since Karen worked for Grandines. Then Greg would want me to drop Grandines, and the FBI would want me to drop the Devinskis. Nobody would be happy—especially not me. So I said nothing.

"What? It's really noisy here, I can't hear you."

"Nothing important. What time will you be home?"

"Late. I have some more sixth-graders and their parents coming in today. Like we need to speak to all of them. But Natalie—" He paused, said something to someone in the room with him.

"Natalie *what*?" I said, more sharply than I needed to.

"Natalie insists that we interview every single witness, or at least, she's interviewing every single witness, and the judge agreed to let us depose them on the spot with their parents present so we wouldn't have to call them to trial, unless it is absolutely necessary." Again, I heard a burst of talking on his side of the line, laughter, somebody coughing, then laughter again. "Look, Tamsen, I have to go. I'll try to call you later. I'll see you tonight."

"Okay," I said. "Tonight." But the line was already dead.

chapter seventeen

I spent the next hour or so lying on the office sofa watching the fire and worrying. The log burned up before its allotted two hours, but I didn't have the energy or inclination to write to the company to complain. Actually, I was relieved that I could get out of there, go home, and decide what to do next.

Jason had expressed suicidal ideation. In other words, he'd said he was having ideas about committing suicide. At some point, the boy had clearly had ongoing homicidal ideation, because he'd procured a murder weapon, secreted it on his person, and eventually carried out the shootings, elevating his homicidal ideation through the other levels that psychiatrists always document—intent and plan. Given the extreme violence of which I knew little Jason was capable, he definitely belonged in a psychiatric hospital right now.

The child psychiatrist's presumption of a seizure disorder was another complication which the Devinskis and the lawyers would have to address. As a treating psychiatrist, it was inexcusable for Dr. Statton to speculate on Jason Devinski's mental state at the time he committed his crimes. Now the doctor had documented her theories, and if and when a trial ensued, she'd end up in court confusing everyone.

Seizures could be caused by so many different factors—drugs, toxins, fluctuations in blood sugar and electrolytes, head injuries, even fever. What Dr. Statton had referred to was a partial complex seizure, also known as temporal lobe epilepsy, in which the affected individual carries out some purposeful-looking but usually meaningless action. The person seems to be conscious and aware of his behavior, but actually isn't. The only partial complex seizure I'd ever seen with my own eyes was in a little girl who would suddenly stare into space, lift her left arm above her head like a ballerina, and then gracefully lower it to her side. I was in medical school, rotating through pediatrics at the time. It had taken a team of about twenty doctors—psychiatrists, neurologists, and pediatricians—to finally figure out that she was having seizures. For months, the psychiatrists kept trying to blame the girl's bizarre behavior on being the middle child in an already overstressed family. The neurologists kept referring her back to the psychiatrists, and finally the pediatricians insisted that the neurologists *do something*. It had been amazing to watch all the feuding doctors in action. I could just imagine the feeding frenzy that would occur now that somebody had suggested that Jason's murderous rampage might have been the result of an undiagnosed seizure disorder. . . . But this part of the evaluation was not my responsibility. It didn't matter what I thought. I had not been asked to comment on Jason's mental status at the time of his shooting spree, or even now or ever. All I was supposed to do was evaluate his parents. I was supposed to determine if something in Karen's or Peter's biology or behavior might have incited Jason to violence. Piece of cake.

I bundled myself back up and headed home. The one really inconvenient thing about living where I live now is that the subway is far away. On the beautiful fall days when I had first moved in with Greg, I didn't mind the walk, watching the people, soaking up the sunshine, and anticipating the rest of the evening with a pleasure so obvious that I knew strangers could read it on my face. Now the days were so short and gloomy. By the time I reached our building, my skin felt scratched and my eyes were burning from being squeezed shut against the weather. I was exhausted, and I knew it wasn't just from the walk. A psychiatrist knows the effect that emotional stress and turmoil can have on the physical self.

It was not yet one o'clock. I put on my sweats and filled the teakettle. It started whistling just as I finished preparing lunch. I took a big bite of turkey sandwich, and a big gulp of tea, and then, of course, the phone rang. "Unavailable," said the trusty little caller ID built right into my phone. Useful thing. Ninety percent of the time you had no idea who was calling, and the other ten percent were people you would have wanted to talk to anyway.

"Dr. Bayn?"

"Speaking." Nobody "doctored" me at home.

"This is Special Agent Kathy O'Neill from the FBI. Jim Mahoney told you to expect my call."

"Yes. Hi." Well, what was I supposed to say?

"I tried your office. The answering service said you had left for the day." Her voice held an unmistakable question.

I answered it. "My morning appointment had to cancel."

"Oh? I'd like to meet with you, if I could, Doctor. When would be a good time for you?"

I visualized the empty white pages of the next week's appointment book. "Umm . . . any time next week?"

Kathy laughed as if I had told her a great joke. Did FBI agents have senses of humor? In the movies they are always dark and humorless. "I was hoping today, tomorrow at the latest."

"Oh." I hadn't realized that this matter was so urgent. Hadn't the diversions at Grandines been occurring for months already? "I'm available now," I said slowly. So much for playing hard to get. "I'm not really doing anything . . . I'm not busy right now."

"Oh, terrific." She sounded enthusiastic. "How about around two o'clock? Or two-thirty. The weather really stinks, it might take us a little longer."

"No problem," I said. At least she was giving me enough time to finish eating. "Do you know where I live?"

"Sure. See you later."

"See you," I said, like a pathetic echo. Kathy hung up before I could ask her who "us" was.

When I'd awakened that morning, I was a regular person with a career and a life. Now I was about to be debriefed by the FBI. I felt as if I had journeyed a million miles and, like Gulliver, found that everything was not what it appeared to be.

I sipped my tea and ate my suddenly tasteless sandwich, and waited. I tucked my mohair afghan around my shoulders. The apartment wasn't cold, but I felt paralyzed, as if my bones had been replaced by a frozen skeleton dug out of some archaeological find. I felt the way I had the day that my grandfather died. I was only seven, and he was in his eighties, nearly blind, in a nursing home. He had vascular dementia, but somehow he always remembered me. I'd known he was dead as soon as I woke up that morning. When the phone rang a few minutes later I knew who was calling and why. It wasn't the first premonition I'd ever had that came true, and it wouldn't be the last. As a mental health professional, I couldn't officially give credence to anything that couldn't be scientifically quantified, or I would get kicked out of the club. But it unnerved me that I had the same feeling of impending doom right now.

I finished my lunch and cleaned up, but I still had an hour until Kathy O'Neill and whoever else was part of the "us" was scheduled to arrive. I needed a diversion, to coin a phrase.

I rummaged around in my bag until I found my appointment book, then looked up Gwendolyn Conklin's phone number in Kentucky. I called her office and got a machine, so I left her a message with all my phone numbers, asking her to call me. I wondered how the boy out there, Sammy Towland, was doing. Had he told Gwen that he wished he were dead? How horrible it must be to be a child without innocence. I wasn't supposed to get involved with Jason, but how could I ignore these tragic kids?

Then I lay on the sofa, my book open on my not quite flat enough stomach in a backbreaking feat of literary gymnastics, and waited with my eyes closed for something to happen.

chapter eighteen

Fifteen minutes later, Kathleen O'Neill called me back.

"Cancel our appointment," she said without preamble. "Jim Mahoney will be coming instead. I have to go to another meeting, but I'll call you in a day or two."

"But . . . he said . . . you know, debriefing . . ." I was blathering like an idiot. I composed myself. "Did something happen?"

"There's been a development," Kathy replied. "Jim'll be by later to tell you about it. I'll talk to you soon. Happy New Year."

She hung up before I could ask what development. I tried calling Greg but he was busy. To keep from speculating, I logged on to the Internet and signed up to have various electronic and printed information about Bermuda sent to me. I was waiting for yet another beautiful pink sand beach to load onto my screen when the phone rang at my elbow.

"May I speak to Tamsen Bayn, please?" The male voice had an English accent. Could it be—

"Speaking," I said breathlessly, expecting to hear that Antony Hastings-Muir was calling from Bermuda.

"Oh, thank goodness I got you. I have a terrible problem. Terrible news. I didn't know where else to turn."

"Who is this?" I asked, although by now I thought I knew.

"Gordon. Gordon Ranier. You know, your father's—"

"Agent," we finished in unison.

Ugh. What a disappointment. Looks and sex appeal before talking to him, 10; personality, as determined afterward, 2. The wise course would be to keep that rating system to myself.

"What happened?"

I guess I expected that his problems would be as superficial as he was. So his next words shocked me.

"My son," he said softly, his voice breaking. "My son, Oliver."

"Your son?"

"My wife. My ex-wife."

"What are you talking about? Gordon?" I could hear him breathing heavily into the phone like a pervert. Then I recognized the sounds as sobs.

"What happened?" I asked again, that horrible feeling back in my gut.

"She fell. She was pushed. Into the subway tracks."

"What? Pushed her into the tracks? Where? Is she— was she—"

"In London, just this morning. Or afternoon there, I suppose it was. She's alive. She, oh God, she lay down in the middle of the tracks. In that filth, you know? The train passed right over her. But she's alive. But he—my child— her child—" Gordon was crying openly now, from what kind of pain I couldn't even begin to contemplate. All of his carefully cultivated smoothness had vanished.

"Is there anything I can do?" I wouldn't ask who pushed her. I wouldn't. I didn't want to know.

"There were witnesses," he went on, as if I hadn't spoken. "It's been on the news in Britain all day. It's evening now. She's unharmed, really. She thought fast. She was so lucky. She—"

"Were you looking for a psychiatrist? For Oliver, I mean, or for his mother, or, you know, for yourself?" Not that I was full of recommendations of psychiatrists who happened to be in London.

"No, I just thought, I don't know, that you could help. Help me."

"Yes, of course, I would be happy to help you," I said, without thinking.

"Because I don't think I can go on like this any longer."

No. No no no no no. Eleven of the most horrible

words in the English language: "I don't think I can go on like this any longer," rivaled only by their frequent synonym, "I *can't* go on like this any longer," or even, "I can't go on like this," or sometimes, economically, "I can't go on." Words that psychiatrists shudder to hear, words that conjure up visions of interminable nights spent convincing patients to sign themselves into hospitals, of fighting with the medical doctors about how stable the patient really is, of struggling to read electrocardiograms and whisking people off to the medical emergency room or interviewing the families of beautiful teenage girls lying intubated in the intensive care unit, their razored wrists bandaged.

Gordon Ranier would not kill himself, not if I could help it.

"Where are you now?" I asked.

"Home. I'm home. Can you come over?"

"Yes. I'm coming." I glanced at my watch. Just two P.M. Special Agent Jim Mahoney would be here any minute. "But I have an appointment now, Gordon. Will you be okay until I can get there?"

"I'll be okay. I have no booze in the house."

"Good. Are you thinking at all about hurting yourself?" I paused, waited.

"No. No, of course not."

"Or killing yourself?" I continued. People's thoughts could be extremely concrete, especially in times of stress. He could have been thinking of killing himself painlessly.

"Killing myself? No, of course not! That's not what I meant."

"What did you mean, then?" I was trying to be gentle, but I had to decide whether or not to call 911.

"It's just . . . I'll tell you when I see you."

"Okay. How about if I come over at around four-thirty, five?"

Gordon gave me his address. He lived all the way back in my parents' neighborhood. I looked out the window. Snow continued to fall. If I owned cross-country skis I could just ski back uptown.

"I'll see you later," I told him. "Don't do anything rash."

"I'll try." Gordon hung up before I could ask him anything else. Which was good, since I didn't really want to know.

How had Gordon described his son the first time we'd met? One of those Britishisms that I'd found so pretentious. Brilliant? Splendid?

Tremendous. That was it. Oliver was a tremendous boy.

I hoped he was tremendous enough to handle this.

chapter nineteen

Gordon was obviously in the midst of a crisis and had asked for my help. It wasn't hard for me to understand why he had called me and not one of my parents. But I had this other situation, Jim Mahoney's visit, his "debriefing" of me, and I didn't think that standing up the FBI would be a wise career move. I changed out of my sweats and back into my black clothes. I stretched out on the sofa and imagined Gordon's beautiful wife (I was sure she was beautiful), sorry, ex-wife, flattened between the train tracks with a subway car inches from her face, praying that she would miraculously survive. It certainly beat the alternative, though, of having that same train turn you into unrecognizable pulp. I couldn't let myself consider who might have pushed her. It was usually some paranoid person prematurely released from a mental hospital. There was no reason to think this case was any different, but my stomach gave a lurch even as I tried to convince myself. I took a deep breath. I was doing a lot of that lately, taking deep, cleansing breaths, but the New Age relaxation technique didn't seem to be working. The thought of a nice vodka tonic crossed my mind, but, like capital punishment, it wouldn't be a good long-term solution.

I was surprised when Jim Mahoney arrived exactly at two-thirty, considering the blizzard outside. I let him in, watched him stomp the snow off the nerdy rubber boots he wore over his shoes. Somehow on him they seemed like one of the great overlooked inventions of the twentieth century. I sat down at the dining room table, a pad of paper and a pen in front of me. They made me feel more secure, even though I thought Mahoney would be the one who would need to take notes.

"We've kept this quiet," he began without ceremony. "You have to keep it to yourself. And I mean, tell no one, not your parents, not your boyfriend. He's not here, is he?" He looked around, as if Greg might be hiding under a piece of furniture.

"No, he's not here. He's much too busy with work."

"Okay, good. All right. This morning an attempt was made on Ginny Liu's life."

"Again? I thought she was doing better. Is she—is she okay?" He had said "attempt," after all.

"She's alive. But you see, now we have a problem. Mrs. Liu was under our protection."

"So how did someone make an attempt on her life?"

"Someone disconnected her intravenous line. Of course, nothing happened to her. She's breathing on her own, she's been opening her eyes, and she seems to recognize her parents, who have been at her bedside since they arrived from San Francisco yesterday." Mahoney avoided my question so cleverly that I almost didn't notice.

"Who could have done it?" I asked. "And how could they get past the guard?"

"It had to be one of the people cleared to see her, Tamsen." Mahoney looked toward the window. "We believe something is happening inside Grandines Pharmaceuticals, and the Lius are in it up to their eyebrows. And frankly, Ginny Liu may die if we don't find out what Grandines is hiding."

"If you know that something bad is happening there, why can't you subpoena someone or bring them in for questioning or something?"

"We've been questioning everyone. We can't get any information other than what the newspapers already have. I have agents in Arkansas investigating the plant, the one that was supposed to destroy those drugs that never showed up. I have people applying for jobs at Grandines, qualified people, for advertised positions, but Grandines has a hiring freeze until after the New Year. I'm told it's routine."

"They hired me," I pointed out.

Mahoney made a note in his little book.

"Why don't I call them?" I suggested. "I'll tell them I need to know more about the position, and how their company works. So I can be comfortable representing them in public. I met the director of marketing."

"I don't know, Tamsen. I think it would be safer for you to wait for them to call you. More discreet."

"But their drug is supposed to become available on January ninth. That's in less than two weeks. I don't know anything about it, really—I mean, I know ostensibly how the drug works, it's an SSRI—but I don't know how they plan to advertise it. You know, all those 'Ask Your Doctor About' commercials. I need to be able to address those kinds of issues. Don't I?"

"Can't you get that information from what they already gave you?"

I shook my head. "You'd be surprised how many medications are sold every day where the mechanism of action is unknown. Pick up a copy of the *PDR* someday. You'll be amazed."

"*PDR?*"

"*Physicians' Desk Reference*. It lists thousands of drugs. Lots of them, believe it or not, work even though we don't really know why they work. I can't think of a special reason why this new Grandines drug, Curixenol, would work against alcoholism when other, similar drugs don't. I need to know how Grandines Pharmaceuticals wants me to deal with that issue."

"Okay." Mahoney sighed. "Think you can search Ginny Liu's office while you're over there?"

I gave him a look that I hoped said, "Don't push your luck." I doubted that there was anything in Ginny Liu's office worth finding that hadn't already been made to disappear.

I called.

Daphne Williams was in, and she sounded pleased to hear from me. She probably sounded that way all the time.

"I'm just a bit confused about what the Curixenol team expects from me," I told Daphne, in what I hoped was a confident and professional-sounding voice. "I would really like to get together with whoever would be the main person. I suppose it would be Jonathan Grandines? He's the director of marketing, I think?"

"One moment, Doctor," Daphne said.

The on-hold music was Mozart, both sophisticated and yet easily recognizable to the average holder. Plus, listening to Mozart was supposed to make you smarter. I listened to an entire movement before Daphne returned.

"Dr. Bayn? Mr. Grandines—Mr. Jonathan Grandines—would like to know if you are available for lunch tomorrow?"

"Lunch?" I repeated. "Tomorrow? What time?" I looked at Jim Mahoney, mouthed the word "tomorrow" to him. He nodded his head yes.

"About one o'clock? We're closing for the holiday at twelve, but unfortunately Mr. Grandines has some pressing business to take care of before then."

I would have to forgo some of the beauty procedures I'd scheduled in preparation for New Year's Eve. Open-toed shoes were not in my immediate future anyway, and the FBI needed me. My trivial little self-indulgences suddenly seemed ridiculous. I'm sure that the ex–Mrs. Gordon Ranier wasn't thinking about her nails as she fell onto the train tracks.

"How about—could we possibly make it one-thirty?"

"One-thirty? Hold, please."

She was back quickly, not giving me time to get much smarter, and confirmed my appointment with Jonathan Grandines for one-thirty tomorrow, New Year's Eve Day.

"I'll make a reservation for lunch," she said. "Our executive dining room will be closed."

We said our Happy New Years and good-byes, and I

hung up the phone and waited for Mahoney to congratulate me on my first significant achievement as a spy.

All he said was, "Did she tell you where the lunch will be?"

"In a restaurant."

"They can't have it there? Well, never mind, okay, here's what I want you to do. I'll page you at about two o'clock. Call me back, pretending I'm your answering service, and tell me *exactly* where you are. Just so we know."

That uneasy feeling was returning to my stomach.

"Just in case," he said.

"In case of what?" I asked, all ingenue.

He paused for a second, then said, "Try to find out how they sell their nonprescription drugs. We know, of course, how they are supposed to do it. But I'd like to hear his version."

"In case there are inconsistencies?"

"Inconsistencies," Mahoney said. "Or lies."

chapter twenty

I got my coat so I could leave with Jim Mahoney. He asked me where I was going. When I told him I was headed back uptown, he offered to give me a ride. He had a car waiting.

Snow fell in wet clumps. Cars were abandoned, buried in drifts all over the city. We sat in the backseat of a big black sedan, unremarkable in every way except for its two-way radio and my assumption that the driver was armed. Every time we turned a corner, I was sure that we would plunge into a snowdrift and be able to move no farther. Amazingly, probably because of the relative lack of traffic, we made it back uptown in just under an hour.

On the way, I told Mahoney a bit about the reason I was going to see Gordon.

"This guy is just . . . distraught, I guess is the best way to put it. His ex-wife was in a terrible accident, and he's concerned about his son. He wanted to talk." I had to explain that the incident had occurred in England and how I knew Gordon.

"You're pretty busy," Mahoney commented. "This distraught guy, and your work for Grandines, and now for us. And you're mixed up with that twelve-year-old killer case. Have you had a chance to meet him yet?"

"Just the parents so far. I don't think I need to meet the boy at this point."

"Adult monsters are bad enough. Kid monsters—unbelievable what these kids are up to these days." Jim Mahoney told the driver to drop me off first.

"Want me to wait?" he asked. "In case everything is not okay?"

"If . . . sure, if you wouldn't mind," I said, surprised.

Gordon lived on East Sixty-ninth Street. We pulled up in front of the address he'd given me and I got out of the FBI car. The snow sucked at me like cold quicksand. I ducked into the lobby of the building and waited as the doorman rang Gordon's apartment.

"He doesn't seem to be home." The doorman's name tag read "Norman." Norman looked like a retired guy who was working as a doorman to fill his long days.

"He just called me," I said. "He's expecting me."

The doorman looked me over. "Let me try again."

"No answer," he reported.

"Can I just go up? I'm a doctor, and he called me with a medical emergency."

"Sorry, against the rules." Norman was taking his retirement job very seriously.

"I'll be right back." I wasn't up for negotiating. The last thing I wanted right now was to come right back. Gordon's refusal to answer his door was not a good sign. I hoped he hadn't gone out for a fifth of something. In the brief time I'd known him, Gordon had struck me as being too self-centered, too arrogant, to ever become authentically suicidal. Still, stress and fear do weird things to people. So I went back out into what was by now a full-fledged blizzard, to ask Jim Mahoney for a little help.

"Everything okay?" he asked me as I climbed back into the car.

"No. Gordon's not answering, and the doorman won't let me go up. I need to make sure he's not lying up there unconscious or something. I'm not his doctor, but when he called me, I accepted responsibility for him."

Mahoney gestured for me to get out of the car. He followed me into the lobby and flashed something at the doorman. "FBI," he said, just loudly enough for Norman the doorman to hear. A small man with two huge dogs, Siberian huskies or malamutes, got out of the elevator and tugged a black knit hat over his shiny bald head. He didn't even glance at us as he crossed the marble lobby, skirted the table with its million-dollar flower arrangement, and headed for the door. I couldn't even imagine what the inside of his apartment must look like, with those two furry creatures in residence. Now, there was someone who would need decongestants.

"Excuse me," Norman said as he held the door for the would-be musher. At least the dogs wouldn't mind the weather. Norman let the door close, then looked from Mahoney to me and back to Mahoney again.

"Okay," he said.

"We'll need the keys to his apartment," Mahoney said.

"Oh, I don't think I can—" He stopped talking when he saw the look on Mahoney's face. "One moment. I'll see what I can do." He picked up a phone and pressed a button. After a pause he began speaking quietly into the receiver.

"Thank you so much," I whispered to Mahoney. "I really appreciate this. I couldn't stand it if something happened to him, if I had come all this way and couldn't help him."

"Well, I was here. You know what they say, one good turn deserves another."

The elevator doors opened again and a short thin gray man emerged. He was wearing gray work clothes, grayish boots, and his head was covered with wiry gray curls. His skin had that sallow gray look of someone who spends all his time indoors.

"Hello, I am Pedro, the super. I will come with you to Señor Ranier's apartment." He pronounced it "apartament."

"Thank you," I said gratefully, including Pedro, the doorman, and Mahoney in my generalized thanks. A woman in a mink coat entered the building and waited with us at the elevator bank. I couldn't wait to see Gordon, make sure he wasn't bouncing off any walls, and go home. Alcoholics could be sober for years—then, in a minute, ruin everything.

The fur-coated lady got off on the fourth floor, and we continued up to the seventeenth. The building was a modern one, and although they tried hard with doormen and flowers, it would never have the charm and elegance of the prewar buildings like my parents'. The lobby had smelled faintly of mold, and the elevator carpet crunched beneath my feet.

"Seventeen-M." Pedro led the way down the narrow carpeted corridor. I could hear the electronic murmur of televisions or radios. Here and there a pair of boots or an umbrella sat outside an apartment door; across from Gordon's apartment, which was at the end of the hallway, one of his neighbors had left a stroller. But for the most part, the seventeenth floor looked deserted. Certainly no neighbors were about to say whether or not they had seen or heard anything suspicious. Not that I expected Gordon to go running out into the hallway screaming, "I'm going to get drunk and kill myself."

Pedro rang the bell; no answer. He thumped on the door with his fist. "Señor Ranier?"

If Gordon didn't hear the bell, he probably wouldn't hear the pounding either.

"Unlock the door," Mahoney instructed Pedro.

"Sí, señor." Pedro recognized authority when he encountered it. The key slid into the lock, turned. I heard a click.

"The same key opens both locks," Pedro explained, turning the top lock. He grabbed the knob, twisted, pushed. The door remained closed.

"Okay, maybe I locked one by mistake." He looked at the key, turned it, pushed, took it out, put it in the bottom lock, and said, "I am sorry, this door was unlocked. I just locked it. I am sorry." He pushed, and the door swung open.

I followed Mahoney into the dark apartment. He fumbled for a light. I thought I could hear water running, but the kitchen was quiet in front of me. "Gordon? Gordon, it's me, Tamsen, are you here?" I jumped as something black and furry shot out of a doorway and crossed the room.

"A cat," I whispered, relieved. In this city, it could just as easily have been a rat. "Gordon? Please come out. We need to know you're all right."

"The lady is a psychiatrist," Mahoney informed Pedro, who seemed to understand the situation instantly.

"I go look inside," Pedro told us. "You wait here. This apartment, M-line, one bedroom, one bathroom. Maybe he just taking a shower."

We had entered a small open foyer. In front of us was the kitchen, to the right was a door that I assumed led to a closet. The arched doorway to my left led into a living room. Gordon's taste ran to the modern and minimal. He had a black leather sofa, white rug on wood floors, glass coffee table, expensive stereo and television on a black lacquer wall unit. The dining alcove held a black table and four chairs. A cup and plate waited on a placemat. A bread basket held half a baguette. Everything neat and tidy and in its place.

At the exact moment that I finished my inventory I heard a scream.

"Señor! Doctora!" Pedro bounded back into the foyer and let loose a stream of Spanish. He was gasping something about the Virgin Maria, but that was all I could understand.

"What is it?" Mahoney demanded. "What happened? Is he here? Is he all right?"

But with one look at Pedro's face I knew that Gordon Ranier would never be all right again.

chapter twenty-one

The next few hours were a blur. Jim Mahoney stayed with me the entire time, summoning the police, explaining what had happened. The emergency medical technicians who arrived within ten minutes did their best, but it was too late. They informed me that Gordon had slashed both his wrists so deeply that the bathroom was awash in blood. The medical examiner arrived, a cold old man who looked like he'd rather be anywhere else. He disappeared silently to the bathroom where Gordon's body lay.

Two uniformed officers were joined by two detectives. All were initially suspicious at the FBI's presence, but Mahoney explained that he was with me on another matter and he'd merely offered me a ride in the bad weather.

"I wasn't actually his psychiatrist," I told a detective. "I was just a friend. He called me, he was upset, asked me to come over. He said he wasn't going to do anything to hurt himself." Meanwhile, my analytically trained mind was thinking: He must have really been angry at me to make me the one to find him dead. Suicide is an extremely aggressive act. But what had I done? Nothing could have been worth killing himself.

We finished giving our statements and eventually we were allowed to go. I'd sat, numb, on the cold leather sofa for most of the time, holding Gordon's cat on my lap, stroking his fur. The cat was a surprise, a regular black cat with just one tiny spot of white between his eyes, and two white feet. If I had ever considered Gordon's possible taste in pets, which I hadn't, I would have pegged him for a designer Persian or Siamese.

"You gonna take her, Doc?" the younger and nicer of the two uniformed officers asked me.

"Him," I corrected automatically. I hadn't really considered the cat's fate. I watched as the EMS guys removed Gordon's body in a black plastic bag. The medical examiner had ordered the body moved to the morgue. When the detective asked when the autopsy would be performed, the pathologist's only comment was, "Take a number."

The scene would be sealed until some more forensics specialists could get there, meanwhile Mahoney and I gave our fingerprints for comparison. "It's just routine," everyone kept saying. Unlike the many times I'd been fingerprinted to work in various hospitals and jails, this procedure left my hands clean.

"The cat, Doc?" the young policeman reminded me.

"Um, okay, I guess," I said. "I'll take him for now. Is—is the litter box in the bathroom?" I felt embarrassed that I could think about ordinary, life-simplifying things like the cat's litter box, when the cat's owner was dead.

"Wait here," the officer said. A few minutes later he returned with a bulging plastic bag. It contained the empty, washed-out litter box, a plastic container of that special clumping cat sand, and a few cans.

"I found the cat food in the kitchen," he explained. He looked sheepish, as if he knew that I wouldn't refuse to take the cat since I felt that it was my fault that Gordon had killed himself. He left the living room and I heard him opening and closing doors. He returned, triumphantly waving a blue plastic cat carrier. "I figured he'd have one."

I put the cat in the carrier. He went in reluctantly, but I think he knew that his owner was dead and it was time to move on. I didn't even know his name. He was black, black as Coal? Black as Tar? Black as Ink? I'd call him Ink. No, Inky. Focus on mundane things. Don't think about the life you failed to save.

Finally, Mahoney and I got into the elevator, the two of us alone, the cat carrier between us.

"I'm sorry," Mahoney said gruffly, not meeting my eyes.

"You couldn't have known," I said. "I—I didn't think he'd do anything." To my extreme humiliation, I started to cry. "I never had a patient suicide," I said. "Never. They say it happens to every psychiatrist sooner or later, that you can't prevent it one hundred percent, that if they really want to kill themselves they will. But he said—I thought—" I wanted to say that Gordon had no reason to kill himself, that his wife and son were both all right, that whatever problems they'd had could be made better, that every child needs both his parents. But I couldn't seem to get any of the words out. "It's my fault," I sobbed. "All my fault."

Mahoney put his arm around my shoulders. "It's not your fault, Tamsen. You weren't his doctor. You couldn't have known. And anyway . . ."

"Anyway, what?" I asked. The elevator stopped, and I juggled cat and bag and pocketbook while I tried to find a tissue to wipe my eyes. I ended up using my coat sleeve.

"Nothing," Mahoney said. "Please. Go home, get some sleep. You'll feel better tomorrow."

Norman the doorman had left the lobby, replaced by a younger guy who barely glanced at us as he held the door open. Maybe he didn't know we had come from the same apartment as the body bag, or maybe he knew but didn't care. Outside the snow was blowing even worse than before. The FBI car had gone. I dimly remembered Mahoney giving someone instructions to send the car away. I was miles away from home in a snowstorm with a cat. Now what?

"I need to get a cab," I said, pushing toward the curb. Right, like there were cabs just lining up to drive all the way back downtown in this blizzard. On this narrow side street we could have been in the New York of a hundred years before. The parked cars were white mountains, and no tire tracks were visible on the street itself. All was quiet and still. Lights from buildings cast circles in the swirling snow. I half expected a horse-drawn sleigh to come rounding the corner, crammed with rosy-cheeked Victorian children wearing fur earmuffs and sipping hot chocolate. The city was shutting itself down for the onslaught.

The most logical thing to do would be to spend the night at my parents' house. It was close; I could walk. I was sure they hadn't gone anywhere, because the airports were closed; anyway, I had the keys.

"I'll go to my parents'," I told Mahoney. "They live nearby. Thanks for everything."

"Tomorrow," he said, a pained expression on his kind face. "Do you think you'll be up to this lunch with Jonathan Grandines?"

I had forgotten that I had anything to do for the rest of my life other than get out of the snow. In its plastic cage Gordon's cat was meowing loudly, and, I thought, a bit sadly. "You think he'll be there? I think they'll be closed tomorrow, with this weather. But yes, if he's there, I'll go."

"Good girl," Mahoney said. "We'll be in touch in the morning."

"I'll be in my office at eight," I said wearily. Across the street I saw a couple walking a dog, heard them laugh, watched them stop to kiss in the snow. I didn't even know if we were allowed to have cats in Greg's building. Our building, I amended silently.

He's dead, a little voice seemed to jeer in my mind, *and it's your fault, and all you can think about is yourself. Selfish.*

Inky yowled.

"No," I said out loud.

Mahoney looked at me curiously. He was wearing a hat, one of those old-man black felt hats with a brim, but the snow was blowing into his eyes and nose, and I could see that he was just a guy on the other side of sixty who shouldn't be standing out in a snowstorm for me.

"Thank you," I repeated. "I'll be going. Do you live nearby?"

"Just two blocks south," he replied. "I'll be fine."

I headed left toward Madison. On a normal snow-free evening, the walk to Seventy-seventh Street would take about eight minutes, plus maybe another two for the lights. Tonight with the cat and the stuff, not to mention the un-shoveled sidewalks, it would take longer. I was freezing and bone-tired and, obviously, using the bathroom in Gordon's apartment had been out of the question.

I concentrated on making it to my parents' home alive and undamaged. The doorman let me in without ringing upstairs, since he knew me and knew I could drop in when-ever I wanted, but I rang the apartment's doorbell even though I had the key. I had been responsible for enough surprises today.

My mother opened the door. She was wearing a silk robe, red, her favorite color, and had the cordless phone tucked between her ear and her shoulder.

"One moment," she said into the phone in Romanian, her native language. "What happened?" This question was directed at me.

My mother was going to be mad that I had brought her an unexpected cat.

"Sorry," I said. "Can I stay here tonight?"

"What happened to you?" she asked again.

"Oh, God," I said, and then those sophisticated-big-grown-up-psychiatrist-in-private-practice tears started again. *"Tata?"* Dad, her dad, my grandfather, the one I hadn't yet had a premonition about, the one safely in Florida. "I'll have to call you back later," my mother said into the phone, and clicked it off. "What's wrong, honey?" she asked me.

I looked at her through my tears. "Tell Daddy he's go-ing to have to find a new agent."

chapter twenty-two

Once the floodgates opened, they didn't close for a long time. I went to take a shower, came back, and curled up on the sofa. My mother brought me tea and a toaster-ovened Swiss-cheese sandwich. My father was playing with the cat, teasing it with some red and white string from a bakery box.

"It's my fault," I kept saying, and they kept saying, "No, no, you couldn't have known," and then I would cry more because I was crying from my guilt and my anger and my shame rather than from any real sadness at the loss of Gordon. I hadn't known him well, we weren't close, we'd had lunch together once. "Why would he have called *me*?" I wailed in frustration, knowing there was no real reason.

"Did you call Greg?" my mother asked. "He'll be worried."

My father brought me the cordless phone. I couldn't remember the two of them ever being so solicitous.

"I lost a patient once," my father said softly as I punched in my number.

"You're in the memory," my mother said. She meant the phone's speed dial. Of course. She called me twenty times a day. For once I didn't mind.

Greg picked up right away. "Tamsen? You're at your parents' house?" The handy-dandy caller ID was doing its job. He sounded confused. "Are you okay? What happened?"

"I—oh, God, so many things have happened," I said, standing up and walking toward the kitchen. I didn't want my parents listening. "I had to go see Gordon—remember Gordon Ranier, my father's agent?"

"That sleazy British jerk? Yeah."

"You don't need to sound like that. He's dead."

"What? *Dead?* An accident? A heart attack? I haven't heard about any new homicides." As part of his delightful job as the deputy chief of the Career Criminal Unit, Greg was notified of every new homicide in Manhattan, even if they weren't assigned to him.

"Suicide." I kept my voice low so he couldn't hear the tears in it. "He called me, he was upset, he needed help, and by the time I got there he had killed himself."

"Come home," Greg said.

"I can't. It's too late, the weather is too bad, and I have to be back here at eight o'clock in the morning to see the Devinskis in my office." I picked up my mug and drank some tea. My mother was always offering cups of things to distraught people. Wasn't that what they did in England for people who were upset? In Agatha Christie books, everyone was always making everyone else strong hot cups of tea. Well, my parents had both learned English by reading Christie, probably some of it had rubbed off on them. When I was a kid I had made my way through a whole shelf of them, with Romanian words penciled in over some of the harder English ones. The thought of English people drinking tea just made my eyes fill again. Gordon was English. Not that I knew whether or not he'd drunk tea.

Greg was talking to me, and I had missed it, lost in my loose associations of irrelevant thoughts. "What?" I asked.

"I'll come to you," he said. "If you want me to, that is."

I was silent. Of course I wanted him to come here. "But—the weather—you won't find a taxi, you have to take the subway . . ." I ran out of objections. "Yes, please," I said. "I need you."

"I'm on my way," Greg said.

I disconnected as I walked back into the living room and handed the phone to my father. He put it back in its little cradle and sat down next to me.

"It was when I was a resident," he said, as if he hadn't been interrupted.

My mother said, "More tea, honey?"

"No, thanks." I took a bite out of my untouched sandwich. I watched as my mother left the room.

"She was a clinic patient," my father said. "It was soon after—um, no I guess it was when your mother was pregnant with you."

"When she was still a surgical resident?"

"Mmm." He nodded, lost in thought. My mother had wanted to be a surgeon, but she got married, and pregnant. (I'd always had my doubts if they'd happened in that order.) Her department had let her work until the last possible day. She went from the operating room to the delivery room, and a couple of hours after I was born, her residency training director came to visit her, bring her flowers, admire the baby (me), and kick her out of the residency. She had been the only woman in her year, and after she got pregnant with me, that program didn't hire another woman resident for five years. It was one of the walls that always stood between us.

"Cheryl. Cheryl Slatkin. She was an identical twin. Cheryl was my patient, Tracy was another resident's.

"They were in and out of the hospital all the time. Now I guess you'd diagnose them with severe obsessive-compulsive disorder, but in those days, we had other diagnoses, severe reactive schizophrenia or some such nonsense, I don't remember." He shook his head. "Tracy was in the hospital this time, and we all knew her, whenever we were on call we'd stop by and see her. You know how certain patients become the department pets. And Tracy and Cheryl were young girls, maybe eighteen, nineteen, when it happened. Pretty. Pretty and crazy. And we all thought we'd be the one to cure them."

I nodded, knowing what he meant. In my residency certain patients would come back over and over. Whichever resident got them would try to find the right miracle combination of medication and therapy to fix them. But some patients are just not fixable. Some people are so disturbed that no amount of modern medical science can really help them.

My father called to my mother, "Regina, can you bring

some seltzer?" Then he continued. "So, Tracy got fixed up that time, and my colleague discharged her. He let me know how well she was doing, that I should put Cheryl on the same meds, blah blah blah. Which in those days was not a tremendous challenge. We spent most of our time talking to our patients. There weren't many meds available, a few neuroleptics, some tricylic antidepressants, and a lot of tranquilizers.

"I called Cheryl, to tell her that her sister was coming home, that she was doing really well. We made an appointment for the next day. She sounded good, Cheryl, like she couldn't wait to see her twin.

"They lived on the eighth floor of a building in the Bronx. They had a terrace, you know? So, the parents went to the hospital to pick up Tracy, and when they pulled up to their building they saw the police, the ambulance . . .

"Tracy told me later that she knew right away. She said she felt something was wrong as soon as her parents came to pick her up, which would have been almost exactly the moment that Cheryl jumped."

My father sighed. "So you see, sweetheart, it happens. I spoke to that poor girl only two hours before she killed herself, and she said she was fine. I asked her, Are you okay, how are you handling things, all the right questions, and she still killed herself."

"You can't watch them all the time," my mother contributed, returning with the seltzer and some chocolates. When in doubt, feed. It's a Jewish-Romanian–Agatha Christie thing.

"Tracy Slatkin killed herself too," she remarked casually. "When I was chief resident. She killed herself while she was out on a day pass from Bronx State."

My father stared at my mother as if she had suddenly sprouted horns. "You never told me," he said. "Why didn't you tell me? That was thirty years ago. All these years I thought that at least one of them had made it."

"I didn't know, Bernie. I didn't know she was your patient. She wasn't actually your patient, in fact. Cheryl was

your patient." She poured some seltzer into a glass and
handed it to me. My mother had become a psychiatrist
when my father's psychiatric residency training program
was the only one available to her. She'd never been motivated by compassion. She'd needed a job.

I watched them in silent misery. Patients will kill
themselves, and decades later we'll still feel responsible.
Nobody could change that fact. If we felt responsible, we
always would. If we didn't, we never would.

I felt responsible for Gordon's death. I knew I always
would.

chapter twenty-three

I woke up the next morning with Greg's arms around me and the smell of coffee drifting into the dark room. For a second everything felt normal, then I remembered where I was and why I was here. Greg had come in after midnight. His arms were like a life preserver, holding me above the surface of the treacherous water that was the beginning of the Gordon nightmare.

"I brought you something," Greg said to me as we drank coffee in my parents' kitchen. "But you can't use it for anything. Jason Devinski is a minor. You can't let on that you saw this tape. You'd be amazed, Tamsen. If you talked to him now, you'd think he was a different boy."

"Tape?" I asked, but Greg was already pressing a video-cassette into my hand and kissing me good-bye. I wandered into the living room and slid the tape into the VCR.

I fast-forwarded through the static and suddenly figures appeared. I hit play. It took a few seconds for me to recognize the distorted female voice in the background as Natalie Diamond's.

"Jason, would you tell me what happened at school?"

"Nothing." The tape was black-and-white. The grainy boy shook his head once, then sat still. He was looking at his hands, handcuffed together on the table in front of him.

"Where did you get the gun, Jason?"

"From my mom's boss. I *told* you already. How many times do I need to tell you the same stuff?"

The press had reported that Jason was cold, with no remorse. The little boy on this tape was talking about killing other human beings in a voice that could have been computer-generated.

"Are you sorry that you killed them, Jason?" Natalie's voice, again.

"Sorry? What is 'sorry' supposed to mean? What's the difference?"

There was more, but I switched the tape off. I felt as if my blood had turned to ice.

By five of eight I was in the office waiting for the Devinskis. The snow had stopped, the airports had reopened, and my parents were on their way to the Sunshine State for their annual New Year's Eve bash. The little cat had been fed. I'd left him curled up on the white sofa, a black fur ball highlighted by a ray of winter sunshine. I sat at my desk and looked at the Bermuda ticket. I hadn't mentioned it to anyone. I had to decide what I wanted to do about it. If I told Greg he'd tell me not to go, to dump Grandines and forget about the pharmaceutical industry and that if I really wanted to go to Bermuda we could go there on our honeymoon. And he would be right. Whatever had exiled Dr. Hastings-Muir had occurred here. Only he didn't know that the FBI had enlisted my cooperation, and I couldn't walk away from Grandines Pharmaceuticals right now. But I couldn't walk away from Jason Devinski either. Everyone was waiting for my explanation for the murders Jason had committed. And in truth, I was the most curious member of the audience.

Where were those Devinskis? I picked up the phone and dialed their number. The voice mail asked me to leave a message. I hung up. Nothing was going according to my plan. My high-profile forensic evaluation was being thwarted by events I wasn't even hearing about. My glamorous consulting job was turning into an undercover cloak-and-dagger operation to help investigate something that I didn't even understand. A casual acquaintance had asked me for help, and instead of intervening quickly, as I should have and could have done, I let him kill himself. I was tempted to call everyone and just say forget it, and use that Bermuda ticket to go lie on the beach until I was baked to a crisp. I wondered if they needed psychiatrists in Bermuda. Maybe I could just stay there.

Lost in my reverie of self-pity, the ringing doorbell startled me into banging my knee on the desk as I sprang out of my chair. Finally. I opened the door and welcomed Karen and Peter Devinski. Both looked terrible, with matching wild hairdos and bloodshot eyes.

"Hi." I smiled as warmly as I could. "I'm glad you could make it. How's Jason?"

"He's okay." The exhaustion was audible in Karen's voice. "He's in the hospital. In Bellevue. Under police guard, since he's a criminal defendant."

"He's already had a CAT scan," Peter said. "He doesn't have a brain tumor or anything." He left off the "Thank God," but I heard it there just the same.

"People are saying awful things." Karen entered the waiting room and slumped onto the sofa, coat still on. She didn't seem aware of her surroundings.

"Come in." I gestured to the consultation room. "Coffee?"

"No, thanks," they said in unison.

Peter said, "We've been up all night drinking coffee."

Something in the way he spoke cut right through to my heart. This couple had one child. They had loved him, nurtured him, stood by him, done everything they could to give him a wonderful life. They couldn't understand how their golden child had betrayed them, how he could have turned from their sweet infant into a ruthless monster. They had come to me looking for more than explanations for the court. They were looking for an explanation for *themselves*. I desperately wanted to provide it for them—but I had no idea what the hell it was.

I pushed the vision of running away to a deserted beach out of my mind. "Okay." I studied the chart on the desk in front of me. "Last time you had just finished telling me about your decision to have Jason, and about your depression, Karen."

Karen nodded.

"Anything else you can remember about those early days? When did you go back to work?"

Karen had taken six weeks of maternity leave, then they hired a warm and loving Jamaican nanny to take care of Jason. Grandines hadn't exactly jumped on the family-friendly bandwagon, with such limited maternity leave. Today they'd have to let her take twelve weeks off.

"She was with us for six and a half years," Karen said. "I mean, she wasn't me, but she was wonderful. She took care of Jason until we moved to New York."

I wrote this information in the chart. So far I hadn't heard anything alarming in Jason's history. His parents weren't perfect, but they had far fewer problems than the parents of the kids I'd treated as a resident in the Bronx. Karen and Peter had good professions, education, plenty of money, and had given Jason the best of everything. I didn't get it.

"Was he spoiled?" I asked.

"I guess," Karen said.

"Not really," Peter said at the same time.

I smiled encouragement that I didn't feel. "Well, which one was it?" I asked patiently.

"Neither," Karen said. "Both. We gave him everything we could. But he was always a good boy. We took him places, traveled with him. He plays the piano, you know? He's really talented." She started to cry.

"Did he ever give any indication that he was violent?" I was treading into murky territory again, but it was important. If they had known that Jason had an inclination toward violence or antisocial behavior and had done nothing about it, then by omission they would be partly responsible. The Devinskis wouldn't be the first well-educated, well-informed, and well-meaning parents to be blind to their children's deficits.

"He was gentle," Karen insisted. "I know what you're thinking, that we just didn't notice—that Jason was wild and badly brought up and that he set fires and tortured animals and wet his bed and we just didn't notice. But I swear to you, he didn't and we didn't. Didn't not notice, I mean."

I waited, curious.

"I've been reading about it," she said apologetically. "At night, when I can't sleep, I read. I know about the triad of bed-wetting, fire-setting, and small-animal-torturing." Karen was referring to what many psychiatrists and psychologists believe are childhood signs that predict adult antisocial personality disorder.

"Well, he did wet his bed occasionally. But not for long. It stopped by the time he was five or six. That's normal, isn't it?"

I nodded. As much as I tried to find some hidden agenda or hidden pathology in these parents, so far it remained elusive.

"Let's talk a little about your alcoholism," I said to Peter. "If that's okay with you?"

"Sure. But I haven't had a drink in years. Never even wanted one."

"Do you go to AA or something?" I'd heard this "I never even wanted a drink again" line from other former alcoholics, but I'm always skeptical. It's like someone who successfully lost weight telling you that she never craved a chocolate truffle again. It sounded good, but I just didn't believe it. I knew that people could stop drinking, lots of alcoholics became sober, but it didn't mean they never *wanted* a drink. They'd just learned to deprive themselves.

"No. I never went to AA. I was in a support group. It really helped." He fell silent, then reached over and took Karen's hand. Again, I felt that wordless current between them.

"Any family history of seizures?"

"No," they said together.

"Karen, did *you* ever have a problem with drugs or alcohol?"

"A problem? No. I have a glass of wine sometimes, but never at home. You know—because of Peter. I don't want him to be tempted."

"How about drugs? Do you use any, um, recreational drugs?"

"Oh, God no! Are you crazy?" She took a breath, looked embarrassed. "Sorry. I did try pot in college. But I wasn't like that. I was kind of . . . nerdy. I was on the volleyball team, though. That was kind of cool. Moderately cool."

"And she played the clarinet in the orchestra," Peter added. "She still plays in a quartet."

"Not anymore," Karen said. "I told them to find a replacement for me. I . . . can't." She looked at the floor, then at the empty fireplace. "You think he could have set fires or tortured animals without getting caught?" Karen's blue eyes shone with tears. "Without us even knowing?"

"I don't know," I answered softly. I remembered the cold boy I'd seen on tape only an hour ago. "I couldn't even guess. What do you think?"

"I'm starting to think that I didn't know him at all. That all this time my sweet boy was just a stranger. Did you ever read that book when you were little about the girl who was stolen at birth and replaced with a fairy? Maybe someone replaced Jason with a devil."

She must have seen my eyebrows disappear under my bangs, because I certainly felt the look of surprise on my face.

"Metaphorically speaking," Karen said. "I'm not crazy. I'm just . . . *crazy*. Know what I mean?"

I did know. She felt as if she were losing control, as if she couldn't predict reality anymore. I had felt that way once or twice in my life. When my fiancé died the day before our wedding, I thought I would lose my mind for sure, permanently and irretrievably. But I survived, and while I would never have chosen Daniel's death, I got Greg. I don't especially believe in predestination, but I don't *not* believe in it either.

"Explain it to me," I said, pen poised above paper. I had to get some new information, for my report and for Agent Mahoney.

"You asked about drugs. I never took them, but I imagine that this must be what it feels like." She glanced at her husband, who seemed to understand her telepathically.

Peter said, "I think I'll give you some space, honey." He gestured toward the closed door to the waiting room.

"Okay," Karen said.

Peter left the room and pulled the door shut behind him.

"He can't keep hearing this," Karen explained to me. "It's destroying him. I told him before we got here that if and when I started to get too sentimental and weepy for him he should take a little break."

"He seems very supportive."

"Oh, he is. He would have stayed, but I seem to spend most of our time alone together crying. He deserves a break." Karen paused and looked at her hands. Even from where I sat I could see the skin was rough and dry, cuticles jagged, fingernails bitten. I hadn't noticed her biting her nails. It must be an old habit that she had recently gone back to for secret comfort.

"I feel like none of this is real, as if it could just go away at any moment." Karen was describing a typical emotional reaction to acute trauma. "We had . . . a perfect life. I didn't realize it at the time, of course. We had great jobs, plenty of money, we have a beautiful apartment, we go on wonderful vacations, we just . . . I don't know, we do everything we want to do. We work hard." Another glance at the soundproof door, behind which her husband waited. "At least, I work hard. And we've been successful. Jason is a straight-A student, he has been since kindergarten. Nobody ever complained about his behavior. He doesn't have a lot of friends, but this is Manhattan. These kids today, I don't know, their time is so scheduled, so overbooked, they don't have much time for friends. You should hear him play 'Für Elise.'" She started to cry again.

I waited, patiently. This always happened: I'd do an evaluation for the court and end up listening to all the person's problems and becoming a sponge to soak up all their unbearable emotions. I know psychiatrists who don't have

an emotional bone in their bodies, funny bone notwithstanding, who can perform evaluations without so much as
a whisper of empathy. I can't. I still haven't decided if it's a
strength or a shortcoming.

"I swear to you," Karen said indistinctly through her
sobs, "I *swear* we didn't know. We didn't do anything wrong.
He must be sick. He must be. Maybe someone gave him
drugs. What's that stuff that my company is in trouble for?
Methamphetamine? Maybe someone gave him that."

"What did you say?" I heard my voice coming from the
end of a long tunnel, a tunnel under a mountain under an
ocean.

"Maybe someone gave him methamphetamine. It
causes violence, doesn't it? I can't think of another explanation. I can't think of *any* explanation."

After the murders, Jason must have been tested for
drugs. Drug screening was routine, even in the juvenile detention center. Nine-year-old kids were taking drugs and
working for the gangs these days. Something so prevalent
wouldn't be overlooked.

"Did they test Jason for drugs?" I asked quietly.

"They didn't find anything, as far as I know. It's just a
shot in the dark. I really don't know what happened."

"Have you heard anything at work about this methamphetamine problem?"

"I haven't even *been* to work, not since that night in the
restaurant. I'm sure that's not it. I'm sure they're not even
having a problem. It's just some administrative foul-up.
How would they get so careless?"

How, indeed. "So you don't know anything about this
diversion stuff?"

"No. Parker had a lot of meetings with his security director. That's all I know."

I couldn't think of any more questions. I knew that Jim
Mahoney was counting on me for information, but I didn't
think that Karen could supply any. But what if— No, it was
too outrageous to consider. Legitimate drugs made billions

for the companies that produced them. Curixenol alone would put Grandines on the pharmaceutical industry map. It would be complete foolishness for them to . . . No. I wouldn't even consider it.

I asked Karen to invite Peter back in. When he was seated beside her, I told them, "Listen, I don't think I need any more information from you right now. Why don't you go home and get some rest? You need to be able to take care of Jason. I'll call you if I have any more questions."

Both nodded. "So what do you think you will say in your report?" Peter wanted to know.

"I don't think that either of you has any mental condition that impacted on Jason's actions."

They looked at each other. The silence stretched on. "What will that mean for Jason?" Karen asked.

"I don't know," I admitted. "For now, I'm putting you in the hands of Dr. Bluecorn and your attorney. It's up to them. But I don't think it will hurt you in any way to have a report absolving you of any complicity in Jason's behavior."

"But it won't help him, will it?" Peter asked.

"I don't know," I said honestly.

"Thank you, Tamsen." Peter got to his feet and zipped up his parka. "I know it's been helpful talking to you, if nothing else."

"When all this blows over—if it blows over—we'll have lunch in the Grandines employee cafeteria." Karen bent her head and fumbled with the buttons on her coat, probably to hide the tears that filled her eyes again. "On me, okay?"

"Just hang in there," I said. "It's not over till it's over." Trite, tired old words, but never truer.

Karen gave me a hug. "Thank you. Thanks for everything. And call us if you think of anything else."

I showed them out and closed the door behind them. I decided to call Grandines to see if my lunch with Jonathan was still on. Daphne was in and she assured me that it was.

"Mr. Grandines is looking forward to it," she said brightly.

"Thanks. Happy New Year, if I don't see you."

"You won't. I'm leaving now. I'm taking my kids to Paradise Island."

Kids? I would never have guessed. "Have a great time."

I bundled up and locked the door behind me. I still had time for my appointment and a manicure was sure to make a good impression on Jonathan Grandines. The salon was three long avenue blocks away. Even though the sidewalks had been mostly shoveled and salted, I slipped twice. I wasn't watching where I was walking closely enough. I was lost in my warped imagination.

Methamphetamine causes violence, Karen had reminded me. I thought again about the possibilities. They were just stupid ramblings of an overactive and overstressed mind. I shouldn't mention them to Jim Mahoney.

Or maybe, I thought as I slipped a third time, maybe I just should.

chapter twenty-four

I emerged from the beauty salon feeling like a new woman. Not until I was halfway home did I realize that I had forgotten about the cat. He could stay alone for the rest of the day, but he would need to be fed. I'd have to bring him to our place. My father liked the cat, but my mother had made it clear that Inky wasn't going to be a permanent fixture in her home, even if he matched the piano.

I changed into my "interview suit," navy blue with gold buttons, and rushed to my lunch. When the taxi dropped me off in front of the Grandines Building, I paused for a moment, breathing in the icy air. This neighborhood was making a comeback, it seemed, with a trendy-looking restaurant right across the street, and two buildings that looked like ancient-warehouses-newly-converted-into-lofts making up the block. I wondered what the loft apartments looked like inside.

I entered the spacious marble lobby of Grandines headquarters, where a uniformed guard sat behind a curved marble desk, reading a tabloid. No one else was in sight. The lobby had the hushed, abandoned feeling of a mausoleum. My heels clicked on the black-and-white marble checkerboard and echoed through the vast space as I approached the desk. I don't like crowds, but I'm a city girl and I feel safe in them. Quiet deserted places remind me of abandoned hotels and the transformation of normal people into psychotic murderers.

I told the guard who I was and what I wanted. He gestured toward the elevator. "You can go up," he said, returning to his paper.

I took the elevator up to twelve, where I had met with

all the Grandines honchos last time. The door next to the unoccupied receptionist's desk stood open. I looked around. The magazines were in disarray and the flowers drooped in dirty water. I wasn't sure if I should go in or wait. I approached the door. I heard voices coming toward me, and froze.

"You can't get away with this." The man's voice seemed high and agitated.

"I'm not getting away with anything." The other voice was smoother, deeper, soothing.

"I've been loyal to you for over ten years. You have some nerve—" The higher voice was cut off by a third, indistinct one.

"Yes, I absolutely agree," the smooth, deep voice said. The voices were much closer now. I didn't especially want to be caught eavesdropping. I headed back toward the elevators, then changed direction. I was standing nonchalantly by the defunct flower arrangement when the three men entered the reception area.

"Dr. Bayn," the deep-voiced man said, and I swung around. A tired pink petal fell off its stem and fluttered to the carpet. With Parker Grandines were a bushy man I had never seen before and Ray Liu.

"Ray," I said involuntarily, surprised.

He looked at me blankly. "Tamsen Bayn," I reminded him. "I visited Ginny the other day. How is she?"

"Umm, better," he replied, looking at me nervously. "Yes. Well, I'll be going now." He glared at Parker and the other man, then strode to the elevator bank. I stood motionless by the dying flowers. On the street below, two parka'd, gloved, and mufflered individuals were trying to dig what I assumed was a car out of a snowbank.

"Good luck, Ray," Parker Grandines said as the elevator doors opened. I turned around and faced the room again. I guessed that Ray Liu had just been fired, and I had been an inadvertent witness to his humiliation. Funny, I'd thought he was in jail. Maybe he'd made bail already. I'd have to ask Mahoney.

Grandines and his remaining companion walked toward me. The fuzzy dark man's arms swung at his sides like clubs. Wiry black hair covered his head and face, and gave the impression of continuing far down beyond his tight white collar and carefully knotted striped tie. Despite the expensive-looking suit, he looked like he would have been more comfortable in an animal skin. He looked like the kind of man who would drag his woman to their cave by her hair. I shivered.

Parker must have noticed, because he said, "The heat's been turned down already, for the holiday weekend. It's getting cold in here. Tamsen Bayn, meet Vasily Stolnik, our national director of security."

The bear-man approached me with an outstretched paw. The back of his hand was covered with the same furry black. I shook his hand. His grip was strong. I had a sudden urge to wash my hands.

"Nice to meet you," I said politely.

"I invited Vasily to lunch with us." Parker took my elbow and turned me toward the elevators. "I think he can be helpful in clearing up a few questions you may have about Curixenol and some of our current . . . misfortunes."

"Misfortunes?" I echoed, but nobody answered as the elevator doors opened with a little *ding*. Saved by the bell. "But . . . I thought I was meeting Jonathan Grandines for lunch."

"Jonathan couldn't make it," Parker told me as the elevator doors slid shut. "I hope Vasily and I will do as substitutes."

We rode down to the empty lobby in a silence disturbed only by the soft whir of the elevator machinery and the bearlike breaths of Mr. Stolnik. I could smell cologne and the lingering odor of stale tobacco. Didn't he know he was supposed to be hibernating this time of year?

We stopped in the lobby to bundle up. My black coat and red scarf looked coarse and common next to their cashmere-and-wool blends.

"We're just going around the corner," Parker Grandines

told me. "It's too treacherous outside to go far and I gave my driver the rest of the day off."

This was a man who wouldn't just hail a taxi, I realized. For this man, a taxi was the equivalent to a chartered bus to Atlantic City, the kind that gave you a roll of quarters "free" with your ticket.

Grandines stopped in front of a nondescript building around the corner. The traffic was still light, but at least here I could see some signs of human life: a few cars, a genderless parka'd person walking a tiny black dog. Parker Grandines held the door open and I entered the restaurant, followed by the two men.

The host greeted us in a melodic and effusive Italian accent. Several businessmen sat at the bar, talking and smoking. One was gesturing with his cigarette toward the screen of his laptop computer, open on the bar in front of him. I took in the scene with mounting anxiety. I'd expected to meet with Grandines Pharmaceuticals' director of marketing. How exactly had that mild job-related request metamorphosed into a lunch with the director of security and the CEO?

"Ah, signorina, let me take your coat," the very handsome Italiano said. "I am Roberto Conti, and this is my humble establishment. I welcome you." His voice was like a caress. I took a deep breath to keep from laughing. I had a funny feeling that the closest Roberto Conti had ever been to Italy was Arthur Avenue in the Bronx.

Roberto ushered us into the dim recesses of his restaurant, past a couple with a blond baby spattered with tomato sauce, who sat in a high chair waving his spoon and saying sweetly but emphatically, "More, more."

We were settled at a square table covered with a crisp white cloth in a corner of a back room. Nobody else was dining here today. Just then my beeper went off.

"My answering service," I explained, with just the right degree of humility, I hoped. "I'll need to call in."

"I have a phone," Parker offered, pulling a tiny black state-of-the-art cellular from inside his jacket.

"Umm, thanks, that's okay," I said. "I was just about to go wash my hands anyway." I owned a cell phone too, but I almost never used it. There's nothing more annoying than seeing people sitting in restaurants or walking down the street, talking into their little black boxes as if something really important were going on.

The two men looked at each other, and I realized that Stolnik had not yet said even one word in my presence. Did he suffer from elective mutism?

"Of course," Grandines said.

Stolnik finally spoke, "Okay, we wait for you." He had a distinctive accent that I'd recognize anywhere. Stolnik was Russian.

I rose from the table. Instantly, Roberto was at my side, showing me to the ladies' room. I went in, never one to pass up an opportunity. When I came out, I found the pay phone, called the number, and was relieved when Jim Mahoney himself answered.

"I'm in a restaurant on Spring Street, called Conti's. An Italian restaurant. There's another guy here with us. That security guy, Vasily Stolnik."

"Oh, the former KGB colonel," Mahoney said. "I've heard some, shall we say, interesting things about him."

"KGB?" I said, and then wondered why I was surprised. America, the world, was full of these men, middle-aged, smart, ruthless, and, sadly for them, unemployed. A director-of-security position would be just the kind of job such men hope to find. Some of the lucky ones were driving taxis around the city. The unlucky ones were driving taxis in Moscow.

"Anyway," I continued quietly, "everything is fine. The only weird thing is that I'm not meeting with Jonathan Grandines. Parker is here. He said Jonathan couldn't make it."

"Hmmm . . ." But Mahoney didn't say anything further.

I continued. "They mentioned their misfortunes. I think they're going to talk to me about the diversions.

Listen, I've been gone a long time already, and we haven't even ordered yet. That Stolnik guy looks hungry. I'd better get back."

"Okay. Call me when you get home."

I hung up and turned around in the dim alcove, and walked right into what felt like a brick wall. It was Vasily Stolnik.

chapter twenty-five

"Oh, hi!" I said, in my best imitation of someone who wasn't shaking inside. We were in a public place. I knew I had no rational reason to fear this animallike man.

"You have emergency?" Stolnik demanded. "You go to office?" What was it about some of these Russians, anyway? Doesn't the Russian language use articles? I'm pretty sure that Raskolnikov felt torment in *the* soul, not just *soul*.

Whenever I get stressed, my thoughts race. We call it "flight of ideas," in psychiatric jargon.

"No, everything is fine." How long had Stolnik been standing there eavesdropping?

"I go to wash my hands. You are sure everything is okay?" He was persistent. Next thing I knew I'd be sitting in some underground room with my eyelids taped open, a blinding light thwarting my view of my tormentor. "We eat, *da*?"

"*Da*," I agreed, relieved that he was letting me go without any further interrogation. Maybe he hadn't heard me on the phone with Mahoney. I followed Stolnik out of the narrow alcove back into the dining room. Another group of suit-clad men had been shown in during my absence. Four of them, drinking what looked like scotch and laughing. I felt safer.

Roberto took our orders himself. Parker Grandines ordered a cold antipasto platter for the table, and recommended that I try some veal dish that probably had a week's worth of calories in it. I politely declined, and chose the linguini with shrimp Fra Diavolo. I don't usually eat pasta, too many carbohydrates, but I was sure that on this day I was burning them up at a record rate, from stress. In the past week I had been eating them at a record rate too, so hopefully I was breaking even.

"You were mentioning your misfortunes," I said, shaking my head as a waiter came over to fill our wineglasses. The waiter ignored me and in a moment the large goblet was full of a deep ruby liquid.

"Cheers," Parker Grandines said. "To a long and lucrative working relationship."

I raised my glass and clicked with the two men. I felt as if I had wandered into an alternate reality. Psychiatrists just don't do business lunches. Medicine is really a very unglamorous profession, Monica Quartermaine of soap opera fame and her three-inch heels notwithstanding. The last time I had drunk alcohol at lunch had been on a Club Med vacation five years ago.

"*Nazdorovya,*" I said, smiling at Stolnik bravely. "Health," the traditional Russian toast.

"You speak Russian?" His bright blue eyes, almost hidden in his hairy face, registered surprise.

"No, just a few words." I didn't add that I was too embarrassed to repeat the other words I knew, once Greg had told me the meaning of those quaint Russian expressions that escaped his lips in city traffic or behind highway maniacs.

The four men at the table across the room were getting rowdy. A couple of sips of the wine had given me courage too. "The diversions? You were going to tell me what was going on, and how it would affect my position with you."

"We don't think it will affect your position at all," Stolnik answered. "We have wonderful new medication, Curixenol, for people who cannot stay away from this stuff"—he swirled his wineglass, then drained it—"and it should do quite well in market. Problem with pseudoephedrine should not concern you. I think no more diversions in new year."

"Your job is really a fun one," Parker Grandines assured me. "You will come to meetings, come with us to hospitals where the representatives give presentations. We have several more dinners planned, for psychiatrists in the tristate area. We may even have some opportunities for you to travel around the country to promote Curixenol, and to talk with clinicians and get some of their feedback on how their patients are doing on it. And of course, we have you lined up for *Good Morning America* and the *Today* show."

"What?" I couldn't believe my ears.

"Our scientists assure us that Curixenol is going to revolutionize psychiatry. It will be on the formularies of all the hospitals and managed-care companies. In fact, that's something else that we hope you will be able to help out with, talking to the pharmacy people about their formularies." Parker smiled benignly and tore a chunk off an Italian roll.

A hospital formulary is a list of medications that a hospital has in stock and can dispense if staff physicians order them. Not all medications are available in all places. Price is the dominant factor in what medications are available where. I had always worked in teaching hospitals, where the formularies are kept fairly up-to-date, regardless of the patients' ability to pay, but I've read about facilities where the only medications sanctioned by the administration are twenty years out of date. In recent years, a new trend has begun. Managed-care companies develop their own formularies. Participating physicians are limited to only certain medications before they even see patients. Some pharmaceutical companies have started managed-care divisions, in which representatives are sent around to various insurance companies to convince them to choose that company's drugs for their formularies, in exchange, naturally, for favorable prices. It almost makes me long for ancient times when the neighborhood medicine woman would make medications out of the flowers and plants in her backyard, tailoring each potion to the needs of each patient, with minimal expense. *Almost,* I said. I like modern conveniences too much to ever want to share a grass hut with mice and bugs.

"Do you have some materials I could review on the

drug, dosage, the results of the clinical trials, side effects, contraindications, that sort of thing? So I can be knowledgeable about the medication when I'm asked."

The two men glanced at each other. "The package insert should provide all the information you need," Grandines said. "Didn't Ginny Liu drop off our prelaunch marketing materials for physicians?"

"Well, yes," I admitted. "She gave me some promotional materials, but the only real scientific information is on those package inserts. And the printing is so hard to read. Isn't there a normal-size version?" Package inserts for prescription medications are invariably printed on tissue paper, in such tiny letters that you need a microscope to read the information there. I wanted a nice, legible, easy-to-understand summary of their new drug: the user-friendly version, not the one the FDA insisted Grandines provide. And I wanted to ask them to give me something so I'd have to remain in touch with them.

"Oh, we should have something like that around. We'll have it messengered to you early next week."

The waiter placed the platter of antipasto in the center of the table and a clean white salad plate in front of each of us. "More bread?" he asked.

"Please." Grandines gestured toward the platter. "Help yourself, please."

The serving plate was laden with salad greens, olives, fresh mozzarella, roasted peppers, marinated artichoke hearts and mushrooms, proscuitto, and cherry tomatoes. I filled my plate. I could get used to being taken out to lunch all the time, as long as my companions didn't always end up committing suicide a few days later. Neither of these men struck me as the suicidal type. Of course, neither had Gordon Ranier.

The waiter returned with more focaccia and two other kinds of bread, plus breadsticks. Tonight was New Year's Eve, and Greg and I had been invited to a party. Too bad it wasn't a costume party; I could have gone disguised as a blimp.

"So, you were telling me about the pseudoephedrine diversions," I prodded.

Again that glance, surreptitious, between the two men. Had I been looking at my plate or at one of the murals of Italy, I would have missed it.

"You know, Tamsen." Parker Grandines paused. "You don't mind me calling you Tamsen, do you?"

I shook my head no, but he didn't really give me time to answer.

He continued. "It's really an internal problem. Vasily, here, is on top of it, and we are really, seriously confident that this problem will be resolved to everyone's satisfaction within the next few days. We're actually cooperating with"—another pause, dramatic this time, and followed by an intake of breath and loudly whispered words—"the FBI."

"*Da,* FBI very good, quite helpful for us." Stolnik gave a throaty chuckle that sounded like a growl. "I would never believe, twenty-five years ago when I was colonel in Russia"—he pronounced it *co-lo-nel*—"that I would be co-operating with FBI. Cooperating voluntarily." He shook his head and rolled his eyes toward the ceiling, lost, no doubt, in pleasant memories of torturing innocent people or CIA agents. He gestured toward the antipasto platter. "More?" The question was directed to me.

"No, thank you," I said, and Parker also shook his head. Stolnik transferred the rest of the appetizer to his plate, and demolished it with gusto. Those violent memories were encouraging his appetite.

"Yes? You had a question?" Grandines didn't miss anything.

"I was just admiring Mr. Stolnik's appetite," I said.

I was rewarded with a big grin from the appetite's owner so I guessed I hadn't said anything wrong. One of the reasons I had gone into medicine in the first place was that I thought that if you did your job right, all the politics and bullshit of the business world would leave you alone. Ha. I wondered briefly what my father was going to do about his book, now that Gordon was dead. What exactly did an agent do, anyway? It sounded so Hollywood. Did I need one, now that I was booked to appear on the morning talk shows? Or was that only for movie stars? Yet another entire area of my education that had been neglected in medical school.

Our entrées arrived and I stared at my plate in dismay. I had a friend in college who once confided that she never ordered shrimp in restaurants because the portions were always so—*shrimpy*. This dish overflowed with pasta and jumbo shrimp, each one the size of a hot dog. I sighed, and speared a shrimp with my fork. I would do my best.

We sat and ate for another forty-five minutes. Stolnik, bizarrely, turned out to be friendly and warm. He entertained us with tales of his work in Russia, although he never actually mentioned the three famous initials. The quartet in the opposite corner remained, quite drunk by now, ties loosened, jackets shed. Their bonhomie seemed to be rubbing off on Stolnik and Grandines, because they, too, were laughing and had started on a second bottle of wine. I didn't remember drinking much, until I stood up.

Just at that moment, as I was mentally remarking on how dizzy I was feeling, Parker Grandines answered his little phone. He hung up, then said, "I'm so sorry, Tamsen. I must be going. Vasily will make sure you get home."

Home was close, a five-minute taxi ride without traffic. "When did I drink so much wine?" I asked Stolnik. "I only had one glass."

"The service here is very good. Very unobtrusive." He winked.

Grandines had disappeared even before I had a chance to thank him for the lunch. I looked at my watch. Four o'clock! I had to get home. It was New Year's Eve. We were going to a party. I had a sexy dress.

"Where can I drop you off?" Stolnik guided me out onto the sidewalk, one hand gripping my elbow.

"Thank you, but it's not necessary. I can get a cab. Oh, damn. Sorry."

"What? Did something happen?"

"No, no. The cat. I—I'm taking care of a friend's cat, I left it at my parents' place and they're away, I have to go pick it up."

"I drive you. Is no problem. I have car. I go home after."

I could hardly refuse. He didn't seem at all drunk, while I was having extraordinary difficulty keeping my eyes open. He steered me to the parking lot on the opposite corner. He drove a big ostentatious Town Car, which the attendant brought over with deference. "You have happy New Year, Señor Vasily," the parking lot guy said.

I sank into the leather seat and put my head back. This was a comfortable car, much more comfortable than my little compact import. Stolnik asked me where we were going. I told him the address, and that's the last thing I remembered until it was too late.

chapter twenty-six

"Where are we?" I mumbled. My head felt thick, in a way it hadn't since college—and rarely then. How could I feel so trashed after a little red wine?

Darkness had fallen, and I sat up in the front seat of the fancy car. Disoriented, I looked at my watch, struggling to see by the pale light of a distant streetlamp. The interior of the car was silent, except for soft classical music on the CD player. I squinted at my watch. Five forty-five! Where had we been for almost two hours?

"Oh, the lovely doctor finally wakes up. I am sorry, I did not imagine you are so sensitive."

I looked over at the river. The afternoon rushed back at me—the huge meal, the wine, the jokes about the nameless agency for which Stolnik had worked in the former Soviet Union. "Where are we? I need to get the cat and go home."

"Ah, the cat." Vasily looked at me without concern.

My heart started to pound faster. "Where—what— what happened? Is something wrong with the car?" Obviously there was, since it wasn't moving.

"We go. Soon. First you tell me who you work for?"

This wasn't happening. I was still asleep. I'd never touch alcohol again as long as I lived. "I work for myself. I'm in private practice." Hadn't I called Jim Mahoney to tell him where I'd been? Where were the FBI when you needed them?

Vasily made a tsking sound with his tongue against his teeth. My grandmother used to make a sound like that when I'd been naughty as a little girl. "You should not drink so much wine at lunchtime. What will your handsome boyfriend say when he hears you were with another man for so many hours?"

"What? Two hours. Less. Take me home. I have nothing to say to you. Anyway, where are we?" I struggled to control the hysteria I could hear in my own voice. My initial confusion was growing into a sense of complete disorientation; the mild annoyance and twinge of fear I had felt when I'd awoken was swelling into full-blown panic. "I thought you were a nice guy."

"I am very nice guy. I don't take advantage of you." Vasily made a vague gesture toward my open coat. "I am married man, family man. Grandson, yes, in Buffalo. Son in university there, he will be doctor, like you. I am family man. You are nice young girl. You don't worry."

I tugged my coat over my knees. "Could you please tell me what is going on here? Where are we?" Maybe if I asked it a million times, he'd answer.

"We are in Bronx. Spuyten Duyvil. Near Harlem River. Good place to talk quietly, no one comes here in winter."

"Let me out. I want to go."

Stolnik watched me with a smile. "You don't get out here. Is not safe. I take you home after we talk."

My right hand was still on the door handle, which refused to budge. I swung my left hand out toward Stolnik's fairy face, but he was too quick for me, and caught my fist midair.

He surprised me by lifting my hand to his lips and giving it a gentle kiss. I felt the beard on my skin. I shuddered. *Please, not this.*

"*Sărut-mâna,*" he said. It was a Romanian expression. Some of my parents' friends still used it, although rarely. It meant "Kiss your hand," and was considered a term of politeness in Romania. Instead of "Nice to meet you," or "Thanks for the cake," Romanians say, "Kiss your hand."

"I spend many years in Bucharest," Stolnik informed me. "I don't wish to hurt you. I know you are only daughter to your parents. I also have only son. So I tell you message, which Jonathan Grandines give me for you. I only do my job. You know, jobs for men like me are not so easy to find."

I stared at him in total disbelief.

"Grandines Pharmaceuticals very good company. They have now internal problems, no concern of yours. You don't ask questions. You do only your job. We want pretty face to tell world that our new medication is good. Is great, wonderful, will make many people well and happy and make our company much, much money. Will make *you* much, much money, if you do not ask too many questions." I thought he winked, but in the shadows it was hard to tell. Then he said, "Is most important to earn good living. We do what we need to do. *Da?*"

"Okay," I said. "I won't ask any more questions." *I won't work for you, either.* My brain was finally grinding into action, and I felt that challenging Stolnik in any way would not exactly be a good move, career or otherwise. "Can you take me home now? Or just drop me off at a subway? Or a diner or something. I need to call home." I thought about my cell phone, cozily plugged in for recharging—in my study.

"Oh, we called. Your nice lawyer boyfriend knows you are going to be late."

"We? Who is *we?*"

"I call secretary, tell her to call him. Tell him you have emergency with patient, in hospital. *Da?*"

"Da." Please take me home. My hand was safely back in my lap. *Take me home.*

Stolnik turned on the headlights and released the brake. The engine had been on, but I hadn't even felt it vibrate. He headed up a hill on a windy road, passing houses on steep lots. Many of them had Christmas lights and decorations. A few turns, and suddenly we were on Broadway, back in civilization. Another couple of turns took us onto the Major Deegan.

It took ages to get home. We didn't speak the entire way. If Vasily Stolnik had wanted to hurt me or kill me, he'd already had ample opportunity. My pocketbook was at my feet. I tried to remember if I had erased the number to which Mahoney had paged me from the memory of my beeper.

I was never so happy to see the awful high-rise Greg and I called home. We stopped in front of the building. Stolnik clicked something under the dashboard, and the door locks popped open. By the time I'd stepped into the snow, he was standing beside me, holding the door and taking my arm to steady me. He pressed something into my hand. "You dropped—"

"My keys! Where did you find them?"

"They fell out of your purse. By the way, I think your boyfriend, he was not at home this afternoon. You know?" Stolnik winked at me. I didn't know what the wink meant. Natalie's image sprang to mind. I wanted to use one of those bad words that Stolnik would understand. He walked me to the door, and opened it before the doorman had time to come over and welcome me.

"But I'm sure the little pussycat is fine." Stolnik waved at the doorman, who went back to his stool and his newspaper. Stolnik winked again. All this winking was making me dizzy.

"Good night," I said, wondering if I should have been screaming for the police instead. I was pretty sure you could only be charged with kidnapping if you didn't voluntarily bring the victim back, but I wasn't positive and I just wanted Stolnik to go away. It wasn't like I didn't know how to find him later.

"It was my pleasure," Stolnik said, as if I had said, "Thank you." "*Sărut-mâna.*" He kissed my hand. "Don't forget." He winked again, turned, and lumbered back to his car.

I watched him drive away before I went to the elevator. What was I going to tell Greg? Tell Mahoney? What exactly had just happened to me?

The elevator came and I went upstairs. I unlocked the door. Greg was on the sofa, beer in hand, television on. He jumped up, anger mixed with the anxiety on his face. "Where have you been? I've been waiting for you all night."

"I was—oh, God, never mind. I'll be right back."

The reflection in the mirror had dark circles under her eyes, pale cheeks, and messy hair, but nothing that a shower and a little makeup couldn't fix. I settled for a splash of cold water and returned to the living room.

Greg was still standing where I'd left him. "You still want to go to the party? You look exhausted. You could have called. It's after ten."

"After ten? It can't be past seven—" I checked my watch. "Greg! It's after ten! I must have misread my watch." I started to shake. "Did you get some kind of a message from me?"

"Yeah, that you had an emergency. What kind of emergency? I can't remember the last time you had an emergency." Greg turned and walked toward the kitchen. I heard the refrigerator door creak open. "Your parents called to say they got to Florida okay. It was eighty-eight degrees there this afternoon." We always laughed at my father's obsession with weather trivia, but now I couldn't even smile. "Want a drink?" he called.

"Greg. Listen. I'm not joking. I think I was kidnapped."

Greg emerged from the kitchen, an open beer in each hand. "You need a drink. I think working with crazy people all day long has finally rubbed off on you." He kissed my cheek and handed me a bottle. Then he finally noticed I was serious.

"What happened?"

"What did he do with me for over five hours?" I couldn't even form a coherent answer.

"What did *who* do with you?"

"This Russian guy."

"What Russian guy?"

I didn't think I could stand to play twenty questions. I recounted what I could recall of the afternoon. By the end of the story I was shaking again.

"Sit down." Greg handed me the beer. I usually only liked beer with food, and only certain foods, but the first sip felt good. My eyes burned with anger and exhaustion, and the beer couldn't possibly help my throbbing head.

"Did he touch you?"

"N-no." I didn't count the hand-kiss, it wasn't considered sexual. "Not that I know. But I don't think so."

I checked my beeper, which had no phone numbers in its memory. Had I erased them? Or had Stolnik?

"We have to call the police." Greg reached for the telephone. "I think you're in shock. You're too calm."

"I'm not calm at all," I said. "But I don't think we should call the police. I have to call the FBI."

"The FBI?" Greg asked me, and then of course I confessed everything—how I'd been approached for information about Grandines and how I'd offered to help FBI Agent Jim Mahoney with his investigation into the missing pseudoephedrine and the Grandines suspicious deaths. For some reason, I didn't mention my brief conversation with Antony Hastings-Muir or the plane ticket he'd sent me. Throughout the story, Greg kept saying "Why didn't you tell me?" and "How could you not tell me this?" I could feel how angry he was. But "Okay, give the FBI a call," was all he said.

chapter twenty-seven

Within the hour, our peaceful apartment became a hive of activity. I had to give these guys a lot of credit: I felt so bad for spoiling their New Year's Eve and all of them remained stoic, calm, and unruffled. Special agents took our statements and our fingerprints, and then began to methodically search our apartment—for what, I didn't know. Unless—

"Greg! I just thought of something." We were sitting on the sofa with the television on low, waiting for the ball to drop in Times Square, signaling the start of another year. Three more minutes.

"Hmmm?" Greg didn't like being asked to sit in a corner and not ask questions, it went against his prosecutorial nature.

"Stolnik told me you weren't home this afternoon."

"I wasn't home. I was at work."

"I know, I know. But I thought he was trying to be coy—to hint you were with Natalie or something."

"No, I didn't meet with Natalie today," he said with the guilelessness of the truly innocent.

"But what if he really meant to tell me that he knew you weren't home because he'd been *here*? What if he took my keys and got into our apartment?"

"But why would he?" Greg looked baffled.

"I have no idea. Looking for something, maybe?"

"Dr. Bayn?" The deep voice belonged to the forensics team leader, one Rick Harriman, Special Agent, FBI. I jumped off the sofa. On the television the crowd was screaming. "Ten! Nine! Eight! . . ."

"Happy New Year," Agent Harriman said politely. Although Jim Mahoney was the agent I was working with, this guy was a technical expert who'd been called in for the occasion. "You probably should think about getting some things together. We'd like to move you to a hotel for a few days."

The FBI were not inclined to answer too many questions, but it wasn't hard to deduce what had happened. Someone, although probably not Vasily Stolnik himself, had used my keys to enter my apartment and . . . look for something? But what? Again, I kept banging into the same obstacle—illogicalness. But what if—

"Greg! What if they want to *listen* to us? Maybe they bugged our phones." I reached to pick up the handset of the cordless phone resting on the table next to me, but Agent Harriman barked, "Don't touch that!" with such authority that my hand froze in midair. I withdrew it, shaking, into my lap. My key chain held keys to this apartment, my office, and my parents' apartment. Stolnik had made a cryptic comment about the cat being fine. Were all my usual haunts now off limits? I conveyed my fears to Harriman, who said brusquely, "That's why we're putting you in a hotel."

"May we get our things now?" I asked him. Harriman beckoned to another agent who followed us all into the bedroom. I watched as Greg pulled a gym bag out of the closet and started throwing clothes into it. Harriman left us with the other, younger agent, who stood leaning against the doorjamb. He was young and blond and fresh-faced, but his unmoving eyes gave me the creeps.

"We could still go to the party," I suggested, and Greg snorted. I didn't mind skipping the festivities, even though a New Year's party would have been fun. My friend Belinda would be there; she'd wonder why we hadn't shown up. And once, in a previous life, before strangers had invaded my home and my life, I would have immediately phoned her to tell her that we weren't going after all. Stolnik must have put something in that wine. I would never have fallen asleep for five hours, especially not in a stranger's car. But why drug *me*?

"I need to change," I said to the FBI agent, who

nodded. In the bathroom, I pulled off my suit, changed into sweats, and then I came back into the bedroom and started putting clothes and toiletries into my own bag. I felt as if I were watching a movie of myself; all my actions felt slow and fake. I really hated the way these FBI people weren't telling me anything. I got the impression that they were just cogs in a big wheel and they knew it, and so they affected a hush-hush superiority to cover up the fact that they really didn't know what the hell was going on.

A wave of panic seemed to crest out of nowhere. In just one day, I'd had a weird former KGB agent kidnap me, sneak into my home, and manipulate my mind, and now I was going to spend this New Year's Eve on the lam. Or was it already New Year's Day? Shaking my head to symbolically clear it, I threw some lighter clothing into the bag with my usual winter uniform of black leggings and sweaters; after a moment's consideration, I added a bathing suit. Brushing past the special agent, I mumbled something about needing a book, and I ran into the study, found my passport, and threw it in the bag too. I had that ticket to Bermuda tucked between the pages of my planner, if Stolnik hadn't found it. I wanted to keep my options open. Greg was busy packing up his briefcase with work-related papers, and didn't notice. Good. I didn't want to have to defend my highly irrational intention to visit Antony Hastings-Muir. At least not right this second.

Ten minutes later we'd handed over sets of keys and been bundled into a waiting unmarked FBI car, no questions asked. Or, to be specific, I'd asked a million questions that remained unanswered: Who did the FBI suspect had entered our apartment? What did that person want from me? What would happen to Vasily Stolnik for abducting me to the Bronx? Why had Grandines chosen me out of all the psychiatrists in New York for their little PR project? But whatever subject I broached was totally ignored by our grim-faced guard. Greg kept urging me to relax and not ask so many questions, which I found incredible—he of the inquiring mind. But I suppose he knows a little more about how the FBI operates than I do.

Traffic was light. On the other side of town, a few hundred thousand people had watched the ball drop in Times Square, but here by the East River all was quiet. People were elsewhere, celebrating. We turned the corner right down the street from my office and pulled up in front of a hotel I'd never set foot in. For whatever reason as yet unknown to me, we merited five-star accommodations on the East Side. The FBI agent who'd accompanied us entered first, and we revolved in after him like obedient lemmings. I stood to one side as I watched the agent negotiate with the night manager. Both spoke in low voices, while dressed-up rich people, looking fairly drunk, wandered through the small lobby. Piano music and laughter drifted toward us from the bar. I tried not to look like a freshly picked-up floozy. Actually, with my beautiful outfit of sweatpants tucked into boots, my hair standing up as if I had recently stuck my finger in a socket, and the remains of my afternoon makeup smeared around my eyes, I suspected nobody would mistake me for a recent conquest.

"Come on," Greg said, putting an arm around my shoulders. "He got us a room. A suite, actually, it was all they had." A suite in this fancy hotel unbooked for New Year's Eve? The FBI must have important connections. The secret agent stuck to his role and slipped away into the night, after cautioning us not to speak to anyone or to let anyone into our room besides the FBI.

We rode up in the elevator in silence. The bellman showed us to the room without comment, unlocked the door, and with one look at me visibly decided to skip the orientation tour.

Greg discreetly stuck a bill into the young man's hand, saying, "Thank you."

"Thank *you*," the bellman said. "Happy New Year!" He permitted himself a surreptitious glance at the money. "Yes, *sir*. Happy New Year!"

He let himself out and I looked around the room. Greg stood very close to me. "Happy New Year, baby."

I leaned into his shoulder and closed my eyes. "Happy New Year," I said softly. "Oh, God. What's going to happen now?"

"Tomorrow, you mean? We'll hear back from the FBI about who was in our house and why. And then we'll go from there. But for now . . ." He unzipped my parka and helped me out of it. I sank into a cushy armchair, upholstered in velvet, and yanked off my boots.

"But for right now . . ." Greg took off his jacket, and draped it over a tapestry-covered chair that resembled a throne. "We'll have to make the best of it."

chapter twenty-eight

I woke up in the New Year with Greg's arms around me. "Woke up" was a euphemism—I'd tossed and turned all night imagining that the next time Vasily Stolnik took me for a ride I'd end up on the bottom of the East River wearing cement flip-flops.

The disorientation lingered, starting to feel familiar, like a scab. I looked around. The heavy blackout drapes had been left open about a centimeter, which illuminated a slice of room decorated in expensive greens, creams, and golds. We were somewhere at the top of the hotel—I'd never noticed which floor—and the narrow beam of sunlight meant that the weather was, at least, dry. Fortunately, New Year's Day did not behave like an actual holiday; most stores were open, and the day wasn't particularly family oriented. You could disturb the FBI with impunity.

"Now what?" I asked, as soon as I estimated that Greg was conscious enough to comprehend me. My heart had started pounding again, and it wasn't because of his proximity.

"What?" That guy could sleep through the nuclear holocaust. Lucky.

I wriggled out of his grasp and slid out of bed. "I have to do something," I announced.

"Tamsen. The FBI is investigating. That's why they're called the Federal Bureau of *Investigation*. You can't do anything. Come back to bed."

I was the one who'd been thrust into this mess. Greg just happened to be along for the ride. He was supposed to be prosecuting Jason Devinski, not investigating the company Jason's mother worked for. No wonder Greg had been able to take full advantage of the five-star hotel and the whirlpool bath and the little luxury amenities while I remained on full alert. As soon as I could I was moving to a P.O. Box and getting a big scary dog. No more all-night vigils for me.

I didn't even bother to feel silly as I dragged the tapestry-covered chair in front of the door. We had been set up, or I had, by Vasily Stolnik, for reasons yet unknown. I was too nervous to take a shower when someone was running around the building with a master key that could so easily end up in the wrong hands. Who would mess with the fiancée of a prosecutor? Whom exactly was I dealing with?

A room-service breakfast of coffee and carbohydrates had magically appeared in the living room part of the suite by the time I emerged from the marble bathroom. I looked at the tray suspiciously, and Greg burst forth with a Russian expletive too dirty to translate.

"It's breakfast! I ordered it! It's fine! Stop being so melodramatic! We won't get anything accomplished if you waste your energy on feeling sorry for yourself."

It suddenly occurred to me that Greg would never allow me to see if he was worried about me. All of his anger and the distance I was feeling between us could be a result of only one thing: his fear that something could happen to me. This whole thing must be much harder on him than I realized, while he was the model of efficiency and law enforcement.

I took my coffee to a gilded side table and pulled out Jim Mahoney's card. It was eight-thirty, not too early to call. I punched his beeper number into the phone. Then I waited. Even though this hotel offered direct numbers into the guest rooms, nobody called me back.

"Maybe he's still asleep?" Greg suggested.

"I doubt it. Here, I have another number for him." I tried the office number. The automated voice asked me to enter the extension of the person I wished to reach. I left a message asking Mahoney to call me back. I was dying to know if the FBI had picked up Vasily Stolnik and what he'd said. But even with all of my energy focused on the phone, it didn't ring. I felt like a teenager waiting for a boy to call.

"Something fishy is going on here," I said. Greg barely glanced at me; he'd discovered that the television came with a video-game player attached. "Greg! How can you just lie there playing games?"

"Easy," he said.

"Aren't you worried?"

"No." He turned back to the TV, but then finally switched it off and sighed. "Of course I'm worried. But worrying never helped resolve anything. Listen, Tamsen. You were in the wrong place at the wrong time. It's clear to me that these Grandines people have some problems. They obviously don't want those problems, with illegal drugs, to interfere with their legitimate pharmaceutical business. It's very simple. Just tell Grandines Pharmaceuticals you're not interested in working for them and they'll leave you alone."

"But I promised the FBI that I'd try to get some information—"

"Yes, you promised, but then when you tried to actually get the information, the Grandines people became angry and figured out right away that you were sticking your nose where it doesn't belong. Why don't you leave the detective work to the detectives?"

Greg's explanation was the logical one, but I remained skeptical. It was a touch too extreme to drug me, kidnap me, and threaten me. Unless Stolnik just didn't know any other way of interacting in the world, given his long history of using intimidation as a professional tool.

I tried paging Jim Mahoney again. It was after nine o'clock, and I would have thought that someone from the FBI would have at least checked up on us by now, if for no other reason than to make sure we were still here. As I punched in the numbers, I heard a knock on the door. Looking back at that split second, I want to say I had a premonition, but I'm really not sure. My psychic skills are not as finely honed as my psychiatric ones.

"FBI," someone called from the hallway. Greg pulled the chair away and opened the door. I recognized the two agents from last night.

"How was the night?" the young, blond one asked.

"Fine," I answered, although I could tell he wasn't really listening to me. "Is everything all right?" I asked.

The two agents looked at each other. Finally the other man, a balding redhead in his forties, sighed. "We have some bad news."

Now Greg moved over to stand beside me, his arm protectively around my shoulders. "What happened?" he asked, a bit too harshly, I thought.

Again, the agents caught each other's eyes.

"What?" I demanded. "What happened?"

"Jim Mahoney is dead."

chapter twenty-nine

The balding redhead was named Joe Luciano. "It looks like a mugging," he told us. Hesitatingly, probably because Greg was a prosecutor, he told us that Special Agent Jim Mahoney had been out walking his two dogs when he'd apparently been ambushed. The dogs were shot first; then Mahoney was shot after a struggle. He was relieved of his wallet, and possibly a watch, although the FBI agent wasn't positive. "He was out walking his dogs!" Agent Luciano repeated, and his voice finally broke, a bit. "What kind of valuables would he have had on him?" He swung away to try to hide his emotions, but the room was filled with grief.

Luciano and his partner, the young nameless blond agent, left us, explaining that the police and the FBI would be back to talk to us soon. As soon as Greg and I were alone, anger and sorrow hit me again. Jim Mahoney dead! I felt as if I'd been punched in the stomach. "That poor man. He was so nice to me. He was an FBI agent. How could he get mugged? It couldn't be random, he wouldn't let himself be a target . . ."

"Tamsen, the only thing you can do right now is to let the police and the FBI do their jobs. I'll track down whoever is on call on my end to find out if we heard anything yet." He shook his head. "I told you not to get involved with those Grandines people. Think it's really a mugging?" I sat stunned, hearing those last words reverberate in my brain. For once I wasn't paranoid or overreacting. Greg dipped a croissant into a fresh cup of coffee and bit off the dripping half in one huge bite. "These are excellent. Try one. You'll feel better."

Nothing like forty-five grams of refined carbohydrates

dissolved in a stick of butter to cheer you up. A heart attack waiting to happen, as Belinda was fond of saying. Attempted murder by croissant. My thoughts flew. I know now that the shock just hadn't fully hit me. It's normal when you first hear of a tragedy to be unable to accept it. I'd finally achieved total empathy for my patients. I felt on the verge of losing my mind.

chapter thirty

I didn't lost my mind after all. I stayed calm as I prepared to answer the FBI's questions for the second time in twelve hours. A stream of officers, mostly municipal, but some federal, came and went. I learned nothing. The NYPD officers assured me that a mugging in Central Park wasn't considered unusual, even if crime in the city was down. We weren't suspects. They kept saying that Mahoney's death *had* to be unrelated to his FBI work. These cops acted like they knew everything. I fought back the urge to throw one particularly condescending rookie out the window, and I waited. Finally they all left. I ignored the phone when it rang for the ten millionth time.

Greg answered and told the front desk to go ahead and send up Kathleen O'Neill. She was the agent whom Jim Mahoney had originally assigned to me. The agents I'd been dealing with for the past twelve hours worked mainly with forensics. Agent O'Neill would be taking over now.

The knock on our door sounded strong and confident. Kathleen was tall, nearly six feet, with shoulder-length black hair and pale blue eyes behind steel-rimmed glasses. She unzipped her black down coat to reveal corduroy pants stuffed into snow boots, and a black wool blazer over a cobalt-blue turtleneck. Greg invited her to sit. I offered her coffee. As she leaned forward to pick up her cup I glimpsed the gun in a shoulder holster under her blazer. It was under her right arm, and I noticed she stirred four sugars into her coffee with her left hand, which was devoid of any rings.

"I had to drive in from the Island," she said, a kind of halfhearted apology for her lateness, which I didn't understand. It wasn't like we had plans or anything. "Call me

Kathy, please. Mmm, look at those pastries." Greg had ordered a croissant refill when all the police showed up. Politics.

"Have some." At least this entertaining would be cleaned up by someone else.

"Okay, let's start at the beginning." She dipped a croissant into her coffee just as Greg had. "When did Grandines first contact you to work with them?"

I went through the whole story, again, starting with Ginny Liu's visit to my office on Christmas Eve Day and ending with yesterday's joyride with Stolnik to the Bronx.

"I grew up right around there," Kathy remarked. "But on the Manhattan side. In Inwood."

"Hey, I grew up in Washington Heights." It did cross my mind to wonder why the schmoozing, but I guessed that Kathleen was dealing with the sudden loss of Jim Mahoney in her own way. We detoured into a little "do you know" conversation. It turned out that Kelly was a few years older than me, and even though she had also graduated from Bronx Science, we knew none of the same people. But all this bonding had put me more at ease, and I barely recognized her questions for what they really were: an interrogation. Until Greg interrupted.

"Kathy, you're starting to sound as if you think Tamsen is withholding information. What exactly are you getting at?"

Kathy countered with, "What about that British guy that you and Jim found dead last Thursday? How well did you know him, Tamsen?"

"Gordon? I barely knew him. I met him at my parents' party. He was my father's agent. Oh, yeah, and I had lunch with him the other day. Tuesday, I think."

Greg said, "You had *lunch* with Gordon Ranier?"

I almost answered, but Kathy interposed. "So you don't know anyone who might have wanted him dead?"

"Wanted him dead? Of course not. I rescued his cat." Now who wasn't making sense?

"Tamsen, did you kill Gordon Ranier?"

"What?" This time Greg and I spoke together.

"Sorry, I had to ask." She looked a bit embarrassed, but I was starting to believe that all this camaraderie and help-fulness was an act. They probably teach it in FBI school. "Jim told you Gordon Ranier's death is still open? That it hasn't been officially ruled a suicide?"

"He *must* have committed suicide. . . ." Then, in a rush to justify my words, I continued. "Gordon was distraught. His wife was in an accident. He was"—I searched for the right word—"ashamed. Guilty and ashamed, that's why he called me. He felt he had failed his family, so he killed him-self."

Kathy's eyes were the color of the winter sky behind her severe glasses. I noticed wrinkles that I hadn't seen at first, a fine road map of suburbia around her eyes, eyes that seemed to see right into me.

"I didn't understand why he would kill himself," I ad-mitted. "But, you know, people always say these things hap-pen, if they really want to kill themselves they will, and if Sigmund Freud himself were available to help he couldn't stop them from doing it."

"A whole lot of people you meet seem to die." Kathy's voice was dry and toneless.

"I think this conversation is over," Greg said, getting to his feet, while I started at Kathy in speechless amazement. I was even more amazed to see Greg actually stand up and open the door.

Kathy didn't make a move, just scribbled something on her pad. "Don't get all hostile," she said, finally. "I'm not im-plying that you had anything to do with those deaths."

"So what *are* you implying, then?" I was relieved to learn I could still talk.

"I'm not implying anything. I'm just speculating." She paused, looked toward the windows. "Jim Mahoney was a fantastic agent." Now she was looking down at her hand as if the pen it clutched were about to come to life. "I'm sorry."

I don't know why I was surprised that Kathy had emo-tions to deal with. After the emotionless FBI agents we'd met last night, I'd somehow convinced myself they were all like that. But Luciano, from this morning, had been obviously upset. Maybe FBI agents are just normal people, and they're trained to hide their feelings. Maybe I could take some lessons from them. "I liked Mr. Mahoney a lot. He was really nice to me. I think he really believed that I could help his investigation."

"That's what we all thought," Kathy said. "That you could help." But her head was shaking *no* as if she knew that I really couldn't. "But now I know it was a mistake to try to bring a civilian into this mess."

Greg was nodding his head in agreement.

"Kathy," I said. "Excuse me for asking this question. But don't you think somebody else should be investigating Jim Mahoney's death? Don't you think you were a little too close to him?"

Her pale skin flushed, but something about talking to a psychiatrist is very liberating for people. She didn't get angry. She just said, "I'm not investigating Jim's murder."

"You're not? So why are you here?"

"I'm here to talk to you about this Grandines methamphetamine business, and this Vasily Stolnik character. That's all."

"So—then, who's in charge of the murder investigation?" I asked, bewildered.

Kathy made a rude noise and said, "We cut a deal with the NYPD. They investigate, make the arrest, get the collar. Then we'll get to prosecute the perp in federal court."

"Can you do that?" I was shocked.

"Happens all the time," Greg said.

"Politics," Kathy said.

"Okay. So you want to know what it is that I know about—what? Making methamphetamine? Selling it? Transporting it? I can tell you with a reasonable degree of medical certainty what its effects are supposed to be. That's about it."

"Could you tell if someone was using it?" Kathy asked.

"Well. I don't know, necessarily. Without a drug test

you can't tell exactly what substance a person has ingested—or smoked, or shot up, or whatever. When somebody shows up in the psychiatric emergency room belligerent and out of control, you need to do a urine or blood toxicology to see what they've taken. They might have not taken anything."

"What do you mean? Not taken anything?"

"There is such a thing as mental illness. Not every bizarre behavior is a result of drug use."

"Of course," Kathy said, in an "I knew that" kind of way. "So without toxicology you can't tell what drug someone has used?"

"Not really. I can usually make a good educated guess. And there's usually someone else around—the person who brought the patient in, a family member, a case manager, or even a cop—I mean, police officer." She was a cop, too, and I didn't know if it was the equivalent of "shrink," offensive to some, although not to me. "Do you suspect that whoever stole the pseudoephedrine used it to make methamphetamine for his own use?"

"We don't know." Kathy had stopped taking notes and was drawing spirals in her notebook. Now she was coloring them in. Her pen had sprung a leak, and her left forefinger and middle finger were stained blue.

"Who's *we*?" I asked.

"Oh, all the people working on this case. A few more questions, then we'll be done for today." Kathy snapped back into professional mode. She asked us if we used drugs (no), if we had ever been in trouble with the law "outside of routine traffic violations" (no, and I was sure she knew the answer to that question, in detail and in all fifty states, already). "Names of next of kin and their whereabouts?" That question gave me the chills but we both answered it.

"If there's anything else you can think of, please let me know." She handed a card to me, and another to Greg. I looked at mine. It was smudged by her inky fingers.

"Kathy," I said as she prepared to leave, "Gordon Ranier had no connection to Grandines Pharmaceuticals."

"No," she agreed. "But he was connected to Natalie Diamond. Karen Devinski works for Grandines Pharmaceuticals, doesn't she? And of course, Ranier was connected to you, and you went to his apartment with Jim Mahoney. Jim was the lead agent in the pseudoephedrine investigation."

Duh. Okay. An extremely vague Grandines connection. But what did it mean?

I shook hands with Kathy. As soon as she was gone, I asked Greg, "Don't you think Kathy was too close to Jim Mahoney to be continuing this investigation? Dragging Gordon Ranier's suicide into this? She's overreacting. Mahoney was her boss, and she can't deal with his death."

"He wasn't her boss. I don't think the FBI is organized that way."

"but he was her de facto boss." As a *forensic* psychiatrist I could liberally sprinkle my speech with legal jargon. I had once heard a psychiatrist in a state hospital describe what he wore to court on the days he was "trying a case." We don't try cases, we try to convince the court of our psychiatric opinions, with a "reasonable degree of medical certainty." At the moment, however, that phrase seemed absurd. What kind of medical certainty did I have about Gordon's suicide? None whatsoever—I'd barely known the man. And what medical certainty did I have about Mahoney's murder? I'd often heard it mentioned that deaths come in threes. Counting the Grandines scientist who'd been engaged to Antony Hastings-Muir, I'd heard of three. Or should I count Ginny Liu in her place? And then there were the three girls Jason had killed. . . . In my whole life, I'd been to six funerals: two grandparents, a great-aunt, a classmate's father in sixth grade, and a college acquaintance who'd died in a car crash. And Daniel's, of course. Until recently, death had not shadowed me like a bodyguard.

Greg was on the phone with someone from the DA's office. Now he hung up and said to me, "Listen, I'm going down there. It's Connor's case—so it's mine too, in a way."

Connor was one of Greg's deputies and a solid, thorough attorney. Plus his good looks and melodious Caribbean accent had a way with the ladies of the jury. Connor and Greg made quite a team.

"I thought Mahoney's murder was going to the FBI," I said. "To the federal prosecutor."

"Not yet." Greg's face was grim. "My team has a great conviction rate. This crime occurred in Manhattan. So far, it's ours." He reached for his coat, eager to get to work catching criminals and sending them to jail. "I'm going down there. Maybe we can keep it in Manhattan." He handed me my coat. "Let's go. I don't think you should stay here alone."

I felt as if I'd fallen into an icy well. The thought of the crime scene—the yellow tape and the freezing day and the blood on the sidewalk like urban road kill—made that million-calorie croissant threaten to make a reappearance.

"I have a better idea," I said hesitantly, envisioning a respite from all the recent chaos.

"What?" Greg's jacket was on and zipped up, his gloves in his hand.

"I can go to Bermuda."

chapter thirty-one

"Okay," Greg said. "I'll meet you there later with the sun-screen." He held my parka up for me.

"No, seriously," I said. I went into the bedroom, pulled the envelope with the ticket out of my bag, and went back into the living room where Greg was impatiently looking at his watch.

"We really don't have time for this. I can't believe you brought a travel brochure with you. You must have been calmer than I thought—or more disorganized." I suspected that he meant "disorganized" in the way psychiatrists used the term, as in, *This is a thirty-three-year-old schizophrenic female who has been increasingly disorganized over the past several weeks.* Fortunately, I was at least a decade past the average age of onset for schizophrenia.

I held out the ticket.

"Where did you get this?"

I explained.

"Well, obviously you're not going. This Antony could be a nut case too. Seems like everyone connected to that company has a problem. I don't want you having anything else to do with them. Now, put on your coat and let's go."

"You don't *want* me . . ." The first day I ever saw Greg, my first impression, after the visceral, was: "This guy looks like the hero in a romance novel." Looking like a romance-novel guy was one thing; behaving like one, however, was something else entirely.

"What do you think could happen to me? I'll fly to Bermuda for free, meet with this guy, hear the scoop about Grandines, and come back and tell the FBI all about it. They'll take over from there. Maybe at some point I'd need to testify, but . . ." I continued the thought in the privacy of my own mind. The FBI would move in, arrest whoever needed to be arrested for trafficking in methamphetamine, and any remaining parts of the company would be sold off at a loss. Karen Devinski might lose her job, but more likely, the Curixenol division would be snapped up and Karen along with it. Curixenol was the first and only drug in its class, even if biochemically it was nothing special. If any other companies had antialcoholism drugs in their pipelines, I certainly hadn't heard about them. Even if Grandines's generic division went down, Curixenol was here to stay. "I won't stay in Bermuda long. I need to be back for the launch of Curixenol on the eleventh. A week from Tuesday. I'll be careful."

"Tamsen, are you nuts? You're not going. What did he say to you that you let him send you this ticket, anyway?"

"Nothing. He didn't want to talk over the phone, so he sent me a ticket."

"Oh, he sounds like a rocket scientist. Afraid to talk on the phone so he tells you *on the phone* to come visit him so you can talk in private? Forget it, you're not going."

"I am not going to see Mr. Mahoney's dead body, nope, no way. Plus it's cold out, and I'm wearing a dress. I'm staying here."

"So change." Greg's voice was around the same temperature as the windowpane against which I was by now pressing my forehead.

"I'm staying here."

"Okay, fine, stay. Give me your office keys, I want to give them to my investigator. No need for them to break in. I don't think the FBI thought of checking out your office."

I had wanted my parents to install a security system in the office when they first bought it, years before. They had laughed. "Tamsen, honey, there's a doorman standing two feet away at all times. What do we need a security system for?" Now I silently predicted that one would be installed within an hour of my parents' return from their vacation. I couldn't even imagine how angry they were going to be

when they figured out the reason I'd been avoiding returning their calls. But I didn't need them cutting short their
trip and returning to this chaos I'd created. I got the keys
out of my bag, threw them over.

Greg caught the keys nonchalantly with his left hand,
the showoff. "If you absolutely won't come with me, then
stay here." He headed toward the door, stopped. "Oops, forgot something," he said, and came over to kiss me.

At least he kissed like a romance-novel guy too.

chapter thirty-two

As soon as Greg left, I called the airline to see if any seats were available on their flights to Bermuda. The first available seat was tomorrow afternoon, Sunday, with more open the next day. I made a reservation for early Monday morning, planning to return by Tuesday afternoon. Wednesday I had patients scheduled in my office: normal patients with normal problems, like depression, anxiety, and schizophrenia. Not forensic evaluees bent on driving me crazy.

Greg would be happy that I didn't go to Bermuda, but I was disappointed. Today was New Year's Day. It was a traditional time to visit family and friends, but my mind was elsewhere, with a murderous child and an evasive psychiatrist, and a pharmaceutical company that appeared to be run by a megalomaniac.

I'd been planning to meet Jason Devinski. His parents would certainly be going to see him today. Perhaps I could tag along.

"Happy New Year," I said to Karen when she answered the phone. "This is Tamsen Bayn."

"Worst New Year's Eve of my life," she replied.

I wasn't surprised. "How's Jason doing?"

"We're just on our way down to see him. He's still in the hospital." Karen paused, then asked, "Would you like to come?"

That was easy. "Of course." I arranged to meet the Devinskis in the coffee shop in Bellevue's lobby. The walk from the subway was long and slippery. Now I remembered why I always drove when I worked here. I arrived at our assigned rendezvous with twenty minutes to spare and ordered a coffee, which I didn't need. I was wired enough already.

"How you been, Doc?" the waiter asked me in his thick Greek accent. "Long time no see."

I have mixed feelings about Bellevue. Actually, I have mixed feelings about a lot of things. Still, it was nice to be remembered.

Karen Devinski blew into the coffee shop, a jumble of wild hair and flying outerwear. Her husband walked sedately behind her. He was saying something to her, softly.

"Tamsen! Here you are!" Karen sank into the seat across from me, leaving Peter standing awkwardly.

I took my cup and slid out of the booth. "Let's move over there." The three of us sat at a larger table and Peter asked the waiter for coffee. "Is everything okay?" I asked them. Karen seemed awfully agitated.

"Okay? How can things ever be okay?" Karen's voice was louder than I'd ever heard it. Her eyes were shining. She ran a hand through her blond curls, once, twice, sipped her coffee, then arranged her hair again.

"I know you're upset," I said softly. "Did anything new happen?"

"No," Karen replied, "nothing new. Same old shit, different day."

"Honey," Peter said reassuringly, and Karen snapped, "Don't honey me, it won't help."

I'd never seen Karen behave in this way. Was she on something? She'd sworn that she didn't use drugs, but I haven't automatically believed anyone who'd sworn they didn't use drugs since I'd been a first-year psychiatry resident.

Karen signaled the waiter for more coffee. He refilled our cups, even mine, which I'd scarcely touched. My mind was racing faster than the emergency room nurses could triage the homeless to Psychiatry. What was wrong with Karen?

"Let's go," Peter said, standing. "Ready, hon?"

The hospital was relatively deserted, probably because of the holiday, which meant that it only took ten minutes for an elevator to arrive and whisk us up to the adolescent psychiatry unit. The nurse who unlocked the door recognized the Devinskis and waved us in. A few angry kids were watching TV in the dayroom. They barely noticed us as we passed. A bored officer sat outside Jason's door. As we approached, he hastily hid the magazine he was reading. Another officer would be inside the room.

Jason lay in the bed closer to the window. One small wrist was handcuffed to the metal bed rail. The other hand picked at a pimple on his chin. Despite the blemish, Jason was a beautiful child. His blue eyes widened when he saw us. His curly, blond hair was cut close to his scalp, and he had high, chiseled cheekbones poking through the baby roundness, and a cleft chin. *He's going to be a real lady-killer when he grows up.* I gasped, horrified at my own silent choice of words. Jason looked nothing like the newspaper and television photos, all of which had attempted to make the boy look dark and evil.

Peter and Karen approached their son; both kissed him. Jason hugged back with his unbound arm. The officer who was stretched out on the other bed rustled his newspaper.

"He's doing a lot better," the officer remarked, although nobody had asked him. "Must be the new medication."

I hadn't heard anything about medication.

"Jason, honey, this is Dr. Tamsen Bayn." Karen nudged me toward her son.

"Hi," Jason said, as unkillerlike as a boy could be. He shook my hand seriously, as a grown-up might.

"How are they treating you here?" I asked.

"Okay," Jason said. "Better than jail, that's for sure. You're the psychiatrist who's evaluating my mom and dad, right?"

I nodded. "So what medication are you taking?" If he was as smart as everyone said he was, he might know.

"I'm not sure." Jason shrugged. "They won't tell me. An antidepressant."

"Once a day?"

"Yes, an orange pill, shaped like a football, once a day."

Okay, I knew what it was. The most inexpensive serotonin-uptake inhibitor. Chosen for its price, undoubtedly. Fortunately it works fine. "And you feel better already?"

"Are you feeling better, honey?" Karen interrupted us. "Oh, sweetheart, that's wonderful! Where's the doctor, is he here? I want to talk to him, find out what's happening, when we can take you home."

I glanced at Peter, who shook his head mutely. He knew that taking Jason home wasn't going to be an option anytime soon.

"I'm sure that the attending psychiatrist won't be in today," I told Karen. "It's a holiday. There's really no one to talk to." I still have the instinct to protect my unsuspecting colleagues from irate relatives who demand answers to uninformed and unformed questions. And on a double-whammy holiday—a New Year's Day that was also a Saturday—minimum coverage was all anyone could expect, in any department of any hospital.

"We'll let you two talk for a while," Peter said abruptly, and steered his wife toward the door.

"Mind if I sit here?" I gestured toward the end of the bed. The only chair was covered with the officer's jacket.

Jason whispered, "Okay."

The officer ignored me as I sat on the edge of Jason's bed. "There's nothing official about my visit," I told the boy softly. "I just wanted to meet you. To see if you were okay."

"I'm much better," Jason said. "Even though I wish I had killed myself. I did a horrible thing."

"Yes, you did." I nodded. "You have any idea why you did it?" "Blunt" isn't my middle name, but it should be. The officer turned another page of his tabloid. Jason wasn't on the cover, for a change.

"No. No. I don't know. It was like, that guy, my mom's boss, showed me that gun last summer, and I *had* to have it.

I don't even know what I was going to use it for. I just knew I needed it . . . just in case."

"Just in case of what?"

"I don't know." Jason seemed close to tears. "Then, I don't know, I felt this urge, this *thing*, growing inside me, like a monster, that I should take that gun to school. I felt like everyone hated me, and I should shoot them and that would show them. I *knew* that Amanda didn't want to be my girlfriend. I already knew. I didn't have to shoot her. She's just a kid. Maybe when she got older she'd have liked me. . . ."

I didn't bother to ask, *Show them what?* "Did you tell the other psychiatrist what you told me?"

"No," Jason said softly. "Not really. I'm only talking to you because I know my mom likes you so much. And I love her—I love my parents—I didn't want to do this to them. . . . I wish I were dead. . . ."

I waited until his tears subsided. "When did you start feeling so bad?"

"I don't know, exactly. It was gradual. Maybe last summer. Or maybe the end of fifth grade. I'm not really sure."

"What about your lawyer? Did you tell her how you'd been feeling?"

"I told her but I don't think she really cares. She spends more time talking to the prosecutor than she does to me."

I'd have to think about that comment later. " 'Prosecutor' is kind of a big word for you to know."

"I'm smart," Jason informed me. "Of course now I probably don't have a future. Funny how you don't really think about anything except yourself, until it's too late."

I'd never heard such insightful words from a twelve-year-old. In fact, I don't think I'd ever heard them from anyone.

"Jason, does your mom seem normal to you today?"

Jason gave a thin laugh. "She gets like this sometimes. Loud, and bossy. Like she becomes another person, sort of."

"Frequently? Because I saw her yesterday and she seemed fine. Upset, of course, and worried. But fine."

Jason shook his head. "I guess it's just the stress."

Could I ask this child if his mother used drugs? Why not? The teenagers who came to the Adolescent Medicine Clinic downstairs didn't hesitate when they volunteered the information that their mothers were junkies and their fathers were unknown.

"Do you think she ever uses drugs? Your mother, I mean."

Jason looked puzzled. "I never thought about it," he whispered. "Think that's it?"

"I don't know." Then I took the plunge: "Jason, did *you* use any drugs? When you took the gun? When you did the shootings? Or any other time?"

Disgust sparked in Jason's eyes. "You're just like everyone else. I don't know why my mom likes you. You're just like all the lawyers and everyone else, trying to blame this whole thing on drugs."

"I'm sorry."

"Are you? You probably wish I had shot myself, just like that TV reporter who said that I should have taken out my anger on myself."

"That's horrible." I paused, deciding what to say next. I don't believe in talking down to kids. "But, Jason, you know that people are going to say awful things. Now that you're responding to an antidepressant, people will want to know how come nobody noticed you were depressed. You are going to be under a ton of scrutiny—everyone is going to want to ask you questions to try to understand what went wrong in your mind. You need to prepare yourself."

"I think you should just go," he said. "Could you ask my mom and dad to come back in?"

"Can I come see you again?"

"No." He looked at me. "Well, maybe. I'll decide later."

"I'm glad I finally met you. Let me know if there's anything I can do." Empty words, really, since he couldn't let me know, and there wasn't anything I could do. But I needed to offer them. In the hallway, I found Karen in animated discussion with the bored police officer. Karen was insisting that her son was just "troubled" and would be found innocent.

I shook my head and said good-bye. I was more confused than ever. I needed to learn what had prompted Karen's bizarre outburst today. Was it just her personality? Was it stress? Or was it something more sinister, like a hit of crystal meth?

chapter thirty-three

I took a cab back uptown. When I inquired at the hotel desk, I learned that Greg had checked us out and that our belongings were being held in a storage room. I was just around the corner from my parents' apartment and my office, and I wanted to check on the cat.

Alfredo, the head doorman, was in the lobby, wearing street clothes—a fat down parka over a pair of dress pants a little too shiny to be real wool. His thin, flimsy-soled tasseled loafers looked as if they belonged on a disco dance floor. He was trying to communicate with the young uniformed Croatian (or was he Bosnian?) who had pulled holiday doorman duty.

"*Hola*, Alfredo," I said. "What's happening here?"

Alfredo rushed to explain that the police were investigating a break-in—in my office. "But we don' know how it could happen," he added. "We no let anyone into the building past the lobby, Tamsen. Doctora," he quickly amended.

My office was a hive of activity. Crime-scene experts were buzzing all over the place. Black fingerprint powder covered every available surface. A young deputy DA finally noticed me.

"Dr. Bayn!" He was *that* young. We shook hands. "Josh Finkelstein, from the DA's office. We're almost done here. Mr. Jolson called this in for you, left me the keys. I hope it's okay."

"Did you find anything?"

"Well, yes." The young lawyer looked worried. "I think we'll be calling in the FBI, actually. I heard it's not going to be my case. It will go to a federal prosecutor." Now he looked relieved.

"What did you find?"

"Well, *I* didn't find anything, it was the police and the investigators."

I was wasting my time with this kid. "Is there an officer in charge here?"

Josh looked offended, then pointed to a tall man talking on a cell phone in a corner.

Just then Greg appeared; behind him stood Kathy O'Neill.

"Let's get out of here," Greg said to me. "Too much commotion. They're sealing the office until further notice."

"What did they find?" I asked him as he hurried me out the door.

"Phone taps. Someone bugged and searched your office. I'll bet it was that Stolnik guy from yesterday." He added a couple of very rude Russian words, and handed me my appointment book. "I rescued this for you. You're probably going to want to reschedule your patients."

I took the book, and said, "Greg, I went to see Jason Devinski."

He looked at me with anger evident all over his face. I knew why Greg was angry, although I doubted that he himself knew exactly why. I wasn't supposed to meet Jason and either feel sorry for him *or* wish retribution on him. Once I'd met with Jason, my evaluation of the Devinskis was bound to be biased, if only unconsciously. On cross-examination, both lawyers could have a field day with me. And cross-examining the psychiatrist is often the highlight of the trial. Lawyers *love* to make doctors look bad.

"I'm not interfering. It's just—I wanted to meet him." I almost told Greg my suspicions about Karen Devinski, but then I realized that he was prosecuting Jason and I couldn't just run around voicing my opinions randomly. I needed to talk to Kathleen O'Neill again. What if Karen were using methamphetamine?

And then I had a really horrible thought.

What if she were making it?

chapter thirty-four

Greg and I ended up checking back into the hotel at the taxpayers' expense. We couldn't return home, and we couldn't stay at my parents' apartment, because the crime-scene investigators wanted to keep everything sealed until they negotiated who had jurisdiction over what. We spent our second night in a regular room, but it was still nice, even though it didn't have a hot tub. The young DA had offered to take Inky back to his mother's house in Flushing until we sorted everything out. Kathleen O'Neill had little trouble convincing the cops that my encounter with Vasily Stolnik, as well as the two break-ins, were related to their first homicide of the year. Poor Jim Mahoney had died in vain, because nobody yet understood the connection. But everyone knew drugs were involved. They always were.

Greg and I argued again about Bermuda. "Let the FBI handle it," he insisted. The next morning we were still arguing, but I was determined to go.

"He sent for me. I told the FBI about him, I told Kathy, and she said they will talk to him. It's just for a day. What could happen to me in a day?"

I had just enough time to get to the airport. I felt sad. I didn't like doing something that Greg hadn't wanted me to do. I didn't need to show that I was independent or self-sufficient. I wasn't one of those women with a complex about proving to the world that she didn't need anyone to take care of her. I had no such complex and I wished that someone would, in fact, take care of me once in a while. But I had just become accustomed to making my own decisions and following my own drummer. What the hell else was I supposed to do? I wasn't Rapunzel, waiting in my tower to be rescued.

Half an hour later, the taxi driver dropped me off at the terminal. In just a few minutes I had shown my ticket and my photo ID and picked up my boarding pass. I started to feel that excitement I always felt in airports, a combination of the thrill of going away and the fear that my flight would be the one out of every three million or so that didn't make it. One out of three million seemed to be pretty good odds for arriving alive. These days, you had a higher chance of dying in a school shooting than in a plane crash.

I needed a book for the trip, so I chose the next-to-latest legal thriller by the richest writer in America. The blonde at the gate picked up her microphone just as I approached. I waited to hear a boarding announcement. Instead, when her voice crackled over the microphone, I heard, "Flight 2173 to Bermuda is delayed at least two hours because of storm activity over the Atlantic. Repeat, Flight 2173 to Bermuda, delayed. We apologize for any inconvenience."

They apologize. Super. I looked around. It was ten forty-five in the morning, but a bar was open on the concourse. I headed toward it. My duffel bag bumped painfully against my hip, reminding me just how stupid and irrational this whole escapade was. I hadn't even telephoned Antony Hastings-Muir to tell him I was coming. Was I crazy?

I settled into a seat by a window. There was nothing to see outside besides baggage handlers and piles of dirty snow, so I pulled my new book out of my bag. A moment later, a beefy man in a suit, tie, and cowboy hat sank into the seat next to mine. He handed his hat to a waitress who'd materialized out of nowhere. She struggled to perch the enormous hat on top of the coat rack.

"Careful with that hat, honey," the man drawled. "It's a gen-u-ine Stetson, top of the line. Almost two hunnert bucks, sweetie pie. Ya gotta set it up there upside down."

I watched as Tex showed the waitress how to fit his gigantic hat onto the narrow wooden shelf. I could have sworn that his hand grazed her butt before he sat down again, but all she said was, "What can I get you?"

He ordered a beer, and then the waitress came over to me, only inches away at the adjoining table.

"A Bloody Mary, please," I shocked myself by saying. Then my neighbor leaned toward me.

"So where y'all from?" The man had booze on his breath and his face was flushed. He seemed to be somewhere around fifty, and that half-century hadn't been so kind to him. I was momentarily tempted to pretend I didn't speak English. In the nick of time I remembered that if I didn't speak English, I couldn't read it either, and I could end up spending the next two hours fending off this Texan in my fake French accent, which was the only one I could do convincingly. "New York," I said, in my regular voice.

"I'm from Texas myself," he offered. "Where y'all headed?"

"Bermuda," I replied, closing my book with a sigh. Why me? You'd think he'd wait until he got on a plane to look for someone to bother. Why do all these horny middle-aged men think a business trip absolves them of all the rules and regulations of normal life?

"No way! Me too. Ever been there before?" He held out a pudgy hand. "Ralph Dupree."

"Tamsen Bayn, nice to meet you," I replied automatically. I shook his hand reluctantly. How could I get rid of this pest?

"Business or pleasure?" the man persisted. "Call me Ralphie, please."

"Business," I said curtly, and opened my book again. The Texan didn't seem to care. He kept talking.

"Me, I go to Bermuda all the time. A little business. And a little R and R."

I tried my best glare, but he continued. "Too bad the flight is delayed. But it will give us a chance to get to know each other—"

"I'm sorry, Ralphie"—well, he had told me to call him that. I almost told him to call me "Tammy," in revenge, but the irony would have been lost on him. "I just had a death in the family, and I'm really not up to talking right now." I pretended to read my book.

I knew I shouldn't drink alcohol before getting on a plane; it wasn't good for me (or for anyone), but I figured the vitamin C in the tomato juice would counterbalance the negative effects of the vodka. Tomaaaato juice had been Gordon Ranier's favorite beverage. Thinking of the suicidal Gordon conjured up a graphic image of poor murdered Jim Mahoney. Then I started wondering how Ginny Liu was doing, and before I knew it, when the waitress reappeared, I had requested a second drink. If I wasn't careful I would end up taking Curixenol instead of promoting it. Then I was struck by a bizarre thought. All the negative press Grandines had received lately about methamphetamine and internal problems had still managed to inform the world that Curixenol was coming. I was reminded of those cola and detergent ads that mentioned the competitors' names more frequently than the products being promoted. Hmmm.

I started reading the best-seller, but it couldn't hold my attention today. I still hadn't notified Antony Hastings-Muir of my imminent arrival. I was sure he was home. When he sent me the ticket, it couldn't have been with the intention of leaving town anytime soon.

I looked around. The bar was full, even though it was a Monday morning. A fair amount of cocktail glasses and beer bottles were scattered among the coffee cups. I pulled my appointment book out of my bag, and looked up Antony Hastings-Muir's number, but I didn't bother to get up to look for a phone. This was ridiculous. If Hastings-Muir knew something about pseudoephedrine diversions, he should tell the FBI or the DEA—not me. I fidgeted. Almost without realizing it, I began drawing on one of the blank pages in the back of the appointment book. Before I knew it, I had drawn a picture of a palm tree.

"Hey, Tammy." Ralphie leaned over from the adjoining table. "That's a nice picture. You like to draw?"

Great line, but it wouldn't work. "Just doodling."

"I know talent when I see it," Ralphie declared. "Here's my card. I'm an art appraiser. I work for insurance companies."

"An insurance company in Bermuda?" I almost kicked myself for asking.

"Bermuda is the reinsurance capital of the world, didn't you know?"

"Oh." What the hell was reinsurance? And more importantly, did I care? I put his card in my bag, where I guessed it would float around with all the other cards people kept handing me, until I threw them all away. I wasn't about to start telling this drunk Texan about my childhood dreams.

"So what's taking you to Bermuda? A funeral, you said?"

"No, the funeral will be in New York. Business," I said again.

His eyebrows rose, and he signaled the waitress for another beer.

"I'm a psychiatrist," I said. "I have a . . . consultation." I'm a terrible liar. I should have stuck to pretending to be French, it would have been easier. I doodled a Texan wearing a beret, trying to convey without words that our conversation was now officially over.

When I was a child I had dreamed of being an artist, but it was one of those childhood things that was left behind after my father told me I could never support myself that way. He also vetoed architect, my related, but more practical, second choice. Ralphie's compliment upset me. I wondered why.

Oh, yeah. I was a shrink, I could figure it out. Shrinkhood was making me quite unhappy lately. Maybe I was dreaming of greener pastures, or at least of painting them. I leaned back and closed my eyes, imagining a beautiful house filled with sunshine and children and laughter. Yellow walls . . . or maybe peach . . . and a stone fireplace . . . or maybe brick . . .

A crackle jolted me out of my daydream. Overhead a voice rasped over the public-address system. Our flight had been delayed until further notice. Bermuda was in the throes of a bizarre, late-season tropical storm. The airline was offering to reschedule all ticket holders for later in the week, as soon as the weather calmed down.

I felt dazed, as if divine intervention had somehow prevented me from embarking on this absurd journey. My vision seemed blurred, as if I were dreaming. Of course, it could have been the two Bloody Marys I'd had for breakfast.

The loudspeaker crackled again, with some other announcement that was irrelevant to me. Beside me Ralphie was talking.

"Excuse me?" I said.

"I was wondering if you'd like to have dinner," Ralphie was repeating. "In Bermuda. Or maybe in New York?"

"Umm . . . I don't know. I don't think so."

"Here, let me give you the name of the hotel where I'll be." He scrawled something on the back of another business card, and handed it to me. I threw Ralphie's card into my bag with the other debris of my life. "Nice meeting you," I said, and scrambled to my feet. I'd had lots of patients who believed in magical signs. I treated those patients with medication. Did that mean that signs don't exist? Did that mean that the cancellation of my flight didn't mean that I'd never been meant to see Antony Hastings-Muir in Bermuda?

I'm always skeptical when I hear someone claim temporary insanity, but I suspected that my desire to fly off to Bermuda might have fit the profile. I didn't hear Ralphie's words as I rushed out of the bar and toward the airport exit. The sun was blinding. I put on my sunglasses, which barely helped.

As I waited in the taxi line I began to appreciate the truth behind the expression "freezing my butt off." Where should I go? Back to the hotel? To my office? Home? I could decide when I finally got a taxi, which judging by the dozens of people ahead of me might take a year. It was now past noon, and I hoped that my head would clear by the time I reached wherever I was going. Finally I was next, and I slid into an overheated taxi and gave the driver my office address. Maybe the coast would be clear by now.

The driver repeated the address in a singsong accent. He pulled the cab a few feet away from the curb, then stopped and made a notation on his clipboard. Suddenly the rear door opened to my left and a hulk of a person hoisted himself onto the seat beside me. I recoiled in fear; the driver, who had just started the car moving again, jammed on his brakes.

"Sir, sir, I have passenger already, please to get out!" the driver stammered, but all I could do was stare at the intruder in disbelief.

"It's okay, driver," the man said. "You can go."

"No!" I shouted.

"It's okay, Tamsen," the trespasser said, flashing something in front of my eyes. "Ralph Dupree, FBI."

chapter thirty-five

"You're an FBI agent?" I sputtered. "Why didn't you just tell me in the bar? Does this have something to do with Jim Mahoney?"

"You could say that." Ralphie settled his large frame onto the vinyl seat. "You can go," he told the driver, who turned and looked at me anxiously for confirmation.

"Yes," I said. "Let's go." The driver jerked the cab into an invisible opening in the flow of traffic. "Why all this cloak-and-dagger stuff?" I asked Ralphie Dupree. "Can I help you with something? Was there something you wanted?"

"Just had a few questions for this Hastings-Muir. Presumably that's who you were going to see?"

I refused to take the bait. "What did you want to talk to Dr. Hastings-Muir about?"

"Just part of our routine investigation of the illegal drug trafficking at his former place of business. You know, your new employer."

"You knew I was going to Bermuda to see him? Why didn't you just tell me who you were?"

"It's more fun this way." Ralphie gave a sinister laugh. "I gave you two cards, and you didn't even look at them." He winked at me, meaninglessly.

"I thought . . ."

Ralphie pressed a third card into my hand. *J. Ralph Dupree, Special Agent, FBI.*

"But—the FBI has no jurisdiction in Bermuda, does it?"

"We need to question Mr. Hastings-Muir, who, incidentally, has been an American citizen for the past ten years."

I nodded. Still, it didn't explain why Ralphie had virtually stalked me through the airport without telling me who he was or what he wanted.

"Where ya off to now?"

"I do have other cases," I answered as haughtily as I could. "I have patients to reschedule. And not every work environment is as . . . hostile as you're trying to make my work for Grandines."

"This Hastings-Muir worked for Grandines," Ralphie said. "Don't tell me you were going to see him just out of some naïve dedication to tourism."

"No," I admitted as the taxi screeched to a halt in the sea of cars waiting to pay the bridge toll. "Nobody ever sent me a plane ticket before."

"Wait a minute, you're telling me Hastings-Muir sent you the ticket? And you didn't mention anything about it to Kathleen? What's the matter with you, gal?"

"Listen, *Mister* Dupree. I don't have to tell you anything. Whether or not I decide to go to Bermuda has nothing at all to do with this pseudoephedrine thing. I called Dr. Hastings-Muir to ask him about this drug I'm representing for Grandines. A totally legitimate medication, nothing to do with methamphetamine or anything. Hastings-Muir, for some reason known only to himself, sent me a ticket. Whether or not I choose to go talk to him is really none of your business."

The taxi sped through the EZPass lane. In seconds we were across the rest of the Triborough Bridge and merging onto the East Side Highway.

"Is that a fact?" Ralph Dupree said, a shade too late.

"Listen, Mr. Dupree. I don't know what you want from me, or what the FBI thinks I can help with. You know I'd be very happy to help you out if I could—"

"I know? How would I know that, *Doctor*?"

"Because I just told you. I told Kathleen O'Neill that I'd be happy to help—actually, I told Jim Mahoney I'd be happy to help, and now he's dead. If there's trouble inside Grandines Pharmaceuticals, which I'm sure there is, it can only have something to do with the manufacture and sale of illegal drugs. That has nothing, absolutely nothing, to do with me. I'm sorry that I agreed to work for them at all, but I can promise you, as soon as I can figure out how to get out of this Curixenol thing, I will."

"Get off here," I told the taxi driver, as we approached the Ninety-sixth Street exit. As the cab swung onto Park Avenue, I turned my face to the window, needing a break from Ralph Dupree. I didn't know what was normal operating procedure for the FBI, but I had a feeling that Special Agent Ralph Dupree was not it.

"So why'd you pull that art appraiser bullshit on me, then?" I turned back to him angrily. "If you're an FBI agent, why did you pretend to be something else?"

"It's a long story," Dupree said, as the taxi pulled up in front of my office. I almost waited to hear it, but instead I said, "Thanks for the ride." I jumped out of the cab and ran into the building. Let the federal government pay for my transportation today. I was so furious I didn't even acknowledge what a pitiful form of revenge I was seeking.

I greeted the doorman perfunctorily as I swept past him toward my office. The crime-scene tape was gone. I shoved my key into the lock, but it wouldn't fit. It took me a few seconds to realize that it wasn't merely my anger interfering with my coordination. The lock had been changed. Well, of course. Otherwise, if Vasily Stolnik had the key, he could use it again.

I took the elevator up to my parents' apartment, but I knew what I would find—no parents, and new locks. I was right. I returned to the lobby and asked the doorman to borrow his phone. Greg was in court. He wouldn't be available all afternoon. I wasn't going to schlep all the way home to find I was locked out there too.

I said good-bye to the doorman and went back outside. It was a beautiful day, but still very cold, not the best day for window-shopping while carrying a heavy overnight bag, which I realized too late I should have left with the doorman. My stomach growled. I stopped at a pay phone;

miraculously, it worked. I tried calling my friend Belinda, hoping that she was in and not in court or somewhere. She was there, said she'd love to have lunch with me. I raced down Lexington. A good schmooze would make a lot of things better.

Belinda Ryan was a divorces-and-closings lawyer whom I'd first befriended when I was a forensic psychiatry fellow and she worked for Mental Hygiene Legal Services. Now she sent me referrals regularly. Since she'd had her baby I didn't feel as connected to her, but I knew we both included each other among our close friends.

Once we were settled into a window booth in the coffee shop, the first thing she did was show me the latest pictures of baby Carly. After I'd oohed and aahed and we'd ordered lunch, I launched into an explanation of my aborted trip to Bermuda.

"Tamsen! What in the world were you thinking? You were going to fly off to meet some guy you don't even know? He could be a lunatic!"

I told her about the FBI then. Keeping my voice low, I filled her in on all the bizarre happenings in my life in the past week and a half. Her gray eyes stared at me from behind lenses that made them look huge, her hot roast beef sandwich growing cold on the plate in front of her.

The direction she took surprised me. "So you say a scientist got killed? I wonder. Waiter . . . could you warm this up for me, please?" The waiter bustled away with her plate. "I wonder if she could have somehow been in on this methamphetamine thing?"

"As far as I know, her death was an accident."

"Still," Belinda insisted, "she'd have lab skills, right? She died in a lab. Maybe she was somehow involved in this . . . what did you call it? Pseudosomething—"

"Pseudoephedrine," I said. "Maybe. I don't know. God, this is all so confusing." The waiter reappeared with Belinda's plate, and for a couple of minutes I concentrated on my grilled chicken Caesar. "Are you busy this afternoon?" I asked Belinda.

"Not especially. I have to work on a motion—this stupid case where they're arguing over ten thousand dollars' worth of assets and it's going to cost them much more to go to trial. . . ." She positioned a piece of roast beef on the soggy white bread, cut through it precisely, and smeared it through the thick brown gravy. It reminded me of a school lunch. You'd never guess that Belinda had grown up in Manhattan and was therefore supposed to have sophisticated tastes.

"Would you mind if I come up to your office for a while and use your computer?" I asked. "I have some things I want to look up, and I can't get into my office. . . ." I imagined I couldn't get into my apartment either. Until Greg got home from work I was homeless. I was mortified by the thought of dropping by Greg's office, searching for keys or solace or anything else. Although we'd met through work, once we'd moved in together we'd agreed that he wouldn't hire me as an expert for any of his cases. Why had I ever said yes to his request that I examine the Devinskis? I should have known that nothing good could come from our collaboration. And so far, I'd been right. I'd just spend the rest of the day in Belinda's office, the way some Europeans had spent the war in Switzerland.

We finished our lunch and started walking back. Belinda wanted to stop in a children's store: "Oh, look at that, could you imagine Carly in that little dress?" When she saw the price tag, though, she dropped the dress as if it had stung her, and hustled me back to her office. She only had a part-time assistant, Pedro, who was nowhere to be seen.

"Use Pedro's desk," Belinda said. "Make yourself comfortable."

"You let Pedro have Internet access?" I asked in amazement. Did she really not mind paying an assistant to surf the Net while he was supposed to be working? His job was supposed to consist of typing and filing and arranging appointments and court appearances, not chatting or shopping or gambling or looking at pornography. . . .

"He's a good kid," Belinda replied, red-faced. "I know I'm too nice to them."

"Them" referred to the twenty or so part-time helpers who'd left, one after the other, as soon as Belinda required them to perform actual work. She had great difficulty delegating responsibility. Like me, she preferred to do everything herself.

All kinds of subversive information was available on the Internet—bomb-making instructions, for example. I wondered if you could find out how to make methamphetamine. When I logged on, the welcome screen greeted me with "Top News Stories." *Child Murder Suspect Remains Hospitalized in New York* was the only story listed. I refrained from clicking on the link. When the "What do you want to search for?" box popped up, I typed in "methamphetamine." In seconds, the computer coughed up over two hundred thousand hits. This way was not going to work. I considered, then typed: "How to make methamphetamine."

Oh, my goodness! Recipes, right on the screen. I clicked away in astonishment. Methamphetamine only required three ingredients. *Anyone* could do this at home! I felt a tightness in my chest. I couldn't tell if I was thrilled or terrified.

I summoned Belinda, who bounced into the reception area with an open folder in her hand and a red pencil behind her ear. She bent toward the screen, then looked dismayed. "Look at this. It tells you exactly what pills to purchase, how to add this lithium thingy . . . and check this out. It requires something that you get from farms. Forget it. No farms in Manhattan." She shook her head. "I must have been wrong. They couldn't be manufacturing methamphetamine in a genetics lab. Guess the scientist didn't have anything to do with it." She went back into her office. "Call me if you need me."

I looked at the ingredient list. The drug required a pure form of ammonia that needed to be stored cold, and that wasn't available casually. Farmers used it to fertilize crops, and stored it in huge tanks. I'd heard a story about it on NPR. I searched the Web for "anhydrous ammonia," and learned immediately that farmers in the Midwest had reported numerous instances of their supplies being siphoned off in the middle of the night. You needed much less ammonia to whip up a fresh batch of crystal meth than you needed to fertilize a hundred thousand acres of corn or wheat.

I jumped when Belinda appeared next to me in her coat, lugging a stack of files.

"Time to go home," she told me. I pensively gathered my things together. It was almost five o'clock. Three hours had zipped by while I toured cyberspace.

We agreed to meet for lunch again the following week, and I left Belinda for her walk home in the twilight. By the time I descended into the subway, despite Belinda's skepticism, I was almost convinced that the Grandines geneticist had been synthesizing anhydrous ammonia in her laboratory when she died. But if the scientist had been the one making and selling methamphetamine, and she was killed, then who killed her? How did Ginny and Ray Liu fit in? And why kill an FBI agent?

It was time to stop sitting around impersonating an innocent bystander. The events of the past week had shown me in horrifying detail that as little as I knew about whatever was going on, somebody else clearly thought I knew more than I did. Maybe I'd stumbled into this mess unwittingly. But now only my wits could make it all stop.

chapter thirty-six

Although I suspected my keys wouldn't work, I tried anyway. Nothing. From the other side of my door I heard a scuffle, then a mewling sound. I rang the bell.

Greg opened the door in his usual uniform of sweatpants and ancient college sweatshirt.

I fell into his arms just like one of my romance-novel heroines and put my arms around him. It took me a second to realize that Greg was standing stiffly and angrily, not responding to me at all.

I pulled the door shut, and sat down hard on one of the dining room chairs. The little black cat ran up to me, and rubbed against my legs. Greg must have retrieved him from the young DA. I reached down to pet the cat, then pulled off my boots. Inky crouched near my feet, purring, then jumped up as if he were weightless and cuddled on my lap. Greg watched me silently.

Then I noticed my surroundings. The place was a mess: books pulled off the shelves, dirty cups and plates scattered around the living room, pizza boxes on the table in front of me. Greg went into the kitchen. I heard the clink of ice cubes falling into a glass, the *whish* as he opened a bottle of seltzer. He came back with a drink that looked as if it were mostly scotch. He stood in front of me, drinking, his legs braced apart as if he were about to go a few rounds with Mike Tyson.

"Did you have a good trip?" he asked. "How many hours in the air? Six or so, altogether? You must be tired."

"I didn't even go," I replied. "I doubt I'd have made it back and forth in one day. What happened here?"

"Cops are not known for leaving the premises as pristine as they found them."

"Oh." I'd almost forgotten. "Listen, I had this idea about that geneticist—"

"What the hell were you trying to prove?"

"Prove? Nothing. I tried reaching you at your office but you weren't there."

"Of course I wasn't there. I was in court. Some of us have jobs."

"That was uncalled for."

"Where were you all day, then, if not in Bermuda? Did you forget that just three days ago you were abducted by some lunatic? Did you forget that every time you turn the corner somebody drops dead? Did you forget that someone was in our apartment and that your phones were tapped? What's *wrong* with you? Running off on some pleasure trip?"

"I have to find out what's happening at Grandines. I was just trying to help."

"Help? What kind of help is this? I should have known better."

"Should have known better than what? What are you talking about?"

"Why do you think that I was able to get a second forensic team in here—and in your parents' house *and* their office—on a holiday weekend?"

I looked at him blankly.

"Jim Mahoney, Tamsen. Remember? FBI agent, dead as a doorknob?"

"That's not an expression," I mumbled, although it might have been. I couldn't remember ever being angry enough with Greg to be intentionally nasty. What was happening?

"Fuck you, Tamsen. You fucked up an FBI investigation into a major drug scam, you go around talking to people who tell you things because you've got this 'Oh, I'm just an innocent psychiatrist who wants to help' expression on

your face, and then you're surprised when they want to shut
you up. You try to find connections where there aren't any.
You—"

Poor Inky gave a terrified meow as I got to my feet in a
rush. "Excuse me?" I raged. "Excuse me? 'Fuck you'? Would
that be an expression of your love? That's the welcome that
I get?" I was shaking with anger. I barely heard the words
behind the anger.

"Okay. So I used the wrong expression. 'Dead as a
doorknob.' 'Fuck you.' Whatever. The point is—"

"The point is *nothing,* dammit. The point is *nothing!*" I
was furious. Blood was pounding in my ears, in my eyes. I
felt as if my head would burst. "I was doing my *job.* I wasn't
interfering with anything. I got out of your way so you could
do *your* job."

"I said I was sorry."

"You did *not* say you were sorry. And anyway, 'sorry' isn't
good enough." I was mad enough to punch something.
"You're the one who wanted me on this case. I didn't volunteer."

Greg started to say something, but I didn't stop to listen. I didn't need this. I went into the study and threw myself onto the bed in a rage.

The cat jumped up next to me, and I stroked it, grateful for the companionship of someone normal. I heard Greg
go into our bedroom and close the door. A moment later I
heard the television go on.

Eventually I took a shower and went into the kitchen. I
put two slices of leftover pizza in the oven and made myself
a vodka tonic. The white countertops were smeared with
fingerprint powder. The apartment was a disgusting mess.

I contemplated going into our bedroom, climbing into
our bed beside Greg as if nothing had happened. Instead, I
cleaned up the little kitchen, scrubbed all the counters, put
the dirty dishes from the living room into the dishwasher,
and turned it on. I wiped off the base of the cordless phone,
and then located the handset on the coffee table. The red
light was blinking, indicating that the phone was in use.

Who could Greg be talking to? I lifted the receiver to my ear.

"Sounds great," he was saying. "What else?"

"Oh, then we'll take a ride up to Montreal. Did you know they have this underground city—"

I clicked the phone off. It had been a woman's voice, happy, cheerful. Greg's voice had been cheerful too. And those voices were making vacation plans. "We'll" the woman had said. "*We'll* take a ride up to Montreal." *Who'll* take a ride to Montreal?

Was Greg already making plans for a life without me? Was he that angry? Or had I been mistaken about him all along?

I curled up on the unfamiliar twin bed, but even relaxation, much less sleep, remained elusive. I, veteran of only six funerals in thirty-three years, could not have randomly stumbled onto a bunch of corpses by accident. I bolted out of bed. Everyone else—Ginny Liu, the Grandines scientist (learning her name might be a good jumping-off point), Jim Mahoney—had connections to Grandines Pharmaceuticals, as did Karen Devinski, and by extension, Jason. But Gordon Ranier was a wild card. His only connection was to me. If Gordon's death was a suicide, then it didn't fit and I could go back to the FBI's methamphetamine scenario. If Gordon had been murdered, then I was back to square one.

I turned on my computer. First things first. Who was the dead Grandines scientist? How had she died? And why?

chapter thirty-seven

I awoke with a start on Tuesday morning, groggy and exhausted. A phone was ringing somewhere. I shot up in bed, totally disoriented. The ringing stopped, then, after a minute, started again. I almost hit the floor headfirst in my haste and confusion.

The phone stopped ringing. I glanced at my watch. Nine o'clock. Greg must have left for work. I stumbled into our bedroom. The phone rang again.

"What? I mean, hello?"

"I hope I didn't wake you up," a woman's voice said dryly.

"Umm. No. Who is this?"

"It's Kathy O'Neill. How are you?"

"Yes. I mean, fine." Why did I have the feeling she wasn't really making small talk?

"I'll be there in about half an hour." Her tone left no leeway for negotiation.

"Yes. Okay. Fine." Kathleen O'Neill had a way of reducing me to monosyllables. (Yes, I know that technically the word "okay" has two syllables, but you get my drift.)

"See you," she said, and hung up.

I rushed to get dressed. What did Kathleen want? Had the arrogant and annoying Ralphie Dupree already ratted on me? Were they really working together? Could she give me more information other than the fact that one Madeleine Balloy, a thirty-three-year-old Ph.D. in genetics from Harvard, had died, leaving behind a fiancé, and a mother, father, and two sisters in Muncie, Indiana? I'd found the information in, of all places, the Harvard University on-line alumni newsletter. The obituary in *The*

New York Times had been even briefer. Nothing told me what Madeleine had been working on for Grandines or exactly how she'd died. There was no way to know if the departed alumna had died from cancer or a car crash or murder.

I was glad that I had straightened up the living room the previous night. The pizza boxes went out into the garbage room for recycling, I put on a pot of coffee, and I was just applying some lipstick when the downstairs doorbell rang. I know it's silly, but if I'm wearing lipstick, mascara, and earrings, I feel like a grown-up professional. If any one of those three steps is missing, I'm just a kid playing dress-up.

I was ready when the doorman called to say Ms. O'Neill was on her way up. She was in her uniform of slacks, turtleneck, and blazer. This morning her smile appeared forced, her eyes the color of the Arctic sky. Her gun seemed to gleam through its shoulder holster, through her blazer, to burn itself into my consciousness. Cautiously, I offered her a cup of coffee. She surprised me by accepting. Judging by her current attitude, I thought she might accuse me of trying to poison her.

"Nice place," she said, looking around. She added four sugars to her coffee, stirred. No milk. Weird way to drink coffee, in my humble opinion. Watch it, I told myself. Don't get that attitude thing going. Stay cool.

"How can I help you?" I asked, deliberately keeping the usual "I'm just your friendly neighborhood psychiatrist" sound out of my voice.

"Why did you try to fly to Bermuda yesterday?"

"Why?" I repeated. Early in my psychiatric training I'd been taught to never ask questions that begin with "why." If the patient knew *why,* he wouldn't be there, would he?

"Mr. Jolson told you not to go to Bermuda, isn't that correct?"

"Yes." Mr. Jolson. Weren't we getting formal?

"I had this ticket . . . I thought it would be fun." I felt myself turning red. *I thought it would be fun.* That's a good reason to run off to a foreign country in the middle of the murder investigation of a guy you were supposed to be helping. Not that anyone had told me not to leave town. . . .

I had a thought. "You're a lawyer, aren't you?"

"I'm a special agent."

"But you went to law school, didn't you?"

She looked at me. "Oh, all right. Yes. Fordham, if you must know. I'm sure, I'm positive, that I know all the people you're going to ask me if I know, so let's not get into that right now, okay? Consider me a *recovering* lawyer." Kathleen sipped her sweet coffee and the serious veneer returned to her face. "I'd like to know why you left town."

"I *didn't* leave town," I reminded her.

"But what's your connection with this Hastings-Muir?"

I explained that there was really no connection. Hadn't Ralph Dupree been in touch with Kathleen at all? He must have been as creepy and sneaky as I'd first suspected.

"Jim Mahoney really liked you. But you need to stick to doing the job that you're trained to do. You're running around as if you're on *Murder, She Wrote* or something, and it just won't do. People are dying. *Dying.*" Kathy glared at me for a second, then her expression softened.

"These guys are brutal. They have something going on there, at Grandines, something illegal. We were hoping you could bring us information from within the company. I wanted you to report back on any documents you found in Ginny Liu's office, or any comments you might have heard. I really didn't expect that you would fly off to Bermuda on some wild-goose chase."

"I'm sorry. I was only trying to help. I didn't plan to go there to find out about the diversions—"

"It doesn't matter, at this point. We'll have an agent out there to question Hastings-Muir in the next day or two, as soon as the weather clears. That's our job. Not yours."

I waited what I thought was a respectful interval, then asked, "Do you mind if I ask you a few things?"

She shrugged.

"Did you find out who killed Jim Mahoney?"

"Not yet." Her hair swung as she shook her head.

"Was Gordon Ranier's death a suicide?"

"I don't know, Tamsen, Ranier's not our case." She paused, then added, "I did hear something interesting about him."

I waited, psychiatrist-style. Most people can't stand silence and rush to fill it.

"This should be right up your alley. Did you hear about his wife?"

"That she fell onto the train tracks."

"She didn't fall," Kathy said. "She was pushed."

"Who pushed her?" I mentally closed my ears against what I knew would be coming next.

"They say it was her son."

I couldn't feign shock; I'd expected to hear it, eventually. "No wonder Gordon was distraught."

"Exactly."

I'd never even met a single really violent child before, and here I was practically intimate with three, although half a continent separated me from one, and an entire ocean from the other. Childhood violence had finally broken free from the moniker "epidemic." If I remembered my epidemiology at all, it had now officially reached "pandemic" proportions. "What about Ginny Liu?" I asked. "How is she doing?"

"Still alive. Can't tell you more than that."

"Her husband?"

"In custody."

"What? He was arrested? I thought he was just questioned."

"Protective custody," she explained. "He claims that he knows nothing. So far he's told us nothing. His job is tracking those drug shipments—or was. He was fired from Grandines. He swears up and down that even with the DEA and even, get this, UPS involved, they've been *losing* those packages. We have an expert from another drug company, a really major one, who tells us that it can happen. It happens all the time, apparently."

"What about my phones and stuff? They were tapped, I take it."

"Our people took care of it. Your office and your parents' apartment had low-tech, Radio Shack–issue bugs in the receivers. But this apartment, it took our guys a long time to find the tap. It was in the junction box, in the basement. Professional job. We still haven't found the receiver, but without the microphones they can't listen to you."

"So everything is safe now?"

"I think so. Oh, you're going to need these." She held out a little envelope, the kind I remembered from my teenage summers as a day-camp counselor. I opened it, but instead of a tip, six keys fell out. Three had blue dots stuck on, three had red.

"Red's for your parents' apartment. The little one is for the mailbox. Blue, for the office. Courtesy of the federal government."

"I was told the office was sealed until further notice," I said.

"Consider this further notice."

"What about the keys to this apartment?"

"You'll have to ask your boyfriend. He has *all* those sets."

Evidently, the FBI remained in possession of a set of the keys to my office and to my parents' home. Could they do that?

"We're just playing it safe. You have my word that nobody will be entering those places, and as soon as all this is cleared up, you'll have all the keys."

"I have confidential patient records there."

"We're not interested in your records. We're interested in wiretapping and breaking and entering."

"How did they enter? Did you ever find out how that big hairy guy got past the doorman?"

"Yes, it was interesting. The big hairy guy, as you call him—Vasily Stolnik—never actually showed up there. Another guy showed up with some identification claiming he was with the FBI. Creative."

"What other guy?"

"A medium-height, medium-weight guy wearing black pants and a black coat. He might have been thirty or he might have been sixty. He might have had blue eyes or brown. He might have been wearing gloves, and they might have been leather or they might have been wool. His hat might have been the kind for skiing, or it might have been the kind that those French artists wear, pulled down tight. You get the idea. The poor doorman isn't so familiar with written English. He heard 'FBI,' saw some laminated official-looking ID and a shield that, for all we know, could have come from a box of Cracker Jack, and he let the guy right in." Kathleen could have been describing anyone, even the poor late Jim Mahoney.

"So, was he?"

"Was he what?"

"Was he with the FBI?"

She laughed. "A double agent? I don't think so. That poor doorman didn't know anything. Didn't know what hit him, and now he's terrified for his job."

"He should be," I said. "My dad will make sure he gets fired when he gets back." Normally I had sympathy for immigrants trying to make it in this country. After all, I was a child of immigrants. But if the rules say don't let anyone in without permission, it means just that. Not the FBI, not the president, not the pope. People were paying for security. They deserved to have it.

"Anything else?"

"I don't know." I had a vision of a little boy in a ski jacket, shoving his mother into the path of an oncoming train. I blinked to make the image disappear. "What about this place?"

"The tap could have been in place for days, even weeks. Lots of people in and out of this building during the day, cleaning ladies, nannies, repairmen, deliverymen. We just don't know. Sorry."

"Wait a minute," I said. "What about Ralphie? Ralph Dupree? Did you hear about that?"

Kathy shook her head. "I'm sorry about the way he be-haved. He took it upon himself to follow you. Dupree goes to Bermuda all the time for his art-appraisal consultations, so he was the logical one to go to question Hastings-Muir."

I stared at her. "So he really *is* with the FBI?"

"He's my partner," Kathy said with a resigned sigh. "In this case. Only for this case. It's a long story."

I waited, but this time she wasn't rushing to fill the si-lence. She told me she had another appointment, thanked me, and left.

The apartment looked small, cold, and unfriendly. I wandered into the bedroom, our bedroom. The bed was un-made, and Greg, characteristically, had used the entire king-sized space himself. I knew it was only a projection of my anger, but I thought I could sense his hostility and the withdrawal of his love in the very air of the room.

I guessed that by the time these bad guys, whoever they were, had come to my parents' building impersonating the FBI, they were having their little joke, their little snicker in the dark. They already knew that I was cooperat-ing with Jim Mahoney, since they were listening to all my phone conversations here. They probably had listened to Gordon's cry for help. Had they killed him? Why would they? Was it meant to show me how powerful they were? Or were they trying to shut him up? And if that was the case, then what didn't they want him to tell me? As far as I knew, Gordon didn't use methamphetamine. He didn't even drink.

I needed to get out of the house. I'd go to my office and call the Devinskis for a final interview. I had patients scheduled later in the week. I had a psychiatry resident from NYU newly assigned to me for supervision. I had real work to do.

But first I called Greg at his office.

"Yes?"

"I'm sorry. Okay?"

"Fine," he said, and it was obvious that it wasn't fine at all.

"I need keys."

"There's another set. They're on the dresser, in that shell dish thing where I put my change."

I walked into the bedroom with the cordless phone still to my ear, and looked into the "shell dish thing." It was actually a candy dish, which I had brought into Greg's life, along with the nightly ritual of dumping change into it—his change. Before he met me, he used to leave his pocket change strewn all over the top of the dresser, scarring the wood and rolling off into various corners. I had introduced order into his world. Now he couldn't care less.

"I found it," I said, walking back to the living-dining-kitchen area. "Let me make sure it's the right one."

"There should be two," Greg said, still with no warmth in his voice.

"I only found one," I said, feeling angrier by the minute. What kind of a stupid cold conversation was this? The key turned easily in the bottom lock.

"Okay, well, use the one, then, leave the other one unlocked. I have to go." Without another word, Greg hung up on me.

I remained strangely calm. Greg's anger toward me, and my bubbling emotions, were disturbing, but they were small, trivial blips on the landscape of humanity. I had bigger things to worry about—tremendous things, even. Like Gordon Ranier's tremendous son, Oliver. Pushing your mother onto the train tracks, that was tremendous, all right.

chapter thirty-eight

The blinds had been left with their slats open, and every available surface was dusty with fingerprint powder, but my office plants were still green and the couch was still comfy. I set to work cleaning up. I'd have to get extra keys made for the cleaning lady, although maybe for now it would be wiser to just meet her here on cleaning days and let her in myself. She was off this week, since my parents were in Florida; one less thing to worry about.

In the tray of the little desktop copy machine I found a copy of the warrant the FBI had used to enter the office and the apartment. I called the answering service. Several patients had called wanting appointments. I wrote down their numbers. Belinda had called to refer me an embittered couple for a custody evaluation, "and to say hi and are you all right?" The answering-service lady read me the message without emotion. I couldn't bring myself to return Belinda's call. I knew I'd blurt out all the gory details of my argument with Greg. I called all the patients and scheduled appointments for them for next week, called in a couple of prescriptions, and filed some bills. I used my banking software to pay my American Psychiatric Association dues and checked my e-mail. I had a million—or at least fifty—forwarded jokes from my preteen cousins in California. I sent them each a little personal "hello" and then deleted all the jokes unread. They wouldn't make me laugh today. I e-mailed my dad, who was sure to have his laptop with him, telling my parents that everything was fine and to enjoy Florida, and my grandfather, to wish him a belated Happy New Year. I felt this compulsion to reconnect with all my relatives. They wouldn't ask the same kind of questions that

Belinda would, and anyway, I wasn't actually speaking to them in person.

Housekeeping, bookkeeping, and sanity-keeping completed, I sat in my swivel chair and tried to remember what exactly it was that I needed to do next. I looked in the top drawer of my desk, where I'd left the Devinski folder. It wasn't there. Could I have filed it away with the other charts in the filing cabinet? Normally I wouldn't until the case was done. I checked. No Devinski folder. I checked under K for Karen and P for Peter. The file was missing. Great. Just when I had to finish up the case and move on, I couldn't find the chart.

I opened my Devinski document in my computer. My word-processing program gives you information about your document if you ask it nicely. I clicked on "Statistics" to see how many words I had written. I'm always encouraged by a high word count. No words. My document was empty. How could that be? I studied the open window on my screen. I'd never realized that the program told you when the document was created, when it was last edited, how much time you spent on it last, and when it was printed.

When it was printed? I had never printed this document. But I had backed it up on a diskette. Fighting to stay calm, I started hunting through the box of diskettes, hoping that I hadn't been organized enough to tuck it into the folder with my notes. I was sure it was unlabeled—I could never find the labels. With mounting panic, I began sliding diskettes in and out of my floppy drive. It took five tries to locate the right disk. With relief, I read my report on the screen, looking for anything suspicious. Everything seemed innocent and obvious. Virtually everything that the Devinskis had told me had been included in the notes from their other psychiatrists.

Who wanted my report, and why? Had the FBI taken it? I made a backup on a fresh diskette and printed out a hard copy. Then I slipped the pages and the disk into a large manila envelope, and tilted back my chair in contemplation.

What the heck was going on here? Had somebody printed out my document and stolen my file? Were the Grandines people afraid Karen had told me something she shouldn't have? Something about a secret illegal drug operation? Or did they think that Karen had confessed to me that she was involved in the pseudoephedrine business? I decided to lock the report and the diskette in my father's safe. I couldn't wait until next week when Curixenol would be available in pharmacies. Maybe once their new drug took off, this methamphetamine stuff would fade into the background.

I was still pondering this latest weirdness and debating which FBI agent to call first, when the phone rang.

"Gwen! How are you?" I was happy to hear from the child psychiatrist in Kentucky.

"I'm okay," Dr. Gwendolyn Conklin said. "Any news on your little killer? Have you finished evaluating the parents?"

"I think so. I'm not sure. Funny you should call right now. I was just working on their report. You wouldn't believe some of the things that have been going on here." I didn't mention the missing folder or deleted file. Perhaps in all my recent anxiety and turmoil I had somehow deleted it myself. It wouldn't be the first time.

"With this case, you mean? It's been hairy here too. My little boy—Sammy Towland—he's been locked up all this time, and he's been talking like a waterfall or something for the past week. He's really in bad shape. He says he doesn't know why he did what he did. Oh, and now he's in the hospital. They admitted him to do the workup I ordered. Funny, they'll send a woman home the same day she gets a mastectomy, but a healthy kid gets admitted for a little blood work and an MRI."

"Any results on that MRI?" The study would provide a detailed picture of the inside of Sammy Towland's brain. If he had a tumor or any abnormality, it would be identified.

"I haven't seen it yet," she replied. "Why? Anything interesting on your kid—Jason Devinski?"

Greg would kill me if I started blabbing about where Jason got the gun. "I went to see him the other day. He's in the hospital, in the adolescent psychiatry unit. He was suicidal for a while. They're treating him for depression."

"Really? I wanted to treat Sammy too. I mean, to have someone else treat him."

"So why didn't you? Do you think he's depressed?"

"It's hard to tell with kids, you know? But something about his apathy and the way he feels so depersonalized, it makes me wonder if he wouldn't respond to a psychopharmacological intervention." Gwen gasped.

"What happened?"

"Oh, nothing. The baby's kicking me. I didn't know it was supposed to hurt. Anyway, let me tell you, the grandmother said that she 'don't hold with none of these mind-alterin' drugs and my grandson ain't gonna take none of 'em.'"

"I see."

"She tells me that her son—Sammy's father—took some pills for nerves. Claims that they replaced the alcohol that he used to drink. She said, 'An' now what's so bad about some good ole-fashion Kentucky bourbon, that my sonny-boy had to go get mixed up with these newfangled nonsense drugs.'"

"Does she really talk like that?" I couldn't help asking Gwen.

"Well, I might be exaggeratin' just a tiny bit." She laughed.

"So what pills did the father take?" I asked.

"I don't know. Can't find it in the records anywhere. By the way, I got me a court order and everything so my investigation of the parents' records is now officially legit. Ooh, that was a strong one, got me right in the liver."

"What?"

"The baby, kickin' the hell out of me. I can't wait until the pregnancy part is over." She sighed. "Although, to tell you the truth, based on the kids I see, the best part of their lives might be when they're still inside their mamas' bellies."

"Ain't that the truth," I said in my best imitation of Kentuckyese. "Life was a lot simpler then."

"It's a big responsibility," Gwen said. "I didn't really think about it. I got married late, swore I wasn't gonna have kids 'cause my mama had six of 'em. We were always fightin' over the bathroom and the TV and the white meat, ya know? My husband came from a big country family too. We were, both of us, the oldest and the first to go to college. Funny how things work out."

"Yeah." Now it was my turn to sigh. "Funny. I was supposed to be engaged, did I tell you? Now my fiancé isn't talking to me."

"Oh, honey, that's what happens when you love someone. Don't take it to heart."

My silence must have encouraged her. She continued. "You know, you love someone, they can hurt you, the way someone you don't love can't. Don't think my husband and I haven't had our share of problems. You care about that boy, you go talk to him, find out what's eatin' him. You're a *psychiatrist,* for heaven's sake. You know what to do."

"I guess." I wasn't prepared to deal with advice at the moment. "Listen, getting back to the Devinskis . . . They seem like perfectly normal, well-adjusted people. I can't find any history of abuse, drugs, beating Jason or each other, or anything. She started taking a little nortriptyline," a tricyclic antidepressant, "a couple of weeks before she stopped breast-feeding Jason, when he was a baby, but I don't believe that would cause anything bad, especially not something like this. He—the father—admits that he used to drink, that he was in some program in Michigan when they lived there, and it helped him. He's not in AA or anything, sober for the last thirteen years or so. No family history of anything, no—no, nothing. It's just a mystery. The only really bizarre thing I've been able to find is that Jason seems to have obtained the murder weapon from this guy who I personally know is a sleaze bag. Almost like the guy set Jason up."

"How strange. Who was he? Why would he?"

I filled her in on some of what Greg had told me, eliciting her solemn promise not to mention it to anyone. I'd meddled in the Devinski case enough. We promised to call each other with any breaking news, and I hung up the phone feeling only moderately better than when I picked it up.

I was in a horrible mental state. I was filled with nervous energy, yet I remained unable to identify an appropriate outlet for my anxiety. I needed to wrap up my evaluation, and since the Devinskis' folder had vanished, I wanted one more face-to-face contact. Somehow, I had to find out if Karen knew anything about the pseudoephedrine diversions at Grandines. I picked up the phone again.

Karen was home.

"How are you guys doing?" I asked. "Everything okay?" Right, as if their kid were a confirmed murderer and things could *ever* be okay.

"We're hanging in," Karen said.

"Have you been to see Dr. Bluecorn yet? Or rather, has he been to see Jason?"

"He stopped in yesterday. He wants Jason brought to him, to the court clinic. Even though it's a private evaluation. Is he allowed to do that?"

"Dr. Bluecorn is the king of forensic psychiatry. He's allowed to do whatever he wants. But if you think it will upset Jason, or if you object for any other reason, you should tell Bluecorn that he needs to go over to the juvenile detention center, or to the hospital. Do you know when Jason is going to be transferred out of the hospital?"

"No," Karen answered. "They seem to like him there on the adolescent unit, isn't that funny? They're not rushing to send him out."

I thought about this news for a moment. It could work in Jason's favor if the treatment staff believed that Jason was so depressed when he did the shootings that he didn't know right from wrong. But I just didn't buy it.

"I was wondering if you and Peter could come over for a final interview," I told Karen. "I just have a few questions that I'd like to ask. If you don't mind, that is. I mean, I probably have enough information now, but there are a few loose ends I'd like to tie up."

"Sure. We can do it. How about . . ." She paused, and I heard papers rustling. "Would tomorrow be good?"

"Ten o'clock?"

"We'll be there." Karen took a deep breath, and added, "I want you to know how much I appreciate what you're doing, trying to help Jason, to help us. I know that your job is to be impartial—"

"I am impartial," I said. People don't seem to understand that being nice to everyone is still being impartial. "I didn't lie or promise to misrepresent you in any way." The last thing I needed or wanted was for my normally open and friendly demeanor to be misconstrued as a willingness to commit perjury.

"I know you're impartial," Karen said. "I know. But I feel like you're on the side of justice, and your mind is open enough to get the information before you decide which side, exactly, that is. I really appreciate that. I can't help but feel that Bluecorn would say whatever we wanted him to just to get our money. I want him to find the *truth*. This is my *child* we're talking about. If Jason really is deranged, or sick, or evil, I have a right to know. But if he's not, if it's something else, if he made a mistake because someone convinced him to do this terrible thing, or hypnotized him or gave him drugs or something—well, I have a right to know that too."

I was silent. The anguish I'd heard last week was back in her voice. I started to speak, but she interrupted me.

"I . . . I don't really want anyone to know about this, but I started a trust fund, a foundation in the memory of those girls. I went to church—God, I haven't been to church in years—I went to confession, and I spoke to the priest, and he's helping me to do it anonymously. I felt that was the least I could do. I couldn't send cards, or anything. Those parents must detest me. And I would hate it if people thought I was trying to buy sympathy or support. This way is better, I think."

"Does it make you feel any better?"

A dry, unamused laugh reached me over the phone line.

"No. Not really. I can't buy Jason's innocence, or pay to turn back the clock. But he's my child, and I love him. I won't abandon him. If that makes me a bad person, so I'm a bad person. And you know what else? This isn't very Christian of me, or charitable, or good. But if I had the choice, if someone asked me, would you prefer for your child to kill three other people's children, and you get to have him alive, forever, in prison, where you can see him once a week or once a month, or would you be willing to sacrifice your child so those other three would live—" Karen was crying now, and I knew what she was going to say.

"I understand," I told her gently. "What you're feeling is normal, it's totally normal. A mother's instinct is to save her child, first, before anyone else's, even before herself."

"Well . . ." Karen said, sniffling. "Tomorrow, then. At ten. I'll be there with Peter."

"See you," I said and hung up. Every day brought Jason Devinski closer to flesh and blood, and further and further from the monster the newspaper headlines portrayed. I liked his mother. I would have liked to work with her on marketing Curixenol. Too bad we'd met instead under these circumstances.

Now what?

I'd never followed up on my plan to try to speak to Antony Hastings-Muir. Now I knew the phone lines were safe—which made me wonder: What had Hastings-Muir known that made him mistrust the phones in the first place? I'd written down his numbers. It took only a minute to leave messages on two answering machines, one somewhere in Manhattan, and the other out in the middle of the Atlantic.

I fussed around the office, not focused enough to do any real work, not ready to go home. A confrontation was on the horizon, and I felt sick with anticipation. Greg's anger was far out of proportion to my behavior. I didn't understand why he wanted to antagonize me, why he was so upset, so hostile. But all these years of psychiatry have taught me that it's the people who love you who know how to hurt you the most. And although people rarely do things without a reason, not everyone is going to spend years in psychotherapy to discover exactly what those reasons are. Greg would calm down, he'd apologize, and we'd get on with our lives. Because I knew the kind, loving, fun, and funny man I'd known hadn't disappeared forever.

The phone rang twice before I heard it ring, so lost was I in my fantasy of a corrective emotional experience with Greg, the one where he says he's sorry and will love me forever, and that he forgives me for wanting to go to Bermuda and for not telling him about the FBI the moment they'd shown up. When I answered the phone, so vivid was my imaginary reconciliation, I really was expecting Greg.

"Dr. Tamsen Bayn?" I'd heard this British accent before.

"Speaking."

"This is Dr. Antony Hastings-Muir. I got your message," he said obliquely.

"That was fast," I said. "Are you calling from Bermuda?"

"Actually, no. I'm in the city. Just flew in. Would you be free for lunch?"

It had to be a corporate thing. All those Grandines people were constantly doing lunch. In five years of psychiatric training I think I'd skipped lunch more than I'd eaten it.

"Why don't you come to my place?" he went on. "I'll pick something up. We can talk."

Flying to Bermuda had been out of the question, after I stopped to think about it. Did I dare to go to the man's New York apartment? Or was that still a crazy thing to do? I didn't know. But I had to take a chance sometime.

"Tell me where you live," I said boldly.

Twenty minutes later a doorman was announcing me and telling me to take the elevator to the penthouse. I rang the bell of the only apartment on the floor. The man who answered the door wore ripped jeans, a faded polo shirt that looked as if it might once have been yellow, and a lazy smile.

I shifted my pocketbook awkwardly from one shoulder to the other. Anything to avoid those amused blue eyes looking at me as though I had forgotten something—like my clothes.

"I was wondering if you'd show up," the man said. Sunbleached bangs brushed his pale eyebrows, and his golden tan gave no hint of the New York winter. "Come on in," he said, the British accent just pronounced enough to give me goose bumps. "Are you planning to stand in the hall all day?"

"I'm Tamsen Bayn," I offered.

"Yes, and I'm Tony Hastings-Muir. I thought we'd established that." We shook hands formally. He led the way through a small dark foyer into a spacious, sun-filled room. At a right angle to the windows, an L-shaped sofa was positioned to take advantage of the expansive view of Central Park and the Midtown skyline. "Call me Tony," he said. "Please."

"Tamsen," I replied.

"Tamsen it shall be." I didn't understand his smile. I shivered. I didn't think I wanted to understand it.

"You have a great view," I said in the socially appropriate manner my mother had instilled in me since birth.

"You like my apartment? Madeleine loved it. She chose this couch. Let me take your coat," he said, as if he hadn't just mentioned his dead scientist girlfriend in the previous breath. I slipped it off and handed it to him.

"Excuse me for a moment. I'm just making coffee. Please have a seat." He gestured toward the sofa and I sank into it gratefully. Tony disappeared with my coat. I looked around. Beside me on the end table stood an aerial photograph of a house. I picked up the picture and studied it. The house was yellow, with a crooked white roof, and seemed to be built right over the sea. What I initially mistook for a small pond was probably a pool, and beyond it, steps led down to a pinkish sand beach. The water was Crayola-blue. I glanced toward Tony's penthouse windows, white with frost.

"I keep my boat under the house." Tony suddenly appeared, and sat down next to me. He pointed to the part of the house that seemed to be touching the water. "It's like a boat garage. I would have liked to show it to you. You would like Bermuda." I turned to see the blue eyes just inches from my face.

"Thanks for sending me the ticket," I paused. "I'm sorry I didn't get to go . . . but I'm glad we could meet here."

"It would have been preferable if you'd been able to keep our appointment in Bermuda," Tony said in his clipped British tones. "I'd rather not spend much time here. Too many memories, of course. You have some questions for me?"

For some reason, I refrained from pointing out that we didn't actually have an appointment. "I just wanted to ask you about Curixenol. Grandines Pharmaceuticals hired me to help promote it. I didn't know anything about any diversions . . ."

"I no longer have any connections to Grandines. After Madeleine's death . . . they did compensate me well, of course, but I wasn't going to keep working for them, obviously. I don't work for murderers. I'm a scientist."

Tony stood and crossed to the windows overlooking Fifth Avenue, his back to me.

"Murderers?" I asked in surprise. "You mean Ginny Liu?"

"Did Ginny die? I'm sorry to hear that, she was a lovely girl." He sounded sincere, but not surprised.

"No. Not that I know of. Not yet."

Tony turned to face me. He leaned back against the window, folded his arms, and sighed. Then he crossed the room to a carved chest of wood so dark it was almost black. He opened the top drawer and took out a photograph in a silver frame. Crossing back to me in three long strides, he handed me the photo. I recognized Tony, wearing only shorts, seated beside a small blond woman in a black maillot. They posed on the front of a white sailboat that looked big enough to live on, and I guessed from the way his arm circled her waist and the way his fingertips just brushed the bottom of her breast that this woman was Madeleine.

"I keep it put away," Tony said softly. "You know, we Brits, we're supposed to be so good at hiding emotion. But I hide her, instead."

"I'm so sorry. She was beautiful."

"Not just beautiful." Tony sighed. "Madeleine was brilliant. I would have convinced her to stay quiet. They didn't have to kill her."

chapter thirty-nine

I thought I hadn't heard right. "Kill her? I thought—I heard she died in an industrial accident in a lab. Supposedly you went out on workmen's comp for depression or something." Even as I said the words, I realized that I had heard exactly what he wanted me to hear. I didn't know this man well enough to know how he had appeared to others before his fiancée died, just weeks ago, but Tony Hastings-Muir was no basket case who needed long-term disability. I had done plenty of psychiatric disability evaluations. Occasionally someone could fake crazy, but I had never, ever encountered someone who could successfully fake sane.

"She died from getting stabbed in the orbit by a piece of glass, that part is true." Pain flickered across his face again. "Right between the bridge of her nose and the medial aspect of her left eye. You could hardly see the entry wound. Right into her brain. She—she was alive when they brought her to the hospital. Barely alive, unconscious. It was truly one of those freak things. The skull film revealed nothing. The glass, of course, wasn't visible on X ray." His wooden voice and carefully controlled features reminded me of my mother, who also had a tendency to become a "doctor" whenever her emotions threatened to burst through their many cocooning layers to someplace where she might actually have to feel them.

Tony fell silent and approached the window again. It was obvious this man was suffering. He wasn't my patient, and so I didn't have the delicate balance of emotional distance and empathy that came naturally when I was working. I looked away from him, realizing, suddenly, how much pain I was ignoring, not feeling, leaving at the office door after every psychotherapy session and every forensic consultation. It might be the only way to get through my days, but I suspected that somewhere deep inside myself all that empathic pain was festering.

Finally he turned back to me. "Madeleine was extremely methodical in her work. And even you must know that you don't heat DNA on a Bunsen burner! How do you get an explosion without something igniting? Why would she need to light a fire in her lab? Why would she even have the gas on? No, they killed her to keep her from going public and they knew that I would find out. So I took their blood money and I left."

The emotions in Tony's voice sounded genuine. The strangest thing about psychiatry is that some people have a feel for it, and some people don't. I was always blessed—or cursed—with a sixth sense, a "gut" for when people were lying and when they were telling the truth. It wasn't something I could really explain, although I had developed some techniques, or, more accurately, tricks, for report writing and testifying to convince others of my opinions. Still, my reasoning usually stemmed from some basic intuitive feeling. Some people might say that Tony Hastings-Muir was paranoid, that he was unable to deal with his grief over the accidental death of the woman he loved, and was looking to place blame for his loss. Certainly he wouldn't be the first person to lose a loved one and then lose his mind, at least temporarily.

"How *did* Madeleine die?" I asked him.

"She died of encephalitis, two days later. The glass—I don't know, they didn't do a CAT scan right away. Managed care, you know? I heard the surgery department was having their holiday party that night, when Madeleine was taken to the hospital. They were a little short-staffed."

Tony rubbed his eyes hard, with his fists. "She never regained consciousness." He turned away from me again, toward his beautiful window with its beautiful view.

Tony seemed to be struggling to maintain that famous British stiff upper lip. I understood. When Daniel had been killed I'd harbored a fantasy for months that if only I had been there, I could have saved him. I'd imagined myself finding superhuman strength, reaching out to steady the jack, keeping the car from falling on him and breaking his neck. Or sometimes I imagined myself just standing guard, taking the impact of the oncoming vehicle and giving my life to save his. I knew only too well what Tony was feeling.

He turned back to face me. "The thing was, she had found out some things that Grandines was trying to keep quiet. An internal problem they hoped to control secretly."

"The pseudoephedrine thing? The diversions? Had she learned something about that?"

"You could say that." He rubbed his temples, shook his head. "I'm sorry. I'm not normally a man given over to fits of emotion."

His words surprised me. "You're a psychiatrist," I said. "You're used to emotion."

"I haven't actually practiced psychiatry since my residency. I've been doing pharmaceutical research for fifteen years."

"Sounds interesting," I said, hoping to get him to tell me more about Grandines Pharmaceuticals.

"Interesting? You could say that." Tony crossed the room toward me. "Yes. You did have questions for me, I understand. First, though, would you like a drink? I have a good port. Or maybe a cup of coffee?"

Did all of these pharmaceutical types drink alcohol in the middle of the day? I thought of the vodka I'd drunk for breakfast yesterday. "Coffee, please."

"I'll be right back," he said, and I waited on the sofa admiring the photograph of his Bermuda house. Maybe one day we'd become really good friends and he'd offer to let me use his house for a vacation. Stranger things have happened. Although, until recently, not necessarily to me.

Tony appeared with a tray holding a silver coffeepot and a plate of cookies. "It's a long story." He sat down beside me.

"What's a long story?" I asked.

I had to wait again while he changed his position, took a cigarette out of a silver box, and offered me one. I shook my head. "Filthy habit, I know. But I've picked it up again recently. I only permit myself one after each meal." I refrained from pointing out that a cup of coffee and a Milano cookie hardly qualified as a meal. He inhaled deeply, held the smoke in his lungs for a moment, then exhaled slowly, politely, to the side so the smoke wouldn't reach me directly. Finally, caffeined and nicotined up, he spoke.

"Grandines is a small company. A private company. Unusual, these days, because all the pharmaceutical giants are gobbling each other up. They're all massive conglomerates, public companies. Grandines should have been bought up long ago."

"Why wasn't it?"

"I don't know. The timing, I guess. Maybe Parker and his boys couldn't get their asking price. What do you know about the company?"

"I know that they produce mostly generic versions of medications whose patents have expired. They have one really good atypical antipsychotic drug, Xixperdine, that they developed, and they alone manufacture. And now this new antialcoholism drug, Curixenol."

"Yes. And the value of the company depends largely on this new drug, because the patent on Xixperdine will expire next year. I hear that another company is already working on a long-acting injectible form."

I nodded. A long-acting, or depot, form of Xixperdine could revolutionize the treatment of the chronically mentally ill. Too bad Grandines hadn't come up with it first.

"What did Madeleine do at Grandines?" I asked.

"She was a geneticist. She ran tests on new compounds in development to determine their mutagenicity. Or lack thereof. She'd only been there for a year when she died. First job after her postdoc. Stanford. Did I tell you she did her postdoc at Stanford?"

He hadn't, but I hadn't come here to discuss the academic accomplishments of his dead fiancée, spectacular though they may have been. I wanted to know how she fit into the Grandines Pharmaceuticals hierarchy. Could she have had access to information about methamphetamine production? Was it possible that she'd been involved? Still, her work did sound interesting. "Mutagenicity? Like doing all those tests on rats and mice, to see if the drugs cause cancer and birth defects and stuff?"

"Exactly," Tony said.

"I always wondered who did all those tests. Did those Curixenol rats stop drinking alcohol? Or do they just kill them to find out if they have cancer or something?" I'd "sacrificed" a rat or two in college.

"What makes you think she was working with Curixenol rats?"

"Well, that was her job, wasn't it? And you know, everyone is talking about the new wonder drug. But, getting back to the pseudoephedrine—"

"Pseudoephedrine?" His face clouded over, then cleared. "Yes. Well, I did want to tell you a few other things about my work first. I thought you'd find it useful in your dealings with Grandines, especially in your position as the Curixenol psychiatrist spokesperson." He stubbed out his cigarette, and looking longingly at the silver case, drained the rest of his coffee. "More?"

I shook my head. I still hadn't finished my first cup. I was starting to doubt that Antony Hastings-Muir knew anything about the diversions at Grandines. Maybe he really had left the company by reason of insanity. Maybe this whole cloak-and-dagger thing was just an adventure, a way to get some companionship. The picture of his house still beckoned enticingly from the end table. I mean, the guy had a framed photograph of his *house*. How stable could he really be? Maybe he left his job because he was too busy dreaming to do his work. Everyone knows that psychiatrists have high rates of mental illness. And he was so self-assured. Maybe he was manic. Anything was possible. I shouldn't make any premature decisions about Antony

Hastings-Muir. Who sends an airline ticket to a woman he's never met? Is that normal?

"Let me show you something else." Tony returned to the carved wooden chest where he kept his photograph of Madeleine. He brought me a small sheaf of photos, the type of booklet that film-developing places sometimes give you with your order. Funny, I'd have pegged him for a leather-bound-album type.

"Look. This is my boat. She's called *Madeleine's Pride.*"

I admired the boat. I didn't have to fake my enthusiasm; I love boats. Greg loves them too. One day we'll have one. Or I'll have one.

"She's about twenty-five years old, but we took real good care of her," Tony said.

"Did you rename her?" I asked. "After Madeleine?"

"Yes."

"Sailboats don't become obsolete, do they? What was she named before?"

"She used to be called *Nancy's Guest.*"

"*Nancy's Guest*? Who's Nancy?"

"Nancy is my older sister. When I was a child, Nancy always had a friend with her. Every holiday, summers, Christmases, whenever we went to Bermuda, she brought a guest. Hence, *Nancy's Guest.*"

Something in Tony's voice made me look up. I almost opened my big mouth to murmur some soothing psychiatric remark that would make Tony tell me all about the sibling rivalry and the anger that he'd felt when his parents had named their boat after their daughter and not their son. Luckily, I reconsidered. The last Englishman for whom I'd tried to play supportive shrink ended up dead.

"So, about the Curixenol marketing program . . ." The moment was ripe for a subject change. Maybe he could just tell me what to say at the press conference and I could leave. "I mean, I originally called you since you had the job before me—"

"I had quite a different job, actually. Did you know I'd

worked on Curixenol when it was first developed? It was my first project with Grandines."

"First developed? What did you do?"

"I was in charge of the clinical trials. You know, the medication is administered to depressed subjects, and then improvement is monitored, compared to placebo."

"Depressed subjects? You mean alcoholics."

"Whatever," Tony said absently. "All clinical trials are run the same way. I recruited study sites around the country, trained the psychiatrists to administer the medication and do the scoring, and then went around from site to site supervising. It was a pretty good time, actually."

"About Grandines," I persisted. "I feel kind of bad for bringing it up, but do you think I should be worried about their diversion problems? If you're telling me that Madeleine was *killed,* deliberately, by someone at Grandines . . ." I doubted that Madeleine had been murdered, and I would have dismissed the story as the product of Tony's overactive imagination, except for two things: I knew that the Grandines people were hiding something, and I knew that I'd spent several hours unconscious in Vasily Stolnik's car while he made copies of my keys and searched my home and office. So I couldn't entirely discount Tony's paranoia.

"Just do what old Vasily says and you'll have no problems."

"What does Vasily have to do with the promotion of Curixenol?"

"He's involved with everything there. Parker and his boys are trying to whip the company into submission so they can sell it. That's why they're so distressed about this pseudoephedrine thing. It's bringing down the value of the company."

"So who do you think is responsible for the diversions? Think it's Ray Liu?"

"It could be." Tony reached for a cookie. "But I have another theory."

I sat up straighter. "What?"

"Just imagine if someone wanted to screw up Parker's chances to sell the company. Imagine if a potential buyer were trying to drive down Parker's asking price for Grandines."

"I don't understand." He was talking nonsense. "Ginny Liu's husband was fired. Ginny was almost killed—she might be dead already. Obviously, there was some *internal* conspiracy to divert all these shipments of pseudo-ephedrine and sell them to drug dealers, who were going to use them to make methamphetamine. You know, crystal meth, the most horrible and deadly drug on the market? Even worse than crack?"

"It *seemed* like several shipments of pseudoephedrine were lost. But think about it, Tamsen: How often do you think a pharmacy has to return expired cold medications? It's the middle of winter—and a terrible winter at that. Lots of people fall ill when the weather is so severe. Haven't you heard about the increase in the number of cases of flu? You really believe that the pharmacies won't sell out of those drugs?"

"So what, then? You think a buyer—a major pharmaceutical company—could make it look as if Grandines Pharmaceuticals were involved in a drug scandal, without inside help?"

"Diversions, Tamsen. Think about that word. A diversion can be—well, in the pharmaceutical industry, a diversion is a shipment of product that goes wrong, that ends up in hands other than those for which it was intended. But what does it usually mean, the word 'diversion'?"

My stomach gave an unhappy lurch. "A diversion is something that takes away your attention. Something that diverts your attention."

"Exactly. A magician will tell you to watch his magic wand, while his other hand is taking the rabbit out of his pocket and putting it in his hat."

A diversion, to divert attention from the real problem, the real issues. "So where's the rabbit?" I gazed past Tony to a painting on the wall. It was a painting of a yellow house with a white roof that looked like an endless step illusion—the same house as in the photograph. Tony was a man obsessed with his house. Maybe he had a right to be. I'd read on the Internet that the cheapest house in Bermuda cost three hundred thousand dollars. Foreigners had to demonstrate that they had a million dollars in assets to qualify for residency. This house probably represented Antony Hastings-Muir's entire net worth. He was just a psychiatrist, after all. We're definitely near the bottom of the doctor pay scale. And even though Grandines Pharmaceuticals offered to pay me a high hourly rate, I knew there was no way they'd ever pay a psychiatrist the equivalent salary, for fifteen years, when they could get someone for a third of the price.

"Methamphetamine, that's a product with a huge market. Maybe not bigger than the market for cold medications—"

"Small companies with drug patents, that's a product that big pharmaceutical companies want. Why do you think Grandines dragged Curixenol out of storage after all these years?"

"What do you mean?"

"Oh, forget it. I'm just rambling. So how do you like the office?"

"Dragged Curixenol out of storage?" I didn't understand. Tony's expression was unreadable. "You mean Curixenol was developed a long time ago?"

"Mmm. That's usual in the pharmaceutical industry. Drugs are developed but never produced, for one reason or another. You were telling me about the office?"

"The Grandines Building?" I shrugged. Clearly he wasn't going to provide me with any more information today. "It's nice." I stood. It was time to leave. I'd wasted enough time with Antony Hastings-Muir, who'd proven to be a dead end. Good thing I hadn't actually flown to Bermuda to meet with him.

"No, your office." Tony also stood.

"I don't have an office there," I called to him as he went to retrieve my coat.

"Hmm. I'd have thought they'd want you to have mine. All my files are there. My marketing plan, with questions and answers—you could use it. You should ask them."

"I will. Thanks. That would be useful." I followed Tony into the tiny foyer. He opened the door.

"When you go down there, to my old office, could you do me a favor?"

"Sure," I said. "If I can."

"I forgot a photograph there. A portrait of Madeleine and me, in a silver frame. I'd like to have it."

"Of course. If I do go there, that is."

"Take care, Tamsen," Tony said to me, and I stepped out into the hallway.

"See you," I said, but the door to his apartment was already closed. It was only when I reached the sidewalk that I remembered I'd wanted to ask him about the storm in Bermuda. The weather must have resolved quickly. How else would Tony have managed to fly in when all the flights had been canceled indefinitely? And why had Tony wanted me to come to Bermuda, anyway? When you get right down to it, he'd told me nothing at all.

chapter forty

While I'd been listening to Tony's ramblings, clouds had rushed in from somewhere to fill the sky. I trudged over to Lexington Avenue for something to eat, then returned to my office with what I hoped was a still-hot container of soup and made a list of what I knew.

> ### Grandines:
> *Madeleine—scientist—dead*
> *Ginny Liu—sales rep—almost dead*
> *Ray Liu—director of DEA compliance—fired*
> *Vasily Stolnik—seems too nice to be a real bad guy; didn't really press me for info. In debt to Grandines? Subject to deportation? Threatened me—why me? And obviously his heart wasn't in it—*
> *Karen Devinski—marketing director, out of the picture because of son*
> *Jason Devinski—committed crime with Parker Grandines's gun*
> *Break-ins in my office/home/parents' apartment must be related to something Karen has said → or unrelated?*
> *Gordon Ranier—dead on the day I met with FBI agent Jim Mahoney who is ALSO DEAD!!*
> *Antony Hastings-Muir—fired/quit?*

I looked at my list, deep in thought. Except for the fact that it all meant *something*, I didn't know what it meant at all. I paged Kathleen O'Neill and finished my lunch. I was brushing cracker crumbs off my desk and watching the first few snowflakes of the day when the phone rang.

"How ya doin'? This is Ralphie Dupree, we met in the airport."

"Yes, hello."

"Too bad ya didn't make it to Bermuda. I was gonna go today, but I heard there was no need."

"Yes?" When he said nothing, I continued: "Was there something you wanted?"

"Just to talk, Tammy. A nice long talk."

"You know what, Ralphie? I don't think we need to talk at all. And please don't call me Tammy."

"Tamsen, then. Should I come to your office? Or would you like to come to mine?"

"Sure, I'll just hop a plane to Houston." I wasn't planning to be sarcastic. It just happened. "I paged Kathleen. Do you know where she is?"

"She's right here, Tamsen. Indisposed. Would you like to come to my office, or shall I stop by yours?"

"What time will you be here?"

I heard knocking. I asked Ralphie to wait a minute and went out into the waiting room to answer the door. Ralphie was standing there, cell phone in hand. Kathleen O'Neill stood a few paces behind him. She said, "Nice talking to you," to the doorman, and turned toward me.

"You people don't give much notice before you show up," I said. "I wanted to tell you some things I've figured out."

"You figured out?" Ralphie snorted. "Puh-leeze. Don't make me laugh."

By now the doorman's ears seemed to be sticking out straight from his head for better reception.

"You'd better come in," I said to the two FBI agents. I pulled the door shut before the doorman could hear another word. And went back into the inner office to hang up the phone, while the two FBI agents stood awkwardly in the waiting room. Then I showed them into the consultation room, where they sat on the sofa, just at the right distance apart to make me doubt their effectiveness as a team.

They seemed to be uncomfortable with each other. I inhaled deeply, steeling myself for some good cop/bad cop routine.

"Now will you tell me once and for all exactly what you're investigating? I went to see Antony Hastings-Muir this morning—"

"I told you not to talk to him," Kathy exclaimed. "Why'd you do that?" She took off her glasses and rubbed her eyes.

"Tired?" I asked her. "Up late with this case?"

"I have a long commute. Not all of us FBI agents can afford to live in the city."

"You shoulda stuck to practicin' law, sweetheart," Ralphie said. "Or better yet, married a lawyer. Or a rich doctor."

Kathleen stood up. "That's enough," she said to Ralphie. "Enough. I didn't want to work with a chauvinist like you in the first place, but since I'm stuck with you, let's just try to be civil to each other. Can I please hear what Dr. Bayn has to tell us?"

"Fine, fine." Ralphie waved his hand at me in a "so, get on with this nonsense" sort of way. I stood and made a photocopy of my list, and handed it to Kathleen. I watched her as she read.

After a moment, Kathy looked up. "Karen Devinski." She'd surprised me completely. "She ever use methamphetamine?"

"Not that I know of," I said. We were in a gray area. I didn't think I should be telling these FBI agents anything about my evaluation of the Devinskis. "My report will become part of the public record after it's submitted to the court. Can you wait for this information a day or two?"

"I suppose," Kathy said. "I don't know. I'm looking at this list and I just don't understand what you're getting at. And now we can't find Vasily Stolnik anywhere. We told him not to leave town, and he apparently did. We still have a lot of questions to ask him."

I felt a chill.

"Yup, there'll be a federal warrant out for that ole Russian's arrest now," Ralphie said. "It's Leavenworth for him."

"Or deportation," I said. I'd worked on exactly one immigration case, so I couldn't say I knew with any certainty what I was talking about. But under certain circumstances naturalized felons could be deported.

"I'd like to go down to the Grandines Building and look around," I said.

"We've looked around," Kathy said. "There's nothing there that isn't supposed to be there."

"I still have this feeling that the only reason the Grandines people have targeted me is because they think I know something I shouldn't know. It has to be about the pseudoephedrine diversions."

"I'm not happy about the idea of sending you back in there," Kathleen objected.

"Did you have any doctors look at any of the documents you found?" I asked.

Kathy and Ralphie looked at each other. "Medical doctors?" Kathy asked.

"Yes."

She shook her head.

"Isn't it possible that something that looks innocuous might have some significance to the right eyes?"

"There's nothing there." Ralphie was impatient. "Nothing whatsoever. You are barking up the wrong bush."

I shrugged. "Okay. But don't say I didn't offer. How's Ginny doing?"

"Better," Kathy replied. "But not talking yet."

"Can you tell me something?" I asked Ralphie. "Why did you try to follow me to Bermuda?"

"I wanted to be certain about you."

"Certain about what? Why couldn't you just have told me who you were when we met in the airport bar?"

"He tried to tell you," Kathy said. "You just didn't want to be informed."

"Well, if he had told me who he was instead of pulling

that art appraiser shit on me . . ." The man had taken advantage of me. By now those FBI people probably had a detailed profile on me, as if I were a serial killer.

"No, he really is an art appraiser. That's why he's working this case with me."

Ralphie looked around my office. "You know, my daddy
was a doctor. He really wanted me to be a doctor too."

"The bureau actually *recruited* Ralph for a forgery case,
a big one. Long before my time." Kathy shook her head, her
eyes round in mock wonder.

"Yeah, that was back in the days when I was just starting to make a name for myself in the art world. I was young
and aggressive enough to take up their invitation, go to the
academy, become an agent. Full-time in the stolen-art department. Bet you didn't even know the FBI had an art department."

"What has stolen art got to do with Grandines?"

"Well, Tammy—sorry . . . Tamsen, it's like this. Art
gets stolen, disappears, then resurfaces. Sometimes days
later, sometimes months. Sometimes it reappears in the
same city in some gallery, sometimes it shows up in Europe
or Asia. And sometimes the same piece is hanging in two
different collections."

I watched him skeptically.

"Actually, the reason I got involved here, in the
Grandines investigation, is twofold. I had been involved a
little with this Grandines diversion thing, because we suspected that some of the methods that were being used to
make the drug shipments disappear were the same sort of
chiaroscuro that art thieves use. I mean that metaphorically, of course."

"Of course." "Chiaroscuro" is an art term; it means, literally, "light and dark," but it's used to mean the use of
changes in light and dark for a dramatic effect.

"Anyway, as I said, my interest was twofold. One of
my first cases as an FBI agent involved Grandines
Pharmaceuticals."

"They had artwork stolen?"

"No. It wasn't an art case. One of their doctors died under unusual circumstances." Ralphie seemed eager to relate his story. Beside him, Kathleen fidgeted.

"Unusual enough to call in the FBI?" I asked.

"Well. See, that's the thing. You're a psychiatric expert. What do you know about dementia?"

Talk about non sequiturs. "What do I know—what do you want to know? I know a bit. And we're not—I'm not talking to you as a psychiatric expert right now." I looked at Kathy. "Am I?"

"No, no, of course not. Is dementia usually sudden, or is it progressive?" Kathy was interested again.

"It's progressive. If you have a brain injury, you can look demented afterward, and that could be fairly sudden. But Alzheimer's disease, or vascular dementia, they onset fairly slowly."

"Exactly," Ralph said. He looked at Kathy with an "I told you so" expression.

"Getting back to the FBI . . ." I reminded him.

"Yes. Well, I was assigned this case concerning a doctor who worked for Grandines. He actually worked under Dr. Hastings-Muir. He ran clinical trials of new medications."

Kathy said, "Ralph helped investigate—the guy left a meeting in New York fine, and then turned up in another state confused and disoriented. He died a few days later."

"It happens," I said. "Did he have a stroke?"

"No." Ralph's eyes met mine deliberately. "He was injected with insulin. He went into a hypoglycemic coma. When he was finally brought out of it, he was brain damaged. His hospital chart said he was demented, that he'd developed a sudden onset of dementia. We—the bureau—figured out that he was injected with the insulin. A few days later, someone injected him again, and he died. The hospital insisted he'd died from natural causes, brittle diabetes, something like that." He was referring to insulin-dependent diabetes mellitus, a disease that does not respond consistently to treatment. The patients' blood-sugar levels fluctuate widely, and sometimes they die, just as Ralphie had described. But if the doctor hadn't actually been diabetic—

"Someone from Grandines injected the doctor with insulin?" I asked, horrified.

"We never cleared the case," Ralph replied. "And after that I went on to do my art forgery work for the bureau. But it was fitting that I be assigned to this case."

"Do you think there's a connection between that guy's murder and the pseudoephedrine diversions?" This whole story didn't make sense. "When did you say that doctor was—um, died?"

"About fifteen years ago," Ralph said. "Just when I was starting out with the bureau."

"But what has all this got to do with what Grandines hired me to do? Is this methamphetamine-diversion business part of a bigger, underlying problem there?"

Ralph and Kathleen looked at each other. Then Ralph said slowly, "I suppose it's possible."

"Follow the money, then. Don't they teach you that in FBI school?"

"Follow the money." Kathy nodded appreciatively. "See, that's the problem. Grandines is privately owned, by two brothers and one cousin. Those three keep pretty close tabs on their money. And they have lots of people busy spending it. None of the Grandines kids are even in the family business. They're too busy with their support groups for heiresses and having babies with international rock stars and things like that. You know. That Generation L."

"Generation L?"

"L for 'lazy,'" Kathy explained. "They've always had so much that they don't particularly know what to do with it."

"Rock stars?" I asked, a new connection forming in my mind.

"One of them, one of Parker Grandines's daughters, was living with some German skinhead rock star and had his baby, then the guy died of an overdose. Lots of expensive habits to support in that family."

"I'm sure you must have considered this," I said, "but since it's a private company and it's owned by one family, is it possible that—"

"It's possible," Kathy interrupted grimly. "But do I personally believe that the Grandines would go to such lengths to support a kid's drug habit? I doubt it. And none of the Grandines kids, there are about six or seven, are working there now. The last one to work there was a grandson in college; he worked in the New York office during his summer vacation two years ago. This generation is not heavily into work."

I had known a few trust-fund babies in college. Some of them were smart and hardworking, but some were just what Kathy had described—Generation L.

"So—the money?" I prompted.

"We have word that Parker and his cohorts are considering selling the company, to a major international pharmaceutical company. They already have a huge generics division, plus a huge OTC division—"

"OTC?" I asked, then answered myself. "Oh, yeah. Over-the-counter. Yeah, so they're going to sell the company. That's old news. You hear about pharmaceutical company mergers on the news every day."

"Because it's such a smart move," Kathy said. "These pharmaceutical giants buy up the competition, plus, in this case, they'll acquire this fantastic new drug. They'll make millions. Have you heard of Heuer-Robst?"

"One of the biggest pharmaceutical companies in the world," I said.

"Heuer-Robst has tremendous resources. They could finance the acquisition of Grandines Pharmaceuticals through their yearly profits on cotton balls and ear swabs alone." Kathy laughed at her own joke.

"What do you know about this new Grandines drug?" I asked them.

"A miracle drug," Ralph answered. "Cures alcoholism. You take Curixenol, in six weeks you don't ever want to pick up another drink, as long as you keep taking it."

"Are you planning to take it?" I asked, then felt my own grimace as I realized what an idiot I had just been. How out of character for myself.

Luckily, Ralph laughed. "You know, I hate to fly. Especially on commercial flights. So I let myself have a beer. That's about it. And a nice cocktail after a hard day, or a nice wine with dinner."

Hmmm. Lots more information than I'd asked for.

Kathy said, "Not all FBI agents are as smooth as the ones you see on television. Ralph told you, he doesn't do this kind of fieldwork very often."

"I read a lot of mysteries." Ralph chuckled. "It was supposed to be a fact-finding trip, nothing more."

"Okay, so you're not really an alcoholic, that's great. But this company, Grandines, with their wonder drug. You think there's something wrong with Curixenol? But what could the connection be with pseudoephedrine? Curixenol doesn't have pseudoephedrine in it—and even if it did, Grandines owns the factory, they can just make more of whatever they need."

This time Kathy's eyes didn't bother to meet Ralph's. The FBI agents were stymied, and they didn't like it. And neither did I.

chapter forty-one

Somewhere in all of the seemingly random events that had been bombarding me, the key to the disasters at Grandines Pharmaceuticals was waiting, patiently, to be found. I headed toward the subway, my mind spinning. I couldn't pretend anymore that Madeleine's death, Ginny Liu's car crash, and the death of a doctor fifteen years before were all unconnected. But then, how did twelve-year-old Jason Devinski fit into the pattern? Or did he?

The weather had warmed up to a balmy thirty degrees or so, and fat snowflakes drifted lazily to the sidewalks. I stopped by the supermarket, intending to cook a romantic dinner for two that would make everything between Greg and me all right. Normal, I craved normal, and I hoped to find it in a homemade dinner and the bottle of special reserve Cabernet Sauvignon that we'd been saving for a special occasion. I let myself into the empty apartment, changed, and turned on some soft music. By the time I heard Greg's key in the lock, the salad was made and I was slicing potatoes for a fat-and-carbohydrate extravaganza. Greg was the official cook of the family, but I knew how to do it when I wanted to. It was another skill my mother had made sure I possessed.

I watched Greg as he unloaded a few bundles from his arms and hung up his coat. He didn't seem overjoyed to see me.

"Hi," he said finally, standing in the kitchen doorway. "I bought some stuff. You didn't have to cook."

"I wanted to. I wanted to, you know, make everything nice for us."

He came into the kitchen then, and put his arms

around me. His kiss tasted of coffee and whiskey. I didn't comment on the after-work drink; it wasn't the time.

"Well, this is nicer than the dinner that I brought, anyway." He carried in the grocery bag from the dining room.

"Dinner's almost ready." Five minutes later we were sitting at the table, the picture of domestic tranquility. I'd broiled a porterhouse. Greg was a meat-eater.

"This is really good." Greg spoke around a mouthful of steak, swigged some wine like a medieval lord, then shoveled some more food into his mouth. I regarded him silently. I knew he was still mad from yesterday, but being, after all, a woman, I couldn't help myself.

"Is something wrong?" I asked.

"No, no." He chewed, swallowed, sipped, swallowed. His face was a tense blank. I caught his eyes, and tried not to blink. It took only seconds. He laughed. "Okay, okay, you win."

"Would you just tell me already?"

"I need you to do another evaluation."

"Okay." I cut another piece of meat. What I should have said was *Absolutely not,* but instead I said, "Of whom?"

"This is the part you're not going to be crazy about," Greg said. He drank more wine. "I was dead set against it, but the judge insisted. But I promise you, this is going to be the last time."

"This is ridiculous. I'm not volunteering, you know. These evaluations were your idea."

"It's not me, it's the judge. He has this idea that the same psychiatrist needs to see everyone. All the players. I told him it wasn't necessary—"

"All the players? But I'm not a child psychiatrist. Anyway, Dr. Bluecorn is evaluating Jason for the defense, and I'm sure the prosecution will find someone equally famous—"

"You know we've indicted Parker Grandines on charges of accessory to murder. For giving Jason Devinski the gun."

I gulped wine. No. The idea was just unthinkable. "And?"

"So, Grandines claims he did nothing wrong, of course. Doesn't recall telling Jason he could take the weapon."

"Of course he doesn't."

"But you'd know if he was lying, wouldn't you?"

"I . . . I'd know if he was lying? No. I'd have my suspicions. That's all." *That's all.*

"Judge Covington really wants your opinion, regardless."

"Grandines? Your judge wants me to do a psychiatric evaluation on Parker Grandines?" I shuddered. Now I said it: "Absolutely not. That's crazy. I can't do it. Anyway, isn't it a conflict of interest?"

"It's not a conflict of interest if the judge requests it," Greg said, stabbing into his steak as if it were his enemy's heart. He chewed for a few seconds. "But he's insisting. You're going to have to do it, Tamsen."

"What if I don't want to?"

"You can refuse. But then I'll look like an idiot."

"That's what this is all about, isn't it?" I said. "Me making you look bad."

"No. It's more complicated than that, and you know it."

Our eyes locked across the table. I didn't have much of a choice. "When do you need me to evaluate him?"

Greg looked away first. "As soon as possible." He drained his wineglass. "Thanks. I'll tell Covington in the morning."

chapter forty-two

I woke before the alarm clock, imagining the tease of light outside the blinds. Next to me, Greg's breathing was deep, the sleep of the just and untroubled. I'd added yet another sleepless night to my résumé. All I could think of was the psychiatric evaluation of Parker Grandines. I couldn't believe Greg had even broached the subject with me, let alone agreed to the judge's request. But you didn't just say no to a judge, not if you wanted him to appoint you for other cases. Which I did. I wanted to be the forensic psychiatrist everyone in the city thought of whenever something crazy happened. What was I going to do?

I swung my legs out of bed. It was barely six. The phone rang. I grabbed it, hoping to avoid waking Greg, but he was already stirring, hitting the snooze alarm as if it were the clock that was responsible for the annoying ringing.

"Hello?"

"Tamsen? It's Natalie Diamond. May I speak to Greg, please?"

At least she remembered my name, I reflected grumpily, as I tried to jar Greg into a higher state of arousal. He took the phone from my hand with his eyes closed and a scowl on his face.

"Yes?" he said curtly. So far I wasn't confusing this interaction with that of lovers heartsick for each other.

"Yes. Mmm. Hmm. What?" His eyes flew open. "You're kidding. No way. Oh, my God." For Greg to say "Oh, my God" indicated to me that something heavy was happening. Now I was sitting next to him, saying, "What? What?"

"Okay. Don't do anything. You just need to stay there,

don't go anywhere. Don't let them leave. They what?" He
covered the mouthpiece, turned to me. "They're canceling
their appointment with you, at ten."

"Who? Oh." He must mean the Devinskis. "Why?
What happened?"

But Greg didn't answer me. He talked to Natalie, a
conversation consisting mostly of "What's," "Really's," and "I
can't believe it's." When he hung up he had a strange look
on his face.

"What?" I demanded.

"We have a development. The Devinskis are ready to
come to some kind of plea-bargain arrangement. They're
ready to have their son plead guilty if Natalie drops the
book deal and Jason can be jailed in a youth facility."

"Guilty? Just plain guilty?"

"Natalie read Bluecorn's preliminary report yesterday,
and she said it stinks. He's willing to testify that the boy had
an adjustment reaction to the Christmas season, as if that
will get him off."

"Adjustment disorder," I muttered. "Get with the program." If Dr. Bluecorn had bothered to check, he'd know
that clinically significant emotional or behavioral symptoms
in response to identifiable psychosocial stressors were now
called "adjustment disorders." Not "reactions." As if it made
a difference to anyone but the insurance companies.

"What?"

"Nothing," I said. "A plea bargain, okay, I can see
where they'd go for one. But not—I mean, why now, at six
o'clock in the morning? Were they with Natalie all night?"

"I guess. Working on the details of the agreement. The
Devinskis want the case to disappear. *They* want to disappear, as soon as possible. Their apartment is already on the
market."

"But—I haven't even turned in my report yet. And what
about the psychiatric evaluation of Parker Grandines?" Now
that it wasn't going to be needed, I suddenly saw the wisdom
behind asking me to do it. If Parker Grandines was an

accessory to murder, why should he get off scot-free while Jason took the plea bargain and went to prison?

"The Devinskis have had threats made against them. And you can bet wrongful-death suits are going to follow, from the parents of the dead girls or the family of the dead teacher. Everyone's suing everyone else these days."

"If they're trying the boy as an adult, how can his *parents* be sued for wrongful death?"

"God, Tamsen, why do you have to analyze everything to its most trivial details? Someone will sue, and it will be up to the trial judge to decide whether or not the case is valid. I don't know all the ins and outs of suing people for money. It's not my field."

"Well, excuse me. I was just wondering." Why was my voice getting so snippy? Why was his?

"Good thing that this Devinski case is going to be over, anyway," Greg said. "I didn't know if I could even count on you to finish that report on time for me after your little international escapade."

"There was no international escapade, Gregory. I talked to the guy right here in the city for one hour. And my report is finished. I was supposed to see the Devinskis one more time today, but I guess now it'll have to be done without that." I was fuming inside, but I was doing my best not to show it. We were arguing about work. It wasn't supposed to overflow into our relationship. Greg was clearly having difficulty with the entire concept, but as a psychiatrist, I should be, at least theoretically, capable of keeping my boundaries and keeping my cool.

"We still need the report. Part of the deal is going to be that the parents are accepting some of the responsibility."

"The parents? How would that work?" I pictured Jason firing the little gun into the crowd of children, the punch bowl and streamers and decorations and party clothes. Nothing I'd learned about Karen and Peter Devinski had led me to think they were responsible in any way for Jason's bloody actions.

"I agreed to Natalie's request for leniency for diminished capacity. Jason's just a kid. He wasn't raised by wolves."

"But—the parents didn't do anything. Do you want me to *lie*?" Greg just glared at me. "So what's going to happen now?"

"I'll need your report—by this afternoon, preferably. The judge has to be informed of any plea arrangement and approve the deal. He's still ultimately responsible for sentencing. He may want to even have a hearing, I don't know. We'll see."

We'll see, I muttered to myself as I headed off toward my shower. Something was really starting to stink about this case. No, "starting" was the wrong word. It had smelled from the beginning. Now it reeked. And two words kept popping up every time I inhaled: Grandines Pharmaceuticals.

I dressed in a suit, with stockings, shoes, and jewelry, as if I were going to court instead of to my cozy office. I noticed the quizzical uplifting of Greg's eyebrows. After a few minutes he asked, "Hot date?"

"Oh, come on."

"I thought maybe you had a rendezvous with that Bermuda doctor."

"Are you crazy?" I gave him a look that I hoped stung like a bee, and turned back to my makeup.

"No, that would be your specialty. If you can't tell, I must be sane." His voice held no warmth.

I turned around again to glare at him. "I don't get involved with your work. I don't tell you how to run your trials. I don't tell you not to hang out with Natalie Diamond. In fact, the only reason I got involved with these stupid Devinskis was because of *you*. I had other things to do. I had the Grandines Curixenol thing—"

"Oh, yes, let's not forget wonderful Grandines Pharmaceuticals, whose CEO makes house calls on Christmas. For a wacky hourly rate, they bought you, so you could lie and help cover up their illegal activities. I didn't mean to forget that wonderful career opportunity."

"What's the matter with you?" I asked quietly, although my heart was threatening to burst right out of my chest.

"The matter with me? Nothing the fuck is the fucking matter with me." Now he was shouting. "You interfere with my case, you don't find the only important thing that I need you to find, I have to hear from the Devinskis' fucking lawyer that they're keeping secrets from you—"

"What secrets?" I demanded. "I'm not a mind reader." My voice had become louder of its own accord too. "What exactly are you trying to tell me?"

"I'm telling you that you got too involved with this Grandines thing, and that it's a conflict of interest for you to be working for them, and it's dangerous, you knew it was dangerous, and you deliberately disobeyed me—"

"*Disobeyed* you? What is this, the Middle Ages? And *you* were the one who came up with the brilliant idea of having me evaluate Parker Grandines. What about that? Don't you have a court order? Isn't the judge expecting a report?"

Greg continued as if I hadn't spoken. "You know what Natalie just told me? That the reason the Devinskis are going for this plea and trying to get out of the public eye is because they don't want to risk being identified with Grandines Pharmaceuticals. Karen's already handed in her resignation. They know something bad is happening there."

"Maybe Natalie forced the Devinskis to take this plea bargain because she knew she didn't have a case."

"I don't think so. She doesn't quit easily."

"Anyway, you should be happy. You got your precious conviction. Isn't that what being a prosecutor is all about?"

"Happy?" Greg repeated, as if he were trying out a word in a foreign language. "About what? You put me in a shitty situation."

"*I* put you . . . What do you recommend, then?" The icicles in my voice rivaled those hanging outside. I had the impulse to open the window, grab one, and stab Greg with it. I inhaled sharply, horrified. This was the man I was supposed to marry, and I was ready to kill him? Slowly, sadly, I twisted my engagement ring off my finger.

"I'm sorry, Greg. I love you. Really. A lot. But it's just not going to work." I held out the ring, waiting for him to take it. I guess in my heart I thought he'd come over to me, hug me, apologize, and we'd have a rational conversation about what should happen next in Devinski-land, and laugh at how we were letting our work interfere with our lives.

I was wrong.

"You can keep it," he said, his voice low, his eyes somewhere else. "Keep it to remember me by." He walked into the bathroom and shut the door. A moment later, I heard the shower start. I slipped into the study and sat down on the bed. Through the thin walls, I heard the water stop. After a few minutes, I heard the front door open, then close. I heard the sound of the key in the lock. Even in a fight he wouldn't just slam the door and storm out.

I went back into our bedroom and placed the engagement ring in the little shell-shaped dish where I had taught Greg to dump his change. The ring sparkled among the pennies and nickels like a rose in a bed of dandelions. Slowly at first, then with increasing resolve, I packed two suitcases. I'd come back for the rest of my stuff some other time.

chapter forty-three

I guess in many ways I was lucky. I had my own career, my own income, and, thanks to my enmeshed family, I had a room I could call my own. I could come up with a good cover story by the time my parents returned from Florida.

Greg couldn't have meant the terrible things he'd said. Tensions were understandably high between us. We should have aired our grievances and spoken what was on our minds all along. But his high-profile Devinski trial and my questionable role as FBI informer were preventing normal communication. It was as if we'd been forced to speak in some sort of secret code.

I stopped by my parents' deserted apartment first, threw my two bags into "my" bedroom, and went in search of breakfast. I would need to buy groceries, put my things away, settle in. It did cross my mind that my parents might not want their thirty-three-year-old "baby" moving in with them permanently, but I knew for a few weeks they wouldn't object. Or even a few months. The arrangement would annoy me much more than them.

I wished the Devinskis would show up for their appointment. Greg had made it sound like they hadn't fully informed me about something, but we'd been so busy biting each other's head off that I hadn't learned what. I was so beyond caring about any conflict of interest or the ethics of the situation. I just wanted to learn what illegal activities Parker Grandines was hiding.

I went downstairs to the office, and pointedly ignored the doorman who had let the bad guys into the building last week. His job was toast, as far as I was concerned, and he could just hop the next plane for Slovenia or whatever they were calling it this week. I was furious, but I would continue to face the world with a smooth façade of icy calm. I would be the marble woman. Just call me Venus de Milo, with arms.

The phone rang. I had the conscious thought, *I hope this has nothing to do with the Devinskis,* as I picked it up.

"Is this Dr. Tamsen Bayn?"

"Who's calling?" I replied obliquely.

"I was wondering if you'd care to give a statement about the Jason Devinski plea bargain?"

"Who's this?"

"Rory Blank, *Daily News.*"

"No. Sorry, Mr. Blank." I hung up. As soon as I replaced the phone in its cradle, it rang again. This time it was a Mary Jane Somebody or other, from the *New York Post.* If I hadn't been so tense and upset I would have laughed as I called the answering service and told this morning's answerer that I wouldn't be picking up the phone and to beep me with any important messages that did not involve the press. Almost famous. That's me.

As I made the ubiquitous pot of coffee in the tiny kitchenette, I considered whether I could stand to drink it black, like all the reporters did in books and movies. Probably not, unless I dumped in half a cup of sugar the way Kathleen O'Neill did. I wondered what she was up to today, and when I would next hear from her. She'd given me the old "Don't call us, we'll call you," which had to be my least favorite way to work with someone. Would the Devinskis turn up at ten o'clock after all? No. My involvement in their case was over.

The bell rang. Could it be? I opened the door to an exhausted-looking Karen Devinski. Her husband stood behind her, his resemblance to a sheepdog even more pronounced than usual. Peter's big brown eyes were moist and downcast, like a good working animal trained to herd his charges to slaughter.

"So you made it," I said to them. "I got a message that you weren't coming."

"Yes, well," Karen said. "It wouldn't have been right . . ." She fell silent.

The Devinskis had been almost ebullient in our previous meetings, but today they were subdued. I offered them coffee, and as they accepted I had the strangest feeling that they were afraid to refuse it. When had they become so afraid? And why?

They sat close together on the sofa, united in their misery. I cleared my throat and sipped my coffee.

"I'm a little ashamed," Karen said. "A lot ashamed. We pled guilty."

"I heard," I said.

"You're probably wondering why."

"Yes." Ambivalence and subterfuge didn't belong in this conversation.

"I couldn't stand what they were doing to Jason anymore. He was ready to kill himself. He's getting skinny and weak and that shrink, that big-shot famous psychiatrist, he's an asshole. Child psychiatrist, my ass. Bluecorn wouldn't know how to talk to a child if you paid him. Which we did, you know. A lot, a whole fucking lot . . ." Karen's voice had risen with every word. By the last words, she was screaming. Through her tears, I realized she was saying something else.

"What?" I interrupted. "What was that about being better off dead?"

"Oh, nothing. Never mind. We want to *live,* right? We want *Jason* to live. Even though dead sounds pretty attractive to me right now. But it's not a step I'm ever going to take. Been there, done that, you know?"

I let out the breath I had been unconsciously holding as I listened to Karen's tirade. I had seen agitation before, even from her, but nothing this severe. Was she on the verge of suicide? Or was she simply overwhelmed by painful emotions? I hoped she had enough self-discipline left, that I wouldn't need to call 911 to take her to a psychiatric emergency room. Peter reached for his sobbing wife, and Karen rubbed the tears from her eyes.

I admired the tenderness with which Peter hugged her, especially under these conditions. He stroked her frizzy hair, kissed her wet cheeks. I was a little embarrassed to witness their intimacy, yet jealous, too, of the way that he was treating her. I stood up and said softly, "I'll be in the waiting room." Peter caught my eye and nodded. Normally, I would never leave people alone in my consultation room, but in the spirit of locking the barn door after the horse had been stolen, I knew what the Devinskis needed right now was privacy. I still had my questions about them, particularly my hopefully unfounded suspicions about Karen's role in the methamphetamine business, so I left the door open, and positioned myself to notice any movement out of the corner of my eye. If Peter or Karen ventured across the room to where the desk, files, and computer were, I'd be up in a flash. But they remained on the couch. Peter spoke softly as Karen cried, then Peter talked some more, finally Karen said something too, but I refrained from eavesdropping. Instead, I paged through a magazine, admiring all the beautiful houses, once inspiration for my future home, the home that I was planning to share with Greg. May as well stay in the city now; I didn't want to live in the suburbs by myself. Single-family homes don't come with doormen. The minute Curixenol hit the shelves next week, and the minute I figured out who'd been making and selling methamphetamine, I'd leave my job with Grandines (which I'd never formally accepted anyway), find another psychiatrist—probably my mother—to cover my private patients for, and go on vacation for a week. I'd earned it. I'd always considered myself strong and calm in the face of stress, but the last few days had taken some of the serenity out of me.

Finally I sensed movement, and I looked up. Peter stood in the doorway.

"Thank you," he said. "We're ready."

"Want me to come back in? Do you still feel like talking?"

"I think so," Peter said.

"What did you want to discuss?" I sat down at my desk, and waited.

"Our lawyer didn't advise us to take that plea bargain." Karen said. "We insisted. We insisted because my boss said that if I persisted in trying to clear Jason's name, not only would I never work again, neither would you, and neither would Tony Hastings-Muir. He scared me."

I stared at her. "Which boss? Parker Grandines?"

"Well. Not my boss, actually. One of his guys, that Russian guy."

"Vasily Stolnik?"

Karen nodded. "He took me to a deserted office, threatened that I'd lose everything, my home, my husband, my son . . . He said that Parker Grandines is really angry, he believes it's our fault that he was dragged into this mess. I heard that now Jason's judge wants a psychiatric evaluation of Parker—and it's really pissing him off. Pissing Parker off, I mean."

I was hardly surprised that Parker would be angry. But threatening Karen was a little too exaggerated, wasn't it? Although I knew from my personal experience with Vasily Stolnik that Parker tended to veer toward the melodramatic when it came to telling people what to do.

"That Stolnik had some nerve," Peter said, as if reading my mind. "Threatening my wife like that. Karen is an experienced marketing director, she can find a new job in five minutes."

Karen turned to look at him. "Yes, honey, everyone is lining up to hire the mother of the killer. The Killer Mother, you know, like the Queen Mother. Oh, which reminds me. Natalie said the only reason she's dropping the book deal is because her agent died. She told us he committed suicide."

"Queen Mother?" That was a loose association if I'd ever heard one. Until now, Karen hadn't given a single hint today of the erratic, manicky behavior that she'd exhibited at Jason's bedside last Sunday. But this bizarre leap in her thinking, linking two totally unrelated thoughts in an idiosyncratic way, almost made me reach for my prescription pad. Loose associations are a hallmark of psychosis.

"Oh, Natalie told me that her literary agent was English, with one of those accents that makes you go all weak in the knees." Karen's expression was peaceful, too peaceful for a woman who'd so recently been close to the brink of hysteria. She wasn't psychotic. Yet the way her thoughts had flowed from her own predicament to an unconnected British title, to Natalie's—and my father's—agent, as if her thinking made sense to her, scared me. Again I thought about the effect of drugs.

"Now that he's dead she doesn't have anyone to sell her book for her," Karen continued.

I was pained to think that Natalie's decision to allow Jason to plead guilty had been based on the evaporation of her book deal.

There was an awkward pause. Then Peter said, "I suppose Jason won't be coming home for a long time." He took a deep breath. "But if he were, or when he does, I won't even own a television, I'll spend hours talking to him every day, I'll make sure to know who all his friends are. . . ." He turned his head to brush at the tears that had begun to silently flow.

I had once seen a male medical student cry when a mean middle-aged female psychiatrist yelled at him. Peter reminded me of that kid, uncomfortable with his tears, fighting them, but needing to cry them nonetheless. I waited. Experience has taught me that men's tears, even in psychiatrists' offices, rarely last more than a minute. Karen looked around for a tissue and handed the box to her husband. She looked as if she were about to burst into tears again herself.

Peter blew his nose and said, "I'm sorry. It's the stress, you know? I keep thinking about those poor people, the ones in Kentucky. Killed by their own child. In a sick way, I envy them. They don't have to be around to deal with the aftermath of what their son did. And at least, if they were responsible, they were the victims, not some poor innocent girls." The tears appeared again, briefly. "And at least they don't have to deal with reporters pestering them with obnoxious questions every time the phone rings."

"I'm sure that the Towlands would have preferred to remain alive, given the choice," I said. "And they would have wanted to be there to support their son in this crisis."

"Towlands?" Karen asked.

"The family in Kentucky."

"Kentucky. Wonder if *they* ever lived in Michigan?" Karen's own tears had stopped, and her wet blue eyes seemed suddenly to focus. Another bizarre loose association. I was getting worried.

"In Ann Arbor? Nah." Peter dismissed the thought with a shrug, as if Karen had said something logical.

"What are you talking about?" I asked.

"You know we lived in Michigan for a long time," Karen told me. "I worked for Grandines there. Pete was at the University of Michigan at Ann Arbor. But he didn't get tenure, so we left."

"So, what has that got to do with the people in Kentucky?"

"Nothing, probably," Karen said.

"It's just that everyone in that group seems to have problem children." Peter looked at his wife, then continued. "Well, maybe not everyone."

"That group? What group?"

"Group therapy. For alcoholics." Peter avoided my eyes as he spoke.

"I don't know if you remember, Tamsen? About six months ago there was a shooting in Michigan. A boy shot his parents and then went to school and shot at the kids in his class. Then he shot himself. It was . . . it was just awful," Karen finished simply. All the words to describe horror had been used up in this seemingly endless wave of violence.

"And?" I prompted.

"Those parents were in our group," Peter said. "And—

actually, there was another one. It didn't make national headlines; I just happened to read about it in a local newspaper when I went to a conference in Chicago. A boy who tried to stab his parents, but they escaped. The boy is in a hospital now. His father had been in our group. It's weird. I can't help but think that the group had something to do with it."

"The group . . ." I echoed.

"The alcoholism group . . ." Karen looked at Peter without finishing her thought.

"And you think the Towlands were in that group too?" I had a sick feeling in my stomach.

"I don't remember the name," Peter said, "but . . ."

"But what?" I asked.

"There were other groups," Karen said, in a voice so tight and dry she sounded like a stranger. "All over the country. The n was over eight thousand."

"The n?" I asked.

"The number of subjects," Karen explained.

"But *Jason* couldn't have been in your group." I nodded toward Peter. What did a support group for alcoholic parents have to do with violent children? "You told me you stopped drinking before Jason was born."

"I did," Peter said. "Presumably we all did."

Peter and Karen looked at each other quickly, then looked away. Karen seemed to be memorizing the empty fireplace, while Peter stared at a Picasso reproduction as if the key to the meaning of life was about to be revealed there. Only then did I realize what Karen had just told me. "Subjects?"

Karen wiggled her hand out of Peter's and stood up. Karen was ready to tell me whatever secret the Devinskis were keeping. "Years ago, when Peter was drinking, we participated in a drug study."

"A study? What drug was being studied?"

"This is exactly what that Vasily guy warned you about," Peter told his wife. "Parker is already furious with you. Why push it?"

"Then why did we come?" Karen asked him. "*I* certainly don't know why they'd care. What, that people took a medication before it was approved? That happens every day."

"Go ahead, then, honey, tell her about the group."

"I was at the end of my rope," Karen said. "I had been in psychoanalysis for *seven years*. I had finally figured out that I had this need to take care of other people. It was a re-action formation to my unconscious dependency needs."

"Karen," I interrupted her, but gingerly. "I don't need a psychodynamic explanation. Whatever you and your analyst uncovered, that's yours."

"Okay." She finally took a sip of coffee, either to wet her dry mouth or to stall. "Pete and I were together, we had gotten married, but he was drinking. I guess he had some image in his mind of the prototypical professor—"

"Honey." Peter's tone was gentle, but I heard the caution.

"Peter was an alcoholic. He drank every day. He wasn't violent, or anything, but we would go to these faculty things, and he would get drunk and say stupid things. For example, once he told the dean that his wife looked like a chicken, no wonder the dean was screwing his graduate assistant. Things like that."

What was hopefully a professionally encouraging chuckle escaped me. "So that's why you didn't get tenure?" I asked Peter.

"Among other things," he replied.

"I begged my supervisor to let me sign Pete up for the B-22-G study. That was the compound Grandines was developing back then."

"What kind of compound was it?"

"It was an SSRI." Selective serotonin-reuptake inhibitor. This type of drug belongs to a class of antidepressant that increases the amount of available serotonin at the synapse, the space between brain cells, and promotes a feeling of well-being. The first commercially available SSRI in the United States, and therefore the most famous, was

Prozac. "Just like all the pharmaceutical companies, Grandines wanted to get in on the ground floor of the serotonin agonist race. Their researchers developed this compound, B-22-G, and they applied to the FDA to test the drug in humans."

"B-22-G cleared all the early animal tests?" I asked.

"Yeah. No problem. Of course, this was over fifteen years ago. Actually, closer to twenty. So, Grandines applied for an IND—an investigative new drug—to the FDA. You know, the Food and Drug Administration, which has to approve all new drugs before they can be sold." Karen shook her head. "But B-22-G didn't work so great as an antidepressant. When the Grandines researchers did the original studies, they found that the depression scores of the subjects who took it didn't improve much. What they did find, though, was so shocking that it changed the whole marketing plan for the drug, and really changed the whole focus of the company."

"What did they find?"

"You know, people who volunteer to be subjects in a drug study are not supposed to have other problems," Karen told me. "The study subjects are not supposed to use drugs or alcohol, for example."

"But sometimes they lie," I said.

"Exactly. People can be desperate to try the new free medication, so they lie. They say they only drink socially. Whatever social drinking is." Karen paused and sipped her coffee, then placed the cup down carefully without looking at Peter. She bit off a cuticle before continuing. "Grandines ran a study in which they compared the effects of B-22-G to placebo. The subjects all met the criteria for major depression."

She reached for her coffee cup again, but didn't take a sip. "So, half of the subjects—the depressed people—took B-22-G for six weeks, to see if the drug worked as a treatment for depression. The other half of the subjects—the control group—got a sugar pill. You know, all of these kinds of studies are set up the same way. . . . But what happened in this study was very strange. The people in the B-22-G group started experiencing a side effect. One by one they began approaching the study administrators, reporting a decreased use of alcohol. Even the true social drinkers noticed that they'd lost their taste for alcohol. But the alcoholics in the study, they actually *stopped* drinking. The alcoholics thought that they were no longer depressed, of course."

"Which they weren't, since they weren't drinking," I said. Alcohol is a depressant. You feel bad, you drink, you feel worse. You stop drinking, you feel better. Cause and effect. Okay, maybe I'm oversimplifying, but the basic premise is correct.

"Right." Karen nodded vigorously, warming to her subject. "The effect was dramatic. It was unbelievable. So Grandines applied to change the labeling of B-22-G. In other words, they applied for approval to test B-22-G as an anti*alcoholism* drug."

I knew where this was going.

"Grandines began testing B-22-G on alcoholics," Karen continued. "The subjects had to be male, between the ages of eighteen and forty-five, and have had at least two years of problem drinking and two failed attempts at sobriety."

"And I passed those criteria with flying colors," Peter told me.

"I was so excited when I found out that Ann Arbor was going to be one of the study sites. I *had* to get Peter into the study. I tried to get some of the drug to give him, but Tony—Tony Hastings-Muir—wouldn't do it. He said it had to be administered under controlled circumstances. So I begged my supervisor, my district manager, to pull some strings. She was the equivalent of what Ginny is now, but in Ann Arbor. She got us in."

"I understand why you'd want Peter to try the medication. But why were *you* in the study?"

"I wasn't in the study itself," Karen answered, chewing on a nail. "See, Tony had this theory that alcoholism serves a function in the family."

"And he was right." Peter leaned forward. "Fortunately,

we found out that *we* functioned better without its function." Very alliterative. Well, he was a professor of English.

"Tony insisted that everyone taking B-22-G also attend this family group-therapy thing, where we could talk about the impact of the alcoholic person stopping drinking."

"Sounds like a good study," I said. Grandines had implemented this study before managed care completely took over psychiatry, and before even psychiatrists themselves started buying into the fantasy that the right pill could cure anything in anyone. The good old days.

"You know how they tell you in Alcoholics Anonymous that in the first year after you get sober, you shouldn't make any major decisions?" Peter asked, stroking his beard in a manner I'd always associated with Freudians.

I nodded. After working with so many alcoholics and drug abusers over the years, I was familiar enough with the Twelve Steps.

"Well, in this group, they encouraged us to *make* decisions. Now that we were sober, now was the time to do things like change careers, have children, move on." Stroke, stroke, stroke. I hadn't noticed the beard stroking before. Was it an old habit, like Karen's nail biting, that had recently made a reappearance because of stress?

"Yeah," Karen added, her eyes wide. "Remember, Tony had that motto: 'It's time to make up for lost time!' "

"So you decided to have a baby to make up for lost time. And it sounds like some other people in the group had the same idea."

"Strange, isn't it?" Karen said. "We were young. Impressionable. It seemed like a good idea at the time. Most of the people in the group, they already had kids. Some of them were on their second or third marriages already, and they were even younger than us. Their stories really emphasized how alcohol destroys people's lives. We wanted to make up for it."

" 'Make up for lost time,' " I said. "Has a nice ring to it."

"It *was* a good idea," Peter said a little defensively. "We couldn't have known that Jason would . . . do what he did."

"No," I agreed. "You couldn't have known. I guess the Raniers couldn't have known that their son would push his mother onto the train tracks either."

"Who?" Karen and Peter asked in unison.

"Gordon Ranier was Natalie Diamond's literary agent," I said. "He killed himself after hearing that his son pushed his ex-wife onto the subway tracks. It happened in London, last week."

Karen's eyes widened. She looked as if she were about to cry, or maybe scream. She wanted to know the details, and I told her briefly how Gordon's ex-wife had managed to survive the attack.

"None of the parents of these violent kids ever know," Karen said. "This is what people don't understand. They're just *kids*. They don't come with instructions. The whole world wants to blame me, but I did the best I could. You think if I killed myself that would somehow make up for what Jason did?"

I began to answer her, but she snapped, "It was a rhetorical question." She gnawed a nail and said, "Sorry. That was uncalled for." She brushed at her eyes and continued. "People think I must be some sort of monster. They want to blame me for everything. Like this diversion thing. I promise you I had nothing to do with it. Nothing to do with it at all, no matter what you might hear from Parker Grandines or his henchmen."

I stared at her. I'd almost stopped trying to figure out how Karen's brain chose what subjects to jump around to. Had we been speaking about the Grandines diversions? I didn't think so.

"We don't use drugs," she insisted. "I've never used methamphetamine. I don't know anything about how to make it at home using this Nazi method, whatever the hell it is." She looked at her husband, seemingly for confirmation. He nodded his support.

"Who said anything about methamphetamine?" I asked.

"Parker Grandines and Vasily Stolnik." Karen started to cry again. Her husband pressed against her, his arm around her shoulders. "They said that they have proof that I took methamphetamine. They say . . . they said . . ."

"What?" I whispered, afraid of what she was going to say next.

"Jason," she said, choking on her son's name. "That Jason . . . that I . . ."

"That you gave Jason methamphetamine?" I asked.

Karen nodded.

"Did you?"

"Of course not," Peter said angrily. "Are you out of your mind? He's twelve. And we don't use drugs. I mean, we've taken medications, of course. Both of us. But we don't use illegal drugs. What for?"

They'd only told me that they didn't use drugs about fifty times or so. It could be the truth.

"He threatened me," Karen said. "That if I say a word about Ginny . . . a word about the buyout . . . they'll publish the evidence. False evidence."

"I'm sorry. You lost me."

"I can't tell you any more, Tamsen. All I can say is if I do, then Parker will make sure Jason is found guilty. But, Tamsen, he *is* guilty. He shot those poor little girls." Karen stood and walked over toward the window. She brushed the curtain aside. "Look at that. A new year, fresh snow, unlimited possibilities. And my only child a murderer. And I have nowhere to turn."

I started to murmur some words of support, but Karen kept talking. "I wonder if that woman in England is feeling better. I wonder if her son is in jail, if *he's* going to be found guilty of what he did to her. Maybe they can find a psychiatrist who will testify that it was an accident. Since he didn't use a weapon or anything," Karen mused as if to herself, mumbling to the frosty window.

"Kids don't have access to firearms in England," I realized then. "Not like they do here."

"Firearms?" Peter asked, clearly baffled.

For a moment I forgot to breathe. "Nothing. I—I'm sorry." I stood up. "I'm so sorry. I really have to go."

I handed the Devinskis their coats and practically pushed them out the door, not bothering to take offense at the expressions on their faces. "Don't do anything for a couple of days, okay? Please. Humor me, don't let Jason plead guilty yet."

They were asking questions that I barely heard. I didn't stop to answer. "I have to go." I stepped out of the office, and locked the door behind us. "I'll call you. Don't let Jason take the plea bargain."

chapter forty-four

Before I could take another step, I wanted to fully convince myself that Jason was indeed the relative innocent in this matter that I now believed he was. I needed to hear directly from the boy himself the story behind his parents and their life as a family. I had difficulty believing that Jason was the pure evil being that the media portrayed. If he was a victim of something larger and deadlier than anything the media could devise, the first place to look would be the parents. Contrary to recent public opinion, children are not raised in a vacuum. If the parents were innocent, unknowing, ignorant in the truest sense of the word, then I would be compelled to take my suspicions a step further. What could have happened to this child to make him carry out such a hateful and inconceivable act of violence?

Jason was still in the hospital, where the staff liked him. Good. Any and all affection was welcome. I walked past security without meriting a second glance, even though my ID card remained somewhere in the bottom of my bag. When the elevator doors opened, a group of psychiatrists surged out. I knew most of them, but they were so busy impressing each other they didn't notice me.

Jason was lying on his side, awkwardly, since his left wrist was still handcuffed to the bed rail. It seemed unnecessarily harsh to restrain him like that, but I suppose the rules were inflexible in this case. Jason's right hand flipped idly through the pages of a book. The police officer guarding him lay on the other bed, perusing the book propped on his stomach just as idly. As I entered, the officer said to Jason, "Hey, buddy, I'm gonna go on my break in a minute. Want something from downstairs?"

Jason and his captors were bonding. Not that the slimiest characters didn't have likable traits, but so far with Jason, the worst thing he'd ever done seemed also to be the *only* bad thing he'd ever done. He was a sweet, even charming boy. Was he a budding sociopath? Or was the school shooting so out of character that it couldn't even be considered a part of him? I was burning to find out.

"Hi, Jason," I said, keeping any false cheer out of my voice. I've always hated adults who pretend to understand what it's like to be a kid. For me, the insecurity and fears of my childhood are like a phantom limb, starting to itch and ache at the most inopportune times. One of the reasons I didn't choose to pursue a career in child psychiatry was precisely because I saw my own past self reflected in the eyes of too many young patients. "How are you?"

"Dr. Bayn," Jason said, surprised. "You came back."

"Is it okay? Do you mind?" I took off my coat and draped it over the back of a chair, careful not to disturb the pile of books there.

"Not really." He grinned. "Wanna buy me a Coke?"

The police officer glanced at me, then said to Jason, "Frankie is right outside, don't forget. No monkey business." He winked.

"Later, Vito," Jason said. "Don't worry, I'll be good." He struggled to roll up to a sitting position in his hospital bed, his book forgotten.

"Can you get him a soda?" I started to pour change into Vito the cop's hands. He waved it away.

"Ya want anything, Doc? Coffee? They have great blueberry muffins downstairs."

They most certainly do.

"I'll have a muffin." When Jason grinned his face lit up like a sunrise.

"Just coffee, thanks," I said, distracted by the transformation I saw in Jason. "Milk, no sugar. Here." I handed Vito the change again, and he took it reluctantly. He pulled the door shut behind him.

"Nice guy," I said to Jason.

"Yeah, he's the nicest one. That Frankie in the hallway, he's a little quiet. There's another cop, Jesus"—Jason pronounced the other policeman's name correctly: *Hey-Zeus*—"he plays chess with me almost every night. I'm getting really good." I heard the hint of pride in Jason's voice.

"Jason, listen, I know you got upset last time when I was here, when I asked you about using drugs."

He looked down at his handcuffed hand.

"I'm sorry to bring it up again. But this is really important. If someone gave you drugs, for any reason, or if you took them, it makes a big difference. It can make, I mean, a big difference in the outcome of your case. Your mom's company, they have lots of drug-related problems. I'm talking to you now like a grown-up, Jason. I *know* something fishy is going on at Grandines Pharmaceuticals, where your mom works. I know you got the murder weapon from Parker Grandines. I know that your mom is so moody that sometimes she seems like a different person from day to day. And I can see how nice you are. The cops that are supposed to be guarding you, they like you, and you *killed* people—"

"Do you have to keep reminding me? D'you think that I don't know how bad I am?" His blue eyes, so like his mother's, filled with tears. "I know how bad I am. I told you, I feel awful about what happened."

"But, Jason, don't you want to know *why* you did what you did? I know you don't even understand it yourself. On the news they keep talking about violence in the schools and gun control, but I don't see how better school security or gun control had anything to do with what you did."

"I'm just bad. Maybe that's what badness is, when you do terrible things for no reason. Maybe that's all it is." He turned away from me, and wiped his eyes with the corner of the sheet. "Just bad," he repeated, with a conviction that made my heart ache.

"Jason, I don't believe that. You're not bad," I said softly.

"There's no abuse excuse for me, Dr. Bayn. I watch TV.

I know the kinds of things that people do to kids. But nobody abused me. I did this on my own. Maybe I should be put to death, like I put Hannah and Jessica and Ms. Lopez to death. . . ."

"Oh, Jason." My heart felt as if it were being torn in two. "You'll have to live with what you did your whole life. Isn't that enough punishment? Don't you want to know if something else happened to you to make you do this terrible thing?"

"There was nothing else," Jason said. "Nothing. My parents love me. That guy, that Parker Grandines guy, he didn't give me drugs. Nobody hangs around my schoolyard trying to give crank or crack to the kids. That's only on TV. It doesn't happen at my school. I never tried any drugs. No. Whatever I did, I did myself. It was only my fault. I'm just *bad*."

I knew that not a school in America had been completely spared the disastrous consequences of drugs, but Jason had a point. He attended the public elementary school that was currently the most prestigious in the city, and it was located on a busy block within sight of stores and buses and restaurants and hundreds, if not thousands, of passersby. In that school, kids were referred to therapists merely for talking in class, and parents whose kids were found to be nearsighted were advised to consult "several specialists" before doing something as mundane as having their sons and daughters examined by an ophthalmologist on their insurance plan and ordering glasses. The smallest infraction didn't go unnoticed. Perhaps Jason had taken, or been given, something, some drug, on the day of the shootings. But *someone* would have noticed if his behavior had been abnormal for long, before he actually pulled out the gun.

"Getting back to your mom. How long has she been so . . . moody?"

Jason didn't answer right away. "I think she has PMS or something. At least that's what she always blames it on."

"Do you know what PMS is?"

"Oh, please." Jason yawned. "I watch TV. There are

girls in my class." He fidgeted; his handcuff clinked against the bed rail. "I wish Vito would come back with my soda. And my muffin. I'm starving." Then he said, "Yeah, there are girls in my class." He hit the side of his head with his free hand. "My mom has this expression. She says, 'I only open my mouth to change feet.' That's the right expression for now, right?"

He looked so small suddenly, a hungry blond boy on the brink of adolescence, sitting handcuffed in a hospital bed high above Manhattan, that I wished I could put my arms around him and hug him. I didn't, of course.

"I never could play chess," I said instead, picking a plastic chess piece out of the box on the night table. "My father tried to teach me, but I wasn't a very patient pupil." We'd advanced as far as arranging the chessmen in their positions, and learning their permitted moves. It was possible, I suppose, that it was my father's patience that wasn't up to teaching me.

"I can show you," Jason said eagerly. "I think the board fell on the floor." He dumped the chessmen onto the bed.

I retrieved the board and we set up the pieces. I sat on the end of Jason's bed, the chessboard between us. Jason's left hand kept trying to help, straining uselessly against the handcuff.

"Chess is basically a game of war," he instructed me seriously. "You do everything you can to get the other guy's king, first, before he gets yours."

Jason moved a pawn forward. I stared at the board. He said, "Okay, move this one here." He slid one of my pawns forward too. Then he moved his queen to the edge of the board.

"Why'd you do that?" I asked. "Now what should I do?"

"Try this. Move your knight."

I hesitated, then picked up the piece that looked like a horse.

"No, the other one," Jason said quickly, grabbing the knight out of my hand. He pointed to a white square. I jumped the other knight over my pawn.

Jason moved his bishop. "It's a war," he mumbled. "Just like chess."

"What?" I looked at the chessboard in front of me.

"My mom's job," Jason said. "A war. That's what she said to Mr. Grandines. *This is war*. I figured maybe she meant the war on drugs. Since everybody lately is so hot for drugs. *Against* drugs, I mean." Jason's blue eyes twinkled. He shrugged and gestured toward the board. "Now you attack my bishop with your knight." He moved my knight, which looked to me to be in a pretty good position right near Jason's king and queen. Then he all but shouted with glee: "Gotcha!" His left hand strained against the handcuff, trying to stretch toward the chessboard. "Ouch." His free hand plucked one of my pawns out of its place and set down his queen, which promptly toppled over. He righted his queen and shouted, "Checkmate!"

"What did you just do?"

Jason laughed. "I *won*."

"How'd you do that?" I feigned dismay, but his laughter sounded good. Still, beaten by a twelve-year-old, it was humiliating. I should probably learn how to play chess. "One day you'll have to explain to me how you just did that." I began setting up the board again. "Jason. Were you talking about a specific incident when you mentioned the war on drugs?"

"Sort of." He eyed me, probably gauging how far to trust me. "It was when they were talking in the study. My mom and Ginny—that ABC woman who works with her—and that pretty blond lady. She looked kinda like Amanda, actually. Or, I guess Amanda looked kinda like her. You know. Amanda, the girl I shot, the one who didn't die. With that long blond hair."

"Jason. What are you talking about?"

"ABC—American-Born Chinese."

"No, I know what 'ABC' stands for. When did they all talk to Parker—to Mr. Grandines?"

"At that party where he gave me the gun. I thought you *knew* this," he said impatiently.

The door opened. Vito walked in, his hands full with one of those cardboard coffee container holders. "Got you a muffin anyway, Doc." Had I been a criminal, his smile would have pulled a confession out of me there and then.

"Was the other woman named Madeleine?" I asked Jason, but the moment had been lost. Jason twisted the top of his soda off with a whoosh, and started boasting to the police officer how he'd just clobbered me in chess. I smiled, but my mind was elsewhere. I sat on the edge of the other bed, and the officer from the hallway came in to join us. The police officers regaled us with stories of "Mentally Ill Persons I Have Apprehended" as I ate my toasted and buttered blueberry muffin and tried to murmur something appropriate when I was addressed. But all I could hear was Jason's voice reverberating inside my head. *This is war.*

Just what had Jason overheard at last summer's Grandines employee picnic?

chapter forty-five

The fact that Parker Grandines had given Jason Devinski a murder weapon only moments after arguing with some of his employees smelled too much of a plan. The pieces still didn't quite fit together, but I was certain of one thing: Somehow, Parker had known that Jason would use the gun to kill. But how? Karen wasn't telling. Ginny Liu was in a coma. And Madeleine was dead. But I had an idea who might have some information I could use.

I cheated and went back to Greg's apartment to search the Internet White Pages for Ray and Ginny Liu. I hadn't known that Liu was such a popular name. I found no Rays or Ginnys, and I suspected that both names were short for something else. I did find two R's, neither of whom admitted to being Ray Liu. I was momentarily stymied.

I didn't know my way around the university hospital the way I knew how to get around Bellevue, but before I grabbed the keys to Greg's car (forgive me, God, for being such a hypocrite, but if I had to go to New Jersey I'd need to drive), I rummaged through my closet to find a Bellevue attending physician lab coat. Technically, I could admit patients to New York Hospital, but I never had and I probably never would. I felt strange as I pulled into the crowded parking lot and grabbed my ticket, but mostly I felt dumb for having gone all the way home to come right back.

From there on, it was easy. Ginny was in the surgical intensive care unit, but I breezed right past the police guard in my white coat and ID card. The funny part was the way my heart pounded, even though I wasn't breaking any laws. I don't know how people could go through life pretending to be someone they're not, when here I was feeling guilty about impersonating myself.

Ginny looked better than she had last time. The bandages were off her skull, where staples still held together healing scalp. Her head looked like it had five o'clock shadow. I didn't see any respirator or intravenous lines, and Ginny looked asleep, not unconscious, although it really wasn't possible to tell. I didn't see a police guard anywhere.

Ray Liu was nowhere in sight. I approached the nurses' station and introduced myself.

"I think her parents went to the cafeteria," a red-haired nurse told me. "They should be back soon."

"Is her husband here?" I asked, although I wasn't sure if Ray Liu had been let out of protective custody or charged with a crime or was still in hiding.

"I haven't seen him today," the nurse responded. "But he's usually hanging around somewhere. Are you the rehab doctor?"

"No, I'm the psychiatrist." I knew the nurse would automatically assume I was there legitimately.

"I didn't know they ordered a psych consult." She shook her head. "I don't think she needs you, to tell you the truth. Our Ginny is a fighter."

"She's communicating pretty well now, isn't she?" I asked as if I knew, although the fact that Ginny was no longer in a coma was news to me.

"Oh, yeah. Like I said, she's a fighter. She's even on a regular diet already. But she doesn't remember anything about the accident. And the two weeks leading up to the car crash are still fuzzy for her."

I hid my disappointment. "I guess I'll wait for the parents in the waiting room. Thanks for your help. Oh, what're their names? Mr. and Mrs. . . . ?"

"Chang," the nurse told me.

"Do they speak English?"

"Better than we do." She laughed and turned back to her charting. I hit the automatic door opener and left the unit. So Ginny was much better, but couldn't remember what had happened to her. On one hand, not remembering wasn't going to help me get any closer to the secrets of Grandines Pharmaceuticals. On the other, however, if whoever had tried to kill Ginny knew that her memory was incomplete, they might be satisfied with the results of the head injury and not try to do her further harm.

The waiting room was deserted, dominated by a TV bolted high up on one wall. It took me a few minutes to figure out how to turn off the volume. By the time I'd shoved the plastic chair back against the wall I saw that I was not alone. An older Asian couple were standing in the doorway, watching me.

"Mr. and Mrs. Chang?" I asked. They nodded, but by their stricken faces, I realized I'd better say something soothing fast. I'd forgotten I was wearing the white coat. "I'm Dr. Tamsen Bayn. Don't worry, Ginny is fine. I was just hoping to talk to you both for a second."

"Oh . . . yes?" Mrs. Chang said, although her words were clearly a question. "Are you here from the rehabilitation department?" She sank into one of the plastic chairs. Her hands fiddled with the strap of her expensive-looking leather purse.

"No, no. I'm a psychiatrist."

Mr. Chang crossed the room in two angry strides and sat down beside his wife. "We don't need a psychiatrist, Doctor. We have our family. Ginny will receive the best treatment money can buy. Our daughter needs rehab, not psychiatry."

Aside from determining that the Changs had been in this country far longer than my family had, I had no clue which direction to take. I didn't want to offend them in any way. Apparently, the assimilation of generations didn't extend to the acceptance of psychiatry as a necessary medical specialty. "I've known Ginny since I was in training. She came to my office the day she was injured. I'm not here as a psychiatrist. I'm here as a friend."

The lines of tension and anger on the faces of both

Changs eased. "Oh, oh. Well, in that case, we're glad to meet you." Mr. Chang spoke for both of them. I could tell that they would benefit from an hour or two with a competent and considerate therapist, but I didn't venture to suggest it. They would come to terms with their anger and their grief in their own time. Real life is not a Woody Allen movie, and the great majority of people still believe that talking to a psychiatrist gives you something akin to bag lady status.

I repeated the good prognosis I'd heard from the nurse. The Changs' tension lines relaxed a little more. "I was hoping to speak to Ginny's husband too," I told them. "How's he doing?"

"Oh, not good, not good." Mrs. Chang shook her head. "He's a nervous wreck. We told him to stay home today. He's constantly looking over his shoulder. He thinks everyone is an enemy. I think *he* could use a psychiatrist. I didn't know he was so . . . sensitive. In over twenty years, he never gave a sign."

" 'Stress does strange things to people.' " I recited a line from the empathic psychiatrist handbook. "I thought I'd send him a card, but I don't have Ginny's home address."

As if suddenly considering the possibility I wasn't who I said I was, Mr. Chang leaned forward to scrutinize my ID card. I pulled it off my coat and handed it to him. Mrs. Chang said, "Maybe it's not just Ray who's getting paranoid," and managed a brittle laugh before retreating into the safety of playing with her handbag. Just then a policeman stuck his head into the waiting room and said, "Everything okay here, folks?"

"Yes," we chimed in unison. Mr. Chang pulled a business card from his pocket and scrawled something on the back of it. I took it and read the Lius' address. They lived in Westfield, New Jersey. The front of the card told me that Ginny's father was a senior vice president and project engineer for one of the big Silicon Valley firms. I mentally tripled the price of Mrs. Chang's pocketbook.

"Thank you so much." Mr. Chang gave me directions

to the Lius' home, then I wished them all the best with
Ginny's recovery and left before they could ask any more
questions. Then I headed toward my car and New Jersey. I
knew I could make it to Westfield in under an hour, as long
as it didn't start to snow again.

My anxiety mounted as I maneuvered the poorly
plowed roads in the car of the man I thought I'd broken up
with. When I moved in with Greg, we'd decided that we
didn't need to be a two-car family, not in New York, and not
yet. I felt guilty, but I'd return the car to the garage and
Greg would never even know I'd been home again. Not that
he even knew I'd left. I didn't even recognize myself in my
own behavior. I laughed as I repeated aloud the words I'd
said to the Changs: "Stress does strange things to people."

But regardless of our personal angst, Greg was still
prosecuting Jason Devinski. Therefore, Greg was one of the
few people who could do anything to change the course of
this case. I had to convince him to let me keep investigating, to postpone any legal decisions until I could find the
truth, the motivation, behind the crimes Jason had committed.

I found the Lius' home without too much trouble. A
modest-appearing house of yellow clapboard, with white
shutters and Craftsman-style posts and a deep front porch.
It didn't look like the house of someone who was earning
drug money on the side. I recalled Ginny's mother's shiny
bag. This was not a family who needed to break the law to
finance extra luxuries. Something was totally wrong with
my picture of Ray Liu as drug dealer. But that insight didn't
stop my hand from shaking as I pressed the doorbell.

A girl in her early twenties came to the door. Behind
her a toddler bashed some plastic figures together.

"Yes? Can I help you?"

"I'm looking for Mr. Ray Liu. My name is Tamsen
Bayn." I handed the young woman my card together with
the one Ginny's father had given me.

"*Ein* moment, *bitte*. Please, I mean." She laughed,
seemingly at herself, but she locked the door before disap-

pearing into the house. I peered in through the narrow window beside the front door. A minute later, Ray Liu appeared. He opened the door and stuck his head out. "What do you want?"

I was shocked. Ray looked terrible, unkempt, wearing ratty sweats covered with stains. Behind him, the little boy wailed plaintively, "Daddy, Daddy, I need you. I need you to play Power Rangers *right now*!"

"Not now, Alex. Go find what's her name." Ray shook his head. "Lise. Go find Lise." The boy continued to wail while I stood on the porch, freezing in my unbuttoned coat and high-heeled shoes. I'd thought the shoes were a nice professional touch when I'd left the house that morning. Now I regretted not wearing boots.

"Can I come in?" I asked.

"Did Parker send you?" Ray practically barked.

I stared at him. The blond nanny appeared and dragged the youngest Liu off, protesting. "I put on coffee," she called to Ray before disappearing.

"No, nobody sent me. I need to talk to you."

Reluctantly, he opened the door and let me in. "Sorry about the mess," he said, although the house looked perfect to me. The toys and books everywhere just made it look lived-in. I added my coat to the pile draped over the banister.

"I don't work for them anymore," Ray said. I followed him into a sunny kitchen, fragrant with brewing coffee.

"She made coffee." Ray's eyes rolled skyward. "We told her, shape up or ship out. She shaped up. I can't believe it. Sit down."

I pulled a stool up to a center island.

"So why are you here, if Parker didn't send you?" he asked.

"I stopped by to see Ginny today. She was sleeping, but the nurse told me she's doing much better."

"She's not better. Not. Better." He glared at me. "You understand?"

"She doesn't remember anything about the accident," I

said. "She doesn't even remember anything about the two weeks prior to it."

Something flickered across Ray's face.

"And that's my story and I'm sticking to it," I continued. I was sure that Ray was warning me against trying to ask Ginny any questions. Maybe Ginny *did* remember what happened on the day of the accident. Maybe she was scared to admit whatever it was she knew.

"If you want to look at it that way, fine. You should know that you can't predict what will happen after a head injury." Ray turned toward the counter and busied himself pouring coffee into mugs. He placed a gallon jug of milk on the counter in front of me.

"Thanks. Listen, Ray . . . you don't mind if I call you Ray, do you?"

"You can dispense with the bullshit. What do you really want?"

I leaned across the island as far as I could, my elbows flush with the built-in stovetop. "Why did they try to kill Ginny?"

"Because they're a bunch of sick bastards," Ray said, as if it were the most obvious thing in the world.

"Besides that. What did she know? Was it something about the methamphetamine business?" I held my breath. Surely Ray, if he were a drug dealer, wouldn't shoot me in his own home with his two-year-old son nearby.

"There is no methamphetamine business." Ray's eyes were cold.

"I know you didn't try to kill her," I said.

Ray slammed his fist onto the granite countertop. "No, I didn't try to kill her," he said, with that scary look still in his eyes. "Parker's minions did that. I told her, but she wouldn't listen."

"Listen, Ray, I'm a psychiatrist, not a dentist, and you're making this much harder than pulling teeth. Why did Parker try to have your wife killed? What does Ginny know about Grandines Pharmaceuticals' illegal drug business?"

"I told you. There is no drug business."

I sat back and stirred milk into my coffee. I wasn't leaving until he told me. "Here's what I think, Ray. You just listen, okay?"

He nodded sourly.

"Husbands and wives, they talk, right? I know that if something happened at work to upset Ginny, she'd tell you about it."

Ray continued to watch me silently.

"Ginny stumbled onto something there at work. Maybe a memo, or some kind of document. Am I right?"

He shrugged.

"She didn't know what it meant. Or maybe she didn't know what to do with it. So she came to you."

"Yes. Fine. Okay. Listen. Ginny got a promotion. She got a new office, and in a box of junk she found some old papers that she thought were important. She came to me, and I told her to forget about it. So she came up with this brilliant idea to talk to *you*. Because one of her psychiatrist's knows a lot of lawyers, she told me. What a joke. Next thing I turn around and Ginny is nearly dead and Parker makes you an offer you can't refuse. Don't you people care about anything but money?"

The coffee mug slipped out of my hand. Coffee sloshed all over the granite, poured into the crevices of the stovetop, and onto my suit. I righted the cup and slid it away from me.

"What did Ginny find?" My clothes were wet, but my mouth was as dry as the surface of the moon.

"Just some old names. Totally meaningless, if you ask me."

"Do you have it? The paper she found?"

"Papers. Probably a hundred pages. Ginny insisted on putting them in our safe-deposit box."

I glanced at my watch. Three-fifty. "How late does your bank stay open?"

"Come with me," Ray said with obvious resignation. He led the way down a steep flight of stairs into the finished basement, where little Alex was watching a video while his nanny did her nails. She gave us a sunny smile. Alex appeared to be glued to the television and didn't notice us.

We walked through the playroom and entered a study. Sliding doors opened onto a snow-filled backyard. Ray opened a drawer, rummaged through some hanging files. "Here. Here's a copy. This is for you. You take it home, look at it. You'll see it means nothing. Just some old names and numbers from some clinical trials Grandines did a long time ago."

I took the thick sheaf of paper. The originals had been printed on a dot-matrix printer, and the letters were small and faded by time.

"Nothing?" I repeated, flipping through the pages. "Don't you have an idea what this is about? Don't you want to help me?"

"This is my final offer. Take it or leave it."

I took it. I followed him back upstairs.

"I told Ginny it was meaningless. She didn't believe me." Ray took my coat off the stair rail and handed it to me.

"Thank you," I said, although I was seething inside. Ray Liu had to have some idea of the significance of the innocuous pages he'd jumbled into my hand.

He nodded.

"Give Ginny my best, okay?"

"Will do," Ray said, finally warming up a bit now that I was leaving.

The drive home took forever. I remembered Belinda's husband telling me how he felt driving his new baby home from the hospital: "As if I were driving on eggs." That's the feeling I had with these pages in the car with me. Ray had insisted that the information they contained was meaningless. But I knew that because of it, someone had tried to murder Ginny Liu, and had succeeded in killing Jim Mahoney. And maybe even Gordon Ranier. I had to figure out what the list of names and numbers meant.

I took the Holland Tunnel home, aware that I was visiting the scene of the crime that had almost killed Ginny.

Rush hour had started. I thought about how easy it would be to lose my concentration for a moment and miss the car suddenly braking in front of me. Don't let anyone try to convince you that road rage isn't an urban problem.

I pulled into the garage and took the elevator into the building—Greg's building. If he was home already I'd just have to deal with it.

The apartment was empty, except for Inky, who seemed happy to see me, although he's a cat, and I'm no expert on animal behavior. I went right to the study.

I looked carefully at the pages. Each contained lists of names and nine-digit numbers. Some of the names had a C beside them; most didn't. The names were clustered into sections, each of which had a heading: Ann Arbor, Baton Rouge, Boston, and so on.

The names and numbers were difficult to make out, as if the original document hadn't been in great shape when it was copied. From a great distance away, my stomach rumbled. I'd been misinterpreting my hunger pangs as anxiety. I certainly didn't know what Ginny Liu had wanted to tell me about this old document. Were these the people who'd taken methamphetamine? Who'd bought it? Who cared who had participated in clinical trials a long time ago?

I felt defeated. My big quest had been fruitless. I don't know what I had expected, but without a user's manual, this list of names meant nothing to me. I stared at the first page. Ann Arbor. Who had mentioned that city to me lately? I scanned the list. Of course. Now I remembered. There he was, third on the list.

Devinski, Peter.

chapter forty-six

I spent most of an hour scanning the pages onto a diskette. Then I backed up the file on my computer and left the apartment without changing out of my coffee-stained clothes, since I'd taken all my favorite things to my parents'. It was late, and cold, and I was starving and exhausted. But most of all I was worried. Why was Peter Devinski's name on this list? Suddenly, the random places and names were no longer meaningless. I was sure that once I understood what was on that old document, all the pieces of the puzzle would fall into place.

As I stepped out of the taxi on Seventy-seventh Street, a huge man loomed up out of nowhere, right into what mental health professionals like to call my personal space. I stepped backward quickly, twisting my ankle as I slid off the curb and into the slush.

"Sorry, sorry, Doctor, I didn't mean to frighten you."

I looked up. The tall man was holding out a large gloved hand. Ignoring it, I struggled to my feet. "Who are you?" I asked rudely.

"Rory Blank. I called you earlier. I'm with the *Daily News*. I wonder if you have time for a few questions?"

"You must be kidding." I fled into the building before he could ask anything else. If one lone reporter could make me feel as if I were being stalked, Peter and Karen must feel like poor Princess Diana did right before she died.

Back at my parents' apartment, I tried reaching Greg. Five tries, and still no answer to any of my pages. Greg obviously didn't want to talk to me. I called his office, but it was late, and nobody was picking up the phone.

I locked the diskette in my father's safe before changing my clothes. Then I decided to begin at the end. I read the lists of names as if they were chapters in a book—every word, every number, looking for a pattern.

There it was. Louisville, Kentucky. Nine digits. Towland, Reginald.

Sammy Towland was the twelve-year-old boy in Louisville, Kentucky, who shot and killed his whole family last fall. His parents had been named Reginald and Hattie.

I nearly cursed in frustration. If Jason Devinski and Sammy Towland, mere children, had committed their horrendous crimes as a result of something to do with this list, found in a box of junk at Grandines Pharmaceuticals, then Grandines was responsible for the string of murders—not the boys. I had to find Greg before Natalie Diamond cut her losses and went on to find another high-profile defendant and another agent, leaving Jason languishing in the ashes of some plea bargain. If Grandines Pharmaceuticals had been responsible for this violence—and worse, if Curixenol was related in some as-yet-unidentifiable way—time was running out. Curixenol would be for sale next Tuesday—and I had the feeling that it would hit the streets like manna from heaven, as all the alcoholics suddenly found a way to honor their New Year's resolutions.

I was out of cash, and the trip to the ATM would take about as long as just grabbing the subway. I wasn't sure how I would get into the Criminal Courts Building at night, but I'd wait until the morning if I had to. I had to talk to Greg.

I swiped my card through the pesky reader three times before the turnstile admitted me to the platform. Next to me stood a young woman, with long blond hair and wire-rimmed glasses. She was reading *Scientific American*. My thoughts jumped to another dead scientist: Madeleine Balloy, struck by the flying glass in her own laboratory. I considered Ginny Liu, lying unconscious in the neurosurgical intensive care unit. In all likelihood, at least some of her amnesia wasn't faked. I stepped far back from the edge of the platform as the train approached the station. What kind of horror had Gordon Ranier's ex-wife felt, lying in the dirty

tunnel with the subway cars above her, rat excrement up
her nose, and the son who'd just tried to kill her on the platform above? Was it a stretch to make the cognitive leap to
two dead sixth-graders and a dead teacher in the gymna-
sium of Jason Devinski's school, or the dead Towland family
in Kentucky?

The train's wheels sounded like nails on a blackboard
as they screeched to a stop. The doors opened with a *ding*. I
stood aside to let the crowd off. Rush hour was lasting
longer and longer. I wondered if it had something to do with
the popularity of after-hours trading.

I was surprised to find a seat. The woman with the
Scientific American sat directly across from me and I studied the picture on the cover of her magazine as she read. It
was an artist's rendition of a DNA helix, in green, red, silver, and white, against a black background. The caption
read, "Finding God: In Our Genes?" It was last month's issue, redolent of Christmas spirit.

I studied the woman's face, wondering if she was a microbiologist or a geneticist like Madeleine. Poor Madeleine,
blond and brilliant and engaged to that gorgeous rich smart
guy. Poor dead woman engaged to a crazy man, I amended.

The train shrieked as it tore through the granite bowels
of Manhattan, and the lights blinked off, then on, and then
stayed off a little longer before they came on again. My
heart began to thump.

In five days, Grandines's new wonder drug would be
on the market. Curixenol would be a miracle cure for millions suffering from the scourge of chronic alcoholism, a
condition that devastates millions of lives. It was a drug that
would make millions for its inventors, and more millions for
the company that produced it.

It was a drug that had been developed more than fifteen years ago by Grandines, then stuck on a back shelf until recently. I knew this sort of thing happened often, that
for one reason or another, medications took years to reach
the public. Yet nobody had ever mentioned why Curixenol
hadn't been introduced to the market when it was devel-

oped. It was a wonder drug that worked. So why not sell it to people who could benefit from it?

Grandines hadn't called me in randomly, because they urgently needed a psychiatrist for their team. They had called me in because they thought poor comatose Ginny Liu had told me something secret, something that she had figured out was not for public consumption. What if the list Ginny Liu had found was a list of experimental drug-study subjects from fifteen years ago? Peter Devinski had admitted to me that he'd been in a drug study. What did those subjects know? What left them open to manipulation by Grandines?

Had the Grandines big shots feared that Ginny had given me a copy of the list, as she'd intended to? Was that why Parker Grandines raced to my home to recruit me on Christmas Eve?

I shuddered. Ginny's accident *had* been an attempt at murder, and she was still in danger, danger of dying before she had the chance to get better and live. She was in danger of dying the way Madeleine had, a victim of an apparent accident, a senseless waste of human life. And Jason, Karen Devinski's beloved son, had killed—only he hadn't killed his parents. But other kids were killing their parents all over the place. Death by offspring would be a brand-new murder method for some intrepid mystery writer to create.

People murdered for three reasons. Revenge was out. Employees often took revenge against despotic bosses—but a boss against his employees? Why kill, when he could just fire? Love was out; I'd never heard of a love rhombus. Or a love pentagon, if you included Mrs. Grandines.

Only money remained.

Curixenol would bring Grandines a staggering fortune. Curixenol would be bigger than Tagamet, Prozac, and Viagra combined. Overnight, the small, family-owned pharmaceutical company would suddenly be in the same league as all the big boys. I needed to follow the money. But where was its trail?

The train pulled into the City Hall–Brooklyn Bridge

station and I got off as if I were sleepwalking. I emerged into a blast of arctic air and snowflakes large as cotton balls. The cold jolted me awake. I turned around, disoriented, not immediately sure which exit I had taken. In a few seconds I disentangled myself from the city's web and headed toward Centre Street. The snow became thicker, the flakes smaller and faster. I wanted to go home. I was, for the moment, technically homeless. But I was alive, healthy, walking in the city, working on my future and expecting to have one. Ginny had been lying in a hospital bed for thirteen days now. What did Ginny know that made her a victim? Someone at Grandines had tried to eliminate her, in the same ruthless way they'd eliminated Madeleine. Had the same person—Parker Grandines, perhaps—tried to kill Karen Devinski, using her son as a weapon? Did those three women know something dangerous? And what did that dangerous thing have to do with the ancient computer printout Ginny had stumbled upon?

I was so confused. With over eight thousand study subjects, it wasn't a total surprise that a psychiatrist might bump into more than one former participant. But I kept circling back to another recent death: Gordon Ranier's. Gordon had an uncanny resemblance to some of the people involved with Grandines. Like Madeleine, and like those helpless children gunned down by Jason Devinski, and like the family of Sammy Towland, Gordon Ranier was dead.

I started walking faster, feeling imaginary eyes on me. This part of the city was deserted after the workday ended. I resisted looking over my shoulder every two seconds and tried to appear confident.

Now everything that had happened lately began to take on some sort of sinister logic. Now I knew I was a target. I knew I was in trouble. And I was in the kind of trouble that left people dead.

chapter forty-seven

The Criminal Courts Building was open. I guess they were used to attorneys working late. I'd once possessed an identification card that allowed me to enter with the employees, but I'd had to turn it in at the completion of my forensic psychiatry fellowship. I didn't blame anyone for inconveniencing me, though—after all, nobody could guarantee that I wouldn't de-gruntle as the years passed and eventually end up a raving lunatic who wanted to bring deadly force or a Walkman into the building.

The building was even older and more run-down than I remembered it. I was glad I'd come in the evening, when I wouldn't have to debate whether or not I should go visit the forensic psychiatry clinic. The secretaries might be glad to see me but none of the doctors would. I was getting more, not less, controversial every day. The world-renowned Dr. Victor Bluecorn was as Romanian as my parents, but lucky enough to have been brought to the United States before hitting puberty, the crucial time for learning to speak a new language without an accent. Once, near the end of my fellowship, Dr. Bluecorn had recommended that I move to some state that only had one or two psychiatrists, so I could be a big fish in a little sea. I think he fully expected me to take his advice. And here we were now, working on the same high-profile case.

I have this awful tendency to try to justify my existence in times of stress. I spent much less time now than I used to convincing myself that I was pretty enough, thin enough, and smart enough to have a life, but I went through a long phase after Daniel died when my guilt was so grandiose that I believed that his death had been meant as a punishment to me. Whenever something bad happened, I reverted to this "Why me, what have I done to deserve this?" mode of thinking. As a psychiatrist, I was aware of it and tried not to let myself get away with it too often. Most of the time I take absolute responsibility for my actions and their consequences.

So I walked into Greg's office with my head held high. If he'd been here all day, he probably didn't know yet that I had moved out of our apartment. I decided not to mention it.

Despite the late hour, the usual chaos reigned in the district attorneys' lair. Everywhere people were talking, walking, moving. I recognized one or two of them, but I had a feeling that nobody really knew who I was. Some smiled and nodded and hurried off to do their important lawyerly business. At least one murder a day was average for the city. These people were *busy*. Nobody stopped me as I walked past a deserted receptionist's desk toward Greg's office. A corner room with three windows, it was considered a good one, if you discounted the time that he arrived in the morning to find a mouse trapped inside a flowerpot, gnawing on the plant.

Greg's door was closed. I knocked. So much noise was coming from the other offices, the copy machines, and a radio somewhere, that I couldn't hear if anyone said, "Come in." I kept knocking.

The door swung open. "I said, come in." Connor Davis, one of Greg's deputies, sounded exasperated. "Is the food here? I'll go down—oh. Tamsen. Hi. What are you doing here?"

"I have to talk to Greg. Is he available?"

"Come in," Connor said, opening the door wider.

I walked in to find Greg, Natalie, and a guy whom I didn't recognize, deep in conversation, which stopped as soon as I entered the room.

"Hi." Greg was too calm. "Is everything okay? Is there something you need?"

"I—yes. Yes. I need to talk to you about Jason Devinski."

"That won't be necessary." Natalie tossed her head. Her long black hair contrasted nicely with her red cashmere turtleneck, which in turn contrasted well with her face, which had lost all its color the moment I stepped into the room. "His parents want him to plead guilty. Oh, Dr. Tamsen Bayn, this is Hector Suarez, a winter-break associate in my firm." Natalie put her hands in the pockets of her black wool trousers and clip-clopped over to the window in her high heels.

I shook hands with Hector, who looked like he had just turned old enough to shave last week. I didn't know that law students worked during the winter breaks as well as the summer vacation. What dedication. In medical school, if you were lucky enough to have a vacation, you played. Because after medical school the real torture started.

"Nice to meet you, Doctor." Hector looked at me, at Greg, at Natalie, and at the sheepish expression on Connor's face. I knew that Greg and Connor talked, even though they would both deny it vehemently if asked. Real men don't have emotions.

"Hector, why don't you go downstairs and wait for the sandwiches?" Natalie pulled some bills out of her wallet, which matched her bag. I was sure that both wallet and bag were some important brand that I should recognize. Suddenly I felt angry, angry that Jason was going to jail while Grandines made millions, angry that Natalie and people like her could buy all this nice stuff while little children suffered and people died. I know it didn't make sense, but I was furious.

Hector took the bills and left, visibly grateful to be given a task that removed him from the tension in the room. Natalie waited until the door closed. Then she said, "You have no business coming here, Tamsen. This is a legal matter. The deal is up to us. Right, Greg?"

Greg ignored her. Turning to me, he said, "What did

you want to tell me?" His voice was icy, but he was never a man to yield to his emotions when he was supposed to be working.

"I'd prefer to speak to you privately," I said.

"About what?" Greg asked.

"I think that Jason is a victim of . . . of something—"

"Oh, that's profound," Natalie snapped before I could finish. "We're *all* victims of something. Did the parents do something to diminish his capacity?"

"Yes," I shot back. She'd probably hear my theory within five minutes. I might as well attack now. "And, if you're really such a hot defense lawyer, you would argue diminished capacity based simply upon his age, and the fact that he hasn't yet finished his cognitive development—"

"Now *you're* the big legal expert," Natalie countered "Let me handle this deal my way. You are supposed to be impartial."

"I *am* impartial. You won't even let me finish. May I speak to Greg privately now, please?"

"You came to work on your little *relationship*? Cute."

"What the hell is the matter with you, Natalie?" Greg's voice was gruff. "Come on." He grabbed my arm and took me out of the room, leaving Natalie whining in the background.

"Way to go, girl," Connor whispered as I walked past him. I guess Connor liked Natalie as much as I did.

Greg led me into a conference room where a couple of young deputy district attorneys were eating dinner.

"I'm sorry," he told them, "I need to use this room."

"Oh, no problem," they said in unison, grabbing their food and soda cans and wrappers. In less than a minute all that remained of their feast was a streak of grease and a few crumbs. Around here, Greg was the Man.

"I saw the Devinskis this morning," I said to Greg. "And then I went to see Jason. You can't continue this charade. That child was manipulated into those murders."

"He shot them, Tamsen. There were a hundred witnesses."

"Well, then he deserves an NGRI plea." NGRI, not guilty by reason of insanity, the defense that Natalie had originally intended to use.

"He's not insane."

"I know he's not insane. But listen, the plea is really not guilty by reason of *mental disease or mental defect*."

"What mental defect does he have? You didn't evaluate him. You were never even supposed to see him."

"You need to drop this case against Jason and do something to help expose what's happening at Grandines Pharmaceuticals. Their new drug will be available in five days. Grandines won't allow *anything* to jeopardize their profits. If they suspect that you know that Jason became a child murderer because of Grandines Pharmaceuticals . . . You could be the next victim. They kill people. They give them a chance to shut up, try to buy them, give them a job like the one they gave me or a severance package for emotional distress, but if you don't stay quiet, they just kill you. That's their MO."

"Now you're being melodramatic. And ridiculous."

"Just let me talk to the judge. Let me tell him what I know. Please."

"What do you know? Nothing."

"But I—"

"Listen, Tamsen, you've pissed me off enough recently. I told you to drop this Grandines business. It's a dead end. Grandines has its own problems. All I want you to do is evaluate Parker Grandines for the court. That's what Judge Covington wants." He shook his head. "God knows why."

I bit back a venomous retort. I wasn't here to fight.

"I'm *not* involved. I'm not. I just figured out that their drug is—"

"I don't want to hear about their damn drug. What I do need is your report for the judge. Natalie and I are meeting with him tomorrow morning. You don't belong here, and you are supposed to give impartial testimony on the Devinski parents. The judge will want to know if they have the capacity to allow their minor child to plead guilty, if they understand the consequences, and if they have their son's best interests in mind. It will save the judge having to appoint a guardian *ad litem*." A guardian for the child's legal interests, for the duration of the case.

"Well, then, the judge will have to issue a court order asking me to answer that question. I'm putting nothing in the report that wasn't in the original court order."

"Okay, fine. Fine. We'll have a hearing just for *you*, okay? I'll call Judge Covington and ask him to schedule a special hearing just for the psychiatric testimony."

"Don't be sarcastic. This is a child's *life* we're talking about."

"He should have thought of that before he stole that gun and murdered those people. I have to go."

He opened the door and stepped out into the dismal, dirty hallway.

I followed him, after a minute. I watched him enter his office, and then I left the maze of offices and headed for the street. Jason was going to jail, possibly for the rest of his life. And the real criminals, I knew, would go free.

chapter forty-eight

The sidewalks were slippery and the subway was a seven-block walk. I stepped off the curb and hailed a taxi. I'd ask the driver to wait for a moment while I got cash.

On the trip home, the driver told me that until this winter he had never seen snow in his life, except on television or in the movies. If he hadn't told me, his driving would have betrayed him. I was thrilled to get off the roller coaster and go upstairs to my parents' warm apartment. I had forgotten to shop, and ended up making a frozen French-bread pizza for my very late dinner. This had already become my own personal year of living dangerously.

Now what? Somewhere in my bag was the package insert for Curixenol, the mystery drug that had waited patiently for over twelve years to be brought into the limelight by a pharmaceutical company that until now nobody had ever even heard of. The drug Grandines Pharmaceuticals had been studying all those years ago was Curixenol. It had to be. Therefore, Curixenol had played a role in the lives of at least two violent boys—Jason Devinski and Sammy Towland—when they were but twinkles in their daddies' eyes. What was the connection?

Curixenol could have some teratogenic properties. "Teratogenic" means "monster-making," and in the case of these children, it was certainly an appropriate word. Those Grandines big shots had asked me several times if I had read the material Ginny gave me. I'd looked at the Curixenol package inserts, found them full of multisyllabic words that convinced me the drug was safe, and promptly forgotten about them. I realized only now that they'd been referring to the list I'd obtained today from Ray Liu.

I cleaned out my shoulder bag as I hunted for the thin folded pages. You practically needed a microscope to read the tiny print, but finally I found the section I sought: "Carcinogenesis, Impairment of Fertility, and Mutagenesis." I squinted at the words:

"Carcinogenicity studies were conducted in Swiss albino mice and Wistar rats. Curixenol was administered in the diet at doses of . . ." Basically, mice and rats had been treated with Curixenol at doses up to six times the maximum human dose, per unit of body weight. After eighteen months for mice and twenty-five months for rats, the animals were sacrificed and their corpses autopsied for evidence of tumors. *"There were no statistically significant increases in any malignant or benign tumors."* Okay, so Grandines was confident that Curixenol didn't cause cancer.

The next little section was "Impairment of Fertility." It took several paragraphs to say that neither mating nor fertility were impaired by the administration of various quantities of the drug. Well, we knew that, even if anecdotal evidence was not scientific proof.

The final little topic was "Mutagenesis." "Mutagenesis" means "mutation-making." *"No evidence of mutagenic potential for Curixenol was found in the Ames reverse mutation test, mouse lymphoma assay, in vitro rat hepatocyte DNA-repair assay, in vivo micronucleus test in mice, or the chromosomal aberration test in human lymphocytes or Chinese hamster cells."*

What on earth were all those tests? Were they the only tests for mutagenesis? Was it possible to know ahead of time if a drug caused genes to be altered? How was anyone supposed to understand this jargon?

I wished that Ginny were conscious and okay and that I could call her and ask her these questions. But I knew that a drug had to be sound to pass the difficult approval process imposed by the Food and Drug Administration. The answer had to lie elsewhere.

My beeper was beeping somewhere, and I realized that I'd forgotten to take it with me earlier. I followed the noise to the kitchen, and recognized the number of my answering service. I'd been paged three times.

The answering-service lady was annoyed. "You know, Doctor, if you're going to have these hysterical people calling you, you really need to answer your pages. *I* can't be responsible if something happens to one of them." Her voice was excruciatingly nasal. Maybe I should recommend a dose of pseudoephedrine.

I dutifully apologized. Kathleen O'Neill had called twice, and Dr. Gwendolyn Conklin had called once. I couldn't really picture either of them as hysterical.

"Oh, and you had a call from that reporter again." Sniff. "He said he'd try you later. At home."

"Again?"

"They've been calling you all day." You'd think that the woman would be impressed by my sudden fame.

I tried the number Kathleen O'Neill had left, but nobody answered. When I called Gwen Conklin, she answered immediately.

"Is it true? Did your little boy plead guilty?"

"Not yet," I said. "Is that why you called?"

"I heard about Jason's plea bargain on the news. They're making a big deal of it here because of Sammy. I don't know if he's heard, or what he's gonna want to do. And you'll never believe what happened to me."

My chest felt suddenly, inexplicably, cold. "What?"

"I'm on bed rest. I have hypertension. I had contractions. I can't work. I have to stay in bed."

"But the baby's okay?"

"The baby's just fine. But I'm going to lose my mind just lying here all day. My doctor said I could get up in two weeks if everything stays stable."

We chatted for a few more minutes about how helpless and uncomfortable she felt lying in bed all day, while her husband went to work in the morning. Gwen needed to vent.

I couldn't help laughing. "So this is just your *first* day of bed rest? You'll get over it. Now listen to this." Quickly I explained the connection between the Devinskis and the Towlands. "And both of them ended up with violent sons. Homicidal sons."

"A lot of those shootings were in Michigan," Gwen was saying.

"And in Arkansas," I said.

"Only boys," Gwen pointed out. "I never heard of any girls doing anything like this."

"Makes sense. Girls express hostility in other ways."

I thought she would laugh, but she just said, "Did Grandines have a study site in Arkansas?"

"Yes. Gwen, do you know what any of these tests are?" I read her the list of tests in Curixenol's "Mutagenesis" section.

"Never heard of them."

"There's this other woman who was killed. She was a geneticist. If she were alive I could ask her."

"A geneticist," Gwen repeated. "I wonder what it means. . . ."

"I think she was murdered," I said to Gwen, and without warning, everything fell into place.

chapter forty-nine

I tried reaching Kathleen O'Neil again, but there was still no answer. Curixenol would be available to the public next week. I thought I knew what Grandines had done. But I needed to hear it from the horse's mouth. This time when I called Greg at home, he answered. His voice was full of sleep.

"When can I interview Parker Grandines?" I asked him.

"Where are you?" he mumbled in response. "I was waiting for you. We have a hearing scheduled for tomorrow."

"I'm . . . at my parents' place. Listen, I have to talk to Parker Grandines. Can I go evaluate him tomorrow?"

"Parker Grandines is only willing to be evaluated with his attorney present," Greg said, as if through clenched teeth. He sounded more awake now. "In the meantime, I've arranged your hearing with Judge Covington. I'll be there, so will Natalie, and a stenographer. The judge is calling it informal, but he'll be there to supervise." If this were a normal sworn statement from me, the way I'd give a deposition if this were a custody case, it would occur away from a judge. In that case, I'd be providing the attorneys with testimony they'd try to elicit—or withhold—in court.

"Can he do that?"

"He's the judge. He can do whatever he wants. Right now he wants information. He doesn't want anything you might have to say to be misconstrued by any member of the press, or by any—by anyone, really."

"Did Jason plead guilty yet?"

"The judge refused to accept Jason's guilty plea without hearing more evidence."

"What was the deal you worked out? If you don't mind

telling me, of course." I said it without a hint of sarcasm. The only emotion I heard in my own voice was sadness.

"Jason was going to plead to one count of assault for Amanda, the girl who survived, and three counts of involuntary manslaughter, for the other two little girls and the teacher."

"Involuntary manslaughter—so there's no mandatory sentence, right? He would only do time for the assault."

"He would go to a juvenile facility and get out in a couple of years. And we agreed to seal the records, like all juvenile records. It's a terrific deal, Tamsen. Very generous. If it were anyone else making this deal, Bob would have his ass." Bob was the big boss, the Manhattan district attorney.

I almost laughed. "Threw that in as a grand gesture, huh? What good would sealed records do when Jason's name and picture have been in every newspaper and on every TV talk show in the world?"

"Listen, I'm just telling you what we worked out. If you must know, I accepted the deal that Natalie offered me. This whole plea bargain was her suggestion. The judge turned it down. Covington does everything by the book, and this type of deal isn't in his book."

"Okay. So when is this hearing, or whatever you want to call it?"

"Tomorrow morning at ten."

"Okay."

"Umm—is everything okay? Aren't you coming home?"

I didn't answer. I wanted to say yes, I'm on my way, but pride kept me mute.

"Tamsen?"

"I thought I'd stay up here for a few days."

Silence. Then, "I see. Well, see you tomorrow, then." I don't know what he felt, obviously, but as I hung up the phone I felt as if I were having my fingernails torn out, or being subjected to some equally painful form of torture. At least I knew he missed me too. But for some reason I felt it was important that I wouldn't be the first to blink.

Well, I had work to do. I still had to update my report on

the Devinskis. It was approaching ten o'clock, but I returned to the office and sat down at my computer. Then I added everything the Devinskis had told me yesterday, including my hypothesis about Jason's father's use of Curixenol. Finally, I went back to the beginning and made a few changes:

I left the "Psychiatric-Legal Question" intact: *"The purpose of the evaluation was to determine if Karen and Peter Devinski, separately or together, impacted or collaborated with the alleged criminal actions of their son, Jason Devinski."* I also wrote a subquestion for each parent individually.

Then I worked on my "Psychiatric-Legal Opinion": *"Although examination of the Devinskis revealed no abnormalities in behavior, relationships, or child-rearing practices that would have impacted negatively on their son . . ."* I stopped typing. I'd started with "although." Although what? The parents had participated in a drug study years ago. The child was conceived and raised normally. The father no longer drank, although I assumed that he hadn't had access to Curixenol for all these years. Yet Jason and at least two other male children of the study participants had become violent when they reached puberty.

I thought about the possibilities. Until now, I'd been looking at the situation all wrong. I'd thought that the Grandines people were trying to divert attention from their possible involvement in the manufacture and distribution of illegal drugs. I'd even considered the possibility that they'd used the methamphetamine itself to threaten and manipulate employees into keeping quiet. But in this scenario I'd overlooked the critical importance of Curixenol.

I'd promised to call back Gwen Conklin in Kentucky.

"I think I figured it out," I said.

She listened silently.

"Alcoholism is chronic," I concluded. "You'd expect to have to stay on the medication forever."

"That's how they're marketing it," Gwen said. "You keep taking it. Forever."

"So how come all those guys used it for a brief time and then stopped drinking? How come Grandines sat on

B-22-G for over a dozen years before they decided to market it as Curixenol? It worked great. So why not market it right away? Why wait?"

"I've heard it can take up to fifteen years to get a new drug approved by the FDA," Gwen said. I'd heard that too, but at least in psychiatry, we usually knew what was in the pipeline. "Still. That woman was a geneticist. The one that you said was killed." There was a long pause on her end. "Tamsen?"

"Yes?"

"Malcolm drinks," she said. "Drank."

"Malcolm?"

"My husband."

"A lot?" I asked, moronically.

"He took it. Curixenol, they're not handling it like other medications. They were giving out samples in my hospital months ago. They're not supposed to do that but . . ."

For how long had Ginny Liu been telling me about Curixenol? How many people had taken it? Lots of times if drug companies know they have a winner, they start promoting it before the FDA gives its final stamp of approval. But promoting a drug does not mean actually handing out samples. . . .

"I'm surprised that your rep was able to get ahold of it."

"It made Malcolm stop drinking," Gwen said. "I'd threatened to leave him if he didn't stop. And he didn't keep taking the Curixenol. I didn't even think about it twice. I just figured once he stopped drinking he'd feel so good and so happy . . . He stopped drinking, and we decided to try getting pregnant. We had fun trying," she said, but all the humor had leaked out of her voice.

"Didn't you have amniocentesis?"

"Of course. My doctor said everything was fine. But what you've been telling me—they did find something that's worrying me now."

"What?" I could barely get out the syllable.

"My baby is a boy, Tamsen. Oh, God—we're having a boy."

chapter fifty

I didn't know how to answer her. There hadn't been a single case reported in the media of a little *girl* shooting or killing anyone. The bloodbath of the past few years seemed to be limited to sons. Was Gwendolyn's son, too, destined to be a killer?

"Tamsen, be careful," she said. "I wish I weren't stuck flat on my back. On my left side, if you want to get technical. I'd come right up there to help you."

"I know you would. Thanks, Gwen. I'll call you. You be careful too." My hand shook as I set down the phone. I suddenly felt more bonded to this woman I'd never met than to any of the other psychiatrists floating around town.

Many people believe that alcoholism is an inheritable, genetically based disorder. You couldn't expect to treat a genetic defect with a few weeks' worth of medication, and have the effects of the treatment last forever.

Unless that treatment wasn't really a harmless antidepressant.

Unless that treatment was really gene therapy.

On my computer monitor, Leonardo da Vinci's flying saucer lifted off its parchment and flew across the screen. Da Vinci had been considered way ahead of his time. Was Grandines Pharmaceuticals a bit ahead of ours?

I nudged the mouse and my Devinski report popped up. I went back to the psychiatric-legal opinion. "*Although examination of the Devinskis revealed no abnormalities in behavior, relationships, or child-rearing practices that would have impacted negatively on their son . . .*" I stopped for a second to gather my thoughts, then continued: "*. . . the possibility of inadvertent exposure to teratogenic medications at* *the time of conception must be fully explored prior to any judicial decision."*

My fingers felt tired after typing that sentence. It was awkward and long, just the type of thing lawyers liked. It meant, essentially, that the court had better make sure that Jason's chromosomes hadn't been messed up by his father's exposure to Curixenol. And I thought I knew exactly which chromosome had been messed up. It had to be the Y chromosome, the one every male inherits from his father, the only thing that makes a baby into a boy.

I clicked print and then fax, and sent the report directly to Greg at home. He'd probably hear the ring of the fax machine. I sat motionless beside the phone, waiting for it to ring. I didn't think Greg was going to be thrilled with my hypothesis.

He didn't call. I went back upstairs, and I must have slept, but when I woke up the next morning I was still anxious and antsy. Back in the office, I began to prepare for the hearing just three hours away. I hadn't been sitting at my desk scrutinizing the pages of my report for five minutes when the doorbell rang.

To my extreme surprise, Vasily Stolnik was right outside my door, loitering in the lobby.

"I heard you'd disappeared," I said.

"I? I take few days off, visit son. Grandson, he almost walking. I show you photo." He pulled out his wallet and showed me a picture of a chubby blond toddler with enormous blue eyes and adorable dimples.

"Cute," I agreed. "So you came over to show me a picture of your grandson?"

"No, I need to talk to you. Is very important."

"I'm sorry, Mr. Stolnik. I'm busy right now." I spoke the words in the doorman's direction, and harshly, but the pale young Slav just smiled at me blankly.

"I wish for few moments of the lovely doctor's time," Stolnik said charmingly.

"Yes?" I made a big show of looking at my watch, as if I were really busy and important. "I can give you five minutes. But I'm sorry, I have a patient in my office." I sat down on the lobby bench right outside my door. Stolnik sat beside me without waiting for an invitation. Neighbors walked in and out, through the main door that the doorman kept opening and shutting, but they barely glanced our way.

"You are feeling good?" Stolnik inquired. "A patient so early in the morning, you are most dedicated professional."

I nodded.

"You are ready then to begin work?"

"I *am* at work." Deliberately obtuse, I gestured toward my office.

"Work for Grandines. New drug available in pharmacies on Tuesday. We have briefing for you yesterday, but you did not come."

"I'm sorry," I said as politely as I could. "I wasn't informed."

"You have contract," Stolnik said. He reached into his pocket, and I glanced nervously at the doorman and the door a few feet away. "You nervous this morning," Stolnik commented. "Here is contract. Your copy. You forget you signed contract?"

"I didn't forget. I never signed one. I wondered about it, in fact, how come nobody ever gave me a contract."

"Is your signature, right here." He thrust the pages at me. My signature, *Tamsen Bayn, M.D.*, was right there in handwriting that looked like mine.

My shock lasted only a second. Grandines Pharmaceuticals could manipulate research data, try to kill drug reps, and kidnap forensic psychiatrists. Why would I think they'd draw the line at a forged signature? "Let me take this."

He let go of the papers.

"Where can I reach you?"

He handed me a card.

"I'll call you later. I've been appointed by the court to perform a psychiatric evaluation of your boss. I'd really like to get started today. So maybe Mr. Grandines should start looking for another psychiatrist for his Curixenol team."

Stolnik chuckled. "I think Parker expecting you later today anyway. His lawyer is on vacation." He shook his massive, hairy head. "But I am sure that Tovarich Grandines will find way to accommodate you. Is very important for him."

I didn't comment on his pretentious use of the Russian word for "comrade." I think he was trying to tell me, in his own muddy way, that Stolnik and Parker and Jonathan Grandines, and the previous doctor, were all in on it together. Whatever "it" was.

"But I not so sure he will be happy man." He winked. *"Capice?"*

The reference and the implied threat were both unmistakable. "I think you'd better go now," I said to Stolnik.

"Sĕrut-mâna," he said, in a dizzying linguistic switch, and left with a final wink.

I shivered. But I knew what I had to do.

chapter fifty-one

I left the lobby bench for my own office, and had a brilliant thought. Maybe Vasily Stolnik could be forced to cooperate with the FBI. Maybe I could just turn him in and go away quietly. But what would I be turning him in *for*? Kidnapping, drugging me . . . all those things that sounded so ominous were virtually impossible to prove. Once I'd had a car accident in broad daylight on Central Park West. An old man in a giant car pulled out of a parking spot while I was waiting for the light to change. He crushed my fender in front of at least twenty witnesses, literally pushing my subcompact out of his way. Then he tore through the intersection before the light was green and zipped off, while I sat stunned in the driver's seat. Ten minutes later I was filing a complaint with the police, with a detailed description of the car, the man, and the full license-plate number. Think the driver was ever prosecuted? Think again. So I knew what would happen if I went to the police to complain about Stolnik. Nothing.

Then I realized I had another problem. I didn't know where to go for today's meeting with the judge. As I speed-dialed Greg's office, I pondered how I'd interpret my behavior if I were a patient. I was unconsciously looking for reasons to contact Greg. But I filed my ego dynamics away for another day. I fully expected him to be away from his desk, anyway. But he surprised me by answering his own phone.

"It's in the conference room adjacent to Judge Covington's chambers." Greg told me exactly where to go in the fairly recently renovated Supreme Court building, and I wrote everything down, repeating the directions. I remembered from my forensic fellowship days that not all the elevators went to all the floors, and I didn't know if that little quirk had ever been changed. You didn't want to take the stairs in a building where all the criminals' friends and families gathered, even if a metal detector guarded the door, and even if those guys were all innocent until proven guilty. The sad truth was that most of them *were* proven guilty.

Greg asked me to fax him my report.

"I sent it to you at home last night." I was momentarily relieved he hadn't read it yet.

"Could you fax it to me again?" He was very businesslike, as if I were a stranger.

I opened up my report and sent it to Greg's office fax machine. Then I waited for the fallout, feeling cheated that I'd wasted all that angst last night, when he hadn't even read my opinion yet. Why hadn't he checked the fax machine at home? Had he been out all night?

Adrenaline was coursing through my veins. I was ready to rock and roll. I was anxious, but I felt something else too. For the first time in days, I felt confident. Now just to stay busy until it was time to leave. When you wake up at five A.M. from stress, it helps to have something to occupy your mind. I was already dressed, and my makeup was perfect. Even my hair looked nice.

I picked up the list of names I'd obtained from Ray Liu, which I hadn't finished reading the previous night. Reading backward, I'd stopped at Boston. I flipped to the Boston section, feeling that I might as well finish the task I'd assigned myself. But then I spotted something that almost stopped my heart.

Gordon Ranier was the last name on the list.

chapter fifty-two

After I stopped shaking, I realized I was still no closer to the truth. Gordon had participated in a drug study run by Grandines, apparently many years ago. Even if I was right, even if what his son had done was somehow related, so what? Why would that give anyone a reason to kill him? I could speculate all day, but the judge wouldn't want to be kept waiting.

My mother would call today's weather "sun with teeth" (it sounds better in Romanian). Today would be a day with teeth. Usually I loved testifying, loved having the undivided attention of everyone in the courtroom, loved being sworn in as an expert as if I were really somebody important with something to say.

But today would be different. Today, I would have to sit around a table with Judge Randolph Covington, with the Devinskis and Natalie and possibly even Jason. I'd have to answer Greg's questions honestly, knowing that as I did so, I was destroying his case, and with every word setting a more and more dangerous trap for myself. And worse, I'd have to sit near him feeling all the old feelings and wondering for the millionth time if I had done the right thing by leaving.

When I could procrastinate no longer, I put on my coat and set off. I greeted the doorman bravely, trying not to look like a rejected woman running home to mommy. My parents weren't even home, didn't even know I was here, and I'd been avoiding their calls so I wouldn't have to confess what had happened. I had to stop obsessing about my love life, and focus on Jason and the possibilities the future held for him. I had a few huge gaps I desperately needed to fill, before I stated my opinion with a reasonable degree of medical certainty. I couldn't just start blabbing to the judge. Just as in court, I'd have to be guided by the questions the attorneys asked me.

On the subway I sat in a private fog, as if the other commuters were holograms and I were the only real human on the train. I emerged from the train station and was dazzled by sunlight. I put on my sunglasses and walked carefully in my court shoes among the piles of dirty old snow. I should have worn boots, but it was just too cumbersome to schlep my shoes with me and change.

The line at the metal detectors was short again this morning. Maybe it's always shorter in this building. I passed through without beeping and found Judge Covington's chambers right away. I was nervous. Usually a deposition is taken outside the judge's presence. In this case, Judge Covington had ordered my evaluation of the Devinskis, and he wanted to be present to hear what I had found and to ask his own questions. In such an instance, I would have expected a real hearing, in a courtroom, but for some reason the attorneys had agreed that this proceeding should be closed and informal, and that my testimony would be reviewed and used at trial only if it was absolutely necessary. I was starting to learn that real life was sometimes very different from the legal dramas on TV.

A bored secretary directed me to a small conference room. I was the first to arrive. The scarred table and mismatched chairs would have been at home in any state psychiatric hospital. I took off my coat, shoved my hat, scarf, and gloves into a sleeve, and threw the whole jumble over one of the chairs placed against the wall. I sat down at the table and pulled my Devinski folders out of my bag. I practically had their life stories memorized by now, but I was too anxious to sit and do nothing. Every hiss of the radiator and every creak of the floorboards outside the door made me jump.

When Greg finally walked in five minutes later, my heart began to beat like a war drum. I'd never given birth, but I suspected that this was how I'd feel being wheeled into the delivery room. There was no turning back now.

"Tamsen." Greg was smiling, and looked happy to see me, as if nothing were wrong, as if nothing had changed. If you didn't count the dark circles under his eyes and the patch of cheek he'd missed while shaving. "This is Judge Covington."

I shook hands with the judge, who thanked me for coming. Judge Covington appeared to be in his early sixties, short, trim, with gray hair still thick on top, and a whiter goatee. He wore a suit and tie, but no judicial robe. His eyes were a brilliant blue. In contrast, the court reporter, whom I identified by the stenography paraphernalia she carried, was at least six feet tall and the color of mahogany, with shoulder-length hair in a hundred braids ending in white and silver beads. She smiled and nodded to me as she began setting up her equipment at the end of the table.

"Prosecution on this side, okay? Defense here. Your Honor, you can sit at the head of the table." She had her own system for typing into her machine, which was hooked up to a laptop computer. Belinda had once told me that the new system was so entrancing when used in court, with laptops in front of the lawyers, that litigators ran the risk of reading testimony as if it were a story and forgetting to interject and object. "Doctor, you sit here, on the prosecution side, please."

The door flew open again and Peter and Karen Devinski entered, with Natalie right behind them. In the flurry of handshakes and "Good mornings," I felt almost normal, as if this case were routine, as if the outrage that I knew was soon going to be heaped upon me were merely an abstract concept.

"You look tired," Karen Devinski said to me quietly, as the judge and lawyers discussed the format of my testimony.

I slid into my seat, leaving an empty chair between Greg and myself. "I'll be okay." I knew Karen had questions to ask me. Some of them I couldn't handle. Some of them would be answered in the next few minutes.

"Let's begin with you, Mr. Jolson." Judge Covington's voice left no room for argument. "I take it both sides stipulate to the doctor's qualifications."

"Yes, Your Honor," Greg and Natalie chanted. They meant that they both agreed that I could be an expert witness and they would forgo the pleasure of attempting to annihilate my credentials in court.

"Nonetheless," Covington said, "would you please state your name and qualifications for the record, Dr. Bayn?" Normally the court reporter would do this part, but today the judge swore me in himself. When Greg said informal, he wasn't kidding.

The court reporter's eyes were glued to us, not even glancing down at her fingers as they flew soundlessly over the keys of her special machine. She winked at me as I spelled my name, probably sensing my nervousness.

I listed my college, medical school, residency, and fellowship. "I have a copy of my CV," I said, gesturing toward my bag.

"We'll take it," the judge said. "Please mark this as Exhibit One." He handed the CV to the stenographer, who stuck a not-very-official-looking sticker on it. "And your report?"

"Here's a copy, Your Honor." Greg passed it to the judge, who barely looked at it before placing it carefully on top of my résumé.

"Please mark this as Exhibit Two," Judge Covington instructed. The stenographer marked it. The judge glanced at the first page, then something seemed to hook him and he read the whole thing through to the end. He was a fast reader, but the rest of us sat in silence for about ten minutes, waiting.

The judge placed the report on the table in front of him. His expression remained neutral.

"Ready?" Judge Covington looked at Greg, then Natalie. Both nodded. "Mr. Jolson?"

"Dr. Bayn," Greg began, "did there come a time when

you were asked to evaluate Mr. and Mrs. Devinski, Peter and Karen, and give your psychiatric opinion on their mental states?"

"Yes." My heart was ticking like a time bomb.

"Could you tell us what you found?"

Natalie looked at Greg with open curiosity. I knew that he would normally never ask such a general question. Especially when he wasn't going to like the answer.

"Withdrawn," Greg said. "Let me rephrase that. Doctor, could you describe for us the psychiatric history and current mental status of Mrs. Karen Devinski?"

"Certainly." I took a deep breath. This was easy. "Karen Devinski is a forty-seven-year-old married white female, the mother of a twelve-year-old boy, Jason. She is currently seeing a therapist privately. She is not taking any psychotropic medication. She first saw a psychiatrist for psychotherapy during her college years." I went on to summarize everything that Karen had told me about her psychiatric history, and all that I knew from her records. All this information had been available to the court for a long time. I was surprised that Greg wanted me to go over all the details.

"Does Mrs. Devinski have a psychiatric diagnosis?" he asked.

"By history." I took a deep breath to slow myself down, and explained. "I reviewed all the available psychiatric records pertaining to Mrs. Devinski. According to some of those records, she has a diagnosis of major depression, mild to moderate, recurrent. But I *personally* did not observe any signs nor did I elicit any symptoms of major depression from Mrs. Devinski." I didn't feel the need to mention Karen's wildly erratic behavior over the past few days. I'd come to believe that her moodswings and agitation were a result of the massive amount of stress in her life. Belatedly, I realized I should have obtained blood work, including serum toxicology, on both of the Devinskis. Oh, well. If my theory was right, even if they did dabble in methamphetamine, even if they did use drugs, it would soon be irrelevant.

"Okay." Greg nodded. "Now, can you tell us—"

"Excuse me," Judge Covington interrupted. "I'm sorry. I have a question, Doctor. You said that Mrs. Devinski was not depressed?"

"No. I mean, yes, I said she was not, is not, depressed. She does not meet the criteria for major depression."

"Could you explain what you mean, please? With this legal case, and her son in detention, and all the publicity, wouldn't you expect her to be depressed?"

"Well, she certainly has been *unhappy*," I answered. "You're absolutely right about that. At times she's even been despondent."

Karen gave me an encouraging look. I thought she clasped her husband's hand under the table.

"But major depression is an *illness*, Your Honor. We have specific criteria that we use to make this diagnosis. Mrs. Devinski doesn't meet those criteria. She had a little weight loss, and a little insomnia, and quite a lot of agitation, but she had *reasons*. She was under an enormous amount of stress. Mrs. Devinski's emotional response to her son's actions and everything that has followed is totally normal. I would expect her to be tearful at times, enraged. She was, but she was able to cope. She was also able to rally to support her son when he needed it most. She does not meet the criteria for major depression." Across from me, both Devinskis were nodding.

As usual, I had said a little more than I needed to, but the judge seemed to understand my point, and didn't mind the editorializing. When you testify as an expert you get away with a lot of opinions, not just medical ones.

"Thank you," he said. "Please proceed."

"Dr. Bayn," Greg said, "could you tell us the reason you were asked to evaluate Mrs. Devinski? The psychiatric-legal question?"

He had my report on the table in front of him. He could have read the question himself. Did he want to fluster me, make me lose my train of thought, drive me crazy?

I read, "*The purpose of the evaluation was to determine*

if Karen and Peter Devinski, separately or together, impacted or collaborated with the alleged criminal actions of their son, Jason Devinski."

Greg was staring at me. I looked away. What the hell did I have principles for?

"Doctor? Are you all right?" The judge was watching me curiously.

"Oh, I'm sorry. Could you repeat the question?"

"What were your findings on this issue?" Greg asked formally. "Specifically as it relates to Karen Devinski."

"I found that Mrs. Devinski was a good mother, a perfectly adequate mother, and I could not find any connection between any history of depression and her son's criminal behavior."

"Was there any indication that any prenatal stressors, any problems with labor or delivery or anything like that, could have caused psychiatric damage in the child?"

"Objection," Natalie snapped.

Now six pairs of eyes turned to look at her. Why would she object to something that might help her client? From the look Peter and Karen Devinski exchanged, I imagined they were thinking the same thing I was.

"I have a report from Dr. Bluecorn, the child psychiatrist, on this issue, Your Honor. This issue is outside of Dr. Bayn's area of expertise." Natalie set her pen down with an air of finality. She hadn't actually written anything either.

"Worried about appeal, counselor?" the judge asked her. "I'll allow it, regardless."

Now six pairs of eyes were on me. I liked the way the court reporter was paying attention. Some of them really got involved in the proceedings, like this one. Others were no more than human tape recorders.

"No. I didn't find anything like that. Mrs. Devinski did not *knowingly* expose her child to anything known to cause neurological or psychiatric or physical damage."

"Thank you," Greg said, his green eyes on mine. I felt that familiar feeling, again. Or still. Damn him.

"Counselor?" The judge addressed Natalie.

"Thank you," she said. "Dr. Bayn, isn't it possible that Jason was adversely affected by his mother working?"

"Objection," Greg said. "Come on. You just objected to my question about prenatal influences. Now you want her to testify to how *Jason* was affected?"

"Let me rephrase the question, then," Natalie persisted, unruffled. For the first time, I could see why she earned the big bucks. "Doctor, did Mrs. Devinski work while she was raising Jason?"

"Yes."

"Is it possible that she might have missed some parts of her son's development?"

I waited, but nobody objected, so I had to answer. "Yes," I said. Where the hell was Natalie going with this line of questioning? I hadn't forgotten that Natalie had a young daughter, that she shared custody with her ex-husband. Natalie herself was a working mother, a *divorced* working mother, in fact. "She might have missed some developmental milestones. First step, first tooth. Mrs. Devinski may have seen them later in the day—"

"Thank you, Doctor." Natalie cut me off before I could point out that it was entirely possible for a stay-at-home mother to, for example, be in the bathroom at the exact moment that her child took his first step in the living room.

"In general," Natalie continued, "isn't it true that children of working mothers have more problems than those of stay-at-home mothers?"

I laughed out loud. "No," I said, shaking my head for emphasis. "It's not true. No study has found conclusively that either one is better. Or worse."

"So, even though Mrs. Devinski was a neurotic, depressed working woman, you don't believe that her child was adversely affected by this?"

"Objection," Greg said. "Natalie, what the hell's the matter with you?"

I felt my mouth drop open in amazement. I knew that in more than a dozen years of practicing law, Greg had never, ever, committed such a faux pas as swearing during a court proceeding.

"Your Honor," he said. "I'm sorry. This case seems to have brought out the worst in me." He looked at me. I blinked. We'd deal with this issue, as they liked to say, later.

"Proceed, Mr. Jolson," the judge said. Did I see a twinkle in his blue eyes? Of course, he knew that Greg and I were a couple. I had insisted that Greg inform the judge at the very beginning of the proceedings, before I agreed to take the case.

"I object to counsel's last question," Greg said, in control now. "Dr. Bayn never indicated that Mrs. Devinski was a— Simone, could you read that part back to us?"

Simone, the court reporter, read in a voice devoid of emotion, "*So, even though Mrs. Devinski was a neurotic, depressed working woman, you don't believe that her child was adversely affected by this?*" Simone wore a wide gold wedding band. Probably a working mother herself.

" 'A neurotic, depressed working woman,' " Greg repeated. "I didn't hear Dr. Bayn use those words. I heard her say that Mrs. Devinski was a good mother."

"An adequate mother," Natalie countered.

"Off the record," Judge Covington said. "Counselors, I'll see you both in my chambers."

Like marionettes, Greg and Natalie got up from the table and followed the judge into his office.

Simone shook her braids and said, "Well, that girl has one major problem with handsome Mr. Jolson."

"Yeah," I said. "Me."

"They're engaged," Karen said, indicating me.

"Congratulations." Simone's smile was dazzling. "When's the big day?"

"Never," I replied, fighting to keep the bitterness out of my voice. "We broke up."

"What?" Even Peter was shocked.

"I don't really want to talk about it right now," I apologized.

"Was it something to do with our case?" Karen began, then fell silent as the door opened and the judge reentered, flanked by a subdued-looking Gregory and an even more subdued Natalie.

"Okay, we're back on the record," Judge Covington announced. "Please continue."

"No further questions," Natalie said. "Let's do Peter Devinski."

"Do you have any questions, Your Honor?" Greg asked.

"No. Please proceed."

"Dr. Bayn. Did there come a time when you evaluated Mr. Peter Devinski for this court?"

"Yes."

"And could you tell us the purpose of the evaluation?"

I repeated the general question, then read: *"Does Peter Devinski suffer from any mental illness, and if so, how did this mental illness impact on his son's actions of last December 23?"*

"And what were your findings?"

I went through Peter's history just as I had gone through Karen's. "Mr. Devinski has a *history* of alcohol abuse. He became sober around the time of his son's conception."

"So he's not an alcoholic anymore?" This question came from the judge, whom I supposed could butt in anytime he wanted to.

"Well, you know, alcoholics say they're always alcoholics, they're in recovery when they don't drink. But, yes, basically Peter Devinski was not an alcoholic parent. He was never drunk around his son, he never abused Jason in any way, never jeopardized the family's stability because of alcohol, nothing like that."

"No more questions," Greg said.

"I have no questions," Natalie said.

"Umm, Your Honor?" I said. "There's something else you should know about Mr. Devinski's alcoholism."

"Objection," Greg said. "She can't decide unilaterally what information to give you."

"Of course she can," the judge told him cheerfully. "She's the psychiatric expert. Go on, dear. Is there something else you think is important?"

"Well, yes," I said, mentally forgiving him for calling me "dear." "Mr. Devinski took a special experimental medication to help him stop drinking."

"Yes?" The judge was looking at me with an expression of great kindness, as if *I* were the mentally ill one. Natalie was suddenly giving me her undivided attention. Greg's face was red, his eyes blazing.

"Tamsen," he said. "Don't go there. It's not important. We'll handle this another way."

"Your Honor," I said. "You should know that I've been involved in this case more, um, deeply than I would have liked to be."

I had his attention.

"Your Honor, you've heard of Grandines Pharmaceuticals. Mrs. Devinski has worked for them for fifteen years. Grandines hired me as a consultant a couple of weeks ago."

"Yes? Does this relate somehow to Jason's case?" The judge looked puzzled.

"It relates," I said. "Remember how Jason Devinski said he wanted to commit suicide? And then he was hospitalized in an adolescent psychiatry unit, and treated with medication. The medication really helped him."

Everyone nodded, even Simone.

"Well, Jason does have a mental problem. Right now, he's taking antidepressant medication and it's helping him. But I suspect that somehow, somebody from Grandines Pharmaceuticals manipulated this child into murder. You yourself ordered a psychiatric evaluation of Parker Grandines, the CEO of the company. Parker is the one who gave Jason the murder weapon. So the idea that Parker might have done more shouldn't come as a surprise to you. To anyone."

Judge Covington looked at me as if I were crazy, but I was getting used to it.

"I have no proof, though," I continued. "I know there's evidence. But I myself personally have no proof. A geneticist who worked for Grandines Pharmaceuticals died under mysterious circumstances a few weeks ago. So I came up with a theory—"

"Theories are not admissible in court," Greg said.

I ignored him. "Greg—Mr. Jolson—he didn't think I should get involved with Grandines Pharmaceuticals. He thought it would be safer for me to just keep this information out of my evaluation. But I have a strong feeling that there might be a biological explanation for what Jason did. And"—I glanced at Greg, took a deep breath, and continued—"I don't think Jason is the only child who was manipulated."

"Manipulated how?" Judge Covington leaned forward, his blue eyes serious.

I took another one of those cleansing breaths. "I believe that Grandines Pharmaceuticals' new antialcoholism medication, Curixenol, causes a gene mutation that induces violence."

Silence. I continued. "I think that the men who took this drug years ago developed a gene mutation that they passed on to their male offspring. Only boys were affected—only boys whose fathers took Curixenol right around the time their sons were conceived." By now, everyone was staring at me with rapt attention. "I think Grandines Pharmaceuticals knew how dangerous their drug was, but they went forward with the medication because they needed the money. They deliberately misrepresented their product to the FDA to get it approved. I think they've known Curixenol wasn't a simple serotonin agonist—which is what they're marketing it as—since the drug was first developed. They *pretended* Curixenol was safe. They *lied* on their application to the FDA. And I think their geneticist was murdered because she figured this out and threatened to go public. There have been other deaths surrounding this company. I'm sure those deaths have also been because of Curixenol. Grandines Pharmaceuticals is being investigated by the FBI for diversions of a cold medication used to make illegal drugs. I don't believe those diversions ever took place. They were a smokescreen."

"Wait a minute," Judge Covington said. "You're telling me that there *is* a medical reason, a medical explanation, for why a normal boy gunned down four people in front of a hundred witnesses. That's what you're telling me. Right?"

"Right," I said.

"A medical reason because of the parents." Judge Covington was getting it. I nodded.

The judge was silent for a long time as he stared down at his steepled fingers. He, too, wore a wedding band. I wondered if he had a son. "You knew about this, Mr. Jolson?" Judge Covington asked, finally.

"This is all in Tamsen's—Dr. Bayn's—overactive imagination." Greg's jaw was set defiantly; his voice matched. "We don't know all the details. But Tamsen was already threatened once by this company. I don't think this is the right way to handle it. The FBI is aware of wrongdoing at this pharmaceutical company, and they are conducting their own investigation. It doesn't relate to these particular charges."

"Counselor," Judge Covington said, shaking his head. "Counselors. If what Dr. Bayn is telling us is true, if it's accurate, then I have only one thing to tell you."

He paused. My heart was in my throat.

"You kids are trying the wrong case."

chapter fifty-three

"We have to call a federal prosecutor," Judge Covington said. "It would be totally unethical, completely wrong of me, to keep this case in my court, given this evidence. You"—he nodded toward Greg—"knew that I was unhappy with such a young child being tried in the adult courts. Jason's still in the hospital, isn't he?" This question was directed toward the Devinskis, who nodded. "That's probably the best place for him, for now. I want the boy to remain in protective custody, until we figure out exactly what's wrong with him. And there's always the possibility that the state will choose to pursue a conviction."

Greg said nothing.

The judge cleared his throat. "Dr. Bayn, you will be called as a fact witness in this case. You need to make yourself available to the federal investigators and to the prosecution, do you understand?"

"Of course."

"I still expect a full psychiatric evaluation of Mr. Parker Grandines. If you, Dr. Bayn, can obtain information directly from him, as you know, your evidence will be highly useful in court. Do you understand what I mean?"

I understood. Normally, hearsay evidence is inadmissible. But if someone tells a psychiatrist something in a court-ordered forensic evaluation, an evaluation which by definition is not confidential, then the psychiatrist may include this information in his or her expert testimony and the jury is permitted to consider it. Extremely sneaky, for those familiar with the law, but a total no-brainer for the average citizen who isn't normally subject to the complex rules of evidence.

"This session is adjourned," Judge Covington said. I watched Simone, the tall stenographer, pack up her things. Natalie sent a mumbled good-bye in my direction and shepherded the stunned Devinskis out the door before they'd regained their ability to speak. You'd think Natalie would be overjoyed to get her client off the hook, but she looked like she'd rather be cleaning a toilet.

Judge Covington had been slowly gathering up his papers, although I had barely noticed him writing anything during the hearing besides a few doodles in the corner of a page. As a fellow lifelong doodler, I sympathized. I didn't want to be left alone with Greg, but my feet refused to carry me to the door. I felt as if both men were waiting for the other one to leave. Finally the judge said to me, "Nice work, Doctor."

"Thank you," I said.

"Mr. Jolson recommended you highly. I want you to know that you'll be first on my personal list of psychiatrists for future cases." There it was. Evaluate Parker Grandines, and the door toward an illustrious career is open. Refuse, and it's back to divorcing families.

"Thank you," I said, again. "I'll do my best."

"She's a wonderful girl," Judge Covington told Greg, who flushed dark red to the roots of his hair. "You should hold on to her. Have a nice day, kids."

Only Greg and I were left in the empty conference room. I looked out the one window. Outside, the clear bright skies had darkened. Yet more snow seemed to be on the way.

"Well," I said. "I'm—I'm sorry. I guess you wanted to keep the case simple. You would have won."

"You know I don't care about that," Greg said. "Dammit. Why did you leave?"

"I just felt—I don't know. That you didn't love me anymore, that you didn't like the way I was doing my job, as if I wasn't smart enough for you or something. I don't know."

"I have nobody," Greg said. "My parents are dead. I have one eighteen-year-old brother, whom I raised practically by myself, and who is now busy screwing his way through college and doesn't give a rat's ass about me. . . ."

"That's not true. Sasha loves you. He's just a normal teenager, that's all."

"Maybe. But listen. I had *almost* nobody, okay? No relatives, no real friends, all the women I met had these . . . what did you call them? . . . rescue fantasies that they'd take care of my brother and in return I'd take care of them. They didn't really care about me."

I looked away, embarrassed.

"But you—" Greg paused. "You loved me. At least you acted like you loved me. I loved you. I *love* you. And you go pull this shit—I'm not going to go through that again, losing someone I love to stupidity." I knew he was referring to the way his father was killed in a liquor store holdup, by two underage thugs.

"Greg—I—"

"Don't. Just—don't. You're right. We're not right for each other. Maybe I'm not meant to have a wife and a family."

Greg looked at me. I thought he was going to say something else, but after a moment all he said was, "See you, I guess."

"See you." I turned toward the grimy window to hide my face. I knew the words he had spoken moments ago had cost him a big chunk of pride, a big slab of male ego. "I—I'll let you know when I want to pick up my stuff. I'll need to get a van or something. If you don't mind, I'll wait until I find a new place. . . ."

"Call me," he said, and left.

I stood staring at the heavy green door as it swung slowly, until it thudded closed. If I hadn't known any better, I would have thought that Greg's eyes were shining with tears.

chapter fifty-four

Back at my parents' place, I called Kathy O'Neill at her FBI office. She wasn't in, but this time someone answered at the number she'd left me. I asked to have her call me immediately.

Five minutes later the phone rang.

"Where are you?" I asked. In the background I heard the sounds of traffic and wind.

"It doesn't matter," Kathy said. "What happened? Did something happen?"

"Well," I said. "Sort of." Understatement of the year. I heard some talking but I couldn't make out her words over the noise around her.

"I'll come see you," Kathy told me. "Where are you?"

"I can meet you in my office. Whenever you want."

"I'll be there in an hour." She hung up before I could ask or say anything else. All business, these FBI people.

I had lunch and tried calling Vasily Stolnik, but I hung up when I got his voice mail. I hadn't planned what to say in my message. Then I went downstairs to the office.

Ralphie was on the lobby sofa, in a comfortable pose, reading a newspaper. Kathleen O'Neill sat on the bench outside my office, tapping her foot and looking impatient. Divide and conquer, who said that?

I walked right past Ralphie, who lowered his newspaper as if he were a CIA agent making covert contact with the KGB in Red Square. "I'm here," I announced to Kathleen.

"What kept you? My God, you look awful."

"Thank you so much." I hadn't realized how the

sleepless nights and the emotionally draining morning had taken their toll. Ralphie stood and approached us.

"Now, Kathy, leave the poor girl alone, she looks fine. Tired is all."

"I have good news for you," Kathy said. "Ginny Liu is out of danger. She's conscious and talking, although I can't say she's making much sense."

"Oh, thank God." I wondered if Kathleen had learned about my little visit to Ginny yesterday, but she didn't say anything else.

They followed me into the consultation room, which I'd been using lately for everything but psychiatric consultations. I had no more logs, fake or otherwise. I didn't bother with any coffee or hospitality.

Something had changed in the past few minutes. Ralphie and Kathy were waiting patiently. Not a question nor a sarcastic comment slipped from anyone's lips. Good cop/bad cop was over. We were colleagues now.

I turned on my computer and printed out a copy of the final section of my Devinski report, the "Formulation and Recommendations" section. The two FBI agents waited quietly as I made two copies on my little desktop copier and handed one to each of them. I felt like a proctor in an exam, making the students wait with the test under their noses, while I read aloud all the useless information about where to write their names and how to fill in their Social Security numbers. Suddenly, I had knowledge. I had power.

"What you're holding is part of my psychiatric-legal report on Karen and Peter Devinski. Today it was handed in to Judge Covington, and since the case is now being transferred to federal court, you are entitled to have access to most of this information. I'm letting you see this part because it contains information important to your investigation at Grandines Pharmaceuticals. I'm also giving you a list of subjects in Grandines's clinical trials of Curixenol.

"You need to take those pages to a federal prosecutor along with whatever other information you have about Grandines Pharmaceuticals. You should call Greg Jolson, he should have already had at least some preliminary contact with the federal courts. You can call me when you need me." I spoke so quickly and forcefully that I think they were scared to say anything.

"The other thing you might want to know is that I'm going to be doing a psychiatric evaluation of Parker Grandines, for Judge Covington. He's the judge hearing the Jason Devinski murder case. But I'd imagine you'd want to get your own court order for my evaluation, from a federal judge."

They exchanged a glance.

Ralphie said, "Tamsen, we understand how upset you are about the tragedy of this child who killed his friends. But that's not what we're investigating. We'll make a few calls, but really, it's not even clearly our jurisdiction. We're here because of Ginny Liu and the pseudoephedrine."

I wanted to punch them both. "The pseudoephedrine was a smokescreen," I said. "A diversion."

"Yes. A diversion of pseudoephedrine, that was used to make drugs." Kathy was nodding her head as if I were an especially smart intellectually challenged person.

I nodded back. They weren't going to send in the big guns for protection.

"I want to see Grandines out of business. I want to see Parker Grandines and his little band of thugs in prison forever. As far as I'm concerned, *Parker* pulled the trigger on those little girls and the teacher at Jason Devinski's school, and *Parker* killed the Towland family in Kentucky, and *Parker* pushed Gordon Ranier's ex-wife onto the subway tracks. Who knows how many other boys are out there committing violent acts because of him?

"Parker Grandines is the mastermind. He's your bad guy. He accidentally figured out a way to make killers, and he did nothing about it; he *gave* the gun to Jason Devinski to see if he would use it. He arranged this pseudoephedrine thing as a distraction because he knew that after the smoke cleared, he'd have a company stronger and more valuable than ever before."

"Well, you can tell that to the other investigating agents," Kathy said. "Did it ever occur to you that maybe *this* story is a smokescreen? That Grandines is guilty of illegal drug trafficking, just as we've always thought?" Her voice and attitude showed exactly what she thought of my conclusions. The two FBI agents rose and started putting on their coats.

I brushed aside my disgust and disappointment. The FBI didn't believe me. I opened the door to show them out as cordially as I could manage, and after they left I went back into the consultation room and sat at my desk. I called Vasily Stolnik again, to confirm our meeting for this afternoon. This time, he answered.

"Oh, the lovely doctor," he said in his singsongy way.

"Are we on?"

"Certainly. We'll see you at four o'clock." Soft laughter came over the phone line. "His regular attorney is unavailable. In Virgin Gorda. Caribbean. Nice to be a lawyer. . . . Mr. Grandines will bring a substitute attorney today."

"Are you sure Parker is ready? Maybe he wants to reschedule." I didn't know much about incompetent counsel as a basis for appeal, but I wondered if that's what Parker was planning.

"Parker is ready." Stolnik chuckled. "You will see."

I have to admit I kind of liked Vasily Stolnik, even though he was in bed with the bad guys. As he'd told me, it was his job. The director of security surely wouldn't be expected to kill anyone himself, would he?

Then again, Stolnik had learned his craft in Russia during the cold war. Exactly how much was I supposed to trust him?

chapter fifty-five

I had one more person I needed to see before I met with Parker Grandines. I called Antony Hastings-Muir. Of course he wasn't in. I left a message on his machine, telling him to call me ASAP.

Ten minutes later my doorbell rang. "I was in the neighborhood," Antony Hastings-Muir said. "I got your message, so I thought, why not just drop by?"

"Come in. I have some questions to run by you, if you don't mind."

"Have you had a chance to go down to my old office, then?" Tony stepped into the waiting room and I closed the door behind him.

"Not yet. I don't think I'll be working for Grandines much longer. But I am evaluating Parker for the court at four o'clock."

"Really?" Tony sounded stunned. "How did such a thing come about?"

"Court order." I shrugged. I led the way into the consultation room. Tony took off his coat and slung it over the arm of the sofa, then turned to face me.

"What can I do for you?" Tony asked, finally.

"I think you know why Madeleine was murdered. I need you to go with me to the authorities."

Tony stood and crossed the room, and sat on the desk in front of me, swinging one leg casually. "Just like that? Go to the authorities and say what?"

"I think you have proof," I said. "I think you kept it in your office at Grandines. That's why you keep mentioning it to me. You left something there."

Tony leaned over the desk, his face just inches from mine. "It's behind the photo," he whispered.

"What photo?"

"The photo of Madeleine. Get me that photo." He pressed something cold and hard into my hand. It was a key.

This guy was creepy. "I can't get you anything. If you had something important, why'd you leave it there? *What* is behind the photo?" I held the key out to Tony, but he ignored it.

"Gene therapy was Madeleine's field. She figured it out."

"Gene therapy," I repeated. "So I was right. You knew about it all this time, and you said nothing."

"Curixenol is not an antidepressant with antialcoholism properties. It's a gene-therapy agent. You take it, it alters a gene for alcoholism. Now that practically the whole human genome has been mapped, anyone will be able to find the mutation. And this mutation is permanent, unlike with most gene-therapy agents. Most of the experimental gene-therapy agents in development work only during the time they're being administered."

I was horrified. Grandines knew. They knew, and lied about it. My wild speculations weren't so wild after all.

Tony went on. "Curixenol also has this little bug that alters the genes for some brain proteins, structural proteins in the regions that control violent behaviors in men. Y-chromosome genes."

"Right next to the gene for hairy earlobes," I said, my anxiety inadvertently trying to make a joke.

"Well, yes, up until recently, the gene for hairy earlobes was the only Y-linked genetic trait that had been identified. But don't forget about the rest of the chromosome. It's full of information. It's only a matter of time until we learn what else that Y chromosome is for."

"So Grandines pretended that Curixenol was an SSRI because they knew they could never market gene therapy. They tricked the FDA into approving a drug that could never be approved. Curixenol causes mutations of genes that hadn't even been isolated at the time the drug was developed. Oh, my God."

"The FDA hasn't yet permitted a single gene-altering drug to be used in humans."

"No, just in tomatoes. Humans, forget it. Maybe they know what they're doing, the FDA. Tomatoes can't shoot guns."

"Curixenol is flawed," Tony said. "Grandines Pharmaceuticals knows about the flaws. The company should have pulled the drug out of development as soon as they realized what the problem was, but they didn't. Madeleine tried to synthesize an antidote, believing that the drug really was a simple serotonin agonist. She thought that the teratogenic properties—the gene-altering properties—were legitimate side effects."

"But—why didn't you tell this to the FBI?"

"I want to get the proof, first. Madeleine's diskette. It's hidden in my office at Grandines. Behind her photo. Just use my master key to get into my office." He waved at the key, which I'd just placed on the desk.

I went over to the window and looked out at the crowded street. "You have proof that incriminates Grandines." I needed that disk.

Tony slid off the desk. His voice was soft, but he was so close that his breath tickled my ear. I leaned my forehead against my hands and closed my eyes.

"Parker gets off on killing people," Tony said. "He killed Madeleine. He tried to kill Ginny. If we don't expose him, and he thinks you know something, do you really think he won't try to kill you next?"

chapter fifty-six

Whatever answer I might have come up with died on my lips when the doorbell rang. I left Antony Hastings-Muir in my soundproof office and went out into the waiting room. The last person I expected to see when I opened the door was Vasily Stolnik. He held out a hand for me to shake. Like the previous time he'd dropped by unexpectedly, I didn't invite him in.

"Dr. Tamsen," he said. *"Cac dela?"*

I recognized the Russian for "How are you?"

"Normalna," I answered. Normal. Russian for "okay," and approximately the extent of my noncursing Russian vocabulary.

"I have some bad news for you, Doctor," Stolnik said. "Or maybe is good news, *da*? May I come in?" He held up his hands. "I promise, I have no tricks up my sleeve today."

I pushed open my office door and gestured toward the waiting room sofa, but remained standing, unsure if I should be fearful or not. My instincts told me Stolnik wouldn't do anything to hurt me or even scare me again. My experience told me that anyone even remotely connected to Grandines Pharmaceuticals was not to be trusted.

"Let me guess," I said to Stolnik. "Parker Grandines has obtained some kind of injunction preventing me from examining him."

Stolnik laughed. "No, no. Nothing so extravagant. Tovarich Parker has merely slipped on a patch of ice and sprained his ankle. He would like the interview to take place at his home in Great Neck. If is okay with you. He will arrange for car service to bring you. He said he is certain district attorney's office does not wish to wait for psychiatric evaluation. You don't wish to wait until Mr. Parker is *back on his feet*, do you?" He laughed at his weak joke.

"When does he want this interview to take place?"

"Tomorrow morning at ten would be convenient," Stolnik told me. "I have car pick you up at nine?"

I considered. I didn't like the idea of getting into a car paid for or controlled by Parker Grandines. I didn't like the idea of interviewing him on his home turf. I especially didn't like the way Grandines was still calling the shots.

Tony appeared from the other room. "Do you need to use your office . . . Vasily. What are you doing here?"

"Tovarich Hastings-Muir." The two men shook hands. "I was just telling the lovely doctor here that we need to reschedule her appointment with us."

Tony nodded. "You always were one for changing plans," he said to Stolnik, and both men laughed. I didn't get the joke, so I said nothing.

"You are well, then, Tony?" Stolnik asked. "Everything is fine with you?"

"Absolutely," Tony replied. "And with you?"

They schmoozed for a minute, exchanging pleasantries, while I stood by, amazed. I'd thought Tony had left Grandines Pharmaceuticals in disgrace. But now I realized that I must have been wrong, that I'd assumed too much.

"About tomorrow," I interrupted, after I'd had more nostalgia and small talk than I could stand. "Maybe you can give me directions, and I'll get there on my own."

I wrote down the directions Stolnik dictated. He was cheerful and polite, and you'd never guess that he'd once drugged me and dragged me off to the wilds of the Bronx. He left full of smiles, telling me he'd see me in the morning. As soon as the door closed behind him, Tony let out a string of expletives.

"Funny, you acted like you liked him."

"That's not it at all. Dammit, Tamsen. How can you get

into my office if you're not going to Grandines Pharmaceuticals' headquarters? I need that disk. *We* need it."

"I think you're a little fixated on that computer disk, Tony. If Parker confesses to knowing all about Curixenol, we won't need your disk."

"I disagree. The courts love physical evidence. How about if I drive you out to the Grandines estate tomorrow? At the very least, you'll have someone you can trust nearby."

"Thanks for the offer. But I don't think they'd like it if I brought someone with me." I didn't add, *Especially not you.* Anyway, I hoped that by tomorrow I could convince the FBI to accompany me. You'd think they wouldn't want me to go out there alone. Even if they didn't believe Parker was a murdering psychopath, they did think he was a drug dealer. Wasn't that bad enough?

"Call me if you change your mind," Tony said. "If you get the disk from him, call me the minute you get back."

"I'll call you from the car," I said, even though I wouldn't.

I left a message at Greg's office, informing him that my interview of Parker Grandines had been postponed until the morning, and advising him of the change in location. I'd first met Greg when I was a consulting psychiatrist for a defendant he was prosecuting. It shouldn't have been so difficult for me to remain in professional mode. Have I mentioned the popular theory that medical students choose to specialize in psychiatry when they are totally incapable of managing their personal lives?

I went upstairs to my parents' apartment. The evening dragged on. I spent some time preparing for the next day, which consisted of packing and repacking all sorts of paraphernalia to take to my interview with Parker Grandines: a tape recorder, and a copy of the psychiatrists' Bible, the *Diagnostic and Statistical Manual of Mental Disorders,* popularly called the *DSM-IV,* in addition to my usual pad of paper and pen. By eleven P.M., I'd drifted off into a trancelike sleep when I heard ringing from somewhere. By the time I'd figured out it was the phone, the ringing had stopped and buzzing had started. I wove my way to the front door. Who could be dropping by in the middle of the night?

Special Agent Kathleen O'Neill stood in the hallway.

"Sorry to barge in so late," she said, although her voice didn't seem too apologetic. She held out a sheet of paper. "I have good news for you."

Good news, bad news. Everyone was a newscaster. "What?"

"We decided—against our better judgment, I might add—to go ahead with the court order. Ralphie will be there to sit in on your evaluation of Parker Grandines."

I took the page out of her outstretched hand, cringing behind the door in my nightgown. I glanced over the court order. It was fairly straightforward, and instructed me to perform a *"Full psychiatric evaluation on Parker Grandines, including, but not limited to, his psychiatric and social history, his mental status examination, and any other relevant information, in order to help determine the extent of his voluntary involvement in developing and marketing a dangerous drug."* The order was signed by a federal judge.

Before I could ask any questions, Kathy said goodnight. "Wait," I called after her, before she could get on the elevator and disappear. "Did you know that the location of the meeting has changed?"

"Obviously," Kathy said. "Why else would I be here now? Ralphie tried to meet you at the Grandines Building and the security guard told him about Parker Grandines's sprained ankle. Ralphie will drive you to Grandines's Long Island house tomorrow morning. Be ready by nine."

My stomach hurt.

I woke up on Saturday morning to the sound of rain. The window air conditioners had never been removed for the winter, and the icy drops were pinging on the metal like machine-gun fire. I showered, dressed in black, which for once felt appropriate, choked down a tasteless breakfast.

Then I squared my shoulders like some sort of brave wartime heroine in the kind of movie that I would only watch by accident, and headed toward the door.

The phone rang. My parents didn't believe in caller ID. "Tamsen? It's Ralph Dupree. Listen, I have a flat tire." I heard sounds of traffic in the background. Why me? Why today? "You'd better go on ahead and I'll meet you out there. Do you have the directions?"

I told him I did and hung up. My parents kept their car in a garage across the street. I was actually relieved to be spared Dupree's cloying presence on the drive. By the time I crossed the Triborough Bridge I was singing along with the radio.

Great Neck is an upscale Long Island suburb of New York. I'd always thought it was far away, but on this eerily quiet January morning, I made it in about thirty minutes, despite the rain and the ice floes in my path. Grandines's home was right on the water. The driveway seemed to be a mile long. The house was a stone fortress. It looked like something you might see in a documentary about the royal family.

I pulled up in front of the house and parked beside a huge pile of old snow that stood higher than I did. The U-shaped drive could have accommodated another hundred cars. The rain fell in icy sheets, tearing into the mountains of snow and flooding the lawn and the driveway. I didn't see another car, and I felt a momentary pity for Ralph Dupree, who had to change a flat tire in this weather. I wasn't about to wait in the car until he arrived, so hunching under a totally useless umbrella, I made a run for the house and rang the bell.

Parker Grandines opened his own grand front door. "Dr. Bayn. So good to see you. Lousy weather, isn't it?" He stepped aside to let me in. "The maid is off. And my wife is in Boston with our grandchildren. We won't have any unnecessary interruptions."

I felt that familiar twinge in my gut.

Parker took my coat before he led me into his study.

Was this the room where Parker Grandines had offered little Jason Devinski the nickel-plated handgun that had become the cause of so much grief and controversy? The room was tucked into a corner of the house in such a way that two walls were virtually all windows. The other two walls were devoted mostly to bookcases, of a dark, glossy wood, except for a painting here, a door there, and a glass cabinet with a few old-fashioned-looking guns in it.

"You like them?" Parker asked me. "This top one is my favorite. It was my great-great-great-grandpa's service weapon in the Civil War. Still works."

"Is it loaded?" First things first.

"Oh, no. Those are strictly for display. The one directly beneath it is a Revolutionary War relic. I bought it at an auction, for just eight thousand bucks." He chuckled. "A bargain."

A bargain of eight thousand dollars? I wondered if he was going to offer me money today—either to lie in my testimony or to continue in my role as Grandines's Curixenol psychiatrist. His original offer had been generous, but he clearly had money to burn. Which made me wonder even more about his drive to bring Curixenol to market when it wasn't safe. Wasn't he rich enough?

My anxiety level was completely out of proportion to what I was officially here to do. *It's just a stupid psychiatric evaluation.* Although I hadn't been thrilled with the idea of having Ralphie Dupree here as my chaperone, I looked around for him. At the moment I would have welcomed Jack the Ripper on one of his good days.

In the movies, some intrepid lawyer or detective wrangles a confession out of the bad guy, usually while he's on the witness stand in someone else's murder trial. But Parker, arrogant as he was, wouldn't fall for such a cheap trick. I gazed around the luxurious room, at the eight-thousand-dollar bargain and at the partners desk that had probably cost twice that much. Parker was clearly someone who cared for things much more than he cared for people.

Sometimes I think psychiatry is like acupuncture for

the soul. Nobody really knows how—or why—talking works, and you have to poke around a lot of different places until you find the spot where the right jab will cure your patient. But if you have the knack, eventually you get results. Maybe I could find Parker Grandines's trigger points.

"Have a seat, Dr. Bayn." Parker waved toward one side of the desk, then excused himself. I busied myself arranging and rearranging my things on my allotment of the enormous desk. When the door opened again, Parker entered the study, together with his cousin Jonathan Grandines. Parker held a pitcher of ice water in one hand, an empty glass in the other. Jonathan was breathing heavily, and his hair was plastered to his scalp. His clothes were dry, so either he'd just come from the gym, or he wasn't feeling too well. Given the dark suit and striped tie, I doubted he'd been exercising recently.

"Meet Jonathan Grandines, Esquire," Parker said with the closest thing to a grin I'd ever seen on him.

"You're an *attorney*?"

"My regular lawyer couldn't make it," Parker said with that well-rehearsed regret I'd heard from him before. "Shall we begin?"

If I wasn't so nervous, I would have laughed at the absurdity of what I was trying to do. Did I really think Parker Grandines was going to confess to pushing a dangerous drug into the marketplace? Parker didn't even want his regular counsel present. For sure he was going to lie, in a big way. I picked up my pen and wrote the date on the top of a blank sheet of paper.

"One moment, please." Parker Grandines carefully poured himself a glass of water, although Jonathan looked like he needed it more. "I'm ready now, Dr. Bayn. Question away."

Parker Grandines exuded smugness the way some men exude sex appeal. I wanted to smack his well-bred face. Instead I said, "I understood Special Agent Ralph Dupree was supposed to join us. Shouldn't we wait?"

Jonathan started sputtering. Parker said, "I received

word he'd be late. He told us to begin without him." I didn't underestimate the importance of having an officer of the law in a room where the bad guys would outnumber me. I wanted backup before I challenged Parker Grandines with what I knew.

"Let's begin." I opened my mouth to ask a question, and realized my mind suddenly resembled the inside of an empty milk carton. Although it was routine for a forensic psychiatrist to interview someone with no attorneys present, or with only one attorney present, Jonathan Grandines struck me as one of the poorest excuses for a lawyer I'd ever seen. Even if he were planning to lie, why on earth would Parker have agreed to meet with me without competent representation? It wasn't like lying to your lawyer was unheard-of.

"Dr. Bayn? Is everything all right?" Parker's solicitousness was almost believable. Almost.

"I'll start with some history." I felt as if I'd swallowed sawdust, but I forced my mouth to form the initial questions: name, age, profession, blah blah blah. I informed Mr. Grandines that our interview was not confidential and that a report would be submitted to the court. His counsel, formerly the director of marketing for Grandines Pharmaceuticals, and presumably still his cousin, Jonathan Grandines, remained silent. I stared at the blank page in front of me. I could conduct a psychiatric examination in my sleep. That's what residency training is for. It wasn't like I'd never evaluated a multiple murderer before.

The only difference was that this time, nobody seemed to know Parker Grandines was a killer. Besides me. Which left me in a rather awkward position.

"Have you ever seen a psychiatrist or a psychotherapist of any kind before, for any reason?" I asked Parker. He looked at his cousin, who nodded ever so slightly.

"When I went into the army I was screened by a psychiatrist." Parker sipped from his glass of water. Nobody else had water, or even a glass. "I was perfectly sane, of course. Ahem. And I went to marriage counseling a few years back with my wife. That therapist was a social worker, I believe."

I jotted down some notes, wondering why the furtive glance at Jonathan for such an innocuous psychiatric history. I doubted I'd have a reason to get into the specifics of the marital problems, although I would have liked to. I'm not the only psychiatrist to have secret voyeuristic tendencies. "Have you ever taken medication for any kind of mental problem?"

"No, never."

I went through Parker's medical and surgical histories (mild hypertension controlled by diet and exercise, appendectomy at age eight). He had no allergies to any medications and did not take any medications. Some psychiatrists feel you should get to the nitty-gritty right away. I always like to get my history first. I always go from easiest to most emotionally laden. By the time I get to the part of the interview when I ask them about whatever it is they did, they are usually willing to talk to me.

I remembered something. "Is your ankle better? I didn't notice you limping." Although I'd assumed that Parker had invented the sprained ankle as a way to move this entire meeting to his own private sanctuary, away from prying eyes and ears, I thought he'd at least try to fake an injury while people were watching.

"Much better. I'm surprised. I've had a weakness in that ankle since I broke it as a teenager."

I scrawled *h/o* (history of) *broken ankle, teenager* on my list of Parker's medical problems, keeping up the charade. If only the whole evaluation could be so straightforward. People, especially other doctors, often think psychiatry is simple. While it's true that a psychiatrist can minimize his or her exposure to unpleasant medical conditions like gangrenous limbs or gaping wounds, making an accurate diagnosis and providing treatment that works is usually much, much harder than what the typical endocrinologist or dermatologist encounters in an average day. Yet, for those who don't understand the complexities of personality development and mental illness, merely talking to people seems at best like hocus-pocus, and at worst, a complete waste of time. That acupuncture thing again.

Charlatan Tamsen, at your service.

Maybe Parker really did think he'd sprained his ankle. There's a hypochondriac born every minute. Either way, the evaluation would have taken place on his territory and his terms, not mine. I continued: "Is there any history of mental illness in your family?"

Parker didn't even glance at his cousin/lawyer this time, didn't wait for Jonathan's nod.

"I had a sister who was institutionalized," Parker said. "They always said she was schizophrenic."

I wrote it down. "*Had* a sister?"

"She died. From natural causes. Cancer. Both my sisters are dead."

"Any history of drug or alcohol abuse in your family?"

"Not really," Grandines replied too quickly.

"How about in yourself, do you yourself have any history of substance abuse?"

"Why are you asking these questions?" Jonathan Grandines interjected. "My cousin—my client—doesn't use any drugs. What are you getting at?"

"These are just routine questions, Mr. Grandines." My questions were routine; Jonathan's were anything but. I suspected they were both trying to keep any discussion of methamphetamine and pseudoephedrine diversions out of the conversation. But why would they care, if the whole pseudoephedrine diversion thing had been a smokescreen?

Maybe this would be a good time for the mental status examination. Usually I saved it for the end of the interview, but I wanted to get the noncontroversial stuff out of the way.

I wrote on my pad: *MSE*. Then I hit Parker Grandines with some basic questions: today's date, my name, where we were. Parker began to smile, clearly at ease. These were the questions people expected from a psychiatrist. How would you describe your mood most of the time? *Good*. I wrote down that he had a *FROA* (full range of affect).

There is no formal thought disorder. Thought content: Answers questions appropriately. Denies anxiety, phobias, obsessions, or compulsions. Parker Grandines denied any problems with sleep, appetite, or concentration. He denied suicidal or homicidal ideation or intent. He denied auditory or visual hallucinations. I didn't elicit any systematized delusions, not that I expected to; in other words, Parker didn't believe he was the Messiah, nor did he experience the sensation of a microchip or a transistor embedded in his brain, or any one of the millions of possible delusions psychotic people suffered from. I estimated Parker's intelligence to be above average. His fund of knowledge was excellent. (I didn't bother to offend him by asking him to name the president or the governor or the two state senators. I'm always amazed when my colleagues evaluate defendants accused of, say, embezzling forty million dollars from the securities firm they're running, and the only knowledge the psychiatrist requires the evaluee to demonstrate is the ability to recite the days of the week or the months of the year. And judges fall for that!) I wound up my mental status examination by asking a few simple questions of memory and recall, and testing a couple of neurological functions: What's this called? *A watch.* And what's this part? *The band.* I even asked Mr. Grandines to draw a clock, to make sure both sides of his brain were working together. He did fine.

"Have you ever heard the expression, 'Don't cry over spilt milk'?" Grandines laughed. I said, "Could you tell me what it means, please?"

"If something is already done and over with, don't waste your time crying over it. Or worrying about it."

"Okay. And how about 'People who live in glass houses shouldn't throw stones'?"

Grandines mumbled something I didn't catch, but before I could ask him to elaborate, he gave me an appropriate interpretation, which I recorded on my pad. Then I asked him what he would do if he saw a fire in a movie theater and if he found a stamped, addressed envelope lying on the ground next to a mailbox. He gave me the stock answers, which I'd expected. There are traditional right answers for these questions, and some lawyers and judges expect you to always ask them, but for me, unless the person's answer is obviously psychotic, the responses are meaningless. Regardless of his answers, I believed that Parker Grandines's insight and judgment were impaired. Later, in my actual report, after I'd gathered more information, I could elaborate.

Back to Parker's life story. I segued into his social history—only the best education, noncombat military service, followed by early marriage to a suitable spouse, three children, and several grandchildren, all of whom were, if Parker's responses were to be believed, perfect specimens of whatever they were supposed to be. This was the part of the interview where I'd usually ask, "Have all your sexual relationships been with women?" But I chose to skip it. Parker was of the generation that would be put off by a detailed sexual history. And I guessed that was the wrong tree to climb. So to speak.

"Tell me a little about how you spend your time. Any hobbies?" See, just chitchat. Nothing to this psychiatry thing. Piece of cake.

"Hobbies?" Parker looked puzzled, and Jonathan said, "Just how would my cous—er—my client's hobbies have anything to do with the reason we're here today?"

I almost told Jonathan Grandines it was a good thing he didn't practice law for a living. Instead I said, "You obviously like to collect rare things. Antiques. Paintings." I pointed toward the display case. "Guns."

"Oh, my, yes. I never thought of those interests as hobbies, though." Parker smiled at me. Sun with teeth.

I was tempted to ask about the gun Jason had taken, but it was too early in our meeting, and I would have been surprised if Parker had answered. Instead I asked, "When did you become interested in art?" Could there be some connection to the stolen art underground, something else that might have sparked Ralphie Dupree's interest? I didn't

want to miss anything. "That painting looks valuable." If
only Ralphie would walk in right now . . .

Parker sprang to his feet and crossed to the painting. It
was huge, and depicted a fox riding to hounds, or something similarly foreign and bloodthirsty. Then he pressed
something near the canvas and the wood paneling slid
open, revealing a heavy metal door with an electronic lock.

"My gun cabinet," Parker said. "Shall I show you?"

My gut froze. "Umm . . . that's not necessary," I managed to say.

Parker keyed in some numbers and the door swung
open. "Come over here and see, Tamsen. I do keep a few
other valuables in here, but I had this room built to hold my
most important weapons. You're the one who asked about
my hobbies."

I'd seen smaller apartments in Manhattan. One wall of
his safe was covered with deep blue velvet. Various guns
nestled in the notches. But I was more interested in the
shelves on the other wall. Some boxes I was sure held jewelry, or papers—and a clear plastic box held computer
disks. The mother lode. I still thought Antony Hastings-
Muir was a little overobsessed with that diskette he
wanted, but it wouldn't hurt to have it, if I could get it.

"Look, this one is a prototype from one of the oldest
gun manufacturers in North America." Parker pulled a
heavy, dull-looking gun out of its notch. "Beautiful, isn't it?"

It never occurred to me that a gun could be beautiful.
Beauty was definitely in the eye of the beholder. Had I
come any closer yet to finding any of Parker Grandines's
trigger points? Besides the literal, I didn't think so.

Parker left the gun cabinet door ajar and he sat down
in his seat. I took my place across from him. "What else can
you tell me about your family? Did your father teach you
about guns?"

"My father? My father was a pacifist. Believed in gun
control, before anyone had even coined that phrase." He
made a harrumph sound of disdain. My ears perked up.

"You didn't have a good relationship with your father, then?"

Parker looked at his cousin and rolled his eyes. "You could say that. He didn't think I'd amount to much. He was extremely reluctant to hand over the reins of the company to me." Parker spread his arms out wide. "But look what I've done. I've lifted our little company—which really was nothing more than a factory in my father's day—I've lifted it out of relative obscurity and into the national spotlight."

"You're proud of your company."

"Oh, my, yes. When I took over, I decided that I'd never sell out. I wanted to build a pharmaceutical company my family and I would be proud of. And I've succeeded. You'll see. Curixenol will make Grandines Pharmaceuticals famous."

"Are you planning to take the company public? Sell stock, I mean?"

Grandines shook his head. "I haven't decided yet." He glanced at his cousin/lawyer. "Some members of the board of directors believe we should simply sell the whole company, lock, stock, and barrel. I tend not to fully agree."

Until today, I'd been convinced that greed was Parker's only motivation in insisting on marketing Curixenol. I'd ruled out revenge and love long ago.

But life is not a multiple-choice exam. I was starting to think that Parker Grandines's motives could only be addressed in an essay question. Probably one that would take up an entire blue book. Or in my case, even two.

"Your parents are no longer living, are they?"

"No. They died years ago."

"I need to note their causes of death. If you know, that is."

Parker looked at his cousin, then said, "My mother died of liver disease. Cirrhosis. She was about sixty."

"I'm sorry to hear that." I couldn't add, *The plot thickens,* but that's what I was thinking. "And your father?"

"He had a heart attack. He was eighty-eight." Parker

looked as if he wanted to say more, but he just opened and closed his mouth silently.

Time for a tiny little test challenge. "You said there was no history in your family of substance abuse. But now you told me your mother died from cirrhosis of the liver. Was it alcoholic cirrhosis, or some other kind?" Rarely, cirrhosis can be a result of infection, autoimmune disease, chemical trauma, or other insults to the liver. However, despite all the possible causes, chronic alcoholism remains the most common etiology. Moreover, I'd never forgotten another little factoid: for men, the average length of time that elapses between the beginning of alcoholism and the onset of liver cirrhosis is twenty-four years. In women, that timeline collapses to only *four* years.

"I don't really know," Parker said. "But if my mother drank . . . well, she had good reason. She was married to my father, wasn't she?"

Jonathan Grandines said, "Park, you don't need to—"

But Parker barked, "I can say whatever I like. This is *my* psychiatric evaluation. Besides, we were talking about how I saved my company from obscurity and failure, which is where we all would have ended up if it hadn't been for me. And Curixenol."

"And Xixperdine," I added. "You haven't said much about Xixperdine."

"We—Grandines Pharmaceuticals—acquired the patent for Xixperdine from a Swiss biochemist who was dying of some neurological disorder and wanted the money fast. We didn't develop that medication in-house." Did Parker really just snort? "Besides, that was my father's last coup before he died, introducing Xixperdine to the U.S. market." All traces of smugness had disappeared from Parker's face, replaced by glazed, unfocused eyes, bulging veins, and skin so red and hot I could almost see the steam rising from it. What had I said to anger him so?

"Curixenol," Parker practically shouted. "Curixenol is the wave of the future. Curixenol will put Parker Grandines on the pharmaceutical map. My father will roll over in his grave when he sees what I've accomplished."

Back to Parker's father. What had Greg said to me the very first day we'd spoken about Jason Devinski? *So many kids killing other kids, or their parents, or even strangers, lately.*

Parker had hated his father. It was his mother who was the alcoholic—and her drinking had something to do with the father, his behaviors or abuse or something I hadn't yet identified. Four years between picking up a bottle to dying in a back room somewhere. Is that what had happened to Mrs. Grandines, Sr.? Did she turn the color of antique parchment and lose all sense of reason? Or did she die with her faculties intact, knowing the chaos she left behind?

The window panes rattled against a sudden burst of freezing rain. I felt as if some of it had invaded my veins. "What else can you tell me about your father?" I gambled on the assumption that by this point, Parker wouldn't be able to resist telling me. The magic of psychiatry in action. You say innocuous things to people, who then proceed to spill their guts. How many times have I been on line in the supermarket, only to be treated to the life stories of absolute strangers? What if Parker was so hot on Curixenol, not only because it would make him rich and famous (because as far as I could tell, he was already rich, and if you were rich, what difference did it make if you were also famous?), but because alcoholic fathers who took it might later be murdered by their sons? Sick. But not out of the question.

"My father was a bad man."

"Was he abusive?"

"He never laid a finger on me, if that's what you mean. Don't you have other questions to ask me? I thought psychiatrists were always interested in the mother. My mother, now she was a *saint*."

"An alcoholic saint?"

"No, Dr. Bayn. Just a regular saint." Parker's shoulders

seemed to harden. His chin jutted out, his eyes like flint. "My father was a pig." His breath quickened. "But I'll show him."

I took a deep breath. "Show him what?" Parker Grandines was frightening me. He didn't seem to be in this room, but rather off somewhere in his own fantasies. Beside him, Jonathan Grandines sat mutely, watching his cousin through blinking, watery eyes.

"Thought he could entrust his empire to someone else?" Parker looked at me now, back on earth. "Nobody ever did as much for Grandines Pharmaceuticals as I did. As I will. I told you. Curixenol will make us famous. No other company has this technology. No other pharmaceutical company can replicate this drug. Because of me, alcoholism as we know it will be eradicated." Parker leaned forward, both hands on the table. "You wanted to know about my father? My father was the only reason that my mother became an alcoholic and died. Because he treated her like dirt, thought that because he was an important executive with his own company, he could have any woman he wanted, whenever he wanted. . . . He encouraged my mother to drink so she wouldn't interfere with his carousing. . . ."

Parker was right about one thing. We psychiatrists do have to be interested in the mother. "Why don't we take a little break?" I asked him. "Mr. Dupree should be here soon, then we can continue."

"Let's continue without him," Parker said. "What else do you want to know? You want to know about Curixenol? Fifteen years ago my company synthesized a compound to compete with the new antidepressants. Prozac, what have you. Only they screwed it up somehow, and they created Curixenol instead. Modifies an alcoholism gene. Permanently. Our subjects all stopped drinking.

"And let me tell you something else about Curixenol, Tamsen. The labeling says the alcoholics need to keep taking it. That our drug only works while it's in the system, just like any psychotropic medication. But you and I know differently. Even Jonathan here"—Parker gave Jonathan what seemed like a look of contempt—"didn't know until today how Curixenol really works. It changes your genes, Tamsen. It turns alcoholics into citizens."

I was frozen to my chair. Why would Parker tell me this? I wasn't such a good psychiatrist. I wished Ralphie Dupree would hurry up and get here.

"Umm, Mr. Grandines? Are you sure you want to share this information with me?"

"That Dr. Abitor was the first one to realize what was happening, years ago. Figured out the mutation would be potentiated by testosterone. Said any boys with the muta- tion would be like time bombs, ready to explode the minute they hit puberty. Abitor came to me and said we had to pull the compound, pull the study. Go back to the laboratory to synthesize a regular SSRI, one that didn't change people's genetic makeup. He was the first one to concoct this ridicu- lous theory that B-22-G—it was B-22-G back then, we hadn't paid the advertising company to invent the name Curixenol—Abitor claimed B-22-G caused Y-chromosome mutations. He said we had to let the men in the study know, so their wives could abort any male fetuses. Can you imagine the panic that would have caused?"

Dr. Abitor—the doctor who'd died of diabetic coma in the early days of B-22-G. Now I remembered. "So instead you followed the male offspring to see what would hap- pen?" I whispered.

"Parker." Sweat ran down Jonathan's forehead and his hands shook as they tried to unknot his tie. "You told me it was a coincidence that all those boys became killers."

Parker ignored us both. "Only a few of those men had sons. Chances were good that some of them would become killers anyway."

"But you wanted to test your theory?"

"That woman, that geneticist, Madeleine Balloy, she found some irregularities as she was preparing her part for the final submission to the FDA. I told her not to worry about it."

"And then you killed her too." Part of me wanted to get up and run out of the room, to run far away from this place and this maniac. But how far could I get when he had an entire arsenal in his closet? I didn't risk turning my back on him. The best thing to do was to sit tight and wait for the FBI to show up.

"I didn't kill her," Parker said. "Only when she threatened to go public . . . she serendipitously met with an unfortunate accident." Parker laughed, a harsh sound like Velcro peeling apart. "Very unfortunate."

I didn't move from my seat, wishing myself invisible. If only Parker would go to the bathroom or something, I'd go right out the French doors and disappear into the storm outside. The gray waves of Long Island Sound, close enough to touch, were calmer and less menacing than Parker Grandines looked right now.

"Don't you have more questions for me, Tamsen?" He'd dropped the "Dr." along with any pretense of formality around the same time the veins started bulging in his forehead. What could I ask him? My most innocuous questions, about his family and his hobbies, had unleashed a river of insanity. If I asked him his favorite food he might decide to shoot me then and there.

"Maybe we should wait for Mr. Dupree before we continue," I said. "Anyway, I think we need a short break. I'd like to go to the ladies' room—"

Parker opened the top drawer of his desk and pulled out a small gun. "Oh, but I haven't told you about Jason." Held the gun, casually, as if it were a pen, or a tissue.

"What about Jason?" I asked, willing my voice not to break.

"The gun. How I showed him the gun. After he took it, I got another one. See? Isn't it nice?"

I said nothing.

"Isn't the gun nice, I said?" He pointed it at me.

I nodded. "Very shiny," I said, in a dry whisper that didn't sound like me at all.

"I knew if Abitor, if Madeleine, had been correct about

that genetic mutation, then there was a good chance the boy would want to take that gun. And he did take it. Can you imagine? I invented a killing machine. I can breed children to kill."

I looked down at the pages I'd written earlier. *Insight and judgment are adequate.* Joke's on me. To calm myself, to distance myself, I mentally lined up the words as I'd write them in my final report, if I ever got out of here alive, which at the moment didn't seem like a distinct possibility. *Although Mr. Grandines answered standard questions about insight and judgment appropriately, clearly his judgment is severely lacking in certain areas, to virtually psychotic proportions. He admits to showing a gun to a twelve-year-old boy, and then providing the child with the opportunity to later remove that weapon, take it home with him, and use it to kill three people and severely and permanently maim a fourth. The most appalling aspect of Mr. Grandines's behavior is the fact that he knew that the twelve-year-old boy in question had been exposed to a drug which causes a genetic mutation, which in turn can result in violence in male children when they reach puberty.*

And then he pointed a gun at me. No. *At this psychiatrist,* I amended. It wouldn't do to use the first person in an official document.

Fuck it. If I ever got out of here I'd write my official documents any way I damn pleased.

Nope, cursing in my mind didn't help; didn't make the gun disappear, although the weapon was now lying on the desk.

"Just think, Tamsen." Parker laughed his scary laugh again. "I can make killers. How do you think my father would have liked that?"

I didn't think he really wanted an answer.

"Madeleine Balloy claimed we could fix Curixenol, can you imagine? She wanted me to let her work on it, to wait for the final FDA approval. Somewhere I have copies of her files, her scientific equations and whatever else she thought could help save the drug. She didn't see the poetic justice of it all . . . that alcoholic fathers would be killed by their sons . . . after they got sober . . . that the sins of the fathers are visited on the sons . . ."

Parker was crazy. Before I could think of what to say next, a doorbell rang somewhere. Jonathan Grandines, who'd sat so still in his chair until now I thought maybe he'd fallen unconscious, said, "Want me to get that?"

"It must be the FBI," Parker said, and slipped his little gun back into its drawer. "Certainly, Jonathan. Please go welcome Mr. Dupree."

I felt some of the tension drain from my body. Ralphie would come in, he'd have a gun, and we could get out of here. I closed my eyes against the tears of relief that threatened to leak. I'd been afraid to admit to myself that Parker might shoot me before help arrived. Now that Ralphie was here, I felt myself begin to tremble, with delayed shock as well as relief.

I looked up to see Jonathan Grandines come back into the room. His presence registered as wrong, and I didn't have to think hard to figure out why. If I'd been the one to answer the door, I'd never have considered coming back into this danger zone to deal with a madman. I'd have sprinted for my car and safety as if I'd had wings.

The next person to walk in struck me as even more wrong. It was someone I knew, all right. But not the FBI agent I'd been expecting.

chapter fifty-seven

"Good morning." Antony Hastings-Muir nodded to each of us. "Tamsen. Parker. Is everything going well with the interview?"

"What are you doing here?" I'd spent the last hour in such a surreal world that it took a few moments for the shock to hit me. Why had Tony come here? Just to collect a computer disk, which he probably couldn't obtain anyway? Why had Jonathan Grandines let him in? Tony was an idiot, but he was a friendly idiot, and maybe he could get me out of here. I wanted to signal him, somehow, that Parker had lost all semblance of rationality, that he had a gun just inches away in his desk drawer, and to run for help.

Then I noticed Jonathan. He was back in his armchair, sweating and gasping for breath. He looked horrible. Why had he come back to this room? Why hadn't he just left when he had the chance?

"I want to hear Mr. Grandines's version of events," Tony said.

"Don't worry," Parker said, "I haven't given you up. There was no need for you to make the trip on such a miserable morning."

"Parker—" Tony held out a hand: stop.

"Not to mention the fact that you weren't invited," Parker said. "Now that you're here, what should I do with you? Jonathan, what do you think?"

Jonathan gazed up at Parker with glazed eyes. One hand clutched the arm of his chair, the other was clasped to his throat.

"I think he's having an MI." Tony spoke calmly,

rationally, using the correct medical abbreviation for "heart attack." "Shall I summon help?"

"Don't touch that phone," Parker said. "I get it. I know why you're here."

Please tell me, then, because I don't know what the hell is going on. Is Tony going to risk getting shot just for a stupid computer disk? "You don't need . . . what we spoke about, Tony." I was afraid to whisper, but at the same time, I was afraid of what Parker might do when I spoke. I had to get him to leave, to get help for Jonathan, and for me, for all of us.

"Ah-ha!" Parker bounced out of his chair as if propelled by a spring. "Don't tell me you were bluffing this whole time!" He clapped his hands like a two-year-old waiting for his ice-cream cone. "I've got you, Tony, haven't I?"

"Bluffing?" I whispered, mostly to myself. I'd been suspicious of Tony's unquenchable desire for that stupid computer disk. Of course. He didn't care about sharing evidence with the FBI.

He needed evidence against Grandines; insurance against something they could use to bury him. I looked at Tony, so good-looking and, well, suave, with his British accent and streaky hair. In the short time I'd known him, I'd thought several times that he had entirely too much money for a psychiatrist, even one who worked for industry: a house in Bermuda, a boat, a penthouse apartment in Manhattan.

Few things generate that sort of income. I thought of the disk behind Madeleine's photo, the one Tony had left behind in his office at Grandines Pharmaceuticals.

Bluffing.

"You were manufacturing methamphetamine," I said to Tony. "You were the one. And Parker has proof. But *you* don't have the proof he knew about Curixenol. That's why he's got you."

Behind Tony, Jonathan Grandines was trying to say something, but produced only a gurgle. His skin had taken on a purplish sheen.

"We need to call an ambulance for Jonathan," I said. "This minute."

"Don't touch that phone, Tamsen," Tony said. "What am I going to do with you now?"

"Our deal is off, Tony," Parker said, in only a slightly saner tone of voice than he'd been using earlier. "I'll take care of Tamsen."

"You both agreed not to turn each other in? Is that the deal?" I was shaking, more from anger than fear, although the fear was there, like a cellar crawling with things you'd rather not know about.

"I told you I needed that disk, Tamsen. I told you what was on it. The research Madeleine did on Curixenol. Her proposal for repairing the defect in the medication."

"You told me you wanted that information so you could help me expose Grandines Pharmaceuticals. Not so you could protect your own interests." *You're a criminal*, I added silently. *I'm trapped in a roomful of criminals.* The only way their harebrained scheme could work was if they removed me from the equation. I glanced over at Jonathan Grandines. He was sweating and panting and a strange shade of eggplant, and yet nobody but me wanted to do anything for him. Parker must have considered him expendable too. Parker wouldn't want any witnesses at all, even if it meant sacrificing his own flesh and blood.

Where the hell was Ralphie Dupree? If I ever in my life needed an FBI agent, now was the time. If Ralphie were on his way, Parker wouldn't have risked telling me so much incriminating information. Parker couldn't kill me and then tell Ralphie I was going to be late, could he? And Parker wouldn't kill an FBI agent. That was completely different from killing an average citizen.

And then I understood two things with such perfect clarity it felt like an epiphany, in the original, religious sense of the word: Ralphie wasn't coming here today at all. He was never going to arrive in time to save me.

And Parker *would* kill an FBI agent. Someone had killed Jim Mahoney. I was willing to bet that if Parker hadn't pulled the trigger himself, it had been as easy for him to arrange Mahoney's death as it was to make dinner reservations.

Did I dare make a run for it?

Parker said to Tony, "You can't do anything about it. You try to testify that I knew about Curixenol's gene-altering properties from the beginning, I'll just go to the FBI with my evidence about your drug business. Good thing I didn't put a stop to your little shenanigans right away. I knew it would come in handy to have something on you."

"You wouldn't dare to go to the FBI. I'll testify against you anyway."

"You won't be a witness much longer," Parker said, his eyes wild. He opened the top drawer of his desk and took out the little gun again.

"Please," I said quietly. "Please. Put that away. Let's be reasonable." Right. Like telling a psychopath to be reasonable has ever worked, at any time in recorded history.

Parker put the gun back in the drawer, muttering something to himself. He turned to look at his gun cabinet, stared at Tony for a moment, then fixed his gaze back on me. I was used to men evaluating me, mentally taking off my clothes, and imagining doing God knows what else to me—what woman isn't? But Parker's stare was different. I felt as if he were appraising where best to shoot me, how to dispose of me, what the newspapers might say.

You'll get caught. Sooner or later, even if you kill me, even if you kill Antony Hastings-Muir and every single person who might have the remotest clue that Curixenol kills. I thought about all the lives that might be destroyed before the FDA took another serious look at Curixenol, and I felt as if I were submerged under the ocean.

I wasn't ready to die. *I'm an only child. Don't do this to my parents, now that we've finally established a truce after all these years. Don't do this to my patients, who are so fragile, who need me. Don't do this to Greg . . .*

Greg. He'd never know I hadn't really wanted to leave him. How would he know that it was only the stress of working on the same case, the confusion of intersecting professions, that had driven us apart? If I'd finally figured it out, I somehow believed he had too. How long would it take him to realize this court-ordered evaluation had gone so wrong? How long until he missed me?

How long until he found someone else?

I closed my eyes against the insanity collected in this room. A shuffling sound made me open them again.

Framed against the door stood a broad figure topped with a cowboy hat, insubstantial as a mirage. Never had I been so happy to see someone I'd disliked so intensely.

"Howdy, y'all," the cowboy said.

I didn't bother to wonder why he'd shown up after all. "Ralphie! Parker's got a gun!"

chapter fifty-eight

"Parker's got quite a few guns," Ralphie said, in his Texas drawl. "What's happening here? What on God's green earth are you doing here, Tony?"

Tony looked at his feet. "I had some business to take care of," he muttered.

"How did you get into my house?" Parker asked.

"The gun. He has a gun," I said again, without yelling this time.

Ralphie looked around the room, paused when he got to Jonathan Grandines. "What's the matter with him?"

"I think he's having a heart attack," I said. "But Parker wants to kill me, kill us. He has a gun," I repeated for what felt like the hundredth time.

"I have a gun too, Tamsen." Ralphie took it out of his pocket to show me. His was black plastic and looked like some futuristic weapon of mass destruction. I was glad that gun was on my side.

"Aren't you going to put handcuffs on them or something? Tony is the one who manufactured the methamphetamine. The person you were looking for all along. And Parker admitted to me he knew about the Curixenol. He has diskettes in his safe that incriminate both of them. You'll never believe what Tony wanted to do—"

"Thanks, Tamsen. I'll take it from here." Ralphie held out his big gun in both hands, the way you're supposed to if you want to actually hit your target. "Mr. Grandines, I understand you have some information, some computer disks you want to share with the United States Government?"

Parker opened the top drawer of his desk.

"That's where the gun is," I was shouting again.

"Don't even think about it, Parker," Ralphie said.

"Traitor," Parker growled. "I'm not afraid of you."

"You should be," Ralphie said. "Otherwise you gonna be spending the rest of your life in jail."

"Don't forget our little quid pro quo," Parker said. "You can't back out now."

"Quid pro quo?" I asked, but nobody heard me, just like they hadn't seemed to hear my warnings about Parker's gun.

"I don't make deals with crooks," Ralphie said. "I'm an officer of the law."

"A *what*?" Tony bounded across the room toward Ralphie. "You lying scum. We had a deal."

Another deal? What did I miss? My heart jumped into my throat. Something was wrong, here. I'd expected Ralphie to rescue me like the imitation cowboy he was. Instead he was waving a gun around and saying things that made no sense.

Jonathan Grandines was unconscious now, slumped in his chair. "He really needs a doctor," I insisted. "He needs medication. Ralphie. Mr. Dupree. Please. Do something so we can get out of here."

Ralphie ignored me. "Sorry, Tony. I'm gonna have to tell the truth about your drug business. But I can probably help you get a deal from the federal prosecutor if you testify against Parker—"

Tony was agitated, restless, pacing around the room. Nobody made any move to stop him. "You'll offer the same deal to Parker, if he testifies against *me*. And you believe you'll walk away scot-free? No chance, Ralph. You're in this just as deeply as I am. You actually believe I won't tell anyone?" He lunged out toward Ralphie's gun, a wild gleam in his eye. "His proof, I don't have. But I have records of every detail of every gram *we* made and sold."

Tony's shoulder exploded in a fountain of red before the sound of the gunshot registered. I drew back in my seat, shaking. Parker jumped out of his seat and ran for his gun cabinet. The only way Ralphie could keep his career as a drug dealer a secret from the FBI was if he left no witnesses. Including me. I gauged the distance between my seat and the door. Tony lay in a crumpled heap in the middle of the escape route, and Ralphie stood right over him. I'd never make it.

"I'll get a promotion, Tony," Ralphie said, still hovering above Tony, weapon at the ready. "I shot the bad guy. Hey, whatcha think you're doing?" He pointed his gun at Parker. "Stop. Hands in the air."

Parker didn't stop; Ralphie let off two rounds even as he ran toward the safe. One chipped the wood paneling, the other knocked the bloodhound painting to the floor.

"It's a fake anyway, Parker," Ralphie yelled, and stepped into the safe after Parker. "FBI. Hands in the air." That hypocrite.

In that split second I did what any red-blooded American forensic psychiatrist would do in the same circumstances: I flew across the room to the gun safe and leaned all my weight against the door. It shut with a click.

For a long second I was aware only of my ragged breath and the cold smoothness of the safe's door under my trembling hands. The next sound I heard was the gunshot.

chapter fifty-nine

The first part of my testimony was as smooth as a greased pig. I had no idea what a greased pig was like, of course—in my imagination, it was a big slab of bacon trotting around with a ring in its nose—but the expression sounded like one Gwendolyn Conklin might use. The federal government had flown Gwen to New York to testify about the mental status of one Sammy Towland, killer of his entire family and possessor of the Y-chromosome mutation that was the cause of this bizarre, violent behavior. She wouldn't be testifying for a few days yet, but I had been thrilled to meet her, after our long telephone friendship. She had delivered a healthy baby boy only three weeks earlier, and Gwen had already ascertained that he was free of what the press had already dubbed the Killer Gene. The baby was in the corridor with Gwen's husband, but Gwen was watching the trial. She was tall and thin and blond and in about fifty years would look exactly as I'd pictured her as an Appalachian storyteller.

"Look, I can already fit into my funeral suit," she had exclaimed minutes after we met. Apparently in Kentucky they don't wear black quite as liberally as we do here.

I had practiced my testimony over and over, so by the time we got to trial I had perfected it. I'd expected heavy, intrusive cross-examination, but the Grandines attorneys were uncharacteristically gentle—maybe because they didn't have much to argue with. I answered all the questions as an ordinary witness: Where had I gone, whom had I spoken to, what had I said and done? The jury followed the questions and answers as if they were watching the final match of the U.S. Open tennis tournament.

I was a fact witness for the prosecution, but they brought out all of my qualifications as a psychiatric expert in the first hour. Even though the state had dropped its case against Jason Devinski, the two cases were inextricably and forever connected. I'd have to testify in another case too: the one in which Dr. Antony Hastings-Muir would be tried for manufacturing and distributing illegal drugs.

Jocelyn Agostino, the federal prosecutor, wore a different color suit every day, and high heels that clicked on the smooth floor. The jury loved her. They saw a pretty young woman who smiled and spoke in a soft, clear voice, in simple words they could understand without ever making them feel dumb. I knew Jocelyn was older than she looked, and that in the privacy of her office she could be, and had been, merciless when she prepared a witness for trial. She'd tuned me like a banjo, and now she played me like one, for the jury to fall in love with.

Nobody had seriously considered charging me with any crime, of course. All I'd done was lock up two guys with guns in a safe. Well, what options had I had? Talk to Parker and Ralphie about their mothers until they dropped their weapons? Administer emergency electroconvulsive therapy?

Today was already the third day of the trial. "Dr. Bayn." Jocelyn had moved on to redirect examination. "Could you please tell us at exactly which point in your psychiatric evaluation of Mr. Parker Grandines you realized you were in danger?"

"As I said in my earlier testimony"—I was tired of repeating myself, but I supposed the prosecutor had her reasons—"the FBI had obtained a court order for me to evaluate Mr. Grandines, to help determine if he had prior knowledge of the genetic effects of Curixenol. After we'd begun talking, Mr. Grandines became very agitated. Then he started revealing information that I knew could get him convicted. At that point, I realized he had no intention of letting me leave his house alive." Boy, did I sound melodramatic. From the safe distance of three and a half months, I could have laughed—as long as I didn't think about the trail of dead bodies that had led us to this courtroom.

"You said in your earlier testimony that you initially thought Dr. Antony Hastings-Muir was an ally. Is that so?"

I couldn't help glancing at Tony, where he sat near the front, looking pale and drawn, his useless left arm hanging at his side, his right wrist shackled to a corrections officer. "I didn't understand what Dr. Hastings-Muir was doing there." Jocelyn asked me to explain—again—how I'd had the revelation Tony had been making and selling methamphetamine. We continued like that, Jocelyn asking me to describe what had happened at Grandines's house for the fifty millionth time, me answering the questions as accurately as I could.

Judge Hershkovitz said, "If I may interrupt for a moment, Counselor. Did Agent Dupree say anything to you to indicate he was not, in fact, working on the side of the law?"

I glanced at Jocelyn, who nodded. As usual, the judge ran the show. "To me personally? No."

"So how did you come to realize that Agent Dupree was not there to uphold the law?"

"Objection," one of the myriad of defense lawyers called out. I kept mixing them up, in their matching suits and power ties, with their graying temples and shiny shoes. "Hearsay. Calls for speculation." That was the refrain these guys had been singing for all these past days, when they couldn't come up with anything better. But I'd been there. I reported what I'd heard and thought and felt. How could they object to that?

"Overruled," Judge Pincas Hershkovitz said, and banged his gavel with a tiny smile. "You can't object to the judge's questions." The smile broadened. "Please continue, Doctor."

"I knew because of Jonathan Grandines." I paused, sipped my water. I still felt guilty about not helping Jonathan when he'd suffered what did turn out to be a heart attack, although a relatively mild one. It was the stroke he'd had when the FBI showed up for his bedside arraignment in the cardiac care stepdown unit that killed him.

"Doctor?" Judge Hershkovitz reminded me I was supposed to be answering a question in federal court, in front of a hundred onlookers. "What did you know because of the late Jonathan Grandines?"

"His condition was the one thing that convinced me, more than anything else, that Ralphie Dupree wasn't going to come through in the end. If Ralphie had been an honorable man, if he were really an FBI agent with loyalty to his job and his government, he would never have permitted an innocent man to suffer needlessly, the way Jonathan was suffering. I asked to call an ambulance; even Dr. Hastings-Muir said Jonathan Grandines needed medical attention. But Ralphie ignored us. A real officer of the law would have called for an ambulance right away, and would have encouraged me to go take care of a sick man until other help arrived. So I knew that Ralphie Dupree didn't care if Jonathan got treatment, because none of us were going to leave there alive. At least Jonathan and I weren't. And Dr. Hastings-Muir wasn't."

They didn't ask me when I learned that Parker was on Ralphie's hit list, which was just as well. By the time I'd locked Ralphie and Parker in the strong room together, I'd been operating mostly on adrenaline and instinct. I wasn't certain Ralphie had planned to kill Parker, until I learned that the shot that killed Ralphie had come from his own gun, in the struggle that ensued in the dark of the gun safe. The shot had ricocheted off the metal door and right into Ralphie's throat. Imagine, if that door hadn't been so thick . . . I'd been leaning on the other side of the safe's door.

"Safe" is really a dumb word for it, isn't it?

Ralphie's share of the methamphetamine money was nowhere to be found . . . and Ralph Dupree obviously couldn't be reached for comment. But Ralphie's guilt became incontrovertible when ballistics proved that the bullet that killed FBI agent Jim Mahoney had come from Ralphie's gun. Ralphie hadn't infiltrated Antony Hastings-

Muir's drug empire in order to turn the whole thing over to the authorities. He'd partnered with Tony in order to make money. I knew this, because Jocelyn told me, but the newspapers never found out. Some things, like corrupt FBI agents, were better kept secret.

Somehow, the prosecution had won me the right to be present in the courtroom throughout the trial, so I was able to piece the remaining details together as the days passed. Antony Hastings-Muir plea-bargained himself into a comfortable early retirement in federal prison. The hired killer who'd happily slit Gordon Ranier's wrists was easy to identify once Colin Grandines and his brother-in-law Jackson Dwyer came forward to testify. They described how Parker Grandines had contracted with one of their employees, a lower-level security guard, first to cut Ginny Liu's brake line, and later to kill Gordon. They admitted that they had been afraid that Gordon Ranier might spill the beans to me about Curixenol before the drug went on sale. It seemed that many of the subjects from the old Curixenol studies had become suspicious when Dr. Madeleine Balloy contacted them about submitting blood samples. That was when Parker Grandines decided Madeleine had to be killed, as well. The same security guard arranged Madeleine's death. Jocelyn told me privately that the hired killer had served twenty years for manslaughter in Georgia, and had come to New York the day he got out of jail before anyone got suspicious about a slew of twenty-five-year-old unsolved murders in Atlanta. Parker Grandines knew how to pick his employees, all right.

Antony Hastings-Muir had been granted a limited immunity for handing over the Curixenol information. He couldn't be tried as an accessory in the Curixenol scandal. Tony pleaded guilty to some reduced charges for the methamphetamine and all the parties agreed there would be no trial. I was off the hook for that one.

I was fascinated to learn that Tony's family had lost all their money years before, and that they'd been on the verge of selling the Bermuda home when Tony stepped in with his brilliant plan of becoming a drug lord. Everyone had a reason for doing bad. Nothing was exactly what it seemed.

Gordon Ranier's son was tested and had the Curixenol mutation. Preliminary results showed that just treating the boys with traditional SSRI antidepressants worked wonders. The children could be treated while they waited for the cure to be synthesized and made available.

Ray Liu, Ginny's husband, testified that when he approached the FBI with his knowledge of Tony's illegal drug-making and -selling activities, he'd been directed to Ralph Dupree. Ginny recovered, and she testified too. She'd cleared up my questions about the conversation Jason had overheard between her, Karen Devinski, Madeleine Balloy, and Parker Grandines. "I don't remember anything about Madeleine saying 'This is war.' But if Jason said she said it, then Madeleine must have been talking about something else. I didn't know about the Curixenol mutations then. It was only after I found that computer printout that I began figuring out what was going on." Her hair had grown in a bit, like a little boy's. She shook her head. "I wish Madeleine *had* come to me. Maybe she wouldn't have died." Then she looked right at Parker Grandines, who'd elected not to say a word in his own trial on his own behalf. "Of course, maybe Parker would have just killed both of us."

As Parker Grandines was getting buried under a mountain of incriminating evidence, his attorneys were trying their best to arrange a deal: Their client wouldn't be tried on any state charges of murder, manslaughter, or anything else, until he'd served his sentences for the federal charges. Eventually, his lawyers prevailed. Parker was sixty-four. Chances were good that New York State would be spared the expense of a trial, after Parker finished serving his ten-to-twenty-five-year federal sentence for defrauding the public and falsifying documents submitted to the FDA. Jocelyn told me Parker had also pleaded guilty to three federal counts of conspiracy to commit murder: Madeleine Balloy, Gordon Ranier, and Ginny Liu. Those years would be served concomitantly with the Curixenol charges. Jocelyn was disappointed that she couldn't try Parker for the deaths of all of the child killers' victims, but she knew when to cash in her victory and stop.

And then it was over, as suddenly as it had all begun. Everyone went back to work, to school, to life. The Devinskis moved to Montana. Over thirty boys around the country were identified with the Y-chromosome mutation. Grandines Pharmaceuticals was required to pay for medical and psychiatric treatment for those boys for life. But experts predicted that all their future male generations would have the Y-chromosome mutation. What would happen when the families forgot? What about the illegitimate children? What about the families that had already been torn apart?

It was enough to drive you to drink.

The alcoholics in the world continued to have to battle their problem with conventional methods. The drug addicts still found methamphetamine to buy. Public awareness about pseudoephedrine had increased, though, and pharmacies nationwide were keeping a vigilant eye on their inventories.

The world still had its problems. But court was adjourned anyway.

I rode down in the elevator with Vasily Stolnik.

"Can I drive you home?" Stolnik asked me, with his trademark wink.

"I think I'll take a taxi," I said, and he threw back his shaggy head and roared with laughter.

"You really didn't know?" I asked him.

"I didn't know. They tell me success of drug depends on having psychiatrist as spokesperson. What do I know of capitalist advertising?"

I was still a little stung that the only reason Parker had chosen me for the glamorous job of Curixenol spokeswoman was as leverage for what I might learn from the Devinskis about Curixenol's shady, bloody past.

Stolnik sighed. "The truth is, I suspected Parker's reasons. But what can I do? I am humble immigrant."

"You swear you didn't have anything to do with sabotaging Ginny Liu's car? Or with killing Gordon Ranier?"

Stolnik shook his head. "I do not believe is necessary to kill people. I am family man. I love my life here in United States. Maybe I will open Russian delicatessen now. I always like food."

I knew he might be lying—not about liking food, that part I knew was true. But I understood his intention. There are people who are their professions. And there are people who are themselves. As long as you can be yourself, a little professional disagreement is meaningless.

And there was something else. When I'd jumped across that room, back in January, and slammed the safe door shut on Parker Grandines and Ralphie Dupree, my only thought was of Greg. That I was going to die without ever seeing him again. I'd never find out what woman he'd been speaking to late that night when we first argued. I'd never know if we could have made things right.

Truth and justice were important. But I'd realized in that split second that my own happiness was equally—if not more—important. I'd had to take the chance.

I'd only had a key for the top lock. Like I said, I don't believe in omens. But I don't not believe in them either.

The key had turned easily, the door had opened. The apartment was filled with light, music, and the smell of something garlicky simmering on the stove. Inky bounded out of nowhere to rub against my ankles.

"I'm home," I'd called out, tired and disheveled and still a little bit afraid—both of what had happened that day, and what still might. Greg came out of the kitchen, a wooden spoon in his hand. As if he'd been expecting me. "I'm home."

Home.

epilogue

I was finally on a sailboat. Greg and I were taking a course together: "Learn to Sail." We needed an official hobby, a common interest other than work. We'd just been practicing "man overboard." The other students were a fiftyish bond trader so dry I imagined him soaking up the waters of New York Harbor and stranding our boat on a pile of silt, and his thirty-something blond girlfriend who looked as if she were afraid to breathe without his permission. The instructor had one of those New England accents I could barely decipher. I looked at Greg and saw a wicked gleam in his eye.

"Man overboard," he yelled.

"You're supposed to tell me when you're going to do that," the trader whined.

"It's better to be spontaneous," Greg said. Bondy had to make three passes before his girlfriend managed to retrieve the life jacket.

"It's like that in real life," I said. "You don't know when someone's really going to fall off the boat."

Blondie sulked and Teacher looked stern. I can't say we were having a good time, but we were learning how to sail, and in July we were going to France, and we were going to charter a boat. We were going to do things that had nothing to do with work. Lots of things.

Bondy and Blondie wanted to bring the boat in by themselves, and Teacher obviously liked them better, since they were as humorless as she was. I was soaked, and even though it was Memorial Day weekend, the weather wasn't warm. So Greg and I went below and started gathering our things. He'd gotten one of those alphanumeric beepers, and I saw him check a message. A long message.

"It's fun, this having a hobby thing," I told him, trying to keep him with me for a few more seconds. Some big case must have broken. As soon as we reached dry land, Greg would be rushing off to interview a suspect. That's what he does.

"Mmm." He nodded, but his eyes had that faraway look to them, and I knew I'd guessed right. It wasn't another woman, or anything like that. The hints I'd had that maybe he'd been straying had been completely unfounded. He'd laughed when I asked him why he hadn't received my fax of the Devinski report last January: "Only you get faxes on that machine. I never even check if there's something for me." And when I'd confronted him about the woman he'd been speaking to on the phone the night we'd had our first big fight, he'd had to think hard before remembering it was his brother's girlfriend, Heather, aka Nose-ring. I knew Greg was devoted to me. If I had competition, it was from his zealotlike devotion to his work.

"What happened?" I asked him.

"Nothing," he said, then laughed and caught my hands in his. "I know I promised. But you've got to at least consider it."

"Consider what?" But deep in my heart, I think I knew what he wanted as soon as I saw his eyes get that weird glaze. I also knew I could say no.

He steeled himself, literally as the boat lurched, and mentally, I could tell. He was going to ask me. I looked at the ring sparkling on my finger. For that he hadn't gone down on one knee. But for this he might. He was much, much more nervous than when he'd asked me to marry him.

"Tamsen, there was a murder on the A train today. They've just arrested a suspect."

I knew it.

"He escaped from Manhattan Psychiatric Center last week."

No surprise there.

"So what I need . . . what I mean is . . ."

I knew what he wanted.

"You don't trust any other psychiatrists," I said, and when our eyes met, we both laughed, even though a murder on the subway was no laughing matter.

"You know I only trust you."

The sailboat bumped the dock. What could I do? I didn't have to iron his shirts or cook his dinner or clean his toilets. All I had to do was evaluate his defendants.

What we women do for love.

acknowledgments

Exactly as much time will have elapsed between the day I first turned on the computer to start a novel to seeing it in print, as from the first day of medical school to the first day of internship. Far from being effortless, Writing University has been the hardest course I've ever taken. And as with any advanced degree, numerous people have contributed to my education and the granting of this diploma, the book you hold in your hands.

My wonderful agent, Anne Hawkins, nurtured this project through every new obstacle, and was always there for me no matter how difficult the path—or I—became. I'm hardly a woman of few words, but I don't think I can ever adequately express my gratitude and respect for Anne and all she's done for me.

Everyone at Bantam Dell was patient and supportive as this book evolved. I'd especially like to thank Kate Miciak and Danielle Perez for all their hard work and commitment to this project.

Friends, family, and coworkers eventually got tired of asking me about the book, but at least they didn't get tired of me. They are too many to list here, but I'd like to thank each and every one of you who believed in me even when it looked like this writing thing was just a systematized delusion. I would like to say a special thank-you to Lauri Hart, founder and administrator of the Mystery Writers Forum at *www.zott.com/mysforum*. This cybercommunity of fellow writers helped sustain me during this long learning process. Closer to home, I'd like to thank all my friends, especially Marlyn Quinn and Andy Sperber, for surviving the early clinical trials, and my "team," Lori Lessin, Larry Siegel,

Elizabeth Mahfoud, and Paul Follansbee, for making our
"day job" so much fun (or at least bearable).

Finally, my incredible family, whose love fuels everything. My husband, Michael, my most devoted fan as well
as my most honest critic, and my boys, Barak, Matthew,
and Evan—I love you all so much. You'll always be my perspective. This book is for you.

January 2, 2001

SARA PARETSKY

"Paretsky's name always makes the top of the list when people talk about the new female operatives." —*The New York Times Book Review*

___ Bitter Medicine	23476-X	**$6.99/9.99**
___ Blood Shot	20420-8	**$6.99/8.99**
___ Burn Marks	20845-9	**$6.99/8.99**
___ Indemnity Only	21069-0	**$6.99/8.99**
___ Guardian Angel	21399-1	**$6.99/8.99**
___ Killing Orders	21528-5	**$6.99/8.99**
___ Deadlock	21332-0	**$6.99/8.99**
___ Tunnel Vision	21752-0	**$6.99/8.99**
___ Windy City Blues	21873-X	**$6.99/8.99**
___ A Woman's Eye	21335-5	**$6.99/8.99**
___ Women on the Case	22325-3	**$6.99/8.99**
___ Hard Time	22470-5	**$6.99/9.99**
___ Total Recall	31366-7	**$25.95/39.95**

HARLAN COBEN

Winner of the Edgar, the Anthony, and the Shamus Awards

___ One False Move	22544-2	**$6.50/9.99**
___ Deal Breaker	22044-0	**$6.50/9.99**
___ Dropshot	22049-5	**$6.50/9.99**
___ Fade Away	22268-0	**$6.50/9.99**
___ Back Spin	22270-2	**$6.50/9.99**
___ The Final Detail	22545-0	**$6.50/9.99**
___ Darkest Fear	23539-1	**$6.50/9.99**
___ Tell No One	33555-5	**$22.95/32.95**

RUTH RENDELL

Winner of the Grand Master Edgar Award from the *Mystery Writers of America*

___ Road Rage	22602-3	**$6.50/8.99**
___ The Crocodile Bird	21865-9	**$6.50/8.99**
___ Simisola	22202-8	**$6.50/NCR**
___ Keys to the Street	22392-X	**$6.50/8.99**
___ A Sight for Sore Eyes	23544-8	**$6.50/9.99**